USURPER

A Dark Age Historical Fiction Novel

Francis Williams

Independently Published

The characters and events portrayed in this book are fictitious. Any similarity to real persons, living or dead, is coincidental and not intended by the author.

ISBN-13: 9781711265407
ISBN-10: 1711265403

Cover design by: Francis Williams
Library of Congress Control Number: 2018675309
Printed in the United States of America

In loving memory of a truly amazing canine. Rest in peace, buddy. You'll always be missed.

Thank you to all those who supported this passion of mine. To anyone who finds enjoyment in my work, please spread the word. Happy reading!

CHARACTERS/MAPS

Abhartach - Great Chief of the Gaels

Alda - Wife of Amiram

King Aldrien - King of Armorica

Amiram - Lead rower of the Fortuna

Lord Ambrosius Aurelianus - Lord of Powys, Brother of King Uther

Prince Ambrosius Aurelianus - Son of Ambrosius Aurelianus, known as Arthur to his friends

Artorius - Son of King Uther, heir of Powys

Atestatia - Sister of Dagonet

Bishop Germanus - Christian bishop from Rome, leader of Christians in Britannia

Braxus - Second in command to Jorrit

Bors the Younger - Friend of Drysten, Officer of Powys

Catulla - Former slave, wife of Gaius

King Ceneus - King of Ebrauc

Citrio Bardas - Gaius' second in command

King Colgrin - King of Saxons in Londinium

Cynwrig - Childhood friend of Drysten

Dagonet - Scout of Ebrauc

Diocles - Former Roman deserter, friend of Drysten

Drysten - Former lord of Ebrauc, imprisoned by Bishop Germanus for five years

Prince Dyfnwal - Son of King Garbonian and Heledd

Ebissa - Saxon, once followed Colgrin

Prince Eidion - Eldest son of King Ceneus, follower of Bishop Germanus

Fortunata - Deceased mother of Drysten

Eliwlod - Guard serving King Ceneus

Gaius - Son of Titus

Galahad ap Drysten - Son of Drysten

Prince Gwrast - Second son of King Ceneus

Hall - Deceased father of Drysten

Heledd - Wife of King Ceneus, mother to all his children

Inka - Wife of Jorrit

Isolde - Wife of Drysten, mother of Galahad

Jorrit - Frisian who served Drysten before imprisonment

Lucan - Orphan

Maebh - Isolde's dog

Maewyn - Deacon serving Bishop Germanus, Christian name is Patrick

Magnus - Former healer of the Fortuna's men

Marhaus - Slaver who once helped kidnap Drysten's people

Marivonna - Deceased wife of Titus

Mathew - Former priest, officer of Powys

Prince Mor - Youngest son of King Ceneus

Myrddin - Druid of Abhartach's Gaels

Oana - Daughter of Titus, wife of Diocles

Octha - Saxon, once served Colgrin

Phelan - Owns a farm in Petuaria

Rodric ap Aosten - Captain of King Ceneus

Titus Octavius Britannicus - Former Roman Centurion turned mercenary

TorinInnkeeper in Mamucium

Tybion ap Cunedda - Prince of Gwynedd

King Uther - King of Powys

Vonig - Second in command to Prince Eidion, servant of Bishop Germanus

Princess Ystradwel - Daughter of King Ceneus

Britannia 430 CE

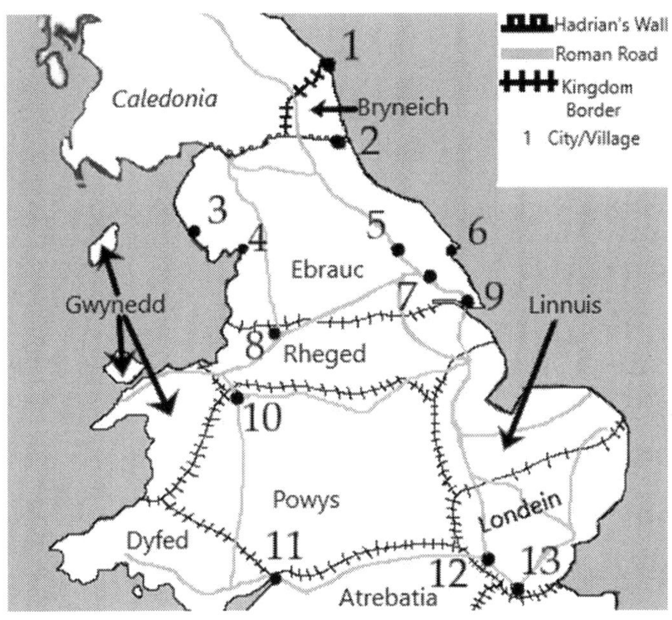

1 - Din Guayrdi - Bamburgh Castle
2 - Segedunum - Wallsend
3 - Glanoventa - Ravenglass
4 - Abhartach's Cave - Dog's Hole Cave
5 - Isurium - Aldborough
6 - Praesidium - Bridlington
7 - Eboracum - York
8 - Mamucium - Manchester
9 - Petuaria - Brough
10 - Deva - Chester
11 - Glevum - Gloucester
12 - Verulamium - St. Albans
13 - Londinium - London

CONTENTS

CHAPTER ONE

The man's incessant stuttering was unbearable. "Lord... I... We don't know where they came from..." he explained. "I strolled off to look on the fish traps when I saw their boats moored on the beach. I did'n know who they belonged to and thought nuttin of it. It's not uncommon fer traders to leave their boats along the beach this time 'o year."

Gaius shot a quick look towards Cynwrig. The king of Ebrauc had sent both of them to investigate the sudden rise in disappearances on their Western coast. Five years ago, Prince Gwrast rode West to put these Gaelic kidnappers to the sword. Most people believed that was the end of it.

Cynwrig inched closer. "When did you first understand what was happening?" he asked of the man. His name was Brynnmore, a man of about fifty years who appeared to be somewhat from what Gaius could tell.

"I was checkin' the ol traps near the water when the screams began. "I ran to hide, Lord, as fast as I could manage," he responded amid his frantic state.

Gaius ran a hand over his head, wondering, maybe even hoping this was just slavers come to steal away more souls than they could auction to the Gaels. "What did you see when you came back?"

Brynnmore met his gaze as much as he could without having eyes left to see. The bloody bandage across his face produced a vacant stare, which unsettled both of the king's scouts. He slowly opened his mouth to speak before sputtering and sobbing nonsense instead.

Gaius placed a hand on the man's shoulder, producing a

slight jump from the man at his touch. "Rest, old man. We can speak further of this tomorrow." He nodded towards a woman whom Gaius guessed to be Brynnmore's daughter, signaling he was done with his questioning for the day.

The woman gently ushered the sobbing man through the doorway as Gaius turned to Cynwrig. "What's your take?"

Cynwrig looked as though he'd stopped breathing as he watched the woman lead Brynnmore down the narrow street. The old man stumbled every so often, with his arms flailing out to find objects for reference. "I do not recall hearing stories of slavers who butcher villagers or gouge out a man's eyes. Bad for business."

Gaius nodded. "My thoughts exactly. Who would want a blind servant?"

"Or a dead one," Cynwrig added with a grim smile.

The two slowly exited the small barracks once used to house Roman cavalry and made their way towards the Northern gate of the fort. The town they journeyed to was once a Roman vicus named Glanoventa, which guarded an essential harbor on Britannia's Western coast. However, now it was solely occupied by native Britons dwelling in the kingdom of Ebrauc, the Northernmost kingdom of Britannia. Both Gaius and Cynwrig couldn't even figure out what the town's current occupants even called their home.

"This place has more fucking *ghosts* than people," Cynwrig whispered.

Gaius nodded as they began passing through the gate of the fort and slowly made their way towards the town. "That would be normal for most places. Not to mention one where half the people were found hanging from trees."

Cynwrig glanced toward the tree line. Small groups of men and women were removing their loved ones from branches or trunks. "Who fucking does that?"

Gaius wished with all his being he could muster enough courage to give his answer. This was one of the rare times in which he was truly afraid. The men who swept through the town were quiet and methodical. Before anyone knew what was happening, they vanished. He had never seen anything of the sort in all his years, and not even the Picts above Hadrian's Wall were known to cause so much harm without at least being seen.

"It's the ones whose bodies weren't found which I am curious about," Gaius finally responded. "These men were certainly *not* slavers. Otherwise, they would have taken many of the ones they instead chose to kill. Most of those bodies once belonged to able-bodied workers or beautiful women. People who would've fetched a nice price. Strange, the descriptions of the missing all share one common trait."

"They were all fat," Cynwrig said with a snort as they walked by a group of sobbing women, all kneeling in front of the statue to a god which neither man recognized. One turned and gave Cynwrig a grim, teary-eyed stare as they passed. "This one was worse than the last."

"Means there could be more than before," Gaius replied. "How many boats did the old man say he counted?"

Cynwrig shrugged. "He didn't. His daughter mentioned two, but the footprints we saw near the tree line would mean they packed at least three dozen men into two tiny boats."

"It would not be possible for them to journey off with at *least* ten prisoners as well," Gaius added.

The two men silently marched to the beach on the Western side of the fort. Each man gave gazed up at the seagulls floating overhead as the salty smell of the sea filled their nostrils. Gaius' group of thirty men made a temporary camp outside the town in the event of the invader's return. But in their minds, each man knew that would be unlikely. The raiders had come and gone in every village they journeyed to, which now came to a total of six. The gruesome tales of kidnappings and the defiling of bodies seemed to escalate with each subsequent raid, and Gaius hated being there to listen to them. Above all, he worried about his next reception with his king. If he journeyed back to Eboracum, the capital of Ebrauc, with little information on hand, there would be a good chance he would lose what good standing he still held.

"There's no fucking pattern for us to follow. These attacks don't even seem to limit themselves to the coast," Gaius murmured in frustration.

Cynwrig let out a heavy sigh. "If we post sentries on the nearest towns, we may be able to provide the villagers with enough warning to flee."

Gaius shook his head. "And limit our advantage? We likely have them with our numbers. We won't if we divide our forces any further."

Cynwrig shrugged as he looked off toward the sea. "Just an idea."

Bonfires were beginning on the beach, with small groups of weary men speaking tales of vengeful Roman ghosts entering circulation among the men. But Gaius didn't believe in ghosts, and from the looks of it, neither did Cynwrig. Even so, what they each silently understood was these raiders were far more terrifying than any fictitious ghost story. These men were real, and terribly so.

"Sir!" a voice called from the village.

Gaius turned to see his lead scout jogging up to him with a handful of villagers, all carrying shoddy hunting bows or farming equipment. "What did you find, Dagonet?"

The scout and his entourage halted in front of Gaius and Cynwrig. The large group of skittish men drew the attention of the soldiers on the beach, all of whom began to stand and equip their weapons. "Tracks, Sir, and a whole lot of em'," Dagonet replied happily. "We can finally catch the bastards."

Gaius smiled as he shifted his attention to his men. "Mount!" he ordered before turning to the villagers. "I know you all most likely lost loved ones, but we will deal with this ourselves. Stay with your families and guard the town until our return. Place all those who cannot fight inside the fort."

Gaius' small force quickly mounted their horses and made their way Southeast, where Dagonet had tracked a small band of swift individuals. They rode a short distance before happening upon what looked to be a makeshift campsite. The remnants of a fire and a handful of footprints were obvious, even at a distance. The site provided a nice overlook of Glanoventa, being rather elevated, while the old campfire lay underneath a pair of trees surrounded by an open field.

Gaius signaled for Cynwrig to remain a short distance away to prevent distorting additional footprints and continued forward with Dagonet.

Gaius dismounted and approached the remains of the site, with the only telling object being a strangely colored pelt bearing a fresh engraving left behind. The odd thing about it was how it was staked into the ground.

They left this for us to find? He kneeled and plucked the strange object from the ground as he turned to his scout.

"I found roughly a half-dozen unique sets of—" Dagonet perked his head up before wheeling around. He surveyed the high grasses behind them, his hand slowly moving toward his bag of arrows at his waist.

Gaius casually looked over his shoulder, unable to detect anything suspicious. "What is it?" he asked warily. He served with Dagonet for the better part of the last five years and understood he was an able tracker. The man had proven his worth many times over and had the eyesight of a hawk. Everyone knew it was entirely possible the man could detect something others couldn't, and that notion terrified Gaius despite his calm demeanor. "What do you see?"

"We need to leave. We need to leave *now,* and we need to go to the king and request more men." Dagonet slowly rose from his crouch and scanned the tall grass around them before giving a quick glance to the town.

"You've been alone in the wilderness far too long. There's nothing here." Gaius did his best to feign bravery, but he found himself slowly reaching for the hilt of his blade as he produced an awkward grin.

Dagonet's eyes slowly began to widen as he glanced

from whatever he saw in the field and over to the rest of the men. "Sir, we're being watched and there's far more than what would be able to fit into this camp." He gave the pelt in Gaius' hand a quick look. "They set a trap for us..."

A shiver began running its way down Gaius' spine. He paced back, suddenly feeling eyes all around him in the thick brush of the field. It felt as though the eyes were gazing into his mind, seeing through his visible calm and shining a light over his inner fear.

At first it was just a feeling, but soon there were whispers all around him. Strange hisses were cutting through the air.

An animal? Gaius wondered. *No... someone's speaking...* It was a language which was both unknown to him, but old in some way. The guttural speech was bringing chills to the man's arms and neck.

All was quiet when the first man went down. A blur erupted out of the tall grass and tackled the rearmost man off his horse, pulling him into the overgrowth nearby. A hand wielding a crude knife showed itself over the waist-high grass before plunging down out of view, soon to be followed by a muffled wail of pain.

"Cynwrig, run!" Gaius screamed.

Thankfully, the man did not question the order, as he quickly turned his horse back towards the town and led the remaining warriors away. That must have signaled the strangers to attack.

Arrows began to burst from the concealment of the grass, most finding a man or the backside of a horse.

Gaius and Dagonet swiftly mounted and turned to follow their men. It seemed they were now out of range of the attackers, but Gaius was too terrified to see for certain.

Where the fuck did they come from? Gaius wondered in panic. They rode the same route as Cynwrig's group, passing by a handful of men squirming below them when Gaius began to slow his horse. The man was grabbing his throat and reaching toward him, pleading for help.

"Don't stop!" Dagonet shouted.

Gaius rode by the dying man and stole a glance behind him, failing to see even one of his attackers.

The horses sprinted their way back until Cynwrig was seen halting just short of the town. Gaius witnessed a man with an arrow jutting from his leg fall off his horse and a handful of men watching in horror. He finally caught up and saw a confused expression on Cynwrig's face as he peered over two more men who were each hit with an arrow a piece. As Gaius approached, he noticed another fall off his mount and quickly turn himself onto his back. He stared into the sky as he clawed at his neck, wheezing and choking. A horse with a broken arrow shaft jutting from its front leg collapsed in a heap, crushing the rider's leg under its weight.

"Poison!" Dagonet screamed with wide eyes.

"Sir, on the hill." The man pointed towards the direction of the camp, with all men halting and looking back.

At first, there was nothing. But that nothing was followed by dark blurs slowly rising from the field, all armed with dark bows that looked to be covered in pitch. A dozen at first, then two dozen, then more were seen rising from the meadows all around them.

"Gods above..." Cynwrig murmured.

Gaius looked over his men, now counting nineteen still standing when he trained his attention back in the direction of the attackers. Off in the distance he saw a horse and rider being led by two black-masked men wearing furs. Both men casually strolled towards Gaius and his men before stopping and spurring the horse forward on its own. The horse slowly walked on as the men behind Gaius watched in silence. A murmur began until Dagonet held up a hand to quiet those whispering behind him.

The horse and rider were now close enough to see it was one of Gaius' longest serving footmen. Only now, he had no head. His head was being held on his lap, with his face still wearing the terrified expression it bore when the man's life was taken. The body slumped over and bobbed up and down as the horse neared. As it approached, Gaius saw the cords of leather tied around the man's waist and legs, keeping the dead man from falling.

"Get the villagers behind the walls of the fort; we're staying the night," Gaius informed his men. "Half watch all night, and get the villagers armed."

Cynwrig rode up by his commander. "There are many more of those bastards than this if the sightings along the coast are to be believed."

"And we don't know where the rest are," Dagonet added.

Gaius returned his attention to the horse drawing closer with a slow canter. "Cynwrig, wait until darkness and make for the nearest garrison. Bring reinforcements back." His voice cracked as he gave the order, betraying the fear his men felt was shared with him as well. "Dagonet, go with him until he arrives, then continue on until you reach Eboracum. You must tell the king what has happened."

"If we fucking make it…" Cynwrig whispered.

"You have to," Gaius replied as he raised a finger towards Cynwrig. "We have no idea how many there are. And if they all fight like this—"

"We're fucked," Dagonet interrupted.

Gaius couldn't bring himself to say it, but he knew the man was right.

"What's that marking?" Cynwrig asked as he pointed toward the pelt.

Gaius had almost forgotten he'd taken the object. After watching the strange enemy disappear back into the grass, he looked down to the pelt in his hands. The leather was a different texture than he'd encountered before, with a brand recently placed in its center. "Written in the tongue of the Romans," Gaius observed. "But horribly done."

Dagonet ushered leaned over for a better look. "Abher… Abhartach?" he whispered.

Gaius nodded. "Who or what is that?"

The men remained silent. Both knew they would likely find out whether they wished to or not.

***

King Ceneus led Maewyn, Bishop Germanus' assistant, into the tavern near the front gate of Eboracum. The tavern-keeper was always told ahead of time when the two would conduct their secret meetings, and made certain to keep a table in the back of the room vacant on each of those nights. The two had been meeting in secret behind Bishop Germanus' back for quite some time. The tavern known as *The Limping Mule* was their preferred setting. The Bishop had ordered the execution of the owner's brother not long ago.

But that was not the only reason for their choice. It may have been near the front gate, but the king could use back alleys between uninhabited buildings to get there. Staying away from anyone who could recognize his exit from the Roman fortress was important for their secrecy. While the king was well-known to his people, Maewyn preferred to keep to himself and mainly looked like any of the other random priests people preferred to keep away from.

Pope Celestine had once sent Bishop Germanus with the task of bringing the islands of Britannia into the arms of the church. All he truly did was spend the last few years funding rebellions in other kingdoms while drinking and whoring. Lately, the bishop was attempting to remove Ceneus from power and instill his son, Prince Eidion, in his place.

The king was always at odds with the bishop. But it was Maewyn who saw Germanus' cruel ways firsthand. Ceneus remembered the moment Maewyn decided he had seen enough. It was the execution of a farmer and his wife. Germanus had believed them to be supporters of the old religion of the Britons despite not having any proof of the claims. Once it was over and the bishop was questioned as to why two lives were taken, he simply stated his desire to remind Ebrauc's people of God's power. It was that moment Maewyn stormed into King Ceneus' estate and vowed he would do what he could to undermine Germanus.

"Spent another night with the servant-girl while he sent

me to speak with tribal leaders," Maewyn announced in a frustrated tone. "Feels as though I do more of his job than he does."

King Ceneus smirked. "I have been saying that for the better part of the last two years."

"Any word from the West?" Maewyn inquired.

The king shook his head. "Still too soon. Though judging from the other reports...."

"The kidnappings are the same as before," Maewyn sadly interjected.

The king nodded, choosing to ignore the interruption as he glanced around the dimly lit tavern. He saw no signs of the mass kidnappings in the festive atmosphere. There seemed to be much more to be happy about in the lands closer to Eboracum. King Ceneus overheard how one of his guards had a healthy baby boy awaiting his return in a village outside Isurium. Another was celebrating a promotion given by Prince Gwrast, the king's second, and favored son. The man proudly showed off his new cloak dyed royal blue.

"Always been a fair-minded man," Maewyn stated. "Though, I expect he still does not trust me."

"Gwrast?"

Maewyn nodded.

"Likely not. But then again, neither do I," the king quipped with a grin.

The two sat quietly for a while longer, with Ceneus cherishing his time amongst his people, and Maewyn cherishing his without the presence of the bishop. To say they were friends would not be accurate, but to say they held similar goals for the coming months would certainly be fitting.

"I've figured it out," King Ceneus began. "I have figured out the enemy we will give Germanus."

Maewyn perked his head up. "One which holds no fear of the man? You would be hard pressed to find such a man now. Even the mercenary from Londinium is smart enough not to go against him, while the Prince from Powys is much too far away to do much of anything."

"We will not be needing either, though the prince recently sent men to visit with Titus as they prepare for war," the king returned. "In any case, I need you to carry a message for me."

Maewyn revealed a knowing smile. "You know the bishop has controlled the prisons for years, don't you?"

"I thought you were the man who does Germanus' job for him," Ceneus returned. "Doesn't that mean you control the prisons as well?"

Maewyn scrunched his face in frustration. The king couldn't tell whether it was due to his comment or the idea Maewyn was the acting religious authority without the recognition normally attached to the position.

Maewyn finally cocked his head as he decided to speak. "You know he will come after you once he is free?"

The king smiled. "I do. It is only fair considering I stole five years of his life from him."

"But you didn't," Maewyn responded.

Ceneus released a heavy sigh. "Germanus may have thrown him into a cell, but he did so in my name. No words would ever be able to convince Drysten otherwise."

"Maybe not," Maewyn began as he glanced around, "but if we make him swear not to come after the royal family until Germanus is gone..."

Ceneus scoffed. "You believe he would honor such a deal?"

Maewyn nodded. "He was raised well. He was raised honorably by his father. He knows the value of keeping his word."

"I doubt he knows it well enough to forget what's been done to him," Ceneus responded with a snort.

Maewyn shrugged and leaned closer. "You have spoken to him during his time in confinement?"

King Ceneus nodded. "Only some. Odd feeling talking to a prisoner you did not throw in a cell."

"I would expect as much. You may know better than I

whether or not he would be willing to help us. So I ask, how can I convince him?" Maewyn whispered.

"Speak of his wife. My eldest boy told him she died in childbirth. He does not know the truth of it." The king felt a wash of guilt as he wondered the hopeless feeling his prisoner had in believing his wife and child died during birth. The same death the man lost his mother and baby sister to many years ago. Though, Ceneus only came to find that small bit of information rather recently.

Maewyn leaned back and nodded. "I remember in speaking with his people he had a great love for the woman. I would expect he would be overjoyed to know she lives."

"As well as his son," Ceneus added. The king knew there was a good chance releasing a man from captivity could have dire consequences for his rule. But it was worth the risk to rid Ebrauc of the bishop and regain the power stolen from him.

CHAPTER TWO

The guard threw Drysten's sole meal of the day between the iron bars of his cell, splattering the bowl's contents over the dusty stone floor. To most people, this would have meant the meal was spoiled and unworthy of a civilized man's stomach. But in the last five years, Drysten learned it was a privilege to eat at all.

He sprang from the corner of the moonlit cell and shoved his mouth anywhere he could see a speck of the chunky white substance thrown to the ground. His frail, mangled fingers ran across the old Roman stone, gracelessly plucking up any morsel of food they could find. Drysten didn't worry about how rotten or spoiled the food was, he simply needed the pains in his stomach to subside long enough for him to finally sleep.

"More of an animal than a man," Drysten heard a guard mention to his comrade.

The distinct bellowing laugh of the guard captain, Vonig, was soon followed by another voice as they each made their way up the stairwell. After a few short moments, the torchlight abandoned the captives of the prison, and Drysten's food suddenly vanished from view. The only souls who could partake in what small amount of nutrients that lay on the floor would be the rats or insects scurrying about the cell. Drysten knew they were now the only ones who could detect its presence. But if he was lucky, he could catch one and have himself a second meal. A feast packed with rare protein. But in Ebrauc's prisons, there was rarely any luck to be had.

After his meal, he finally laid his head to rest on the lone source of comfort in his possession, his father's old bearskin cloak. The brown furs had become tangled and split, creating a crude and barbaric look from the years of separating Drysten's body from the cold stone beneath him.

"Where are they?" he once asked himself. "Why have my people not come for me?"

He knew the answer, but never had the strength to face it. His people were most likely told he had been executed by their ruler, King Ceneus of Ebrauc. He was one of the few men which Drysten vowed to disembowel and hang from the tallest peak in Britannia should he somehow gain his freedom. But the hope of such a privilege left Drysten long ago, as did any other dream or desire he once held. These luxuries left him alongside the muscle he once developed onto his arms and chest, once making him look fearsome and bringing him confidence in battle.

Segedunum... Drysten mused. How long has it been?

He truly did not know the answer. He fought for the king, he won, and he was condemned to a cell for it. He lost his father in that battle, and as thanks for his sacrifice, King Ceneus cast him aside into obscurity. Cast him away from his men, but more importantly to Drysten, his beloved wife.

Drysten worked so hard to believe there was some way she could still be alive. He once etched the figure of a woman and child into the wall of his cell to remind him of a hopeful future. But one day the prince of Ebrauc, Eidion ap Ceneus, had personally come to give him the news. He was a prisoner for no more than a few months at that point. But after he heard of his wife's passing, he no longer wished for freedom. He wished for someone to enter his cell and send him to his precious Isolde and the child she tried to give life to.

"She died in childbirth," Prince Eidion had whispered with a smile, "like your mother. She fought and fought, but in the end..." Drysten will never forget the man's smile widening as his voice trailed off. From that moment on, Drysten ceased to care about nearly anything. Every time he stared into the etching of his woman on the wall, he fell deeper into sadness and felt his sanity slowly leaving him.

There were others imprisoned under the earth, but Drysten rarely had the opportunity to converse with them. In truth, he cared little for speaking. The king and his prince were his only visitors, both coming to gaze upon the woeful being they had created. Through starvation and abuse, they had turned the proud son of an honorable man, and a fierce fighter, into a wretched animal. Drysten wondered if they were proud of their new creation, but truly did not know.

You are worthless. This is where you belong, the disembodied voice declared. *Nobody misses you.*

Drysten's eyes shut themselves even tighter as images of the people he failed quickly burst through his mind. He had long been plagued by the voices of the gods. He had heard them ever since he was a boy. Sometimes it was to his benefit, and sometimes not. In recent years, they had largely driven him to madness with their malevolent whispers.

Get up, son, the voice of his father stated, you have more to do.

Drysten slowly opened his eyes as he peered around his cell, suddenly feeling a slight burst of life flow into his limbs. This was a common enough occurrence, as the voice of his father also visited him from time to time. This time though, it was accompanied by a hooded figure staring back at him.

"Do you recognize my voice, Drysten?" the man asked.

Drysten erupted up from the stone floor and pressed his back into the far wall of his cell. It had been so long since he had a new visitor, one who was not present to perform some manner of torture, that he forgot what the experience was like.

The figure gently placed a hand onto the crossed iron bars of his cell. "I didn't mean to startle you, Lord."

"I… I am not a lord any longer, spirit." Drysten muttered. The years of fearing the unknown had begun to produce tears at the corners of his eyes.

The torchlight illuminated just enough of the man's face to show his slight grin. "That may be true, but we require your services, nonetheless. I assure you, I am completely real, Lord."

Drysten slowly stepped from the wall of his enclosure, unsure of what tricks the king or prince may be playing. He glanced down to the bearskin cloak on the ground, hearing faint whispers of encouragement from his father. He slowly raised his gaze back to the visitor. Behind the man, he saw the spirit of his father, Hall, standing with his arms crossed and a vacant gaze coming from his white eyes. His skin was pale, pale as Drysten had seen it when the man's body was brought before him at the fort of Segedunum. The image slowly unfolded his arms, and a deathly smile spread from ear to ear.

"Drysten?" the hood man whispered. "Drysten, we have work to do, and I require an answer as to whether or not you are capable of doing it."

Drysten stared into the empty eyes of his father, receiving a nod of assurance in response. He then straightened his back and stared into the concealed face of the man gently resting a hand on the iron bars of his cell. "Speak," he rustled.

The hooded man released the iron from his hand and stepped back, causing the image of Drysten's father to slowly fade into mist as it slowly disappeared. The visitor cleared his throat. "The king—"

Drysten scoffed as the mention of his enemy brought a shiver of hatred down his spine. "The king is a distrustful fucking *fool.* What business could he possibly—"

"Freedom," the visitor replied with a reassuring nod. "He will grant you your freedom. In return, you will make war on the Christians who attempt to undermine his reign."

Drysten let out a snort of contempt in the face of his visitor. "Why would I do this?"

The visitor shrugged. "Do all men not wish to be free?"

"The ones with reasons to be," Drysten answered. As the idea he could one day leave this cell began to take shape in his mind, images of his former friends and family floated through thoughts. People he loved, people he hated, and people he wished he knew better before he was taken from them.

"You can be with your wife again," the man said quietly.

Drysten looked to his feet. "Isolde died years ago."

The hooded man's head tilted to the side. "Your... no, Lord. Your wife is very much alive. As is your young boy, Galahad. I'd wondered what Eidion told you..."

"My wife... Isolde is alive...?" Drysten softly whispered. "Galahad..."

"Yes, Lord. Your son was named after a Christian man who briefly fought for the people you once led. He saved a handful of lives, one of which was your wife," the man explained. "Fear not though, Lord. Her and the Christian were simply bonded by your friendship."

"You said... my friendship?" Drysten wondered aloud. He always prided himself on being good with names. It was something his father had explained was important to doing business in foreign parts. He could recall most of the names he'd learned over the course of his life. The name Galahad held no meaning to him whatsoever.

"Aye, Lord. The man was given the name upon his conversion around the time of your imprisonment," the visitor stated in a reassuring tone.

"Who was... what did I know him by?" Drysten asked as he stepped closer to the iron bars between him and this curious guest.

"Matthew," the stranger answered after a moment's pause. "I understand he was known to be a Christian, but the bishop believed him to be a heretic. A Pelagian, in fact."

Drysten hung his head as he remembered the vibrant priest he had once befriended. "He was a good man. Why was his new name Galahad?"

"Named for a holy place to the East, Lord. The bishop re-baptized him in this very river right after you were imprisoned." The stranger stepped towards the bars. "There is much you must hear from your five years down below."

"What of my people? What else has happened?"

The visitor furled looked away, clearly uncomfortable

at the question. "There have been executions. The ones who served your father, Elias and Cyrus, were hung from the gatehouse over Petuaria about a year after you were imprisoned."

Drysten looked to his feet, remembering the times those two men had helped train him to fight and be a good man. Along with a man named Amiram, those two likely had as much a say in his upbringing as his own father. Especially after his mother died.

"There were others as well," Maewyn whispered. "The one known as Heraclius tried to form a resistance to the bishop."

"What happened to *him?*"

"He… was executed as well." Maewyn looked away toward one of the other cells as a soft clang was heard. "His death was slower than the others."

This cannot stand. Drysten concluded. He felt a slight breeze float by his ears as he turned to pick up his father's old cloak. He walked by the man's ghastly image as he bent down and grasped the scraggly fur resting on the ancient Roman stonework. For a moment, Drysten met the vacant, dead gaze of his father's ghost, but failed to discern his opinion on the matter. "I accept whatever duties you require of me," he said as he rose with the bearskin cloak, "but you will take me to my wife."

At that, the visitor smiled and removed his hood.

"I… know you…" Drysten said as he studied the man's face. He had green eyes and a kind smile, a smile he had only briefly seen once before.

The stranger nodded. "I am Maewyn. We met once when you returned from the voyage to Frisia. I am also known as Patrick, though it is slightly more dangerous to use my Christian name in these times."

"You *work* for the bishop! Why should I trust you?" Drysten hissed.

Maewyn scoffed. "I would have moved to kill him were I not a man of the cloth. Of that, you can be certain. We are on the same side whether you believe me or not."

Drysten looked the man's face over, wondering whether he still held the ability to discern a lie. He had been told so many over the years it seemed he no longer understood the concept of truth.

"Have it your way, priest," Drysten conceded. "I'll play your little game until I find my own way."

Maewyn nodded. "I would expect nothing less." He reached into the pocket under his robe and revealed a key. Not just any key, but the key which had unlocked the way for Drysten's torturers for so long.

"How did *you* get it?" Drysten wondered aloud.

Maewyn chuckled. "I did something I didn't know I was capable of."

"Killed him?" Drysten asked with a chuckle.

As the door opened Maewyn looked on Drysten with a shocked expression. "Goodness, no! I lied to Vonig. I explained I was to give someone the rites before death on the order of the bishop."

"You must have an impressive set of morals for *that* to be painful," Drysten muttered as he stepped out of his cage. He briefly glanced behind him, witnessing the strangely cold smile of his father as the image granted a reassuring nod upon his exit.

Maewyn led Drysten up the stairway, occasionally glancing behind him to make sure Drysten was still behind him. "Follow, Lord! Before we worry about you leading a war, you should get yourself a decent meal."

"Are there guards near?" Drysten wondered in a hushed tone.

Maewyn shrugged as he looked up above them. "Doubt it, Lord. Most people do not care for the smell emanating from down below."

"It occurs to me, I have no idea where we are," Drysten announced as torchlight from the top of the stairway began to light up the stone walls on either side of him.

"Eboracum, Lord. Right below the king's baths. There are sewers below the city which lead out to the river," Maewyn informed him. "As well as another one used as a secret passage going from the baths out to the river. The prisons connect the two tunnels."

That knowledge could prove quite useful…

As the two men reached the top of the stairs, Drysten spied a window illuminated by the faint moonlight overhead. The outside air was creeping its way into the room, filling Drysten's nostrils with his first scent of freedom. He closed his eyes as he tried to savor his initial moment of liberation from the cells below Eboracum. It was the city where he was born, and the city he had once fought for.

"Lord, the king is waiting. We need to cover you up so nobody will recognize you," Maewyn declared as he stepped closer to Drysten. He brought a priest's dirty cloak up from the ground. Drysten was pleased to see his liberator had planned ahead. Maewyn approached, carrying the worn robe as Drysten removed his father's cloak from his shoulders.

Drysten snapped out of his daydream and quickly donned the garment, carefully raising the hood over his scarred face and ears. His beard had grown longer than he thought, with the lowest point going nearly to the middle of his chest.

Drysten finally finished and folded his father's cloak into a square, now only looking like a small blanket. "Lead on, priest."

***

Ceneus sat in the study of his estate, patiently waiting for his two sons to join him. He was in no hurry for the conversation he was preparing himself for. He'd been having it with himself in his mind while he waited.

Your freedom for your short-term service, Ceneus thought. *We have a common enemy, you and I.*

Ceneus let out a deep sigh as he leaned forward in his artfully crafted chair, left over from the Roman governor when the unknown man abandoned his post for the continent. He knew what he was about to do would cost the lives of countless men under his rule.

This will be a necessary war, he thought. *It will be necessary, but terrible.*

He stared out the window into the courtyard of the old Roman fortress, watching a pair of his royal guards huddled near a small bonfire. These will be some of them I ask to die for me? he thought. He hated wars. Most of all, he hated knowing the amount of people he would send to die in them. His mind drifted back to the previous night in the tavern, and how he overheard the men speaking of newborn babies and promotions.

"Lord King," a voice greeted from the doorway.

King Ceneus turned to see his highest-ranking officer, Rodric, standing at attention. "Enter," he commanded. *He's beginning to look very much like his father.*

King Ceneus had begun seeing the face of one of his greatest friends in Rodric's face. His father's name was Aosten, and the man was murdered by Ceneus' eldest son. That crime was committed the day of a great battle north of Hadrian's Wall. This horrendous act was pinned on Drysten, the son of the king's commander at that battle. It was the reason used for the man's imprisonment.

The young man of roughly twenty years removed his worn Roman helmet and stepped towards the king. Ceneus watched as he ruffled his long, brown hair and sat in the seat across from him.

"Do you understand why I have summoned you?" King Ceneus inquired.

Rodric nodded. "We're finally going to kick the fuckers out of our home," he replied in a happy tone.

The king grinned. "That we are. I will wait for the rest of our small group to join us until I—"

A pair of voices were heard outside the door. King Ceneus paused until he knew for certain who may be skulking around outside. He was pleased to see two of his sons, Gwrast and Mor entering from the darkness.

"Father," Gwrast, the elder of the two said with a nod.

King Ceneus returned the nod and gestured for both of his boys to pull up chairs of their own. "We are awaiting a pair of others, both of whom will undoubtedly surprise you. We all share the same goals, as this bishop of ours has affected the lives of each man who enters this room."

"Why don't we simply kill the bastard and be done with it?" Mor asked in frustration. He was always the more rambunctious of the king's children.

"We would be fools to anger the pope," King Ceneus responded. "What we need is a man who has no love for the bishop, as well as myself, to openly oppose him."

Gwrast glanced towards the window as he pondered the idea. "I believe we could call on the madman to the South," he stated, referencing the Saxon who declared himself king of Londinium five years ago. "My spies tell me Colgrin is in need of funds for his new kingdom."

King Ceneus shook his head. "The Saxons cannot be trusted. Even now, they raid the towns they pledged to remain peaceful with. And they get away with it by simply explaining the men who carried out the raids have no affiliation with Colgrin."

"Didn't know there were so many Saxon kings making war against Powys," Gwrast replied with a scoff. "One could be forgiven for not knowing of them all."

The king chuckled, but wondered whether Gwrast was opening the messages from the South. There was indeed an unknown Saxon who came ashore in recent weeks, but the king didn't wish to cause a panic by openly preparing to defend against him. Especially since there was still a large amount of land to cross between the South and Eboracum.

"Then who is it you believe can fill the role?" Mor wondered as he shifted in his seat.

The shuffling of footsteps was heard from outside. King Ceneus began seeing two dark shapes drawing closer to the entrance. "A man who genuinely hates me as well as the bishop," he answered as he rose from his seat.

Two hooded priests slowly entered the room, one barefoot and smelling significantly fouler than the other. The first one to enter gave a slow nod and stepped aside, giving the second priest enough room to shyly take two more steps forward as he carefully revealed his face. His bearskin cloak looked ancient with its filth-encrusted hairs folded over itself. Ceneus wondered what smelled worse, the man or cloak.

"*Lord King,*" the dirty, lice-ridden skeleton of a man greeted. The sarcasm toward Ceneus could be easily forgiven. He wore those years poorly. His years of captivity had caused his eyes to shrink into two dark pits under his forehead, with long, matted hair atop his head.

"Maewyn," the king began, "that will be all. Get some rest, as I do not know the next time you will be able to."

"Yes, Lord King," Maewyn replied before bowing and shuffling away to the darkness. Before he passed by the dirtier of the two, he leaned in and whispered something which seemed to calm the newcomer. Maewyn then patted him on the shoulder and journeyed out into the night.

The king saw Rodric and his two sons all sitting in silence with perplexed expressions on their faces. All three of them subtly glanced to one another before the king finally found the courage to speak in the presence of the man of which he had taken so much. "Drysten—" he began.

"Am I?" Drysten interrupted. "I thought my people believed me to be dead. What good is the name of a dead man?"

The king glanced at the desk in front of him as he attempted to find the words. He briefly looked his former prisoner in the eye, catching a quick moment where he seemed to look off at someone else who only he could see.

Must have been driven mad, the king silently concluded. I suppose he may have a point.

"Father," Gwrast awkwardly whispered. "Who is this man?"

The king turned to his favored son. "He was once the son of my greatest, yet shortest tenured commanders. Hall was his name."

Mor perked his head up. "The man from Segedunum?"

King Ceneus nodded. "The very same. This man here is... his son."

Gwrast and Mor each looked on the scraggly man staring into their father's forehead, both unsure of what to make of the sight.

"This... Drysten was the commander who carried the attack forward once his father was killed," The king added.

Mors leaned forward. "Why the fuck are we imprisoning people like-"

"Enough!" the king declared as he raised his hand to quiet his son. He looked over Mor's confused expression and slowly nodded his head. "We did nothing of our own will. That is why we are all here tonight. Since the bishop arrived, that is how we have lived. We are nothing but pawns working under the bishop's direction under threats of holy armies and vengeful gods."

"Aye," Gwrast sadly replied.

The king noticed Drysten's eyes follow something across the room, something totally unseen by anyone else. "Drysten, you swore to kill me, did you not? I assume all men in your position make a vow of that sort."

Drysten's focus snapped from whatever it was following

onto the king. A grim smile began to shape across his face. "You will die," he responded. "Not even your God, or even Bishop Germanus… or these three fools here will stop me from wrapping my hands around your neck."

The king was slightly startled at the intensity of Drysten's hatred, but knew it was entirely reasonable. Gwrast began standing until the king gestured for the three men to remain seated. "Then I give you one last order," Ceneus began. He paused for a moment, as he knew this would end up being a command which he could regret more than any other. "I order you to leave here, gather your strength and… try. But you are to try upon the completion of one task. Kill the damn Bishop and kill Eidion alongside him."

Drysten produced one of the most wicked smiles the king had ever seen. "Yes, Lord King." At that, he slowly turned towards the door, keeping eye contact with Ceneus as long as he could manage before finally turning away to exit.

Both of the king's sons were staring at him in shock, while Rodric was understandably watching the strange guest leave to make sure he would not try and make good on his promise earlier than agreed.

Gwrast slowly rose from his seat and took a step towards the door to make sure Drysten had left before finally turning to his father. "You just told a man to kill you," he said in confusion. "There were likely other ways to go about this without the risk of dying at the hands of a madman. Did you see how he stared off into nothing as though he was being spoken to?"

King Ceneus smirked. "I heard rumors the gods speak to him, maybe they—"

"Gods?" Mor asked in surprise. "That is the first time I have heard you speak of multiple gods since we were forced to change faiths."

The king nodded. "It is. As for the madman, there would have been risks involved no matter the course we chose. This one was simply… calculated. If he succeeds, the Bishop gets killed by an enemy we shared with him, meaning the Pope would not see cause to send a papal army to remove us from power."

Gwrast let out a heavy sigh. "I wish we knew for certain whether or not those threats could even be carried out."

"You've seen the mercenaries Germanus brings to our shores," Mor put in.

Gwrast nodded. "Men who fight for money are hardly a papal army, brother."

King Ceneus nodded. "It's too great a risk. Saxons and Gaels are one thing, but having a whole faith against you is another matter entirely."

At that, the king and his sons had found the man who would bring down the bishop, but possibly themselves as well.

CHAPTER THREE

Drysten spent the short walk from Ceneus' baths listening to the sounds of the night all around him. There was a chorus of insects clicking and birds or bats flapping their wings overhead. But the thing Drysten heard the most was the sound of his father's voice.

"The fool doesn't believe you will succeed," Hall's voice announced as Drysten stepped through Eboracum's Southwestern gate. It was the exit to an old Roman fortress now used by the king of Ebrauc as his residence.

Drysten chuckled. "I know," he answered with a scoff. The voices were only audible to him, meaning a pair of guards in Roman armor and royal blue cloaks suspiciously eyed him as he passed. "Just speaking with our Lord and Savior," Drysten declared as he sauntered by, raising his hands to the heavens shrouded in the oppressive darkness above him.

The two guards scoffed and returned to their private conversation as Drysten walked by. Drysten was thankful he knew the one way he could pass by without any trouble. To them, Drysten was simply another shoddily dressed priest roaming between the fort and the numerous nonbelievers of the town below. How could they know what Drysten really was?

He continued until finally reaching the line of torches leading towards the main walkway of the town. The feeling of freedom was strange to him, as he truly had no idea what his first course of action should be.

"Visit your mother," Hall commanded.

Drysten wondered what could possibly be of help at the

grave of his mother, but knew enough from his many years hearing the voices to understand he shouldn't question it. He immediately changed course towards the grave at which he said his final farewell to the woman at the age of ten. Fortunata was buried outside the fortress mere days before the last Romans finally left Britannia for the mainland. She was quickly laid to rest just outside the Northern walls of the fort, under a cloudless sky on a bright summer's day. Drysten remembered holding his father's hand as they each followed the cart holding his mother.

"It's a beautiful day," Hall had said to his son. "She would have enjoyed it."

Drysten had fought off tears as he peered towards her final resting place. He remembered trying to be so strong until he looked to his father and noticed the small drops fluttering down his cheek. Of all the times he tried, he could barely remember anything else, and even struggled to recall what his mother even looked like.

He waded through the darkness along the wall of the fortress until he finally found the clearing containing the countless graves of the deceased buried outside Eboracum.

"I should have visited you when I was last here." Drysten felt an ample amount of guilt over not being able to bury his father next to his mother. The two were the perfect parents to him in his early years, and his mother was pivotal in teaching him to deal with the voices he heard from above.

Before long, he came upon the familiar sight of a stone column once supporting the roof of an enclosed grave, now weathered into a heap of rubble at his feet. "Only a few feet away," Drysten whispered. He turned and scanned the moonlit grass at his feet, finally seeing the stone block denoting his mother's presence, but this time, there were two more at either side of it.

They could not have run out of space— Then Drysten read the names. The one on the far left of the three read his father's name, 'Hall ap Lugurix, defender of the people and leader of the Fortuna' while the other bore his own.

"Drysten ap Hall..." Drysten read aloud. "The *usurper*."

Drysten didn't know what compelled him to drop to his knees and begin to dig. He suddenly felt the whole weight of the world push him to the dirt as he clawed and scratched at the earth beneath the grave marker which bore his name. He scraped and clawed under the moonlight, hearing wild dogs and people off in the distance, but nothing that would prevent him from finding out what they buried in his place.

"Dig!" a woman's voice screamed.

Mother? Drysten wondered. It had been so long since he'd heard her kind voice, he couldn't have been sure. There was something wicked attached to it.

The voice spurred his weakened body forward until the appearance of a wooden box at the base of the shallow hole. Drysten paused for a moment, glancing around into the darkness, completely unsure of his next action. He glanced back to the warped and rotting wood as he began clearing away the dirt to find its edge. Upon its discovery, Drysten began to heave it out of the hole and rest it atop his mother's grave.

It's too light for them to have put a body inside, Drysten mused. What could they have possibly buried in my place?

Drysten stared at the short chest at his feet. It was barely large enough to hold a child, let alone a full-grown man. He peered through the darkness for an instrument to beat into the wood and settled on a chunk of his mother's gravestone which had weathered off over the years.

"Thank you, mother," Drysten whispered.

He picked up the stone, satisfied the weight of the roughly fist-sized object would be enough to splinter the wood and peer inside. After turning it over in his hand, he finally found the sharpest edge.

Drysten lifted his arm as high as he could manage and brought it down with more force than he thought he was capable of. The top of the rotted wood was all but obliterated, and inside laid something Drysten never thought he would see again.

"Titus' armor... and father's dagger... " Drysten fought tears as he remembered the moment Titus, one of the best men he had ever known, bestowed upon him the exquisite Roman-made armor after Drysten helped the man's people. He ripped the remainder of the top away from the box before finally picking up the metal breastplate, placing it carefully on the grass beside his cloak. As Drysten began to glance away, he noticed the brown dye along the armor had turned to a darker color, with most of the leather looking decayed and haggard. He reached in and brought out an object wrapped in cloth, instantly recognizing it as the sword he had purchased in Ostia during his first journey as the captain of his father's ship, the Fortuna.

He rose from his knees as he gently unwrapped the cloth, revealing the old Roman scabbard encasing his blade. His fingers wrapped around the hilt before he gently tugged the steel out of its sheath, seeing the moonlight glistening over the metal. He thought it was ironic he held a tool of war over the grave of his mother, a woman who detested violence and cruelty. But there would be much cruelty to show in the times ahead, and Drysten knew this without a doubt.

He slowly began donning the items which had once felt so familiar. The armor somehow managed to stay atop his shoulders with the leather straps noticeably loose in comparison to the last time he had worn it. It took him longer to apply his vambraces, as the dexterity of his hands had left him long ago. His graceless fingers fumbled with the laces of his greaves before he finally managed to complete the set.

Drysten needed to create an extra notch in his sword belt to make it stay around his waist without falling, but only needed a moment to puncture a small hole with his father's dagger. Once he finished donning his armor, he reapplied his father's bearskin cloak.

"It's so much heavier..." He knew he once looked the part of a Roman general in the ensemble. But now he guessed he looked much more like a man birthed from someone's nightmares than anything else.

"A nightmare you will be," the brooding voice whispered. Burn it all.

Drysten smirked as he stared into the moonlight, knowing full well what his next goal was. "Get your strength back, and find your people," he whispered to himself. "Find them all and burn everything in Ebrauc to the ground until the king is nothing more than ashes, and... Eidion is a castrated fool wandering the streets."

Drysten was so entranced by his own desires he couldn't hear the footsteps coming from behind him. He stared into the moonlit grass, wondering how long the process of finding his people, gathering back his strength, and removing the king and bishop would take when the guards began approaching him.

"Who are you?" one demanded in a commanding tone.

Drysten's smirk finally faded as he turned to face them. As he surveyed the newcomers, he saw two guards wearing worn, Roman-made metal armor. It was called lorica segmentata when the Empire still used it. It consisted of an upper body piece made of steel plates tied together by leather scraps and was a favorite among those who had once fought for Rome. The pieces were rare, but elegant and trustworthy in battle. These two men not only had the plates, but vibrant royal blue cloaks resting atop their shoulders.

The man in the front held out a torch in his off-hand while in the other was his sword. He had narrow eyes and a grey beard, but Drysten guessed he could handle him in a fight should it come to it. The second was significantly younger, with short hair and a fat face. Both men were shorter than him by about a head, but the younger one looked more capable in a fight.

The guard with the grey beard stepped closer "I said—"

"I heard you," Drysten croaked. It was strange to him to be able to speak with more than one person in a single day.

"Then who are you?" replied the younger guard through a shaky voice.

Drysten cleared his throat and took two small steps forward. "I am Drysten ap Hall." The older guard seemed surprised by the answer, while the younger man seemed altogether indifferent.

"You," Drysten said as he pointed to the man with the grey beard. "You know that name."

The man nodded. "I fought under a commander by that name at Segedunum. I was one of the few who didn't try to run away from that fight." The guard glanced back to his companion before returning Drysten's gaze. "The man you speak of is dead."

Drysten smiled and shook his head. "Maybe that man is dead, but I assure you, who you see before you is whatever's left of him."

"Prove it," the guard demanded as he threw down the torch between Drysten and himself and raising his blade.

"When I arrived here, my people had recently been attacked by a Frisian who later fought by my side. I had to journey into his homeland to save my wife and others from slavery at the hands of a man named Servius. I returned to help my father wage war on the Picts atop a hill to the East of Din Guayrdi, and later retook a fort called Segedunum from them in your king's name." Drysten knew the man likely didn't even know all those details, but figured it couldn't hurt to divulge them.

"I saw your father die. Saw the blade that cut his throat," the man whispered through a narrow gaze.

Drysten knowingly grinned to himself. "If you were *truly* there, you would have seen the blade cut through the armor at his side. *Not* his throat."

The grey-haired man's eyes went wide as he began lowering his blade and raising the torch. "I saw that very thing, Lord." The bearded guard sadly surveyed Drysten's mangled face as he sheathed his blade. "You were supposed to be dead,

Lord. It was said the prince and the bishop executed you in a cell for attempting to usurp the king. They even forced your loved ones to engrave 'usurper' on your stone."

"I did no such thing," Drysten said with a scoff. "Though now, I intend to."

The guard's mouth fell open as his hand moved back to his blade and he deftly pulled it from his sheath. "Come again, Lord?"

"I intend to kill the king," Drysten said with a laugh. He bungled the attempt to pull his sword from its sheath, dropping it from his malnourished hands.

"Ha!" the younger guard bellowed with a smile. "Fucker couldn't be the lord of anything. He's just some damn graverobber, sir."

The older guard furrowed his brow as he watched Drysten stumbling over himself to pick up his sword. "Stealing from the dead joins you with them in these parts."

"Then we should get it over with." The younger guard drew his sword and pranced towards Drysten as though the former lord wasn't a threat. But that was when Drysten struck.

Fool was much too easy to trick, Drysten thought as he nimbly turned and jabbed his dagger through his assailant's throat. He let go of the handle as the boy collapsed into the dirt, squirming and reeling from the pain. Drysten gathered he would be screaming if he were still capable of it, and gently picked up his sword to face the bearded man racing towards him.

"Lord or not, you're *fucked* now," the guard sliced wildly towards Drysten's head, missing by mere inches as Drysten ducked just low enough to avoid it. He thrust the point of his sword into the guard's chest, turning it as the point created a loud thud against the metal armor. In Drysten's healthier days, the man would undoubtedly have been a bloody heap on the ground. But in his weakened state, all he succeeded in doing was cutting a pair of the leather straps along his foe's side as his sword glanced away.

"The guard let out a startled cry as he glanced down to his side. "Fucking bastard!" He turned to swipe again but was stopped when Drysten turned and sliced upwards, catching the man's sword hand, and sending the blade to the ground.

After a yipping cry of pain from the guard, Drysten knew he did not have the strength to break through his metal chest-piece, nor the dexterity to swing for his neck. Instead, he chose another strategy.

"Slice him from the ground up," the echoed voice ordered.

Drysten started hacking into the man's legs, only managing enough force to break the skin and tear shallow grooves in the muscle. The guard was wailing in pain as he desperately reached down for his sword, but Drysten changed from attacking his legs to jabbing his sword point down into his hands.

"Mercy!" the guard screamed. "Fucking mercy!"

Drysten halted, as his victim was now groaning while curled up into a bloody ball at his feet. For a moment, he knew the right thing to do was to walk away. But then he saw the color of the man's cloak and remembered the royal blue meant the man was in the service of the king.

"No," Drysten whispered. He raised his sword up and quickly brought its point down through the side of the man's neck, causing his enemy to immediately go limp.

He let go, leaving it jutting out of the ground as he stepped toward the hole once thought to be his grave. "Glad to know I have some fight left in me," he cheerfully thought as he pushed the box's broken pieces into the hole. "I wonder if graverobbing is still graverobbing when you're stealing your own belongings."

Drysten turned back to his victims and pulled his sword and dagger out of both of their throats before searching them for anything he could use. The grey-bearded man had a small pouch with two silver coins, while the younger one had a pouch with six. On top of that, Drysten also found a silver chain on the older guard and a bone-carved crucifix with the younger one.

Did they have to die? Hall asked his son.

Drysten shook his head as he began making his way around the walls of Eboracum. “No, father, they did not.”

“I thought I raised a good man.” The sadness in Hall’s voice was obvious.

Drysten scoffed. “You did, but you didn’t raise a *weak* one. The second the man drew his sword, I knew I would have to put them down. You would say the same were you even here.”

“I suppose I didn’t teach you fear, either.”

“That came later,” Drysten solemnly replied.

***

The ride East to Eboracum was tumultuous, even by Dagonet's standards. Once he left Cynwrig a short ride East, he continued until he finally made it to Eboracum. It took him two days of pressing his horse harder than he thought the beast could handle. For the first leg of the journey, there were signs he was being followed by the strange Gaels he encountered with Gaius at Glanoventa. Those signs thankfully ceased when he journeyed about twenty miles, with no more dark specks in the grass behind him.

They were so fast... Dagonet recalled as he rubbed his tired eyes. The men who had trailed him were relentless, and he understood whatever enemy who caught him would likely best him in a fight. Whether that was due to the lucky shot of a poison-tipped arrow, or him simply letting one get too close while he slept.

The gates to the fortress of Eboracum was teeming with guards, some wearing the royal blue cloaks of the king, and the others wearing the black of Bishop Germanus. Dagonet rode on at a slow pace until he was almost stopped by one of the black-clad guards. Before the man could manage a word, a guard in royal blue simply waved him in.

"He's with us," the man declared. "You can fuck off back to your bishop if that’s an issue." The black-clad man sneered as he eyed Dagonet riding toward the baths of the fort.

The entrance was manned by a dozen of the king's men. This was more than twice the number Dagonet had ever seen stationed within fifty feet of the place in all his years of serving him. One who recognized him simply waved him on through the doorway, taking the bridle of his horse as he dismounted.

"What's the fuss about?" Dagonet asked as he glanced towards the heavily guarded area.

The guard shrugged. "Two of our boys were murdered last night. Nobody caught a glimpse of the killer."

Dagonet nodded as he entered the baths and made the short walk to the main room. Even these Gaels couldn’t be fast enough to beat me here on foot. Probably just a drunken fight between Germanus' men and Ceneus'.

"Ah! Someone who might actually prove useful!" a man announced upon his entry.

Dagonet instantly recognized the voice as Prince Eidion, Ceneus' oldest son and protege to Bishop Germanus. "Lord Prince," he dutifully greeted with a slight nod.

"What news from the West, man? And don't respond like the other dullards we sent. They spent all day trying to say these men could simply vanish into thin air." the prince stated with a disbelieving scoff.

Dagonet nodded. "I did not see them disappear, Lord Prince, but I indeed witnessed them appear quite suddenly."

The prince scowled. "You simply must not have been attentive enough to witness their presence."

Dagonet wasn't sure, but he thought he could sense a slight twinge of fear in the man's voice. He surveyed his face and saw nothing but uncertainty and exasperation, nothing new to the man in most situations. "I perceive those kinds of things quite well, actually," Dagonet responded with a grin. "Lord Prince."

Footsteps became audible from the hallway Dagonet had just marched through. "I expected your return," a voice stated.

Dagonet turned and saw the faces of King Ceneus, Maewyn, and Gwrast appear in the doorway. "Lord King," he said with a bow, moving to the side to allow their entry.

The king nodded before looking back to Eidion. "Leave," he sternly commanded.

"Do I not have just as much cause to be informed on this matter as yourself, father," the prince asked with a smirk.

King Ceneus shook his head. "No, you do not. As you are not king, you still obey my commands."

"For now," Eidion returned with a wicked grin. He slowly shuffled through the assembling group until he finally disappeared through the doorway. Upon being out of view, an immense cloud seemed to be lifted from the baths, and Dagonet found his way to the edge of the water where he started to strip his armor and rags off to enter.

"Did I say you could?" Ceneus chirped as he began doing the same.

Dagonet scoffed. "I suppose I could remain smelling like shit if it pleases the king."

Gwrast chuckled. "The only shit I smelled was the nonsense coming from my brother's mouth."

The four men quickly entered the baths, with the feeling of the warm water seemingly washing away the troubles of Dagonet's past few days. It was a pleasant feeling to go along with the muck encrusted onto his body going with those troubles. Nobody spoke for a few moments until Maewyn finally trained his attention to the scout.

"Was it him?" the priest asked. "Was it Abhartach's people?"

Dagonet nodded. "The signs were there. The disappearances, the boats, the poison. All of it."

Maewyn glanced to the king. "You did well sending Mor into the West. Though I fear he'll be needing more men soon enough."

Dagonet nodded. “Many more. It seems there could be a greater number than before.”

King Ceneus glanced towards Gwrast. "Can you spare any?"

Gwrast paused for a moment before tilting his head to the side. "Not if we're to protect ourselves from... closer enemies."

Dagonet watched both the king and prince glance towards him, clearly reluctant to divulge something which they felt he shouldn't hear. "More Saxons?"

Both monarchs shook their heads.

“Those Jutish bastards again?”

"This one will stay close to the chest for a time," Ceneus finally responded.

Dagonet nodded before turning to the priest. "What enemies did Abhartach have across the sea? Are there any people who could be called upon simply because they hate him?"

Maewyn shook his head. "There are none, Lord, as most feared him more than hated him. And everyone hated him while he was there."

Dagonet sat up in the warm water. "Most?"

"Dead men cannot help us now," the priest sadly responded. "There was one man, but I have not heard mention of his name in a very long time."

Dagonet splashed water over his head as he let out a breath of relaxation. "From my experience, these raids will incite others. We all know who would jump at the opportunity to invade a weakened Ebrauc."

"Colgrin," the king whispered as he splashed water onto his arms.

Colgrin was the Saxon who somehow managed to rally countless other tribes from Germania and Gaul before invading Londinium, a large city to the South. There were always rumors their original target was Eboracum, but Dagonet could never find out if the rumors held any truth. The man was widely known to be a bloodthirsty savage, with his people committing unspeakable crimes in the South for the last five years.

"We need to deal with this now before word gets out," Gwrast stated.

King Ceneus nodded before turning to Dagonet. "Go to Petuaria. Cross the river and speak with Titus. I know he does not have the numbers he once did, but we need what he can spare."

Dagonet nodded before wiping the small specks of dirt from his legs and arms and rising to his feet. "Yes, Lord King. I will leave at once."

The king smiled. "You've always served me well, Dagonet. Get some food in your belly before you leave, and give my regards to your sister."

"I'll do that, Lord King," Dagonet said as he stepped out of the bath. He dried off on a cloth given to him by a servant, and departed upon being given a fresh set of clothes to wear on the ride to the Southeast.

Dagonet didn't think it fitting the tell the king his sister had disowned him for not wanting to switch to the Christian faith. Her life had become tumultuous after she was saved from being Servius' wife, and the Christians tricked her into believing her life could be put back together if she simply worshipped their savior.

He quickly exited the baths to the street, feeling noticeably fresher than he had upon entering the building. To the right of the gateway leading to the city, Prince Eidion was speaking to Bishop Germanus about something he couldn't hear. The bishop, with his strong brow and freshly shaven face, noticed him by the baths and began approaching him.

No chance of that conversation happening, Dagonet thought as he quickly hopped on his horse and rode through the gate with a grin. Germanus' perturbed scowl was much to the delight of Ceneus' four guards stationed near the gate.

"My regards to our Lord and Savior!" Dagonet shouted as he rode by.

The bishop replied with something inaudible to him as he rode on through the city, eventually making it through the Southern gate and onto the road to Petuaria.

Petuaria was once a Roman fort many generations ago. It was built atop an old tribal town belonging to the Brigantes tribe before most people of the area were living under the Roman flag. Now it was the lone bright spot of Ebrauc in Dagonet's eyes. There was a villa briefly owned by an old commander Dagonet served under. A man he couldn't help but think about from time to time. Hall's principles and honorable qualities were impressive, even by Rome's standards. He taught Dagonet much in the little time he knew him and his son.

The way into town was somewhat soggy, with the rains washing mud from the side of the road onto the worn Roman stonework.

"You'll get some rest soon, boy," Dagonet whispered into his horse's ear. He felt guilty riding the same one for the duration of his trip West. He guessed stopping for an extended time to rest could mean the Gaels pursuing him would finally be given a chance to catch up.

He slowed to a canter as he made his way South, only pausing for a moment to urinate on the side of the road. The sky was clear overhead, a sight which brought relief to the scout. He had ridden through the rain for most of his trip to Eboracum, and had no desire to stomach much more.

After a few hours at a leisurely pace, he found himself trailing behind a haggard-looking beggar in a scraggly cloak. There was something familiar about the man, but Dagonet couldn't tell what it was. He slowed his horse to a walk to observe the man shuffling towards the same destination.

No other place he could possibly go unless he wishes to deal with rebels in Rheged, Dagonet concluded.

Rheged was the land which borders the Southern regions of Ebrauc. It was once a proud kingdom until King Ceneus convinced the Powysians to aid him into conquering it. He cited their king attempting to kill him when he took his crown. Dagonet did not know many of the specifics, but for the last twenty or so years, the land was a disorganized mess at the mercy of bandits and rabid tribesmen in the hills. Rheged's king. Gwrwst Lledlwrn, was thrown into a prison many years ago. This made many people believe Rheged's power had gone with him.

After a while of following the beggar, the town of Petuaria finally came into view. Its stone walls were crumbling away, offering little protection themselves. But Dagonet genuinely believed it to be the safest place in the entirety of the kingdom. The finest fighting men he ever saw lived there. Once the followers of Hall, they now only picked up a sword to defend themselves from raiders, though few dared to attack them. Neither King Ceneus, nor any leader of Ebrauc sought to anger those people, as they were more organized than most of the royal army.

Dagonet watched as the man in front of him suddenly stopped and walked into the middle of the roadway. It seemed the stranger was gazing over the many buildings behind Petuaria's walls. Dagonet thought he could hear the man whispering something to himself.

"Friend! Are you alright?" Dagonet called as he neared.

The man neglected to respond even though he gave away he heard him. He tilted his head to the side before looking back to the town. It seemed his gaze was fixed on the villa.

Dagonet road up beside him. "Is there something you need?"

He finally had a chance to survey the stranger up close, seeing grossly neglected armor and a sword with a rusty handle. He had a black beard which ended in the middle of the breastplate, and scraggly black hair atop his head. It appeared the man had tried to tie the mangled mess up at the back of his head, but only succeeded in grabbing a handful. His eyes seemed vacant in a strange way which made Dagonet uncomfortable.

"You swore to fight for me once," the stranger whispered. "You swore to stand by my side, but where were you?"

Dagonet narrowed his eyes as he attempted to get a closer look at the man's face. "Who are you?" he demanded.

This stranger was known to Dagonet. He could feel it in his bones, but had no idea why. He knew he would remember seeing a man in such a state as this for all his days.

The man produced a smirk over his scarred face. "You likely wouldn't believe me?"

"Try me," Dagonet commanded as he rested his hand on the hilt of his sword.

"You called me lord once." The stranger raised his face higher to let the sun illuminate it. "Take me to my people."

Dagonet gazed over the worn, beaten face of the man in front of him. It shared an impressive similarity to a man he once knew long ago. But Dagonet knew it couldn't be him. The bishop had that man executed in his cell when he took him prisoner and threw him under Eboracum. He even forced the word 'usurper' engraved on his headstone while the funeral was still being presided. It was Eidion who had done the deed.

"Throw down your weapons," Dagonet ordered as he dismounted. "Now!"

The man immediately complied and handed his decaying sword-belt to him. Dagonet turned it over in his hand and easily discerned fresh blood at the hilt of the man's knife, causing him to glance up into the man's vacant eyes.

"Take me to my people," the stranger repeated. His croaky voice sent a faint ripple down Dagonet's spine. It reminded him of gravel being tossed onto wooden planks.

Dagonet simply nodded and gestured for the man to lead.

CHAPTER FOUR

Hall's voice was humming through Drysten's mind as Dagonet followed him toward Petuaria.

"He doesn't believe you," Hall whispered. His voice felt as though it was gliding through the air beside Drysten's head.

Drysten was amused by the remark and betrayed a slight chuckle. "He will."

"What was that?" Dagonet questioned from behind him.

Drysten slightly turned and shook his head, apparently satisfying the scout in the belief he must have misheard him.

The two were now making their way through the stone gate to Petuaria. All those who saw Drysten stopped to look on the gangly creature which had crossed under the gate's arches. One child, a boy, took a single look at Drysten and ran towards the villa.

Drysten looked over the walls of the villa, remembering how it was once his home. *I married Isolde there…* The stone archway had become cracked and broken. The depiction of the goddess, Britannia, had worn down as well. It was a sight that brought a sense of sadness and woe into Drysten's heart.

"Take me to Diocles," Drysten ordered.

Dagonet returned a suspicious gaze, with Drysten beginning to see the man finally daring to believe the truth of his identity. "You… who else lives here?"

Drysten turned towards the town, thankfully seeing a handful of familiar faces staring back at him. Oddly, many people were pausing their day to day tasks and looking on him as he took a pace forward. He cleared his throat, and began pointing from person to person. "Magnus is the one kneeling by that home; he took care of the Fortuna's sick. Those two men with bows in hand, walking towards the river are the Cretans, Petras and Paulus." Drysten slowly turned to Dagonet, seeing his perplexed expression and desire to believe Drysten's every word. "Those two may well be the best two marksmen on the islands. Their sister's name is Petronela, and they originally wished to build a home by the tavern, though I do not know if they strayed from that desire."

Dagonet quickly raised his hand to quiet him, glancing among the small number of people who may have heard the exchange.

"*Now* he believes you," Hall whispered.

Dagonet frantically surveyed the many faces of the townspeople before grabbing Drysten's shoulder and leading him around the back of a newly constructed home. The thatch had not completely dried, with Drysten noticing a few green strands of water reeds as he was being dragged past them.

"Lord," Dagonet whispered, though Drysten could not discern whether he was panicked by his presence or relieved, "We need you to look like a beggar. Take off... is that Titus' armor you have on?"

Drysten nodded. "It is, though I doubt he'd want it back in this state." He glanced down and noticed the spot on the chest which once held the impression of a bull. He couldn't tell whether it had been broken off or simply crusted over with muck.

"Lord, take it all off. Take the cloak and everything but what rags you have on," Dagonet ordered.

The scout found a pile of stacked timbers around the back of the home and began to fashion a hiding spot for Drysten's belongings. He piled them in such a way there was just enough space underneath to slip the armor and sword belt before covering it with another couple of logs.

"Can you take me to my woman now?" Drysten inquired.

Dagonet gave him a confused expression. "I thought you wished to find Diocles."

Drysten glanced towards the pile of logs near his feet. "I have... been... alone. I don't know... "

"*Weak!*" the voice seethed. "The usurper pines for the loving embrace of a woman to soothe his soul. How will you kill the bishop and the prince while at the tit of a woman? "

Drysten's head began to ache as the voices slowly became louder. The world seemed to vibrate, and his vision was getting smaller and smaller until he finally collapsed. The noises of his mind were blaring; but they seemed to make the world a quiet enough place in which he may be able to rest.

"Son, get up!" Hall screamed. "You must *always* get back up!"

"No! Stay where you are! *Weak* and pathetic being..."

Drysten frantically looked around for his father, forgetting he once stood next to his lifeless body in the fort on Hadrian's Wall. "Father... " he whispered.

Dagonet rushed over and picked him up, throwing an arm over his shoulder and attempting to drag him behind a pair of bushes. The only thing Drysten could hear from the man was something about his clothes no longer being fresh.

"You're wasting time! Find them and kill them!" the voice hissed.

Drysten peered around, seeing only Dagonet. "Kill who?" he begged.

Dagonet awkwardly gazed into Drysten's face, clearly believing he was mad.

"Usurper! Usurper! Usurper!" The voice cackled madly, numbing Drysten's ears as he watched Dagonet whisper something to him and run off behind the row of houses. "Fool! He'll betray you! They'll all betray you! They left you to die, and now you wish their comfort!"

Drysten shut his eyes as tight as he could as he silently begged for the voices to cease. It was common for them to ring out in the way they were; this was just the first time they did so outside the comfort of his cell. He could feel the tears beginning to stream down his face but didn't know if he was sobbing.

A woman's voice cut through the hissing and screaming of the voices in his mind. "Drysten... " she whispered.

He slowly opened his watery eyes and looked up, wondering when he had been placed with his back to the wall of the home. He looked to his side, immediately noticing a pair of legs under a ragged gown. After slowly raising his gaze, he finally saw his wife after five long years without anything but her memories. He couldn't manage anything more than a nod as she slowly crept closer, egged on by Dagonet and another man turned around behind them.

"How are you alive?" she said through teary eyes. "We were told you were executed by the bishop. We even buried your belongings by your father and mother."

"Surprised they let me have a grave," Hall bitterly muttered.

Drysten looked away from Isolde. "They let you have a grave because they blamed Aosten's death on me."

Isolde seemed startled. "Who spoke to you...?"

Drysten meant to answer her by couldn't remember what she'd asked. "I was alive the whole time. They told me you died giving birth to our son."

Isolde's eyes widened as she fixed her gaze toward Dagonet, with the scout returning a sad nod.

Dagonet looked around the corner of the house before helping Drysten lift himself from the ground. "Remember, you're a filthy beggar who's not worth anyone's time. You're not stupid enough to cross in front of the villa because you *know* how the prince treats beggars and vagabonds." He glanced around the corner one more time before looking back. "Follow us at a safe distance, but do not look anyone in the eye. Keep your eyes down, or someone may recognize you."

"Somehow," Drysten responded with a chuckle. He glanced to Isolde one more time as she began walking forward with Dagonet, flashing an awkward smile as she walked by him.

"It's good to have you back, Lord," a voice said from behind him. He was so fixed on Isolde he forgot she arrived with another. He turned to look on the smiling face of Magnus, his ship's doctor who once served under Drysten's father as well. "You look *better* than I remember," he said with a smile.

Drysten snickered as he glanced down to his ragged, filth-stained hands. The area around his groin was moist. "I suppose I'll need to bathe before Isolde will stand to be near me again."

"Lord, she silently begged to whatever gods she worships for them to give you back. She won't be complaining about the state of you now that you're here," Magnus replied. "Maybe keep that to a minimum." Magnus gently ran his fingers of the 'FVG' brand on his own forearm. Magnus, Isolde, and a few others bear the brand. Magnus received it while he was the property of a slaver a few years before joining Drysten's father's crew. "Our people need this," he sadly whispered. Drysten saw his mind journey somewhere else for a moment before he finally returned. "I'll be right behind you, Lord."

Drysten nodded, but wondered what Magnus could mean when referring to his people needing him. How could anyone need him at all when he was in this state? He turned and began the slow march through Petuaria, moving as though he were an emaciated homeless man in need of charity. He realized the irony in the fact that he sort of was.

I understand the king would wish to bring me out of confinement under the guise of a priest, but why must I act as a lowly wanderer near my own people? Drysten wondered. He stepped from the shadows and into the street, with strangers granting him disgusted looks as they passed him by. He glanced to his right and found his woman peering behind her before Dagonet looked to turn her back around and ushered her forward.

"To the ferry, Lord," Magnus whispered.

Drysten nodded before lowering his eyes as he walked towards the river, quickly approaching the villa he once called home and stealing a look inside.

"Kill him!" a voice screamed.

Drysten froze as he looked through the entryway. There stood one of the men who repeatedly tortured him in his cell for the last five years. Many of the scars across Drysten's face were gifts from this man. "Vonig," he whispered.

"Lord, *keep* moving," Magnus urged from behind.

Drysten felt his face contorting with anger as he managed to will himself forward. Vonig glanced in his direction but only saw a haggard pile of rags, while on his lap sat a woman who seemed to be a whore.

I will kill you, Drysten thought as he journeyed on, *it will be slow.*

Two children began playing across from him until one glanced his way and turned white in the face. The two were clearly startled as they moved off towards a series of shoddy homes near the docks of the town.

The faint sound of Isolde and Dagonet arguing were heard. From what Drysten could overhear, Isolde wasn't sure of Drysten's identity. She said something about his appearance only being vaguely like that of her loving husband.

Can't blame her, Drysten thought, *the years have not been kind to me... or you for that matter.*

Drysten looked over the state of his woman, only then noticing the raggedness of her clothes. They were obviously not as bad as Drysten's but were not fit to be worn by someone of Isolde's status. The wife of a lord should have been afforded much better comforts than the ones she was given.

When the group finally reached the ferry leading to the other side of the river, Magnus quickened his pace and strolled right next to Drysten. Gazing over the scars given by Vonig and Eidion over the past five years.

"You've had a rough go of it, Lord," Magnus whispered.

Drysten nodded. "Hopefully not any longer."

Magnus chuckled and glanced behind him, satisfied nobody was watching them as they walked down a dirt pathway to the riverbank.

"Dag," Magnus called, "I think we're out of view."

Dagonet turned around and nodded once he saw nobody was following them. "Onto the ferry, Lord."

"How is *this* supposed to hold all of us?" Drysten asked, gesturing toward the shoddy pier. It was clearly old enough to have been built by the Romans many years before they eventually departed from Britannia.

Dagonet shook his head. "It won't. Magnus will have to go back to the village. I believe this will hold three people safely, considering one weighs no more than a large child."

Drysten glimpsed down and saw his ribs were easily discerned through his haggard garments. "Fair enough. Lead on."

Dagonet led Isolde and Drysten onto the ferry, then used a long wooden pole to push off from the riverbank. The distance between the sides of the river wasn't far and the three reached the other after a few short moments. Drysten peered behind him, seeing Magnus wave and turn to the village once they reached the other bank.

"He'll be getting the men together," Dagonet stated. "This way, Lord," he said as he gestured to the dirt pathway leading from the river. "Titus has a villa on this side of the river."

Drysten nodded and looked to Isolde, seeing her lower her gaze to avoid his own. "I promise you; I am who I say I am."

A tear began in the corner of Isolde's eye. It was obvious she wanted to believe him but was smart enough to understand the chances of him lying outweighed those of him telling the truth.

Always too smart for your own good. Drysten wondered if he should describe the journey he took to rescue Isolde and more of his people from the same slaver who once owned Magnus. He ultimately decided it could do more harm than good at the moment.

The walk from the river to the villa owned by one of Drysten's old friends seemed longer than it actually was. The sun was just beginning to go down when the old walls finally came into view. Where the villa in Petuaria was a luxurious home still fit for a Roman statesman, this one was anything but.

The walls were all cracked and broken, with large chunks laying at its base. The roof had no tiles in view and was largely comprised of thatch from water reeds. It was a strange look, but understandable when considering the only people able to repair such buildings departed Britannia with the Romans long ago.

Drysten knew this building would once have been looked on as homely. Considering his home for the last five years was a cell, it may as well have been the imperial palace. He glanced to Dagonet and Isolde, both staring back at him.

"What is it?" Drysten wondered.

Isolde glanced to Dagonet before beginning to stammer. "You… you were… speaking to yourself again."

Dagonet gave an awkward nod. "Your father."

Drysten felt the blood rush to his cheeks from embarrassment. He finally understood the voices which plagued him all his life had now taken a hold on him. Something which hadn't been an issue since he learned to suppress them around the age of ten.

"Bring me to Titus." Drysten did his best to project an air of authority, but wondered if he simply made himself look like a mad beggar. "Please…"

After glancing to Isolde, Dagonet sighed and pointed ahead to the villa. The three marched toward the gate, which looked as though it had been battered inward some time long ago.

"Citrio!" Dagonet called.

After a moment, a blonde-haired man with tired eyes walked from a small guardhouse near the gate, immediately looking on Drysten with a quizzical look. "Who the fuck is this?" His gaze lowered to Drysten's groin. "The fucker pissed himself, Dag! Who—?"

Dagonet took a step forward. "Open the gate you dullard or I'll kick it over."

Citrio returned a heavy groan. "Please don't. It takes *forever* to get it back on its hinges."

Drysten chuckled, earning a slight scowl from Citrio as he unlatched the iron and pulled the gate open. Drysten began to enter until Dagonet placed a hand on his shoulder.

"Best to let me go first, Lord. Wouldn't want Titus to get startled by a ghost," Dagonet stated as he gently patted Drysten's arm.

"You're worse than a ghost," a voice announced. "You're nothing more than a disappointing memory to these people. He won't even allow you to walk ahead of him."

Drysten fought the urge to reply to the voice as he returned a nod to Dagonet and stopped just inside the gate. He watched Isolde walk in behind him, giving a glance to Drysten as she walked by.

***

Titus spent the better part of an hour fighting through a bowel movement before eventually giving up. It had been a long two years since the stomach pains began. They worsened once the well-water dried up and his household was forced to use the water from a shallow spring nearby.

"Old man!" a voice called.

Titus sighed as he instantly recognized it. *That bastard wants more of my people to die in the wilds of fucking Ebrauc. Or would it be Rheged this time?*

"Titus, where are you?" the voice added.

Titus hoisted his breeches and walked over the packed dirt floor as he exited the latrines, finding his way into the atrium of his shoddy home. The sun was a welcome sight when considering the rains of the last few days. *So many leaks in the roof and nobody able to fix them properly.*

"There you are!" Dagonet happily stated from the entrance to the villa's main building.

"What is it now?" Titus grumbled.

Dagonet smirked as he gestured toward the entrance to the villa. "I have someone with me you may wish to see."

"Unless it's the Powysian prince come to liberate us, I highly doubt that," Titus returned with a scoff.

He referenced Prince Ambrosius Aurelianus, the man from a neighboring kingdom who promised to bring Titus and his people away from Ebrauc should they request it. He glanced behind him and saw the large dog owned by Isolde bouncing his way outside, tail wagging as he disappeared through the doorway.

"You brought the girl back?" Titus wondered aloud.

Dagonet nodded. "She is here. Where's her boy?"

Titus shrugged. "Oana took the boy out while she gathered nuts from the nearby woods. Some air would do him good."

Dagonet let out a sigh of relief, of which Titus couldn't understand the meaning. "You need to come outside."

Titus raised an eyebrow and began shuffling towards the entrance to the villa. He placed a hand to his side as the stomach pains worsened for a moment before quickly subsiding.

"I'm going to warn you, this will startle you if this man is indeed who he says he is," Dagonet whispered. "He has certainly convinced me."

Titus smirked. *Must be a Caesar raised from the—*

"It's been a long while, Titus," the haggard beggar of a man stated.

"Drysten..." Titus whispered. He glanced to Isolde, noticing her antsy demeanor. It was clear to Titus she must not have dared to believe this man's identity.

The group watched as Isolde's large dog, Maebh, sprinted from the entrance of the villa to his master. The beast's tail wagged with a fury as Isolde knelt. He spun around a handful of times until locking eyes with Drysten, halting his excited display of affection. Titus watched as Drysten smirked and lowered himself to Maebh's level.

"I wouldn't do that. He bites strangers..." Titus warned.

Drysten shrugged as he extended a hand, allowing Maebh to smell it. The dog slowly crept forward and caught a whiff, perking his ears up in interest.

Titus stepped forward. "Drysten, he—"

Maebh leaped at Drysten and wagged his tail just as madly, whining and spinning as he did so. He knocked Drysten onto his back before jumping onto him. Drysten was even able to flip the dog over and scratch his belly as Titus stole a glance to a shocked Isolde.

"Isolde, I think you can believe him now," Dagonet stated.

Isolde slowly began to sob as she knelt and wrapped her arms around Drysten. The man appeared shocked at first, then returned her embrace. Maebh laid across Drysten's lap with his legs to the air as he awaited more attention.

Titus chuckled at the sight before glancing to Dagonet. "You truly couldn't recognize the man?"

Dagonet shrugged. “How likely is it a man can return from the dead?”

Titus nodded and limped towards the couple still tied in an embrace. “The both of you are staying for dinner?”

Isolde smiled as she looked away from Drysten, who Titus noticed was staring at something behind him. “I believe we will,” she replied. “Where is our son?” she asked with a wide grin towards Drysten.

Titus gestured south towards the far-off wood line. “With her aunt collecting nuts or some such thing. Should be back shortly.”

Titus saw a sliver of happiness cross Drysten’s face as he stared off into nothing. Nobody but Titus was able to see it, but Drysten seemed to be conversing with someone when Isolde stood up in front of him. Titus glanced to Dagonet as the scout approached him, gesturing for the men to take their conversations inside.

“We have much to speak of, friend,” Dagonet whispered. “The silent ones have returned.”

Titus’ bowels suddenly began to stir at the news the cannibals from the West had returned. “Why the fuck are they here? Did they not think to stay off when we executed their king?”

Dagonet shrugged. “I never believed him to be their king, and there also seems to be more of them this time than there were before. I counted a few dozen I could see. Aside from that, the boats we found signaled there could be many more.”

Titus followed Dagonet into the atrium of the villa, gently resting a hand on his abdomen as a pang of discomfort hit him. Thankfully, he had learned to conceal such feelings long ago. He halted to let Maebh run by as he wandered towards the table their meals would be placed on.

“He always does this,” Isolde cheerfully stated to Drysten. “If he was blind, he could still tell the time of day by his stomach.”

“Sounds familiar,” Drysten replied as he entered.

Titus noticed the awkward glance Isolde gave her husband, but knew she couldn't truly understand what the man had been through until he eventually decided to tell her. As Titus examined the ghost being led into his home, he saw the outlines of ribs, the scars of torture, and the gaze of a man who had endured too much to be the same man he once was.

"Drysten," Titus found himself saying, "you have a home here now. We will get you back to fighting shape for what comes next."

What eventually would come next was a mystery. It could be wars, or a suicide by a tortured man overwhelmed by freedom. Titus had seen both.

Drysten returned a thankful nod. "I promised the king one thing before my release."

Dagonet turned around with an obvious interest. "He's the one who released you?"

Drysten nodded. "He made me swear an oath in exchange."

That king is truly an odd one, Titus concluded. Puts too much stock in the oaths of his enemies.

"I am to kill the bishop, the prince, then the king," Drysten explained with a smile.

Titus scoffed. "You're telling us the king made you swear to kill him?"

"No," Drysten replied with a shake of the head. "I simply told him that part was not negotiable."

Dagonet glanced to Titus during the awkward silence. Isolde must have noticed the uneasiness created by her husband, and gently tugged his arm towards the table. It was being set by Titus' daughter-in-law, Catulla, and her son, Lucius. Lucius was named after a man who perished under Drysten's command, but was close to Titus' son, Gaius, in their early years.

"Where is Marivonna?" Drysten asked Titus as he stepped closer, clearly worried judging by the tone.

Titus felt his limbs weaken as he remembered his wife.

"Died of a fever the winter after you were taken. Did not go... peacefully."

But that wasn't even the beginning of it. Not really. He knew to spare a man who endured torments of his own from the grisly details, but Titus couldn't help reliving the horrific times between Marivonna becoming ill and her passing, all in an instant, as usual.

He remembered how she had first developed a cough before quickly becoming bedridden. She couldn't keep food down and was sweating profusely for nearly a month before Titus had found her. He was bringing her broth from the kitchens in the hope she would somehow regain her strength, but the draft from the cracks in the wall whisked her soul off before that could happen. Titus remembered the overwhelming grief he lived with every waking moment of the next few months. This grief was only broken once little Lucius suddenly crawled over to him. Titus was so overcome with emotion at the sight he couldn't help but pluck the boy up from the ground and hold him tightly to his chest, sobbing until Catulla came to retrieve him.

"Titus?" Drysten whispered, snapping Titus from his memories, "I'm so sorry..."

Titus nodded. "As am I, boy." He saw the sorrow in Drysten's eyes, and had the brief thought there could still be a warm-hearted man underneath all the scars and filth.

Titus knew he would be responsible for putting the meat back on the man's bones, but understood it was the least he could do for him. Drysten once saved the lives of Titus' people, ordering men to protect a ship filled with the loved ones of Titus' men. That was the day Titus made the oath to serve Drysten, though he had few opportunities to do so since.

Drysten glanced behind him. As Titus wondered what the man saw, the pitter-patter of feet was making its way from the front gate. Titus faced the newcomers, seeing his daughter Oana, her husband, Diocles, and Drysten's son all walking up.

Diocles was the first to notice Drysten, clearly not recognizing the man based on his skeptical look. He gently tugged at Oana's arm and ushered her and the young Galahad behind him. "Mind telling me who this one is, Titus?" the man wondered.

Titus snickered to himself. "How is it the man with the oldest eyes here is the only one to recognize him?"

Dagonet wandered next to Drysten. "I myself recognized the smell," he said with a smile.

"Indulge me then. Who is this mess?" Diocles questioned.

Galahad was now grasping the rags of Oana's dress as they both remained silent. Titus' daughter seemed a natural fit for motherhood, and he wondered why she was not gifted a young boy or girl to call her own.

"I do not blame you for not recognizing your lord, brother," Drysten said with a smile. "But I assure you, I am not a ghost."

"Certainly don't smell like one," Diocles quipped, causing Dagonet to produce a smirk. Diocles stepped closer as a hint of recognition crossed over his eyes. The Greek inched away from his wife and glanced towards Titus, who returned his stare with a knowing nod. "How are you alive?"

"I persisted. There is not much more to it than that. They wished for me to die of my own means, and I simply denied them the satisfaction," Drysten answered.

Diocles stepped closer and peered back to Galahad, gesturing for the boy to step forward. "You'll be wanting to meet this one then."

The boy is terrified of his own father, Titus examined. "Perhaps we should—"

"I will meet my son now," Drysten interrupted through a hushed tone. The man stepped forward, slowly shuffling towards the young boy now standing next to Diocles.

How strange it must be for you to stand near one father figure and look on another, Titus mused.

Galahad looked up to Diocles with wide eyes. "Who is that, father?"

Drysten froze. Titus saw the shock in the man's eyes. Looking from Drysten to Diocles, he saw the Greek slowly kneel to Galahad's level and smile.

Diocles placed a hand on the young boy's shoulder. "I know I have likely been the closest thing you have ever had to a father. But the gods do strange things to us in our lives, and one of those things is bring your real father back from your Otherworld."

Titus knew Diocles did not practice the faith of the druids like Isolde, or any other faith for that matter. He knew out of respect for Isolde, he should enforce the beliefs she wished instilled into her boy, and reference the Otherworld where the boy's ancestors now wait for the day he would join them.

"This man here," Diocles gestured toward Drysten, who slowly shuffled closer, "is the man we have all spoken of before you've gone to sleep each night. The one who will love you unconditionally."

Galahad looked from Diocles to Drysten. Titus wondered what the boy was thinking and couldn't help but guess this whole experience would be rather overwhelming. As that thought crept into his mind, he saw the boy's face contort as his eyes began streaming tears down the sides of his face.

Isolde walked from behind Titus towards her son, giving Drysten a reassuring nod as she passed him. "This is a happy day!" she began as she knelt beside her son and Diocles, who was still holding a hand onto the boy's shoulder.

Titus knew no amount of reassurance would soothe the boy until Drysten managed to clean himself up. "Perhaps the boy would see more of a resemblance to his father if we… readied a bath for the man," Titus suggested as gestured to Drysten.

Dagonet nodded as he waved his hand in front of his nose. "I agree."

Titus chuckled as he glanced to Drysten staring off into

the empty space behind Galahad. *Who do you see that we cannot?* he wondered.

Drysten gave a subtle nod before turning to his wife. "I believe he is right. I am willing to bet this is not unlike when my father came back from fighting for the Rome. I barely recognized the man. Not to mention Galahad has never laid eyes one me."

"Very good idea," Titus began. "The boy will no doubt become more accustomed to your presence once we get some more meat on your bones. Don't want him thinking he'll grow up to become a skeleton do we!"

Titus saw Drysten smirk, but again stare off into nothing.

***

King Ceneus rubbed the space between his brow as he glanced out the window of his study. Rodric was seated in the corner with Gwrast. Both men never leaving the king for exceedingly long after the two bodies were found in the graveyard near the fortress. The sight disturbed Rodric, who was led there by a handful of guards under the employ of the bishop. King Ceneus didn't like working with those men, but they had been the first to find the bodies.

"Lord King," Rodric began, "I fear there may be more consequences of your decision—."

Ceneus raised an eyebrow at the comment, causing Rodric to stop mid-sentence. "Go on."

Rodric stood and shuffled towards a window, tilting his head from side to side as he gazed around with tired eyes. Content in the knowledge that nobody was listening in on their conversation, the king watched as his highest-ranking officer turned back. "This man has known nothing but cruelty for the last few years. We should expect him to respond in kind to our people."

"I know," the king responded with a sigh.

Rodric shrugged. "We need to find him—"

"It's too late for that," Gwrast interrupted. "The man is already with his people and you know it."

Ceneus felt himself letting out a long, slow sigh of frustration. He knew his son and captain were right. Drysten was more resourceful than Ceneus anticipated, and the cruelty on top of that could spell ruin for more than the bishop's people and himself. "The man can do us a great deal of harm," the king began as he stood from his finely crafted chair. "But any harm done will be done against the bishop first. That is when we strike at him as well."

Gwrast nodded. "You are king, so we follow your guidance. But this man… " his voice tapered off as he slowly shook his head.

"We put another piece in play which holds an immeasurable amount of hatred towards Germanus and Eidion. I know he will do everything he can to rid us of them before turning his attention to me. Besides, we may be able to convince him I didn't want him imprisoned in the first place," Ceneus replied.

Rodric scoffed. "So you'd rather he kills you for being unable to control the affairs of your kingdom?"

Ceneus gritted his teeth and glared into Rodric's eyes. "If you were anyone else's son..."

Gwrast raised a hand, drawing the king's attention away from Rodric. "Even if you're right, the man still has well trained and seasoned men at his back. Aside from the royal guards, we don't have a way to match his strength," he interjected. Ceneus could tell his son was frustrated judging by his outstretched hand and stern tone.

Ceneus nodded. "The bishop has more Roman-trained men venturing across the sea as we speak. They were originally purposed with rooting out more non-Christians, but Drysten's people should keep them more than occupied."

"Are these men fighting for the bishop or the pope?" Rodric wondered aloud.

Ceneus felt himself cock his head to the side. "My spies managed to open some of the messages coming from Rome. I would venture to guess they fight for the pope."

Gwrast scoffed. "I doubt these men coming to Ebrauc are much more than deserters or mercenaries."

Ceneus shrugged. "Either way, Bishop Germanus' strength matches our own. We needed to free Drysten to try and change that."

The three men sat quietly for some time. Rodric was fidgeting with the clasp securing the royal blue cloak about his shoulders, while Gwrast harbored a blank expression as he stared out the window. Ceneus knew those close to him had the will to act against Germanus, but wondered if they had the wherewithal to do so effectively enough to make a difference.

"Word from Powys, Lord King," a cheerful voice said from the doorway. Ceneus turned to see Maewyn nod as he entered with the king's other son, Mor at his side. "Prince Ambrosius has wed your daughter. They believe she's pregnant as well."

Ceneus couldn't help but grin. He loved his daughter more than any of his other children, especially Eidion, and knew she would indeed be a wonderful mother. "I wish I could have been there to see the wedding."

"Might've been killed once you arrived, father," Mor said with a snort.

Ceneus shook his head. "Though the prince knows I am at fault for the bishop's presence, he understands I wish to correct it. When we met in Isurium last summer, he made an oath to aid me in exchange for Ystradwel."

"Always wondered why she left so damn quick," Gwrast stated with a snort.

Maewyn smirked as he lowered himself into a chair next to Rodric, who gave Gwrast a subtle glance as the priest sat. It was obvious to the king there was still a feeling of contempt towards Maewyn, whose presence reminded Rodric of one who ordered his father's death.

Gwrast returned Rodric's glance with a grin. "When can we expect the Powysian to provide us with an army? We will undoubtedly need one if we are to fend off the Gaels as well as whatever resistance the bishop can muster."

Ceneus shrugged. "I have no idea. The king of Powys has not shown us the same amount of… friendship as the younger Ambrosius has. All I can say, is the prince has sent his best man and a small company to meet with Titus."

Ceneus nodded. "Rodric will represent me at their meeting. When can we expect them?"

Maewyn shrugged. "A couple of weeks. The Powysian in command was tasked with tracking a small band of the Gaels before arriving. It seems the people of Ebrauc are not the only ones living in fear of them."

"That's comforting," Mor put in.

The idea the strongest kingdom in Britannia was also

worried about the Gaels was cause for worry by itself. The idea they sent men away from their wars with the Saxons to do something about them meant they were likely a larger threat than even Ceneus knew.

“I wouldn’t worry greatly,” Maewyn added. “Arthur has shown himself to be quite adept at picking his officers. The man in charge will undoubtedly catch and kill whoever they’re chasing.”

Ceneus nodded. “One can only hope.”

CHAPTER FIVE

Drysten spent the last two weeks at Titus' villa cleaning himself up. He now looked vaguely like his old self, with steady meals already bringing more color into his once lifeless face. He noticed Isolde was finding it easier to look him over since his ribs began disappearing back into his chest.

To bring some life into his arms, he even established an early morning routine consisting of sparring with Diocles and Citrio. These sparring sessions brought a sense of purpose back to Drysten, who now viewed them as tests until he would inevitably find himself fighting against Bishop Germanus and Prince Eidion.

At first, he lost to both men easily. But the knowledge of what had been happening to those who once followed him spurred him on. He found out his old friend, Heraclius, was killed over the course of many days at the hands of Vonig. Drysten even knew when it was, as the man who had tortured him as well once left for a few weeks to deal with another errand. The man had been drowned after there was no more blood for Vonig to take from him.

This knowledge helped Drysten to find a kind of strength he didn't know he had. The first inkling of this came when Citrio disarmed him with a powerful blow from above, knocking Drysten's old blade from his hands. Citrio must have thought the fight over, but Drysten did not. He leapt forward and brought Citrio up from the ground before heaving him over his shoulders and slamming him down to his back. Suffice it to say, Citrio felt ambivalent about sparring with Drysten again for a few days.

"A visitor for you, brother," Diocles announced as he entered the atrium of the villa. Drysten had been reading Titus' old journals from his Roman campaigns in Africa. "It's a... priest who says he knows you. A priest and one other."

Drysten glanced away from the journal in his hand. *Maewyn...*

"Should I send him in, Lord?" Diocles questioned.

Drysten nodded. "I will see him alone."

Diocles nodded and exited the atrium before returning with the hooded priest who first granted Drysten his freedom. "Are you certain you don't need me to hear what is to be said?"

Drysten shook his head. "That will be all."

Diocles produced a dejected look as he departed, with Maewyn giving him a reassuring nod as he passed by.

"I was wondering when I would see you again," Drysten began. "I've spent the better part of a month regaining my strength for what's to come, and never heard more than a whisper from you. I was beginning to think I would have to go about this alone."

"We had a deal, Lord. Your killing the guardsmen left Ceneus with a certain amount of grief. He considered it his fault they died the way they did," Maewyn answered.

Drysten nodded. "Wasn't it his fault? He did free me."

"I suppose so. He likely didn't believe you'd begin your conquest of Ebrauc so soon."

"One of his faults seems to be believing there are men less driven than himself. The truth is quite the opposite." Drysten craned his neck and looked past Maewyn. He thought he could hear Diocles whispering to Titus, but wasn't certain.

"Either way, it's good to see you've been regaining your strength," Maewyn responded. "I fear you will have need of it soon."

Drysten stood and glanced to the corner of the room, seeing the image of his father staring back at him as he walked towards the priest. “Why is that?”

Maewyn cleared his throat. “Our Lord is just and will bring judgment to the apostates! They will be beaten, burned, and altogether broken!”

“I will just assume you were reciting the bishop’s words and not your own, priest. I happen to enjoy some of these apostates,” Drysten returned with a sneer. He had only recently figured out what an apostate was, that being a person who does not believe in the Christian God.

Maewyn chuckled. “Of course I was. The man wishes murder on the people of Britannia. Christian or not, this cannot stand.”

“And it is my duty to stop it,” Drysten whispered.

“Quite right,” Maewyn said with a nod. The priest turned and looked to the entrance to the atrium. “Rodric!” he called.

Drysten watched as a man only a few years younger than himself entered the room. *He was with the king and his sons the night I was freed…* The man was followed by Diocles, who Drysten chose to let stay until this newcomer’s intentions were clear.

“Rodric will aid you for the moment,” Maewyn explained. “Considering you have no men as of yet, he will help you find them.”

“I have men,” Drysten responded.

“And where are they?” Maewyn replied with a smirk, staring around the vacant room with outstretched hands.

“Messages have been sent to Powys for my people to return.” Drysten glanced to Rodric, still standing in the entrance as if hoping to be sent back home. “I have no use for this man.”

Maewyn sighed. “It would be wise to use what help you are being given, Lord.”

“It would be wise for you and yours to remain as far away from me as you can. You strayed much too far from home, priest,” Drysten whispered through a smirk and harsh tone.

Drysten glanced to Rodric, who had crept a hand onto

the hilt of the Roman spatha at his waist. He was clearly wondering whether he should draw the blade and remove a threat from his king's lands but must have been deciding against it based on his conflicted expression.

Maewyn gave an uneasy glance to Rodric and shuffled his feet. "Bishop Germanus has brought mercenaries from Gaul. They will ride down this very road tomorrow. At dusk, or possibly a little later I would expect."

"Hardly enough time to muster a force on our own, Lord," Diocles put in. "Not to mention the timeframe your new friend here gave us isn't all that specific."

Drysten glanced to his friend and responded with a slight nod. "It seems we will... need Rodric's help, priest," Drysten announced as he glanced to the priest. "How many can we expect?"

"Fifty strong Frisians at your disposal, Lord," Maewyn replied.

Drysten cocked his head to the side as he wondered whether one of his old friends was with them. "Is Jorrit—"

"He is!" Maewyn cheerfully interrupted. "The madman leads them under Prince Gwrast's command, but ultimately falls under Rodric's and the king's control."

If Jorrit is coming to aid me, I may be able to turn him away from this prince he serves, Drysten thought.

Drysten remembered how Jorrit was forced to make an oath to King Ceneus in return for asylum. The Frisian had originally invaded Britannia alongside the Saxon king, Colgrin, who now resided in Londinium. When he found most of his people had been slaughtered by a slaver under the employ of Colgrin, he took the king's wife along with the men under his command and sailed to Ebrauc to escape him.

Drysten chuckled to himself as he thought of meeting his old friend. "I look forward to seeing him again."

Maewyn nodded. "I suppose you would look fondly on reuniting with many of your people, Lord. I have been doing my utmost to find where they have journeyed since your imprisonment."

Drysten raised an eyebrow as he glanced to the priest. "You're doing all this on my behalf?"

Maewyn hesitated before nodding. "It may be a small kindness in the grand scheme of things, Lord, but this kindness is not without its own motivations. It is my hope you come to understand the king was not responsible for what was done to you."

After rolling his eyes and glancing to Diocles, Drysten sighed and looked to Rodric before raising a finger to Maewyn. "I... will keep an open mind, priest, no more than that."

Maewyn smiled warmly as he gave Drysten a pat on the shoulder. "That is all I ask," he began as he turned away. "I will be returning to Ebrauc now, but make use of Rodric how you can. He is quite capable. Takes after his father in that way."

Drysten gazed to Rodric as the man stared off into a mosaic on the wall. "Who was your father?" he questioned.

Rodric briefly glanced into Drysten's direction before returning his gaze. "The man your father was rumored to have killed."

"Aosten," Drysten whispered. "I met him once. He seemed like a good man."

Rodric glared into Drysten's eyes. "He was," he sternly replied.

After a sigh, Maewyn looked between Drysten and Rodric before shaking his head. "I told you, boy, this man had nothing to do with your father's death. Any lies you were told by the bishop are just that, lies. Hall was a good man, and the reports I received from the battlefield indicated it was the prince who murdered your father."

Rodric clearly wasn't certain the priest was telling the truth, but Drysten knew it for certain. He glanced to Hall's ghost staring at Rodric and didn't see regret or anger at the man's presence. He saw pity. Whether or not this image of Drysten's father was a figment of Drysten's imagination, he still wouldn't have believed Hall committed the crime he was accused of.

Upon receiving no response from either man, Maewyn nodded to them both before finally making his exit.

***

"I had never been... hunted like this," Gaius explained to the king. He arrived in Eboracum in the early morning hours to divulge what had occurred with the Gaels two weeks prior. Since that day in the meadow, he had to deal with the disappearances of his men. All one at a time and without a trace.

King Ceneus rose from his seat, his face dimming as it drew away from the candlelight. "Tell me the word again."

Gaius shifted uncomfortably in his chair. "The pelt had... Abhartach etched across it."

"But we killed him," Ceneus said to Maewyn, standing near the window.

Maewyn shrugged and looked back to Gaius. "You're certain that's what it said?"

"I am." Gaius nodded. *Of course, I'm fucking sure. Why are you always in these little meetings, anyway?*

King Ceneus clicked his tongue as he angrily turned away. "Who do we have available?"

Gwrast peered out the window. "The Frisians are all in the—"

"They're unavailable," the king interrupted.

Gaius raised an eyebrow as he looked to the king. He was turned, and Gaius couldn't see his face, but from his tone he could discern there was something the rest of the room wasn't supposed to know. I'll have to remember this moment, I think.

"Who else can we call upon?" the king wondered aloud.

Gaius shrugged. "My father still has about forty men he could muster. May take a day or two."

Ceneus glanced to Maewyn, who Gaius noticed was giving him a strange look as if to disagree. He looked back. "You will wait for a day until you journey to your father. I think a little rest may do you some good, as well as give all of us the time needed to find more souls to send against the Gaels."

No, Gaius thought. *That will be too long. I left Cynwrig in charge of the fight in my absence, and the man cannot defend the West on his own. Not for long.*

"You see a problem with this?" Ceneus inquired as he turned.

"I... no, Lord King. I will wait a day before journeying South." Gaius lowered his head, knowing he would go against the king.

"Good," Ceneus whispered. "Get yourself fed." He gestured a hand towards the door, signaling for Gaius to leave.

Gaius stood and offered a "Lord King" as he turned to leave, giving Maewyn a suspicious glance as he finally passed through the doorway. The sun shining on his face gave him a momentary feeling of comfort. As he closed his eyes and let the sun warm his face, he saw flashes of his men choking on their own tongues from the strange poison on the arrows. The arrows fired from seemingly nowhere, and the terrified feeling that came with it.

How do you kill someone you can't see? Gaius wondered.

He slowly paced through the courtyard of the old Roman fortress, briefly glancing to the principia. He wondered why the old administration building was only used by Bishop Germanus as he noticed the man staring out the window with a blank expression. Two of the bishop's men were standing guard at the front entrance to the building, with a handful now exiting. Gaius had never seen these men before, which was strange considering how the bishop's men seemed to have greater control of Ebrauc than those under King Ceneus' command.

"More just arrived this morning," a voice said from behind Gaius. It was not difficult to place the voice, as the man's entitled tone always produced an uneasy feeling in nearly everyone who heard it.

"Lord Prince," Gaius said with a sneer. "How wonderful to see you again." Gaius hoped his sarcasm would register with the prince, but knew he was somewhat dimwitted, and it likely did not.

Prince Eidion smirked as he stepped beside Gaius. "They will be riding South tonight. I believe by your father's villa if

I'm not mistaken."

Gaius shrugged. "Makes no difference to me where they choose to travel, just so long as there are no more arrests by these newcomers."

"Arrests?" Eidion said through a widening smile. Gaius noticed the man's blonde hair was longer than the last time he saw him. Now, it seemed to shroud his shoulders and hide a bit more of his face, something Gaius was pleased by.

"You know of the arrests as well as I do. You've been seen dragging those who worship the old ways off to their deaths on the order of the bishop. I've ridden by the shallow graves in the West, with more appearing closer and closer to Eboracum," Gaius returned.

All Eidion chose to respond with was a slight wink as he stepped towards the principia. Gaius watched him nod to the man who Gaius believed to be the leader of those who recently arrived to serve the bishop. Their black cloaks were freshly woven and dyed. The cloth was still stiff around their shoulders, making Gaius wonder if these men were simply mercenaries who defected away from the failing wars of the Romans.

Would make more sense than the bishop having the men he claimed to. If that were the case, we would all be living under the leadership of the pope by this point, Gaius determined. He glanced toward the gate leading to the city before finding himself wandering toward the newcomers to the bishop's army.

A kind-looking man of about forty years noticed him approaching. "How goes it, friend?" the man asked though a beaming smile.

Gaius nodded. "Beautiful day for a march. Have room enough for one more man?"

"Only if you follow orders til your destination," the man returned as he extended a hand.

Gaius took the man's hand and gave a brief shake before releasing it and looking the man in the eye. "Name's Gaius. I'm only going to the other side of the river. I heard you're going that way as well."

"I am Quintus, and you are correct." Despite the man's name, he was clearly not a Roman. His hair was long, where a typical Roman's was cropped short. He also stood taller than most Romans Gaius had ever met.

Must be a Gaul. Perhaps even from Germania, Gaius concluded. "I'll follow your orders despite the fact I outrank you," he returned with a smirk.

Quintus shook his head. "Germanus told me anyone wearing blue is a subordinate."

Gaius shrugged. "I'm a lord of the king's. Either way, we can simply argue over it on the way to wherever you're off to."

Quintus smiled once more, and the two men began moving toward the main section of the city.

***

The Frisians arrived around the same time the sun set. Jorrit had the same reaction to Drysten's presence as everyone else. First came disbelief and shock, but Jorrit finally ended up showing the same strange version of happiness as everyone else. Along with Jorrit, Drysten was happy to see Magnus and the Cretans, Petras and Paulus, sauntering up with a handful of his father's men still dwelling in Petuaria.

"Good to see you, Lord!" Magnus began. "You look better since you've gotten some food in you."

I wish people would stop saying that, Drysten thought with a sigh. "Thank you, brother." Drysten clapped a hand on Magnus' shoulder as he stepped towards Jorrit, who was speaking with his second in command, Braxus, as well as Rodric.

"Lord," Braxus greeted with a nod. His tribal tattoo now extended from his neck down to the wrist of his sword arm. A long scar also could be made out under the fresher dye on his skin.

"Good to see you're still alive," Drysten returned, referencing the fact Braxus had almost perished during the great battle at Segedunum The man apparently stepped close enough to death to be briefly stacked onto a pile of bodies when he was returned the Petuaria.

Braxus smirked. "Not for lack of trying, Lord."

Jorrit nodded toward the men awaiting their orders outside the villa's gates. Titus hated the idea of all the fully armed men congregating in the open but must have hated the idea of having them inside the walls of his home even more.

Jorrit waited until Braxus was out of earshot until training his attention back to Drysten. "You know you'll have to explain where the fuck you were."

Do I owe you this? Drysten wondered. "I'm sure we will have time for that after we're through with the Christians. I'd rather we focused on the task at hand for the time being."

Jorrit drew in a long breath as he gave Drysten a skeptical glance. Drysten saw how the man's large, dark red beard was now sporting streaks of grey, much like the long hair sprouting from his head. "These men we're fighting are Romans. They arrived earlier in the week, all dressed in black."

"So they are the bishop's men." Drysten glanced to the sun, almost dreading the moment he would find himself fighting trained warriors when he had not yet fully regained his strength.

Jorrit glanced toward the entrance of the villa, gently patting Drysten's shoulder and gesturing a hand in that direction. "Someone wishes to speak with you."

Drysten sighed, believing it to be Diocles about to attempt and convince him to stay indoors. He slowly turned and saw Isolde and his son standing there waiting to speak with him. "A moment," Drysten murmured to Jorrit, who nodded and walked towards Braxus. He turned and shuffled towards his family, wondering why he couldn't find the words to speak to his own wife and son. The only thing he dreamed of for the past few days was the message he was about to send.

"Our little one wishes a word with his father," Isolde said with a smirk, ruffling Galahad's short hair.

Drysten nodded and went down onto a knee, relieved the boy no longer cowered in the presence of his own father. "What worries you, son?" he whispered.

Galahad glanced to his feet. It was clear the boy didn't wish to speak, leading Drysten to believe it was his mother's idea to come to him at all.

"Seems my grandson did not inherit your outgoing personality, son," Hall whispered into Drysten's mind. The malicious voices had mainly left Drysten these last couple of weeks. Curiously though, he still heard the whispers of Hall rather frequently.

Drysten snickered to himself and placed a hand on Galahad's shoulder. "That's alright, boy. The quiet ones normally smarter than the loud ones. Just be sure to listen when you choose not to speak." Galahad looked to Isolde and leaned his head against her leg.

"You know I have been trying to get him to speak more," Isolde commented with a mildly irritated expression.

Drysten shook his head. "The boy may simply turn out to be a man of few words," he returned, glancing down to Galahad. "The wisest ones always are," he said with a wink, causing a small smile to cross his son's face.

"You'd do well to stay away from the fighting. Your son wouldn't want to lose his father so soon after meeting him." Isolde did not bother to hide her annoyance.

Drysten understood why, as it was ultimately his decision to participate in the ambush. He was given the choice not to, but nobody would understand the pent-up aggression needing to be released. When he closed his eyes, he still heard the voices of Eidion and Vonig as they would slice little slits into his ears or prod him in the chest or back with a scorching hot poker. Now, Drysten would have an opportunity to inflict worse than torture on those who chose to follow those men.

"I love you, papa," Galahad suddenly whispered in his tiny voice.

Drysten's heart melted as he realized his son spoke out of his own volition. He quickly brought his boy into his arms and held him tight, with Galahad doing the same.

"When can we expect your return?" Isolde said through a wide smile.

Drysten let go of his son and ushered him back near his mother's side before looking to Isolde. "Once they've been dealt with," he responded, not wanting to be specific around his son. He was still too young to hear of wars and killing.

Isolde nodded. "Be careful, love."

Drysten stood and walked to his wife. "I love you. I'll see you both soon."

At that, he kissed his wife, and turned to start a war.

CHAPTER SIX

Gaius outstretched his arms as he rode South with Bishop Germanus' men. They set off later than planned, as a handful of those now under the bishop's employ disappeared immediately after arriving in Eboracum. They were found in *The Limping Mule* with Gaius' help. When Quintus let it be known the men were missing, Gaius knew were soldiers typically congregated. The marching column departed the city not long after.

Gaius was surprised by how cheerful the men were. After overhearing what they'd been paid for one year of their presence, Gaius began to understand why. The men cheered as Quintus and Gaius both rode to the head of the column before they broke out into an old marching song of Rome.

Quintus spent much of the ride questioning Gaius about the Gaels, not allowing Gaius to forget the painful memories of late. The frustrating thing Gaius quickly learned about Quintus, was he believed he knew everything. The atrocities Gaius had seen seemed to be mere stories to him. Gaius knew everything he was saying was being taken much too lightly by this stranger to Britannia.

"I don't know," Gaius said, responding to the question of how many men attacked him. "They came and they went. We couldn't count them."

Quintus leaned back in his saddle and glanced towards the sky. "The Gauls fight much the same way. I regularly tell my daughter of those times before she goes to bed each night. She loves scary stories, much like all children. But they're just that, Gaius, *stories*."

"The Gauls know how to fight because they use their

homeland to their advantage. They know the way through their forests and where the freshest water can be found. The Gaels can be placed in any environment and strike without notice. *That* is not normal for any foe in unfamiliar territory," Gaius returned.

"They may simply be impressive trackers and nothing more. Besides, I have yet to meet a man who cannot be killed, Briton," Quintus said with a laugh. He ran a hand over his long, brown hair as he spoke.

Scary stories may entertain you now, but wait until they become all too real, Gaius thought. *I almost can't wait until you encounter Gaels for yourself. I'll be sure to come and find what's left of you.*

"Tell me of your father," Quintus ordered. "It heartens me to know there are still good Romans worth meeting in these shit-stained islands."

"I'd rather know more about you and your men," Gaius responded.

Quintus gave Gaius a quizzical look before glancing over his shoulder. "What exactly do you want to know about *us*? Can't imagine we'd be all that interesting."

Gaius scoffed. "Heavily armed band of men show up, and that's *not* supposed to be?"

"Fair enough." Quintus glanced down to the ring on his finger before taking it off and handing it to Gaius.

Gaius took it and turned it over in his hand. "I Adiutrix?"

"The legion we fought for," Quintus explained. "Most of the men here were once—"

That was when the first arrow struck Quintus in the neck. Two more flew from the overgrown grass on the left side of the road as Gaius wheeled around and saw men bursting from the same direction. They were led by a fierce warrior who released a blood-curdling war cry toward the Romans. A man who Gaius was well acquainted with.

"No prisoners!" Jorrit screamed as he cleaved an axe into the legs of a horse, sending it squealing to the ground. Gaius watched as the Frisian wretched the axe free and cleaved the rider's head in two with ease.

"Traitor!" Gaius screamed as he drew his sword. He began spurring his horse toward the Frisian commander until two hands brought him from his saddle to the dirt below. As he fell, Gaius saw two more arrows wisp through the air above him before hearing a pair of screams.

"Stay down, brother," a familiar voice whispered. "You're lucky the Frisians noticed your presence, otherwise the Cretans would have killed you first. You know how they love to aim for the officers."

Gaius raised his head to see his brother-in-law, Diocles spring up and swipe his blade across the throat of the man who was riding behind Gaius mere moments ago. The spray of blood spattered across Gaius' face, and he slowly looked further behind him to see the Frisians ripping men from saddles and running them through with their spears.

Braxus, a man who was a friend to Gaius, even decapitated a man and threw the head towards two more who turned to flee. Of course, those two men were quickly shot in the back by the Cretans before they made it to safety.

Gaius rose from his knees and looked over the carnage. Men were begging for mercy all around him. He turned his attention just up the road. A beaten looking man, who curiously had no blood on him, approached him. The stranger looked vaguely familiar, but under the scars and unruly hair, Gaius could not figure out why.

"You still wear my father's armor?" the stranger said in a cheerful tone.

Gaius glanced down to the blood spattered lorica segmentata he was given after the battle of Segedunum. One he was fortunate enough to stay away from until he journeyed North to see the aftermath.

He hesitated before lifting his gaze as he finally understood who he was speaking to. "Lord... Drysten?" He rose to his feet as the man smirked and nodded before walking toward him and patting his shoulder. His eyes were vacant, and the boyish cheer he once radiated had been replaced with something else. Something strange. Gaius knew he saw enjoyment in the man's eyes as they hovered over the dead and dying Romans who had only just arrived to serve the bishop.

"Get used to the sight," Drysten uttered to Gaius. "There will be much more death for these filthy animals in the times ahead."

Gaius turned back to the bloodletting. One man was on his back, holding a hand to his side as blood pooled below him. He looked Gaius straight in the eyes and the life slowly began to fade from him as Jorrit sauntered over. The Frisian paused for a short moment before he finally brought his axe down in the man's chest. An uneasy feeling began in Gaius' stomach as the last of the men were executed. He looked to Drysten to see a wicked smile emblazoned across his face.

"Leave one alive," Drysten ordered with a finger raised.

Braxus heard him and nodded. The Frisian was about to bring his blade down into the neck of a downed Roman, but instead reached down and brought him up from the ground.

Jorrit looked over the dead and dying, nodding with obvious approval. "Kill the rest," he ordered before walking to the lone prisoner. "This one will live long enough to *sing* for us, boys!"

The prisoner whimpered as Jorrit cupped his hands on the man's cheeks and howled into his face. Even despite his fear, the man remained defiant and refused to speak. All he did when Jorrit released him was turn and glare straight into Gaius' eyes. It was the most hateful look Gaius had ever been subject to in all his years.

Man must think I planned this, Gaius concluded. He began to speak, but was startled back into silence by a loud, liquidy gurgle coming from the ground at his feet. He knew what he would see, but Gaius trained his gaze to the ground all the same. Quintus was somehow clinging to life with one of the Cretan's arrows still jutting from the front of his throat.

Paulus noticed the same thing as he began unstringing his bow and tossing it to his feet. The Cretan nodded and muttered something to his brother as he sauntered over. Without hesitating, he gripped the shaft of the arrow and pulled it free from Quintus' throat, causing a wheezing sound from the vacant hole left behind. Gaius saw the last noise the man would ever make, as his eyes glazed over, and his squirming stopped altogether.

Who will tell his daughter? Gaius found himself wondering. He ran a hand over his face and found blood caked to his forehead.

"Take their heads," Drysten ordered. "We need to send a message."

Gaius glanced to Diocles, who was sporting an uneasy expression as he stepped towards his lord.

"Surely their deaths would be message enough," Diocles whispered.

Drysten shook his head. "No, it is not. Not in this situation, brother. You must trust me." Diocles scanned over the massacre before resting his gaze upon Jorrit. The Frisian noticed his reluctance and stepped forward.

"I will see to it myself," Jorrit stated.

Gaius saw Drysten nod and glance in his direction before stepping close to Jorrit and whispering in his ear. Jorrit's eyes seemed to widen as he looked back to Drysten with a perplexed expression. This surprised reaction added to the uneasy feeling brewing inside Gaius' stomach. He found it hard to focus on the speech of any one man, but one thing he overheard clearly had produced the same stomach pains inside himself that afflicted his father.

"A wickerman?" Gaius muttered.

That was what he had heard. Drysten gestured to the tree line and ordered two men to begin building a wickerman. The wickerman was how the ancient Britons and Picts executed their Roman prisoners. They would place the men inside a tall, wooden man made of twigs and branches before setting it ablaze. The last thing the imprisoned Romans would see was the rituals of the old ways as the Britons sent their souls to the gods.

Gaius saw Drysten nod and glance off to the West before gesturing to Braxus to take the prisoner to Titus' villa. Braxus nodded and placed a sack of twine over the man's head before taking his arm and moving South.

Gaius knew he had no choice but to join them. Even though they were on the same side in the fights against the Gaels and Christians, it still felt wrong to him.

***

Drysten led the prisoner into Titus' villa, yanking his arm to steer him through the front entrance. He was accompanied by both Braxus and Diocles, both men somewhat antsy after the conclusion of the ambush. Drysten found it hard to care about their misgivings. He knew they wouldn't understand why he did what he did in the aftermath. But those were concerns for another time, as Isolde was leading Galahad up to his father as the men entered Titus' villa.

"Thank you for not taking any risks just yet," Isolde whispered as he released Galahad's hand. She was looking over Drysten's leather armor borrowed from Citrio, and was satisfied by the lack of blood it carried.

Drysten smiled and ruffled his son's hair as the boy wrapped his arms around his father's leg. Drysten glanced to Braxus and nodded for him to move the prisoner inside, releasing the man's arm as Braxus ushered him on. Drysten reached down and placed a hand on his son's head as he followed the men inside.

"Go back to your mother," Drysten whispered with a smile.

Galahad peered up and released Drysten's leg as he shuffled away toward Isolde.

"Has your eyes, son," Hall observed.

"I wouldn't know. Never seen my own eyes. Not with much clarity, anyway."

"Lord?" Braxus asked, overhearing Drysten's solitary conversation.

Drysten shook his head and pointed toward the prisoner. "Leave him here," he ordered.

"What information do you hope to get from him?" Braxus asked as he tossed him to the ground inside an empty room.

Drysten shrugged. "Anything really."

Braxus nodded. "And what about after?"

"Depends how helpful he is," Drysten responded.

Diocles entered the atrium of the villa, marching toward the prisoner's lodgings as he nodded toward Drysten and Braxus. He took the prisoner and set him down on a box before removing the bag covering his head. He was young, younger than Drysten was the first time he fought.

Couldn't be more than fourteen, Drysten concluded.

The boy glanced around, with Drysten noticing the top of a tribal tattoo poking out from underneath his neckerchief. Braxus tapped Drysten on the shoulder and gestured for him to follow. He led Drysten back to the atrium where Jorrit was standing in wait, and antsy judging by the way he was grinding one hand into the other.

"I have duties to attend to in the city. This is likely the last you'll see of me until the king no longer needs extra guards around the principia," Jorrit explained.

"What use does he have for extra guards?" Drysten wondered aloud.

Jorrit sighed. "The Gaels returned once word got out their king was executed."

Drysten smiled. "You didn't execute their king," he explained. "The man I was imprisoned with was merely one of the king's bastard sons."

Jorrit's eyes went wide. "Gods be damned..." He rubbed a hand over the back of his neck. "I knew killing him was a mistake, especially when I saw one of his men standing in the crowd before I took the man's head."

"You saw one?" Drysten asked.

Jorrit nodded. "Hard to miss them. No hair, scars everywhere..."

"No tongue either," Drysten added.

Jorrit raised an eyebrow. "How did you know that piece?"

"When we took Segedunum, there were a handful of these specific Gaels among the dead. All had their tongues taken out. Those are what Abhartach calls his 'hunters'. His son explained the rituals to me during our time in captivity."

"Hardly useful to take a soldier's tongue," Jorrit responded. "What purpose does that serve?"

"Obedience for one. But they mostly did so to make certain they are the quietest of their fighters. They are the scouts, and all are about as good as Dagonet on his best day. He chooses them based on how many people in neighboring villages they can kill without being caught. They strive for the honor of being picked to be one of his most feared warriors," Drysten explained.

"Why couldn't it just be more Saxons to deal with?" Diocles whispered. "At least they aren't crazy in these ways."

Jorrit glanced to Braxus as he shook his head. "This isn't a comforting thought."

Drysten shook his head. "No, it isn't."

"It is rumored the two murders in the city were done by those men. Nobody saw the assailant, and nobody heard the murders happen. The brutality is similar to what we saw in the West." Jorrit seemed to shake off some uneasiness as he spoke.

Should I tell them? Drysten wondered.

"Ha!" the voice screamed. "Let the fools fear the ones in the West. They will have cause to soon enough."

Drysten glanced to the corner of the room and saw the image of his father. He looked even more decomposed than he had in Eboracum's underground. He stared back in silence while casting a malicious grin.

"If..." Drysten began, trying to find the words. "If the Gaels have sent men this far East, there could be real trouble ahead."

Diocles nodded. "Not only for us."

"For Germanus as well," Drysten said with a smile.

"One can only hope the Gaels are not picky eaters," a voice said from the entrance to the villa.

Drysten turned to see Gaius and Titus marching up to him. Both clearly shaken. Drysten wondered if it was due to the idea Gaius was almost killed, or possible the news of the wickerman.

Drysten chuckled. "I would venture to guess they prefer

Christians. Abhartach's son alluded to it a few times. Something about feeding their gods with those that wish to remove them."

Diocles made a disgusted face as he looked on Gaius, who also seemed somewhat ill.

Titus didn't seem fazed by the idea. "I heard rumors of the man when I fought other Gaels with your father. I don't think Abhartach had a presence in the army we defeated, but I cannot be sure."

"Did any of your men die of poisoning?" Drysten asked with a scoff.

Titus hesitated but ultimately shook his head. "Not that I can remember."

Drysten shook his head. "Then I'd say no. That would have stuck out." He noticed Gaius staring into the room with the prisoner and fidgeting with a small copper ring. His eyes seemed glazed over, and Drysten wondered if the stresses of the last few weeks combined with what just occurred were taking a toll on him.

"He cannot be allowed to leave," Drysten told Gaius. "I'm not going to execute him, but he cannot leave until the bishop is dead. If news got out of who really attacked Germanus' men… "

Gaius returned a shallow nod. He glanced to his father and wandered further back into the atrium. Drysten wondered if he was the only man who understood how Gaius felt. How overwhelming the presence of others could be in the times a man needed to be alone with his thoughts.

Drysten watched Gaius stop by a narrow pillar in the atrium's center and lean his back against it. As he watched, Drysten found himself thinking of Abhartach's bastard son. His neighbor in the prisons of Eboracum. He missed his talks with the Gael, who only divulged his identity to him the night before he was to be executed. To Drysten, the man seemed a unique combination of madness and genius all bundled into one grotesque shell.

Man taught me much, Drysten thought as he half-listened to Titus and Diocles speak of the prisoner. He looked on the face of Galahad as the boy ran up to him. It was then and there he understood what Abhartach, the father, would do to the people who killed his son.

"Father, mother said you were fighting!" Galahad stated. The boy looked excited, something which brought a strange feeling to Drysten's heart.

Drysten shook his head. "Not this time, my boy. This time we were doing something much more important." He noticed Titus and Diocles glance at one another out of the corner of his eye.

Galahad cocked his head to the side in obvious curiosity. "More important than fighting, father? Mother said fighting is how men win."

Drysten looked up to Isolde, who was standing in the atrium with Oana. "Your mother speaks the truth, but there are other ways to fight." He looked down to his son, still confused judging by his gaze. "It doesn't matter now, boy. Someday, many years from now, I will explain my meaning." Drysten ruffled the hair on the top of his son's head and pointed to Isolde.

Galahad smiled as he turned to run toward his mother, all the while being watched by Hall's ghost. Only Drysten could see the man, but he found himself wishing there were others who could understand what toll these images took on him. To be the only man who has a certain type of knowledge can be a special thing, but it can also be the greatest burden imaginable.

"Lord Drysten," a strangely cheerful man said from behind him. Drysten turned to see Maewyn, clearly weary from the journey South and looking as though he raced to Titus' home. "Lord is it true?"

Must have ridden by our handiwork, Drysten thought. "It was not the Gaels, priest. It was simply us." Drysten did his best to sound reassuring but knew Maewyn was still somewhat skeptical.

"How did you know what Abhartach's men do to the ones they kill?" the priest asked in an uneasy whisper.

Drysten smirked. "I was in the cell beside his son for a long while. Your bishop saw to that."

Maewyn cocked his head to the side. "You did much speaking to the man?"

Drysten nodded.

"Then would you have any idea as to why he has returned." Maewyn was no fool, and Drysten was certain the priest already knew the answer.

"You will never be a father, so I know you won't fully understand. I am a new father, and I can tell you with the greatest certainty that I would burn anything... everything to avenge the death of my boy." Drysten took a step towards the priest. "Maewyn, you did a foolish thing by standing idly by and allowing the bishop to believe killing Abhartach's son was the right course of action."

Maewyn sighed heavily as he glanced to the ground. "I did no such thing, Lord. We all believed he was the father, not the son."

"Why did you believe that? The man was roughly the same age as me," Drysten replied.

Maewyn raised his head and gestured to the Frisians. "You were leading men just as effectively if I recall correctly. Your age did not seem to prevent you from doing nearly anything."

"Suppose not," Drysten said as he saw Braxus bringing food to the prisoner. "I would have words with the man we captured. See yourself inside and find some food."

Maewyn glanced around before shaking his head. "Titus does not believe me to be a trustworthy companion. I think it would be best—"

"Titus swore himself to me before I was thrown into a cell. I am the lord here now," Drysten replied. He was somewhat shocked by his authoritative tone, but knew at its core, the statement was technically true.

Maewyn, still looking ambivalent, gave a slight nod and shuffled away as Drysten began to walk towards the room containing the prisoner.

"You believe you are lord here?" a man whispered. Drysten instantly recognized it to be Gaius.

"Yes," Drysten replied as he turned, "I do. I remember your father's oath, as does he. Otherwise, if he did not, I would not have had a home here."

"My father took you in because he pitied you, nothing more." Gaius' eyes narrowed as he stared into Drysten's. "The only lord here happens to be my father. You are nothing more than—"

"That's enough, boy!" Titus' voice boomed through the atrium, bringing silence from anyone who heard it.

Drysten turned and saw Titus hobbling over, still limping from the leg injury he sustained around the time he made his oath. Drysten pitied the man. Titus was once a great Roman officer, fighting everywhere from Africa, to Judea, and finally Britannia. But now, he was reduced to a hobbling old man living in a decrepit villa.

That is what Rome is now, Drysten thought. *An overly glorified shadow of its former self.*

Gaius straightened his back as he turned his gaze from Drysten. "This fucking—"

"He is your lord as much as he is mine, Gaius." Titus struggled to keep his balance for a moment, with Jorrit seeing this and walking over to help. "I'm fine. Leave me."

Gaius shook his head and pointed to Drysten. "Father, you cannot trust a man who has been all but dead for five fucking years and now comes back acting as though times have not changed."

Voices began whispering messages of cruelty into Drysten's mind, but somehow, he managed to shut them out and focus on Titus.

"Son," Titus began as he placed a hand on Gaius' shoulder, "I trust Drysten because when we had nothing, he trusted us to help him in any way we could. At the very least, we are canceling out a debt I never thought we would have to pay."

"And how much more will we have to pay?" Gaius hissed. He glanced to Drysten and began shuffling away, holding eye contact as long as he could before Drysten was behind him.

"Wait," Drysten commanded.

Gaius scoffed as he turned back around. The room was quiet as all eyes were fixed on Drysten. "Lord?"

"That ring. It looks like my father's," Drysten stated. "Which legion were they with?"

Gaius looked down to the ring before returning a strong glare toward Drysten. "I Adiutrix. Why does that matter?"

Drysten looked to Titus. "Is this legion still part of Rome's army?"

Titus shook his head. "No, they definitely aren't. They were with us when we followed Constantine, then turned against us and helped siege Arelate. I'll never forget that place." Titus stared off for a moment. "We always considered that to be the reason Constantine lost."

"But do they still fight for Rome?" Drysten insisted as he stepped closer to Titus.

"Why does that matter? They're here anyway." Titus adopted a quizzical look.

Drysten smirked. "Because if they aren't, then Germanus is simply purchasing the services of mercenaries. In turn, if these men are simply mercenaries it means he doesn't have an army of Christians fighting under the Pope."

Titus raised his gaze to the ceiling as he visibly tried to recall who these men could really be fighting for. "I... would think they fight for the Visigothic king. Theo...doric or some such name. He managed to secure the loyalty of many legionnaires once Honorius drove out the non-Christian politicians and generals. They needed someone to pay them, and many likely wanted to fight against Rome once Honorius' people killed their families."

Gaius let out a hollow gasp. "What purpose would killing

the families of your soldiers have?"

Titus sighed. "He wanted to ensure their loyalty by holding their families as hostages. I cannot say for sure why the men surrounding him allowed that."

"The Rome we all know from the stories is... dead," Drysten sadly declared. The tales of great generals and emperors he once heard from his father meant nothing to the people who ran the empire now. It seemed the brilliant minds, both military and political, had all left this world.

Gaius glanced to his feet, clearly thinking something similar to Drysten. Drysten began wondering how much of a problem Gaius would prove to be, but knew if Titus was still behind him, the man would be manageable. He watched Gaius disappear into the villa, likely to join his wife and son somewhere inside.

"He is simply shaken, Lord," Titus said in a hushed tone. "He has had a troubling few weeks from my understanding. Tonight did not do anything to soothe his mind."

Drysten nodded as he looked over Titus. He seemed to be greying quicker in the last couple of weeks, almost as though the talks of war were taking a toll each time they occurred. "I will not take any offense, brother. But I am not foolish enough to ignore his words forever."

Titus nodded. "Understandable, Lord." He patted Drysten's shoulder before turning back to follow his son.

"He will be yet another issue to deal with," the voice whispered.

Drysten knew there was no earthly being speaking those words to him. *Which god are you, I wonder?*

"The one you believe in." The voice faded out as it spoke, leaving Drysten with the understanding it had left him for the time being. He wondered which god it could have possibly been, as he believed in the existence of many gods. Their presence in this world was seen by many, and Drysten wondered whether there was simply a select few who were just called different names by different people.

“Lord,” Diocles said as he stepped forward. “Gaius is a good man. He is a good man, but a proud one.”

“So was I once. At least he gave me something useful before he stormed off like a child,” Drysten responded as he glanced down to the ring taken from the raid.

Drysten nodded as he slowly shifted towards the entrance to the villa, wondering what new problems he’ll have to face on top of those he already knew of. There was one thing which brought him a small bit of joy.

The confirmation Germanus was a fraud.

***

Eidion followed Bishop Germanus through the courtyard towards the old Roman baths now used as the king's residence. It had been little less than an hour since the messengers arrived with word of the patrol's ambush and dismemberment.

"This brazen disregard for the Church's authority will not go unpunished!" the bishop screamed as he walked through the entrance to the baths. "We will punish them all for this mess they've created for themselves!"

Eidion noticed the bishop seemed pleased with the outcome of the ambush. Almost as though he'd been hoping for something of this magnitude to happen for quite some time. *I wonder what you'll do now. This new slaughter will give the Christians an excuse to persecute everyone they view as an outsider.*

Two guards in royal blue cloaks denoting their service to King Ceneus halted them by the entrance to the baths. The steam was seeping out at the top of the door's entrance. Eidion always hated the stifling feeling it gave his chest to be so near the warm pool of water.

One familiar-looking guard stepped forward and raised a hand, with Germanus failing to stop and running his chest into the man's outstretched glove. "The king is in a meeting," the guard declared.

Bishop Germanus' eyes went down to his chest, where he swatted the guard's hand to the side. "I would have you gutted and thrown into the river for denying me—"

"Are you the king, Your Excellency?" the guard asked with a smile.

Germanus scoffed. "My authority is absolute. I don't need to be the fucking king to enter—"

"As a matter of fact, you do." The guard stepped forward and brushed his royal blue cloak aside to show his hand on the hilt of his sword.

Bishop Germanus glanced to Eidion, who took the hint and stepped forward. "You will move," he commanded, though he wasn't in the mood to say or do much else should the need arise. He truly didn't care one way or the other if the guards moved, as he hated his father and loathed the moments they were in each other's presence.

The guard shook his head and smiled. "The king specifically forbade you entering as well."

Bishop Germanus began to stammer, something Eidion had never seen. "If… I will be having words with your king—"

"Our king, Your Excellency." It was obvious the guard was simply trying to get a rise out of the bishop. If Eidion didn't hate his father quite so much, he may have actually found it entertaining to see Germanus stammer like a simpleton. "While you stay in his lands, eat his food, and fuck his women, he is your king as well."

Suddenly, the door opened. Rodric, the king's captain was standing on the other side wearing a knowing smile. "That will be all, Eliwlod. The man's veins seem about to burst."

So, that's how I recognized you. You're the bastard cousin, Eidion thought with a smirk.

Eliwlod was the son of King Garbonian, the current king of Bryneich. After Ceneus stole the crown from the man and banished him to the North, Eliwlod was born to a servant girl Garbonian had taken a liking to before his eventual defeat. Eidion wasn't certain King Garbonian even knew his son existed.

Eliwlod turned back to Bishop Germanus and winked before moving aside and allowing him and the prince through. "In you go, Your Excellency."

"I will remember your insolent tone," Germanus returned through gritted teeth. All the comment succeeded in doing was causing a huge smile to cross Eliwlod's face.

I like that one. A shame I'll likely have to kill him someday, Eidion thought. He yawned as he entered the room behind the bishop. He surveyed the room and sat at a vacant table with only a few scraps of food on a dinner plate. *Seems my father had a guest. He likely needed more time to usher them out the hidden doorway so we wouldn't know who.*

Eidion glanced over the steaming pool and saw the head of his father poking up from the shallower end, near the steps. His hair had grayed considerably these last few years, though Eidion was puzzled as to why. A man in his position was afforded every luxury imaginable, save for a proper family. The whole kingdom knew the king hadn't had one of those since before his coronation.

"Son," King Ceneus said as he stepped from the pool. "I hardly see you without your lapdog next to you." The king referred to Vonig, Eidion's highest ranking officer, and leader of his household guard. It was true Vonig was normally at Eidion's side, with that simple fact contributing to unsavory rumors likely started amongst Ceneus' men.

Eidion scoffed. "That is because he is doing the work of your own people, father. Allowing such barbaric attacks on your own patrols—"

"My patrols?" King Ceneus asked as he glanced to the bishop. "My patrols are all roaming to the West. I have only a handful of men to the South, and none of them wear black cloaks and harass the locals of that area. Those men were not mine at all. They were yours," he returned as he gestured a hand toward the bishop. "I was under the impression you wished for me to stay out of your affairs, Your Excellency."

Bishop Germanus glared into the king's eyes. "Don't twist my words, Ceneus. You know full well that I require your help, just as you require mine."

Eidion watched his father roll his eyes and turn away as he rose from the water and moved toward his robe. The fabric of it was old, but still looked softer than anything the prince had ever had. "What do you know of the attackers, father?"

"He speaks!" Ceneus said with a laugh and outstretched hands. He donned his robe and turned to face his son and the bishop. "Nothing you don't. I know no more than yourselves, though I confess I care quite a bit less."

Bishop Germanus scowled as he stepped toward the king. "Of course. Why would a man care about his own people being slaughtered in his own kingdom?"

King Ceneus scoffed and shook his head. "They were neither my people, nor were they killed in my kingdom. They were slaughtered in Rheged, and they were mercenaries paid for by the taxes you levied without my consent."

"I do not need your consent, Lord King, for I serve a higher power than yourself," Germanus returned while signing a strange gesture from his chest to his head and arms. Eidion always wondered what it signified, as all Christians did it. "I also find it funny you do not care for the barbarity of the attack's aftermath."

Eidion noticed the king perk an eyebrow at the comment. "What... barbarity is that?" Ceneus questioned as he stepped toward the bishop.

"Their heads were taken, and a handful were gutted. A small wickerman was created and the heads were placed inside." Germanus failed to conceal his uneasiness, as he was rubbing his arm the whole time he spoke.

King Ceneus noticed this as well. "I will admit, these attackers should be found before they cross our border." He glanced to Rodric, sporting a confused expression which made Eidion wonder what words must have been spoken prior to this meeting. "Send scouts, and find Dagonet. He will lead them."

"Yes, Lord King," Rodric obediently returned.

Ceneus glanced to the bishop and dismissively waved a hand to signal for his departure until Germanus interrupted. "Where is Maewyn?"

Eidion saw a slight uneasiness inside his father. *Seems both of you are holding secrets against one another...*

King Ceneus faced the bishop and smiled. "If I knew, I would likely have my spies watching him in the same manner they watch you. As far as I know, he is still in the city attempting to build that fucking... shrine you so badly wished for."

"I... expect you may be right. It is hard, time consuming work to assemble the faithful in these parts." Bishop Germanus glanced to Eidion as he spoke, giving him the silent order to find Maewyn's whereabouts.

Eidion rose from his seat. "I have other matters which require my attention, Your excellency." He turned to his father. "Lord King," he muttered as he turned to exit.

King Ceneus rose a hand to halt him. "I have a task for you, son."

Eidion froze. It had been so long since his father had tasked him with anything. It was strange to feel needed in some way, and Eidion wondered why a small part of him felt happy, or even lucky in the moment. "What would that be, father?" he wondered as he turned back.

"The Gaels have returned, as I am sure you are aware. I would task you with rooting them out before their kidnappings begin growing in scale." King Ceneus glanced to the bishop, who was clearly annoyed he would be without his most trusted officer. But the king was still the king, and this was not yet a Christian nation governed by the Church. No matter what delusions Germanus held.

"Why do you want me on this little errand? What of Gwrast?" Eidion wondered aloud. "Why have you not tasked him with this?"

I have," Ceneus responded. "I would have you both working to expel the Gaels. Gwrast in the West, and you closer to Eboracum. Mor cannot be troubled with this, as he oversees defending the North from the Picts that still climb the wall and ravage our homesteads."

Bishop Germanus stepped forward. "I would have him remain here, with me."

Ceneus smirked. "I would not."

Eidion watched as the bishop and the king glared into each other's eyes, wondering what game was being played between the two. His father undoubtedly wished for the bishop to be weakened and vulnerable, while the bishop knew his grip on the nation would shrink while his men were being attacked and his most trusted man was away. "Vonig will stay behind,

Your Excellency."

Bishop Germanus glanced to the prince and gave a slight nod. "Then away with you. I suppose those invaders pose as much a threat to myself as they do to Ebrauc."

It seems I have not lost all my importance to you, father. That is... strange. Eidion nodded and shuffled toward the door.

***

Titus felt the throbbing in his leg worsen as he descended the three steps to the kitchen. His wife had once suggested a walking stick when the wound was freshly healed, but Titus knew that would be the first thing he looked back on to identify when his body finally began breaking down for good. He glanced up to see Catulla hard at work in preparing enough food for both the residents and the guests who would be staying the night.

"Daughter," Titus greeted. He always enjoyed greeting Catulla this way. She was born a slave, then married who many would see as a nobleman. Titus always wondered whether she felt out of place but could never truly tell.

"Lord," Catulla said as she turned with a smile.

"Where is the little one?" Titus asked of his grandson.

"Isolde and Oana have put them down for the night. Lucius and Galahad are inseparable, almost as though they were brothers from birth." Catulla grinned as she looked back down to the pot she was stirring.

Hopefully, that will last longer than the friendship between their fathers, Titus hoped. He thought back to the tense exchange between Drysten and Gaius and hoped that would be the end of it. Sadly, he was no fool, and understood it likely wouldn't be. He knew what would happen to his son if he pushed a man like Drysten too far.

Titus glanced down to see Maebh sitting at his feet, eyes fixed on the food being prepared. The dog was about five years old, but still had enough youth in his soul to act as he had when Isolde first brought him from Frisia. He would routinely take their sandals off into dark corners or under beds.

"What'll it be, beast?" Titus said with a chuckle.

Maebh perked his ears up and met Titus' gaze for a moment before being distracted by a shuffling sound coming from the atrium. He turned to see Maewyn entering the kitchen, nodding to both himself and Catulla as he entered.

"It is nice to see you in good health, Lord," Maewyn said

with a smile.

Titus sighed and gestured to his leg. “Is that what this is?”

“You’re alive, Lord. That is much better than some can say.” Maewyn glanced to the pot and waited for Catulla to nod before picking up a clay bowl and sauntering over. It seemed to Titus the man hadn’t eaten in quite some time.

“You’re right, I haven’t,” Maewyn said, seemingly reading Titus’ mind. “I had a woman preparing my meal before I was sent off by the king to speak of Abhartach’s attack.”

“Abhartach’s?” Titus asked in confusion.

Maewyn nodded. “We originally believed—”

“It was Lord Drysten who led that ambush. Gaelic demons had nothing to do with it,” Titus interrupted.

Maewyn nodded as he clicked his tongue and tilted his head back. “He explained as much to me. While I don’t condone such barbarity… I must admit, it was quite effective at instilling a little fear into Germanus.”

Titus glanced at Catulla, who clearly had no knowledge of what Maewyn was speaking of. Titus always tried to keep his loved ones as far from the ugly side of life as he could. “We will speak of it later,” he told her. He then shifted his attention to Maewyn. “Lord Drysten was imprisoned with the man’s son. That is how he’s learned of their… methods.”

Maewyn began turning white in the face. “He told me as much just before I came to find my dinner.”

“I wonder what the real Abhartach would think if he saw someone… imitating his methods,” Titus replied.

Maewyn gently placed the half empty bowl onto the nearby table and looked off toward the vacant doorway. To Titus, he seemed distressed in some way. He watched the priest slowly close his eyes and lift his head toward the ceiling before releasing a long sigh. “Something terrible is about to happen. Something terrible indeed.”

Titus nodded, though he truthfully didn’t know why he shared the priest’s belief.

Maewyn began moving to the door. "I must leave, but keep watch over Lord Drysten."

Titus nodded. "That's what everyone here has been doing since the man returned. With his vacant stares and lack of speaking, he's driven poor Isolde mad. I just wonder what's going on inside the man's mind."

"I wonder," a voice said from the doorway.

Titus turned toward the entrance to the kitchen to see his exhausted son staring back at him.

Gaius glanced to his father as he approached his wife. "Lucius is asleep?"

Catulla nodded. "Went down with his brother not long ago."

"That boy is no member of our family," Gaius stated as he threw his head back in frustration. "We do too much for them."

"We do what is owed," Titus hissed to his son.

"And when does it become too much?" Gaius glanced to his wife, who looked uneasy as she stared back.

Titus let out a heavy sigh. He wanted to scold his son for defying his wishes, but for some reason he didn't have the will to. He simply stood in front of him, feeling the throbbing in his leg begin to die down.

Strange, Titus realized as he looked to his leg. *It's been a constant nuisance since...*

Suddenly, he found himself staring into the thatch roof of the kitchen. His son was kneeling over him, clearly worried judging by how wide his eyes were. He was speaking, but Titus could only hear whispers too faint to understand. He blinked and found he was in his bed, with his whole family around him. Among them was Jorrit and a handful of his Frisians. Braxus was speaking with Jorrit while giving Gaius a suspicious stare.

Drysten was closer, standing over a crying Galahad as he began to pat the boy's shoulder. It was the most human thing Titus had seen Drysten do since the man returned from the dead. Isolde was doing much of the same with Oana right beside them.

"What..." Titus croaked.

More whispers were heard as he shut his eyes. He opened them to see the Greek standing over him, with nobody else in the room. It was no longer night, as the sun was peaking its way through the cracked window. Just enough of Diocles' face was illuminated to show he'd been fighting off tears.

"I will take care of them, father," Diocles whispered. "I will take care of them all. Even Galahad. I know how much you enjoyed having him around with little Lucius."

"When..." Titus tried to speak but wasn't sure if he was heard.

"It has been a week since you tried to leave us," Diocles stated as he sat beside Titus. "I'm so sorry, but nobody knows what's happening to you."

But Titus understood what was happening. If I have been in this fucking bed for a week, I expect I'll soon be put in the ground for much longer.

"Father?" Diocles whispered.

You always enjoyed calling me your father. A shame your true father never knew his son. I imagine he would be proud of his boy. Titus couldn't tell if his happiness translated to a smile, or simply a feeling in his soul.

CHAPTER SEVEN

Maewyn awoke that morning to a knock on his door and a man cloaked in royal blue asking for his presence in the Roman baths. He had been spending the last few days trying to oversee the construction of a church just outside the front gate of Eboracum and found it hard to shake the sleep from his body. After donning the modest robe typically worn by men in his position, he slowly made his way outside to the morning air.

Men and women were beginning their day by walking to the market stalls for food or other things needed to survive. It was a welcome sight for the priest, as he rarely had the chance to see the people of Ebrauc during the times they weren't living in fear. At this moment, life seemed normal.

Either these people have no idea what kind of danger they're in, or they do and they're simply braver than the Romans of these times, Maewyn thought as he began shuffling toward Eboracum's fortress.

Maewyn overheard laughter coming from behind him, and immediately noticed Prince Gwrast was near. His voice was unmistakable to the priest, who saw much of King Ceneus in the prince. His men lauded him for his bravery, while the women of Ebrauc all wished he would act more like other members of his family. Maewyn always thought it was strange how he was the only monarch he'd ever seen who preferred not to womanize. It was one more way Maewyn knew he was a man of good morals. Something of a rarity in these days.

The soldiers under his command were all standing near the front gate of the city. It was widely known when Gwrast was in Eboracum, he normally camped outside with his men instead of spending the nights behind the safety of Eboracum's walls. Maewyn guessed it was due to the presence of his overbearing mother, but never knew for certain.

Gwrast spied the priest from afar and kindly waved as he walked over. "Bright and early."

Maewyn snorted as he glanced to the overcast sky. "I would have relished the opportunity to stay in bed a bit longer."

"As would I, but there seems to be something important happening." Gwrast chuckled at a small dog who pranced by with the cooked leg of a bird in its mouth as the two walked.

"Fewer rats than there used to be," Maewyn observed. Rats were common in any city, but it seemed Eboracum had always had more than its share.

"Likely due to the cats and dogs roaming about," Gwrast returned.

"Or the fact there's more people living inside the city's walls," Maewyn responded.

Gwrast smiled as he glanced around. "A happy sight when you remember what this place looked like mere months ago."

Maewyn tilted his head to the side as he spied Gwrast's older brother exiting a tavern just ahead of them. "Be happier without him being here."

Gwrast sighed heavily as his gaze rested on Eidion. "Spends more time with whores than your bishop. Does it make handling them easier when they're knee deep in servant girls?"

Maewyn chuckled as he shook his head. "Not really."

Both men went quiet as Eidion spotted them. "Good morning to you both!" Eidion shouted. "I'd wager neither of you spent your night in as good a company as me." He quickly caught up and clapped his younger brother on the back before bumping past Maewyn.

"Lord Prince," Maewyn grunted as the man marched ahead.

It wasn't long before the three men finally entered the fortress. It seemed both Gwrast and Maewyn were still in a morning daze, while Eidion was more jubilant than usual.

"Wonder what happened to the Roman," Gwrast said through a yawn.

Eidion scoffed. "The man was old as dirt. Probably died in his sleep."

Gwrast chuckled. "Hopefully, his son is simply given the same position. I always trusted him more than his father."

Maewyn glanced back to Prince Gwrast before ushering both men in front of him. They had just reached the baths as Bishop Germanus emerged from the principia, bible in hand. Maewyn wasn't certain if Bishop Germanus could honestly be considered a Christian. But what he did know of the man was he held a strong devotion to the word of God. The flaw was Bishop Germanus decided what the word of God actually was.

"Heard rumors of a kidnapping this morning," Gwrast began as the three entered the Roman baths. "Farmer's wife said her husband disappeared a few miles West of Isurium."

"Likely ran off with a younger woman. Haven't you seen the livestock we have for women around here?" Eidion said with a scoff.

Gwrast chuckled. "I've seen the women you spend your time with, brother. Livestock indeed."

Eidion scrunched his face as he returned his brother a scornful glance.

Maewyn didn't want to alarm the princes, but he knew for certain Abhartach was near. He knew this because Drysten had sent for him. During his time as a slave in Hibernia and Dal Riata, he learned how the various tribes communicated with each other. Not the tribes who were at peace, but the ones who were at war. Wickermen were normally built to send messages of doom to a rival, but Drysten had used it to send a request for help.

Fool has no idea what he's done. What this will cost, Maewyn thought with a sigh.

The three men entered the baths to see Gaius speaking with the king at the small table near the door.

"Welcome," King Ceneus muttered in a sleepy voice.

Gaius turned and nodded to Maewyn and Gwrast before sneering toward Eidion. "A pleasure," he said.

"We need to speak privately, Lord King," Maewyn blurted out.

Maewyn felt the confusion in the room as all members of the meeting looked toward him at once. He felt the blood rushing to his cheeks from the embarrassment until the group was alerted to Bishop Germanus entering the room. Ceneus met Maewyn's gaze and returned a slight nod as Germanus plopped himself down in a seat at the other end of the table.

"What's this about, *Lord King*?" Germanus asked with a scowl.

"Titus has taken ill. Gaius will be taking up his duties," the king answered in a morose tone.

Germanus scoffed. "And this is important because… "

The king and Gaius each glared at the bishop, causing the man to smirk in the knowledge he managed to get under their skin.

"My father served this kingdom faithfully and honorably, Your Excellency. I would assume there should be a small amount of respect for him here," Gaius growled. "Even from you."

Bishop Germanus scoffed and tilted his head to the side. "Yes… well, I suppose the man was more competent than most we are surrounded by."

Maewyn watched Gaius lean back in his seat and wondered how such a statement could have eased the man.

Ceneus must have been wondering the same thing, as Maewyn also saw him widen his eyes and give a slight shake of the head before gesturing to his sons to come forward. "What news of the Gaels have you for me, boys?"

The princes glanced to one another, with Gwrast stepping forward. "I have nothing, father," he sadly stated. "All I have are rumors."

"And what do they whisper?" Ceneus asked as he reclined in his seat. "Rumors can lead to something more."

Gwrast shrugged. "Nothing of substance. I have had my men checking on them as we ventured back to the city."

Maewyn shook his head. "You heard one more recently, Lord Prince. The disappearance near Isurium."

Gwrast snickered. "I doubt that was related, priest."

Eidion chuckled to himself as well. "Livestock…" he whispered, drawing a rare bit of amusement from Prince Gwrast.

The king stood. "I would have Eidion on it, with you venturing back West to keep routing them out wherever they may pop up."

They are closer than you think, you fool of a man, Maewyn thought as he glanced to his feet. *They will find you soon enough. Then you will see…*

"Something to say, Maewyn?" Bishop Germanus questioned before plunging a large hunk of meat down his gullet.

Maewyn shook his head. "Nothing, Your Excellency. Merely wondering how long we will wait before taking the fight them instead of watching our people slaughtered."

"Such drive from you, man," an impressed Germanus returned. "No doubt this comes from your time as a slave to these Gaels."

"I was not a slave to them, Your Excellency. I was a slave to people who feared Abhartach just as much as you should."

King Ceneus gave Maewyn a confused glanced before Germanus cut him off from speaking.

"I would remind you we are the only ones in God's grace here." the bishop outstretched his arms and looked to the ceiling. "And we thank you, Lord, for all that you do for us."

Gwrast snickered. "Could you ask him for an army?"

"God's army is already here," Germanus answered while bringing his hands to his chest. "I would herald it into battle myself if I must."

"What a sight that would be," Gwrast added.

"It would come at great surprise to learn I was once a great commander of Rome. I took up these robes when I had a moment of supreme clarity and grace inside a church. God spoke to me and gave me a divine purpose!" Germanus again looked to the ceiling. "I thank you for that every day and night, Lord."

The men remained silent. The discomfort in the room was unbearable for all but the bishop. Even Maewyn rose with the rest of the men as they began to shuffle away from the bishop's rabid prayers. The man was no Christian in Maewyn's eyes. He simply knew how to play the part of one well enough to trick the Britons.

Maewyn was led out of the baths by Gwrast while Eidion and Ceneus went their separate ways.

"Does he make you... rich?" Gwrast asked in a hushed tone.

Maewyn shook his head as he stepped into the morning air once again. "Doubt he makes anyone but your brother's guards rich."

"Why do you follow him? He's crazy."

"I follow the teachings of my God. I do *not* follow him."

Gwrast cocked his head to the side. "I'm beginning to wonder whether or not you worship the same god."

Maewyn chuckled to himself. "I suggest you worry about the Gaels. I'll see to the bishop's soul."

The two men shared a laugh before going their separate ways.

***

Galahad followed Drysten through the wood line. It had been two weeks since Titus had collapsed in the kitchens and became bedridden. Drysten knew Titus was extremely important to the well-being of his son. Without him, there's no telling the conditions Galahad and Isolde would have lived in.

"Galahad, follow," he sternly said as he walked.

The boy had apparently never been so far from Titus' villa, which was somewhat understandable considering who his father was. If people could identify him, his life would be in much greater peril than it already was by merely living in Britannia.

"Father, where are we going?" Galahad asked. The boy was tired. He had been woken up early in the morning by Drysten and Isolde. Likely earlier than he was accustomed to.

Drysten couldn't help but smile upon being called father. "Petras and Paulus are going to begin teaching you to shoot. They even fashioned you a small bow of your own." Drysten stole a glance behind him to see his son beaming with excitement. It seemed the fatigue had left him and was replaced with excitement. A sight which brought a new kind of joy to Drysten's heart.

While Drysten was indeed happy in the moment, he remembered why they had woken so early. He told his boy the truth, but not the reasoning behind it. Titus was getting ready to meet his ancestors soon and Drysten and Isolde agreed it would be best to take their boy away from the grieving family. Isolde stayed behind, as she had grown quite close to both Oana and Catulla, and she thought she may do some good.

"Where are they?" Galahad wondered aloud.

Drysten heard the faint rustling of leaves as he turned to answer, then noticed it wasn't his boy who made the noise. Galahad was staring into a group of bushes with a confused expression, giving Drysten a moment's pause as he turned. "What is it, son?"

"I... I..." Galahad pointed to the bushes as he stammered.

Drysten stole a quick glance around him when he felt the knife against his throat. "Abhartach..." a man whispered.

In a blur, the man pricked Drysten's neck with a small, wooden stick coated in a shiny substance. The last thing he saw before his world began to fade out, was the crying face of his son, and the two large, scarred hands which plucked him from the ground.

Drysten's father was a faint specter lurking in the background, far off in the trees. "I know you will do great things. Things I was not capable of. Things the gods above have chosen you for."

When Drysten awoke, he found himself wondering if his eyes were open. The place he now found himself in was darker than anywhere else he'd ever been. Darker than any time of night. He glanced around and saw roughly a dozen shapes all sitting beside him. As his eyes acclimated to the darkness, he noticed the heads of those around him were covered with brown-stained sacks. Every one of them seemed to have been propped up with their backs against the wall. Not a carved wall, but stone of a mountain or rock face.

"The one who called us stirs!" a man announced. "Your message was heeded, as I'm sure you will rejoice to hear."

Drysten turned his gaze in the direction of the voice, seeing a small fire's light peeking through the darkness. Its light was faint and distant, but it illuminated just barely enough to show a man approaching him.

"You called on The Morrigan?" the man questioned. "Of the ones we captured, you would be the last I guessed to request our presence. But alas, the ones you find yourself with divulged your identity to me rather quickly." the man knelt down and leaned close to Drysten's face. "It was the hairy one, if you're curious. He told us you commanded him to construct the wooden one." The stranger gestured to a large silhouette Drysten guessed to be Jorrit.

Drysten's head felt fuzzy as he tried to stand. He found neither leg would move no matter how hard he tried.

"Your stiffness will fade," the stranger said.

Drysten could just make out the man was bald, and had no facial hair. Judging by his silhouette, he was burly but lacked in height. "Where am I?" Drysten asked. He was slightly surprised he could speak considering how dead his body felt.

"A cave we have recently taken up residence in near your happy little home," the man responded.

Drysten glanced at the shrouded individuals beside him. "And these people... they're all mine?"

"They are! They are indeed your friends and loved ones. But now, my new friend, you will make a choice." The man released a maniacal laugh with chilled Drysten to the core.

"Gods above..." Diocles grumbled from beside Drysten. "Where the—"

"Say no more!" Drysten ordered. "Do not speak." Diocles, head covered, gave a faint nod in response before Drysten turned back to his captor. "What choice?"

"The Morrigan demands lives as payment for our... kinship." the man answered. "And keep in mind, the more important the life, the more of The Morrigan's favor you will be granted."

"Abhartach..." Drysten whispered. He now understood why he was there. When he was imprisoned by the bishop, he was in the neighboring cell to this man's son. The son described how his father could be called upon, as Abhartach the father left his boy specific instructions to give to anyone who could prove useful.

"My message worked," Drysten said through a weak grin.

"It did, and here we are." Abhartach rose and gestured his hands toward two others who had been standing in the darkness of the cave. "But tell me, why should I heed the message?" Abhartach asked.

"Because I can give you what you want," Drysten explained. "Because I hear the gods and know their will." The last statement was the only time in Drysten's life he professed to understand the voices of his mind. But when Drysten was still imprisoned and claimed to have seen a black-haired woman swarmed with crows, Abhartach's son believed he knew The Morrigan well.

Abhartach scoffed as he slowly leaned his head back, pausing a moment before returning his gaze to Drysten. "How do I know these words speak the truth?"

"Because your boy was instructed to only explain your little ritual to those who were important enough to know of it. And I am important enough." Drysten felt slightly invigorated by some strange sense of authority he didn't know he had. Many considered his gift to be just that, a gift. But he never did. The voices tormented him his whole life, but now he had found a use for them.

"You are an interesting one. I'll give you that," Abhartach affirmed through a thick accent. "We sent a man to my son the night before his killing. That man crept through the passages under the city of stone to find you both, but you were fast asleep like a little babe. What my boy told him, was there was a man who would help bring the downfall of this kingdom. But all services require payment."

"What payment could I possibly give?" Drysten asked.

Abhartach stood and turned toward the far-off fire. "The Morrigan requires payment through a sacrifice. An important sacrifice."

Drysten felt a pang of guilt, and a small voice inside him begged him not to go through with the deal. It wasn't the voices he heard from above, it seemed to be his own conscience. *Anything worth doing is always going to be difficult, he thought as he tried to suppress his conscience.*

"Lord, the children!" Diocles rasped. Like Drysten, he too tried to move but failed after a few groans.

Abhartach shuffled over to Diocles and knelt right in front of him. "Why would The Morrigan wish for us to take the future from our hands. She is a just god, and would never do such a thing…" He placed a hand on Diocles' cheek and clicked his tongue in the same manner a mother would to soothe her child.

"I don't believe you. "Diocles moved his face from the Gael's hands and turned his head to Drysten. "And neither should you, Lord!" he screamed.

Drysten glanced toward the fire in the distance. "Where is my son and the other boy. And who else have you brought here?"

"The children are being cared for; I assure you. As for the others..." Abhartach began moving from bag to bag, ripping the sacks from the familiar shapes.

How did you manage to bring everyone from the villa here at once? Drysten wondered.

"For our services, The Morrigan demands... two souls," Abhartach stated. "Now, choose." He snapped his fingers and a man went from person to person, ripping the bags from their heads.

"Keep your head, son," Hall whispered. "You caused this, but now you will have to stem the bleeding. Choose wisely..."

Drysten felt sick to his stomach as he glanced over the frantic gazes from the other prisoners. It seemed some had also been gagged for some odd reason, but there was one who seemed as though he was still asleep.

Titus, Drysten thought. "Bring a torch. I need light to see."

"I suppose even a man who hears the gods squawking in their minds must still require certain luxuries." Abhartach turned and gestured something before a silent shape began moving toward the fire. He returned a moment later with not only light, but two scared children as well.

"Son..." Gaius wheezed through his delirium.

"Are you okay?" Drysten asked both children, who each nodded through tears.

"They have been fed and watered, God-whisperer. I assure you," Abhartach announced.

Knowing what the Gaels ate made Drysten sick to his stomach. "What did you put in their bellies?" he demanded.

Abhartach released a bellowing laugh as he through his head back. "I know your people have a different… preference than my people. They were given the meat from a hare and wine from your own storage. We are many things, Briton, but disrespectful of a parent's wish is not one." Abhartach walked by both boys and patted their shoulders before peering back to Drysten. "Now, choose."

Drysten looked over the terrified faces of his loved ones. Isolde, Oana, Diocles. All desperately hoping for another way out. Curiously, there was Maewyn, right between Isolde and Titus. But his gaze was different. His eyes were darting between Drysten and Titus. He was telling him what to choose.

"Titus, I am sorry," Drysten stated.

"Fucking… bastard…" Gaius huffed as he struggled to move. "You'll—" and then he seemed to fade from consciousness.

Titus briefly stirred, but stopped as he gazed back to Drysten. After a sickly nod, he too seemed to fade out.

"This one was taken in his sleep! He must have been a great man in his early years, though now he shows me nothing but weakness," Abhartach responded with a perplexed tone.

"He's the finest man I've ever met. He reminded me much of my own father," Drysten murmured.

After a satisfied nod, Abhartach pointed to the old Roman. Two masked men plucked him up from the ground amidst the wailing and begging from everyone around.

There was no talk of payment, Drysten mused as he fought back tears. *If I meet your boy in the afterlife, I'll be sure to show my appreciation for this.*

"Another," Abhartach ordered as he snapped his fingers toward the moaning prisoners, silencing them.

Drysten's eyes darted over the terrified faces of his people. He couldn't see their fear, but he felt he could have reached out and plucked it from the air. He knew there was no easy choice. But the one thing he knew was the women never be options. Aside from them, Diocles was his most trusted man, and the Cretans were not only his men, but his father's. That left Jorrit, Maewyn, Citrio, and Gaius. Maewyn's eyes seemed to want Drysten to pick him, but how could he repay his freedom with a death sentence. Citrio was staring through tears, and Gaius's head was slumped over in sleep.

Gaius could prove an issue later, but he is Titus' only son... Drysten was nearly losing the fight the keep back his tears. Thankfully, he learned how in the five years of confinement.

But there was one other.

"Him," Drysten muttered as he craned his head to the prisoner from the ambush.

The young man's eyes went wide, wide enough for them to be seen clearly in the torchlight. Abhartach gestured a hand in his direction.

"This one?" the Gael asked in surprise. "That one is still young enough to remember his mother's tit."

"He fought against us. Men fight, children do not," Drysten insisted.

Abhartach smirked and nodded. He looked back to one of his men, and the figure quickly walked over and plucked the boy up from the ground.

"No! Please!" the boy screamed. It occurred to Drysten he had never even learned the boy's name. "Don't do this!" he wailed as the hunter dragged him away, moving toward the fire. Everyone in the cave was silent as the boy was dragged off. His wails soon disappeared after one last shriek of pain, and the cave went silent.

"I have another I wish to add," Drysten whispered. "A prince."

Abhartach moved the torch toward Drysten and raised an eyebrow. His head tilted to the side as he inched toward Drysten. "A prince is surely more important than any man here, but the payment has already been fulfilled!" He glanced behind him toward the man who returned from killing the boy before returning Drysten's gaze. "The Morrigan is wise enough to heed anyone's words. You will speak."

Drysten nodded. "The heir to a kingdom. Someone The Morrigan would be pleased with. A wicked Christian."

"Ah… Now that does sound like a man worth her altar. Removing the wicked from our homes is a noble cause indeed!" Abhartach glanced back to two silent men as they inched closer toward him, neither speaking. One blinked and pointed to something outside. "I have a matter to attend to. We will be in contact soon, brother," Abhartach announced in a panic before dropping the torch and storming away with the two men. It gave Drysten a moment to glance at the frightened and distraught glances of his people.

"Lord…" Diocles whispered. "What did you do?"

Drysten peered to his closest friend and tried to speak, succeeding only in returning his vacant stare with one of his own as the crying of his people became more audible. "I…"

"My father… treated you as a son…" Gaius hissed. "And you repay him with death?"

Drysten slowly shook his head. "There was not talk of payment or sacrifice when I—"

Isolde began sobbing, causing a tearing sensation in Drysten's chest. "You killed him," she whispered. "Why did you do such a thing?"

Drysten glanced to Lucius and Galahad as they approached their mothers, and wondered how he had ever seen working with Abhartach as a viable option. How could he not have expected something like this to happen after all he had learned of the Gaels from his own people?

Maewyn glanced to Isolde and Gaius. "It was the only option there was." Gaius began cursing under his breath as Maewyn turned to Drysten. "You did a foolish thing, Lord. The Gaels as a whole are much like the Britons were before the Romans came, but not these. These Gaels are different. They simply roam from place to place and deliver pain as sport. Those are the ones you have aligned yourself with."

Diocles glanced from Maewyn to Drysten. "I will not follow you any longer, Lord. Not alongside them, and not after what you've done."

Drysten had never felt so much shame. He quietly nodded and glanced to the fire, beginning to make out the sound of footsteps approaching. But these were heavier, armored footsteps. Clumsy in comparison to those of Abhartach and his men.

"Lord!" a man yelled. "Lord Drysten!"

Drysten cocked his head to the side as an armored man with a bloody sword ran into the room, madly dashing his gaze from side to side until it settled on Drysten.

"They said I was mad to believe it, but here you are!" The man rushed over while a small group of others adorned in Roman-made Lorica segmentata entered the cave.

"Matthew?" Drysten whispered in surprise.

"Galahad, Matthew, it's all the same to me." He smiled as he leaned over to pick Drysten up and quickly slung him over his shoulder. Drysten must have briefly passed out, as the next thing he saw was Matthew wearing a solemn expression as he knelt over him. He was wearing a polished set of lorica segmentata and a dark purple cloak about his shoulders. He had a ring of silver with an orange stone in its center wrapped tightly around his thumb. He was opening a skin of liquid he then lifted to Drysten's lips.

The feeling had come back into Drysten's arms, and he even had the dexterity required to handle the skin himself without any assistance. He glanced around and saw the dismayed faces of his loved ones glancing back at him.

"I heard what happened. What you did," Matthew announced as he stood. "He was a good man. I fail to see why—"

"Abhartach's son never explained payment," Drysten interrupted, his tone more desperate than he meant to show.

"Yet you accepted his offer anyway," Matthew sternly replied. "We all do foolish things, Lord, but I fear your foolishness may have more consequences than you know."

"How are you even alive?" Drysten wondered. It seemed like a few others wondered the same thing, as both Isolde and

Diocles glanced over to listen for the answer.

"Titus and Prince Aurelianus devised a plan to stage my death. I was taken in by the Powysians," Matthew explained. "Many of your people are there already, though I wonder what they'll say—"

"Hopefully, they'll hang him high enough for his new friends to see him across the sea!" Gaius shouted.

"Leave me," Drysten commanded as he lowered his head. "Take everyone else with you and go."

The unsettling reality of what Drysten had done set in, as not a single person cared whether or not he stayed behind. Matthew simply nodded and gestured for his men, roughly thirty in number, to help the rest of Drysten's people up from the ground.

Matthew then looked back to Drysten before peering around through the trees. "I expect you'll have visitors soon. Tell them I'll be seeing them soon." He then nodded, and ordered everyone to move off.

Drysten looked to Isolde before she and Galahad were led away by one of Matthew's men. "I promised you I'd care for you," he whispered just loud enough for her to hear. "I'm so sorry."

Isolde began to sob as she clutched Galahad at her side. Matthew looked to the man who was trying to usher away and jabbed a finger toward the direction of the others.

Drysten was then alone but felt an unexpected sensation of serenity in the moment. He spent five years away from everyone and wondered whether he missed his solitude. He knew he didn't miss the prisons, but this was a much more pleasant setting than the one he was in before. The birds were chirping overhead, and small animals could be heard roaming nearby. But then a cloud settled over him.

CHAPTER EIGHT

The Morrigan was happy, or so Abhartach said. It was roughly two months since Drysten had joined Abhartach's Gaels. It was strange being the only one besides their leader who could speak. Every single person there, save for Abhartach and himself, had their tongues taken in the ritual before becoming the highest-ranking men in Abhartach's army.

"The herbs have helped?" Abhartach asked as they huddled inside the same cave Drysten had met the man.

"Your healers know what they're doing," Drysten answered. Drysten had not only been given healing ointments and herbal drinks for his strength, but was being trained to fight as one of Abhartach's men as well. He now wondered if he could rival the Cretans with a bow, and knew for certain he was quicker with a blade than ever before.

Abhartach returned a proud nod. "Our druids are the last of their kind. There are few others who know the trade on the big island."

"I expect the Romans are to thank for that," Drysten stated.

"They are. They took the magic from the druids in these lands using the power of the written word, then killed the druids themselves to bring the Britons to heel. Now all that's left of their legacy are shadows and ruins." Abhartach sighed as he glanced towards the entrance to the cave.

Drysten thought back to the first night he was with them. It was then he found out that these people were there to try and bring the old druidic beliefs back to the Britons. Abhartach sent a bastard son to try and find out how likely a scenario that would be, but ended up finding a better reason to tell Abhartach's people back in Hibernia an invasion was necessary. The boy knew if he died, then the druids could say there was a quest for revenge to be had, and that is exactly what they did. But Abhartach did not use this excuse for revenge, he was on the same mission as the Christians. He wanted to bring back the old ways.

"We will be leaving soon," Abhartach explained as he stood. "I have given you ample time to regain your strength. It is time for the final offering to be made." He glanced down to the two skulls resting atop a small altar illuminated by torchlight. The larger skull had once belonged to Titus, or Drysten supposed it still did, he just didn't have need of it. The smaller one was what was left of the prisoner whose name Drysten never learned. Drysten hadn't intended to get the man killed, but he was thankful for his presence. Had the man not been in the cave that night, Drysten would have had a much harder decision to make.

Drysten rose from the ground and followed Abhartach out of the cave. "We will use the old Roman sewers. The priest who set me free told me of a way into the Roman baths from there."

"It will be good to stay out of sight." Abhartach answered with an approving nod. "My hunters are the most fearsome warriors these islands have ever seen, but even they can die if the odds are poor enough," he added.

I remember killing them easily enough in Segedunum. I'll kill many more once you are no more use to me, Gael. Drysten did his best to contain his hate for Abhartach and his people. He quickly grew to hate them once he saw how they lived, what they ate.

"What will you do once The Morrigan is pleased?" Drysten wondered. He instantly regretted asking the question, as it implied Drysten had no intention of staying with them.

"We will journey South and root out the Saxon menace. It will be much easier to deal with the Britons and bring them back to our ways once they no longer have as many enemies to fear," Abhartach answered. "My forces are waiting on the small island between here and Hibernia. Two thousand strong."

Drysten was stunned. *How does a man-eater entice that many fucking people to fight for him?* He wondered. He suspected it had something to do with the herbal magics the druids employed. While he was there, the Gaels seemed to almost worship them in a way.

Drysten roamed alongside Abhartach and his hunters for the remainder of the day. He wore the same animal skins and brown mask as the Gaels. The only thing that set him apart was the bearskin cloak once belonging to his father.

The fifty men finally made their way within sight of the city. The sun was still hovering high enough to illuminate the road, so everyone was ordered to halt near the edge of a tree line until darkness. There were a handful of riders going from the city to the South, but none Drysten could recognize.

Most of those who passed seemed like traders or local tribal guards. Drysten guessed those men were likely from small villages between Eboracum or Petuaria. None of them would pose any serious threat, and would likely run at the first glimpse of the Gaels.

However, one stood out from the rest.

"Dagonet..." Drysten whispered, prompting the man behind him to grab his arm, and angrily put a hand over his mouth. *I'll kill you first when I have the chance.* He glanced back to his friend riding toward Eboracum with one other in tow. *Is that... Cynwrig?*

And it was. It seemed Cynwrig had indeed made himself into a prominent warrior, as he rode with his back straight and his chin up with dignity. There was a familiar golden chain around the Briton's neck. The very same one which King Ceneus had once bestowed upon Drysten before taking the Fortuna into Frisia so long ago.

Abhartach began a slow, deliberate crawl towards Drysten. "They are known to you?" he whispered.

Drysten nodded. "They worship the old ways and should not be harmed."

Abhartach shook his head toward a pair of men who had strung their bows, with them removing the arrows they had at the ready. He looked back to Drysten, nodded, and crept away.

Drysten glanced back to his two friends, his heart immediately stopping. Dagonet had halted and was now staring into the overgrown grass near the tree line. The hunter beside Drysten began to slowly string his bow until Abhartach tapped his heel and shook his head.

Keep moving... Drysten wondered if Dagonet heard his thoughts, as the man clicked his tongue and spurred his horse forward at a faster pace than before.

Abhartach waited until Cynwrig and Dagonet had ridden far enough away before he stood. He looked to the hunters around him and made a series of hand gestures Drysten had yet to understand. The hunters all rose from the ground and knelt at the edge of the tree line. They were now close enough to the road to jog a few paces and reach it, but far enough into the tree line to still have a good measure of concealment.

"Are you nervous to face this man?" Abhartach asked of Drysten.

Drysten glanced to the king, smirked, and shook his head. "I don't fear anything anymore. That was one thing they managed to rid me of when they threw me down below."

Abhartach produced the most wicked and disturbing smile Drysten had ever seen in a man. "That is good. I hope our... relationship continues for a long time. It is rare to find men of your mettle on the islands."

Drysten smiled and glanced to Eboracum, sitting far off in the distance. "The sun is going down."

Abhartach peered in the same direction. "Lead us."

Night came, and Drysten found a loose drainage stone on the Northern side of the city, right outside the wall nearest the fortress. He signaled for two men to pry it from the ground, and after a few moments of struggling, the ornately designed stone was lifted to expose the darkness of the sewer.

Drysten dropped down first. He grew accustomed to the rank smell emanating from underground in the five years down below. The area he was guiding Abhartach's men into was not the same one he was led through with Maewyn, but he still knew enough about it to be a serviceable guide. Every so often he would pause under a drainage stone leading up into the city, and listen to discern exactly where he was.

Those women sound like the whores who roam near the front gate of the fortress, Drysten observed. He turned to his followers and gestured them forward. "We will soon come to a turn. A right will lead us to the Roman baths, and a left will take us to the cells I was kept in."

"To the right then," Abhartach whispered. "We can rehash old memories later."

Drysten led the hunters right and down a long, straight tunnel. No noise was heard, not even from the men behind him. Rats would scurry away from the intruders as they slowly moved through the darkness.

"A light," Abhartach whispered.

Drysten trained his eyes and saw there was indeed a small trickle of light coming from the end of the tunnel. It was barely a flicker, and Drysten could instantly tell it was likely a torch. "There's likely nobody down here. We can keep moving."

Abhartach whispered his agreement and the group resumed their pace. They eventually reached the light to see a torch. It seemed to be a freshly lit one. "I thought you said there were no souls to worry about," Abhartach whispered.

Drysten glanced around and saw a set of stairs next to a small gap in the wall. The gap led outside, presumedly to the edge of the old Roman fortress. Drysten felt his lips curl into a smile, as he knew for certain the stairway led to the baths. "This is the secret way into the king's residence. The exit is behind a narrow crack in the wall, covered by a royal blue banner. The priest told me as much," Drysten explained.

Abhartach moved beside Drysten and began staring up

the vacant stairway. He turned and gestured for the men to follow him up.

***

King Ceneus and Maewyn sat on opposite ends of the Roman baths as the bishop began scolding them both. It had been roughly a day since rumors of Drysten's survival had reached Germanus, but even he needed to check with his spies to see if it were true. However, now he had someone new to rely upon for information on his enemies.

"Titus' boy explained it all to me. It took him some time before he could stomach coming here himself, but he eventually did so," Germanus hissed. "You fools thought giving the bastard his freedom would somehow align him with you. Pathetic wretches. Now we are being forced to work alongside each other. And Maewyn..." Bishop Germanus looked over the priest with a sad gaze.

Ceneus glanced to Maewyn, still clearly shaken from the encounter with Abhartach a couple of months before. The man was normally talkative and jolly, but had recently taken to being silent and withdrawn.

"And now he has the support of the Gaels, the ones who are rumored to disappear before a man's eyes and reappear in a completely different part of the island. I have no idea if they have the magic of the druids on their side, but now they may have something worse."

Maewyn gave the bishop a hollow gaze. "What could be worse than the druids, Your Excellency?"

Germanus scoffed. "A lord willing to guide these rabid beasts through Ebrauc."

King Ceneus had no idea what his next course of action should be. He trusted Drysten just enough to expect the man to kill the bishop, but he trusted him based upon the man he once was. Now, it seemed like an entirely different person left the cell than the one that entered it. "I should have expected this."

"You're right, you fool," Germanus screamed. "You should have!" He rose from his seat and paced from side to side before slamming his fist down next to the bible resting on his table. "Eidion!" he called. "Eidion, get the fuck in here!"

King Ceneus watched as his eldest son entered the baths wearing a perplexed expression. It seemed to Ceneus the boy had no idea what had been learned the last few days. *Germanus must not have told you. I expect he believes our relationship to be somewhat strengthened since I have given you new authority.*

"Your Excellency," Eidion greeted. The prince glanced to his father and nodded, a respectful gesture which the king rarely received.

"You are to raise all my men and venture South," Germanus ordered. "You are to find Lord Drysten and his Gaelic pets and kill them all. There will be no mercy."

"Lord... Drysten?" Eidion said in a confused tone. "That man is—"

"He is very much alive, and it is now your job to correct this insult!" Germanus bellowed. His tone went even more mad as he violently jabbed a finger in the prince's direction.

Eidion, still confused, glanced to his father and Maewyn, both of which nodded in confirmation Drysten was alive. "Where were these men last seen?"

Maewyn stood and walked to a map which had been laid out on a table near the entrance. "Here, in a cave. I can take you, but I doubt they are there."

"Then fucking find them!" Germanus screamed. His voice began going hoarse. The way he was throwing his hands into the air reminded Ceneus of a child who had been denied his evening meal.

"Vonig," Eidion beckoned. The bald captain entered the baths from the doorway and approached the prince. "His Excellency and the king are under your protection," Eidion ordered.

Vonig gave a suspicious glance to Ceneus before eventually nodding. "Right enough, Lord Prince."

The prince nodded and said his farewell before venturing out into the night to muster his men. Maewyn silently stood and followed suit.

"What of the Powysians who stormed in and took the

traitors?" Germanus asked of Ceneus.

The king shrugged. "The only traitor I know of is Drysten. That being said, I have sent Rodric and Eliwlod to Powys for information. Dagonet and his man, Cynwrig, are following them. They will be venturing East to Praesidium to sail along the coast until arriving at Glevum."

Ceneus lied to everyone in the room. He knew the tides were beginning to turn out of his favor. In actuality, Rodric and Eliwlod were going to Bryneich to meet with Ceneus' brother, King Garbonian. It was Ceneus' hope he could entice his brother into helping fight off both the Christians and the Gaels.

"They are all traitors," Germanus muttered to himself.

The king sat in silence for a time, apparently creating a great enough amount of boredom in the bishop for the man to stand and leave. Vonig began to follow but was gestured to sit back down as the bishop walked by. Germanus disappeared through the doorway and was overheard ordering his guards to join him in the principia, likely the safest place in the city.

Bishop Germanus had roughly a hundred people staying in both the principia and the surrounding barracks, while King Ceneus had about forty. The king always preferred for his men to stay with their families on the other side of the river, one of the many efforts Ceneus was making to repopulate Eboracum following the Roman withdrawal from Britannia.

"Would you mind if I eat, Lord King," Vonig asked as he gestured to Maewyn's full plate.

Ceneus nodded and gestured for the man to make his way over to the plate and have his fill. "Why do you tolerate the bishop?"

Vonig chuckled as he broke apart a hunk of bread. "He freed me from the prisons."

"As I recall, you were there for raping a fisherman's daughter during the Samhain celebrations," Ceneus hissed. All Vonig responded with was a sly smile and a wink towards the king, causing a hollow pit to form in the base of Ceneus' stomach. *At least he doesn't know he gave the woman a pair of twins.*

Could never see this whoreson as a father.

The two remained silent for a while longer, with Ceneus wondering how long Vonig would stay in the baths if there was nothing to do. The man was known to frequently visit a certain tavern on the other side of the river for the same handful of whores. Ceneus knew if he grew bored enough, the man could eventually leave him in peace as the bishop had done.

"Lord King," a voice greeted from behind him.

Ceneus sighed and wondered which one of his guards had ventured into the sewers and gotten himself turned around. It happened every so often, with the last one being Eliwlod roughly a month before. He glanced behind him and leapt from his seat, with Vonig doing the same.

There stood two men in worn, mud-stained furs, wearing masks which covered half their faces. Both men had their blades drawn, with the shorter of the two wielding an older sword which looked crudely fashioned. However the other seemed to be brandishing a Roman spatha, and on his waist was slung a dagger which Ceneus instantly recognized.

"Drysten..." the king whispered. He knew he would not be able to contain his fear. "I... We had... a deal, Drysten. It was to be the bishop and my son before you went after me." He grew more embarrassed as every word stumbled out.

Drysten slowly reached for his facemask and pulled it down below his chin. Ceneus had a better view of the scars left from the man's captivity, with a handful being across his ears and cheeks, and a large one going down his left temple. "The Morrigan requires an offering," he whispered

"And she will have it," the shorter man added through a malicious grumble.

King Ceneus felt his eyes go wide as he heard Vonig struggling with someone behind him. He stole a glance and saw two more men equipped in the same fashion as Drysten standing over him with a knife to his throat. "You think you can... kill all three of us at once."

Drysten nodded.

"Eidion is not here," the king said in a weak voice. "I sent him away to..."

"To what?" the shorter man said in a thick accent.

That was when Ceneus finally understood who the second man was. His son was executed on the king's order four years ago, but Ceneus would always remember the strange, wicked tone of the man. "Abhartach..." the king whispered.

"I am, and you will answer," Abhartach stated as he stepped forward.

King Ceneus glanced behind him and saw the two men holding down Vonig were glaring into his eyes. It was the most unsettling sight the king could imagine. Vonig writhing about on the ground as two men stared blankly back at him, easily restraining their captive with little effort. "I won't survive this, will I?"

Both Drysten and Abhartach shook their heads.

This was not how it was supposed to end. There is so much more to do. Ceneus felt the tears beginning to trickle down the sides of his face.

"Now is not the time for sadness. Now is the time to rejoice. The Morrigan will have herself a king!" Abhartach declared in an uplifting tone.

"He once worshiped as we do," Drysten rustled.

Ceneus saw Drysten cock his head ever so slightly as he glanced to who Ceneus thought was his king. It was then he realized what Drysten's game was and knew not to spoil it if he wished to live.

"It is our duty to restore the old ways," Drysten whispered.

"I can give you what you wanted, and much more than that," the king excitedly announced. *This is the best chance I have to kill Germanus.*

Abhartach took a step forward and glanced to Drysten before signaling for Ceneus to continue.

The king darted his eyes from Drysten to Abhartach. "You wish to restore the old ways, and I can help you do this.

The man who sentenced your son to die, and seeks to root out the ones who worship the same way as our ancestors once did is here. He is right inside this very fortress and I will take you to him if you let me live."

Abhartach glanced to Drysten before gesturing towards Vonig.

Drysten's eyes seemed glazed over. "That one is mine to kill."

Ceneus glanced behind him and accidentally let out a shallow whimper as he turned back to Abhartach. "He... serves the man. Any guard wearing a black cloak serves the Christian," he explained. "The men in blue are bound to my family."

Abhartach glanced to the ceiling, clearly considering his next move. However, Drysten had his eyes locked on Vonig, something Abhartach noticed immediately when he lowered his gaze. "You wish to send him to the Otherworld? You couldn't simply wait a moment before—?"

Drysten did not bother to acknowledge Abhartach as he slowly paced forward. Abhartach waved the two men carrying Vonig over, and the king watched the pleading man being brought on his knees. Ceneus hated Vonig, and hated him greatly, but even he wasn't sure he wanted to witness what was about to happen.

"No! Please, Lord. No!" Vonig screamed as he was dragged forward on his knees.

Drysten slowly kneeled beside Vonig, who stared through tears into the man who was about to end him. A smirk began showing across Drysten's face as he tilted his head and peered into Vonig's eyes. "You gave me most of these scars," he whispered. "I will give you some which will never heal."

The king watched as Drysten slowly lifted his mask back to the bridge of his nose and point to the Roman bath. The two silent men brought Vonig over, and dangled his head over the calm water a few inches below.

"Please, Lord. Mercy..." Vonig began to wail.

Ceneus wasn't sure if Drysten heard him, as the man

seemed to be staring off over the other side of the pool. Abhartach noticed this as well and walked over to whisper something in his ear. Drysten looked to the king, then back to Abhartach and nodded as he dropped his sword and pulled his dagger from its sheath at his waist.

"Are you a man of faith, Vonig?" Drysten asked.

Vonig tried to look around, but his head was pushed back down near the water. "I… was baptized by the bishop, Lord."

"Agh!" Abhartach exclaimed as he threw his hands up. "This man pollutes the waters with these… baptisms!"

"The bishop will no longer pollute these waters," Drysten replied through a calm tone. "But this man will."

The king watched as Drysten lowered himself down to Vonig's level, resting a knee beside the pool. He released a low "hm" as he tilted his head to the side. In one quick motion he grabbed the back of Vonig's neck and plunged the man's face into the pool. The gurgles were loud, and Ceneus wondered if anyone outside could hear them.

"Are you a man of faith?" Drysten screamed. "Pray! Pray, damn you!"

Vonig's face was brought out of the water just long enough for him to draw in a breath and see Drysten place the dagger next to his face. He began to whimper before having his head plunged back into the pool.

"End him and be done with it," Abhartach said with a chuckle. "We have work to do."

Drysten paused and glared up toward Abhartach, having no trouble holding the man's gaze while keeping Vonig's head from rising out of the water.

"You do as I say, Briton," Abhartach stated as he grew a perplexed scowl.

Drysten seemed not to care, as he scoffed and began nicking little cuts into Vonig's ears and cheeks.

"Drysten!" Abhartach hissed. "We tarry here too long! I will not lose men because you wished to—"

"You forget who I am, Abhartach! I am the one who speaks with the gods. The *only* one," Drysten shouted as he finally cut Vonig's throat. He dropped his squirming prey into the pool before looking back to a surprised Abhartach. "To business."

Abhartach nodded through a strangely impressed stare before he slowly glanced to King Ceneus. "Tell me how you can be useful to me."

King Ceneus began to stutter until Drysten finally spoke up for him. "He's a king. A king who only recently moved from the old ways."

Is he giving me a way out? Ceneus wondered.

"Recently?" Abhartach wondered aloud.

King Ceneus nodded. "I was once a worshiper of Cernunnos."

Abhartach looked to Drysten. "Do you know of the one he speaks?" he asked.

Drysten nodded. "Cernunnos is the horned god who watches over the forests. The ones who worshipped him were routed out long ago by Bishop Germanus' men." He looked to the king. "One of the king's oldest friends was executed in front of him quite some time ago for worshipping the deity. I later found out his name was Drumond. His demise was the reason the king had to search for outside military commanders. My father was summoned because of this..."

"Cernunnos...?" Abhartach whispered as he raised his head. It seemed to Ceneus he was pleased to hear of the god's involvement in his early years. "And why did you move away from the gods of your ancestors?"

King Ceneus hung his head. "I... was tricked. Tricked by the bishop." He knew the statement was a lie, but not a complete lie. The bishop did trick him. But at the time, he cared little for any god a man could worship. Let alone Cernunnos.

Abhartach walked to the king and paused, staring into the man's eyes with a strangely vacant gaze. It almost looked as though he was looking behind Ceneus. Eventually he began raising his hand towards the king's neck, pausing for a brief moment, then placing it on the man's shoulder. "Then it would seem you are not my enemy..."

Ceneus glanced to Drysten and saw the man give a slight nod before turning to Abhartach.

"The bishop is here," Drysten stated. "We can rid Britannia of his kind for good. We can do this right now if we are quick enough."

Abhartach removed his hand from Ceneus' shoulder and waved a hand forward. The king watched as a long line of men began coming out of the passage to the sewers, roughly fifty in total by the time they all entered the baths.

"Wait..." Ceneus blurted out, causing both Abhartach and Drysten to both wheel around and face him. "My guards are loyal to me but will resist you unless I order them away. The men in blue are trustworthy. I swear to you."

Abhartach glanced to Drysten, who nodded, then turned back to Ceneus. "I will give you a few moments to remove them from my path. But I warn you, once we begin the killing, we will not stop for anyone. Black or blue."

Ceneus nodded and quickly turned to the front entrance. Abhartach's men all watched him as he exited, and for a moment the king wondered if he should simply try to run. That fear was dashed when he saw the bishop's men all piling into the principia, and his own standing guard by the barracks.

"You!" the king screamed. "All of you, come with me. Now!"

A handful of blue-cloaked men glanced at each other before one ran inside the barracks. It seemed like an eternity, but the king knew it had only been a few seconds until all the men began rushing out, most still donning their armor.

"All of you, follow me. The Gaels have been sighted on the road. We need to get to them before they reach the city!" King Ceneus waved a hand toward the other side of the river and hoped to whatever gods may be watching he did so quickly enough.

***

Drysten watched from the doorway as King Ceneus led his guardsmen away from the principia. He wrung his hands together in an involuntary response to his nerves. Drysten knew it must have been hard for someone to witness what he had just done to Vonig, but not as bad as it would have been should Ceneus have experienced it himself. Vonig was just the first man who would be punished for what was done to Drysten. That thought brought happiness to Drysten's heart. A feeling he hadn't had since the day he married Isolde.

As he watched the king peering over his shoulder while leading his guards away, Drysten began feeling conflicted. He didn't understand why he wished for the king to live, simply that he felt the man needed to. Drysten wondered why he believed the king hadn't outlived his usefulness.

Did I not have the stomach for the man's death the moment I left the sewers? Drysten wondered to himself. *Or was I simply holding up my end of the bargain they forced me to make?*

Drysten sighed as the king finally faded from view. There were no torchlights going from the fortress to the other side of the river. Drysten remembered a time when there were, but recent years saw many people leaving Eboracum for the safety of other kingdoms. Even the king's brother, King Garbonian of Bryneich, accepted many newcomers as the Christian raids worsened over the years.

"Are you ready?" Abhartach whispered as he approached.

Drysten nodded. He glanced around the corner of the doorway and gestured for Abhartach to follow once no more guardsmen could be seen. The only light of the fortress came from two torches lit on either side of the principia's entrance, where roughly two dozen black-clad guards were joking amongst themselves, and altogether simply milling about.

Abhartach tapped Drysten on the shoulder and leaned closer than Drysten was comfortable with. "How many more are inside the building?"

Drysten shrugged. "If King Ceneus sent Eidion away, then he won't have all his men. The ones still here are his personal guards."

"That wasn't what I asked you, Briton," Abhartach hissed.

Drysten met Abhartach's gaze, glaring intensely into his eyes. "If you want to know for certain, you can go and count them yourself."

Abhartach looked Drysten in the eye, holding his gaze until he finally began to smirk. Drysten knew the man enjoyed being around someone who didn't fear him, something most people couldn't help. His features alone used to make Drysten uneasy, and that was before he saw how he was just another religious zealot hellbent on preserving his ways. The man's short stature hid his true strength, of which there was a considerable amount. If it weren't for Drysten seeing it himself, he would assume he could take the man in a hand to hand fight. But he knew if it ever came to that, there was a decent chance he wouldn't survive.

Abhartach lifted a hand and pointed around the corner. Two of his hunters nodded and strung their bows as they stepped to the corner of the building.

"Make them fear," Abhartach commanded.

One nodded and glanced around the corner before handpicking an arrow and stringing it onto the blackened bow. He looked back to the other, who did the same, and the two quickly shot around the corner into the group of black-clad men.

Drysten stole a look, immediately seeing two men with arrows in their legs writhing on the ground in agony. A group of others quickly created a barrier between the wounded and the direction the arrows had burst from.

They have no idea what's about to happen, Drysten thought with a chuckle.

More men began coming to the aid of the wounded. Both were now wailing and beginning to make gurgling sounds, with the men around them growing more uneasy.

"Our poisons work quickly, don't they, Briton?" Abhartach whispered. He didn't bother to hide his excitement.

Drysten nodded. "Judging by the men in the shield wall, I'd say they're just now understanding who they're up against."

And Drysten couldn't have been more correct. The tales of Abhartach's poisons spread far and wide before Drysten had even been released from his cell. Germanus' men quickly understood the normally non-fatal wound would now cause the most unsightly death they would ever see.

Abhartach looked back to the two hunters. "More," he commanded before turning to the rest of his men. "Fill them with arrows."

Drysten watched as every hunter burst around the corner, forming a line before firing into the shield wall of Germanus' men. A handful were able to move inside the building before the arrows began to fly. It signaled to Drysten more men would soon be coming to their aid.

And a handful did, but it truly didn't matter. Arrows from the hunters were continuously pelting the shield wall until a couple eventually snuck through gaps between shields.

"Hold them, you useless fucks!" a voice screamed from the third floor of the principia.

Drysten turned to Abhartach. "That is our man." He gestured towards the direction of the voice, and Abhartach nodded before gesturing in the same direction.

"Kill!" Abhartach commanded, and every hunter dropped their bows to the ground and rushed forward.

Drysten followed. It seemed like a flash before he was pouncing through a gap between two shields, black-clad men on either side of him. Drysten began swinging wildly to widen the gap and allow more hunters through. One man was caught in the neck by Drysten's blade, spewing blood down his chest as he thrust a hand to his wound to stem the bleeding.

"Kill that one!" Germanus shouted from above.

Drysten stole a moment and peered up towards the upper level of the principia, holding his gaze in the direction of the bishop. Until that moment, he hadn't noticed, but his mask had fallen below his chin. His identity was now on full display.

A scary sight indeed, Drysten thought.

Drysten smirked before parrying the blow from the man in front of him. The hunters had begun cutting their way through the front ranks of the shield wall, and most of Germanus' men were either trying to cower behind one another, fight like madmen, or flee.

How many of you were even real fighters? Drysten wondered as he stabbed a man in the belly. Barely any of you have the stomach for a fight. Must be hard killing someone other than a woman or child.

Suddenly, the hunters began to break their attack. There were only about ten men left to deal with, but for some reason Abhartach was screaming the order to move back. Drysten followed, and immediately noticed why.

Eidion was leading two dozen men from the darkness of the city. They must have been Eidion's own personal guard, as no man in the group wore a royal blue cloak about their shoulders.

"Drysten! Drysten, we must go!" Abhartach screamed as he wrenched his blade from the chest of a fallen guard.

Drysten swiped toward the nearest man, missing greatly but succeeding in moving the man back far enough for him to turn and run with the rest of the hunters.

Eidion's men had cut off the path to the baths, meaning the only other way out of the city was either to other gate or the tunnels below. Drysten surveyed the path leading toward the gate and saw a line of shields waiting for them, while the path to the building Maewyn had once led him through was vacant.

"Abhartach!" Drysten screamed. "Follow!"

Abhartach nodded and pointed for his men to follow Drysten down through the darkness. Drysten knew there would likely be no more than one or two guards to worry about. No king would waste his men on guard duty in a sewer. Besides, everyone else would likely be behind them to deal with anyone they met. He quickly found the abandoned building which housed the stairway leading down to the prisons. He turned and waved some of the hunters in before him, gesturing towards the stairway in the dark corner of the room.

Abhartach rushed forward after watching about eight of his men becoming trapped between two groups of black-clad warriors, roughly thirty in number. “We will come back to this place,” he hissed as he watched his men slaughtered. “They will never forget what we will do to their people once we do.”

“No. No they won’t,” Drysten added as he made his way down. There was a moment where Abhartach was distracted, and Drysten wondered if he could get away with swiping his knife across the man’s throat. He even moved his hand closer to its hilt, but those aspirations were dashed when one of the hunters grabbed his shoulder and ushered him toward the stairs. “I’m coming, damn you,” he stated.

The familiar smell instantly brought the memories of Drysten’s imprisonment to the forefront of his mind.

“Which one was my son in?” Abhartach asked as they ran.

Drysten paused and pointed to the cell beside his old one, looking in to see the image of his father staring back. Drysten halted for a moment and stared into Hall’s eyes, seeing nothing but disappointment in the face of the greatest man Drysten had ever known. Hall’s skin was almost rotted away, with bone poking out through gaps in the muscles of his face. Hall looked to try and step forward but could only shamble his way a few feet before once again raising his gaze to his son.

“Was I… wrong in believing you to be a good man?” Hall’s asked, almost sounding like he was begging. “Where is the boy I raised?” Drysten heard his voice clear as anything in his life, but Hall’s lips weren’t moving. They couldn’t move. The man’s face was a rotted mess of flaking skin, revealing muscles and bone. The sight proved too much.

Drysten hung his head as Abhartach jogged by. The Gael stopped and investigated the cell his son had once lived in, and Drysten wondered if he too was seeing a similar vision. Drysten harkened back to a conversation he once had with Diocles. The Greek once told him he lamented the thought his mother would be able to see the man he'd turned into, with Drysten now feeling much the same.

"I see there is still room in your heart for remorse. Maybe you can yet be saved from this, son." Hall let out a pained gasp, almost as though he was choking on air. He then fell back a step and vanished from view.

"We need to go," Drysten sadly whispered.

Abhartach muttered something under his breath, and the hunters continued.

"Wait!" a man screamed.

The voice sounded like Drysten's father, but harsher and older. Drysten paused and looked to Abhartach, now seeing this voice didn't come from anyone's mind. It came from a nearby cell.

"Take me with you!" the stranger begged.

Drysten and Abhartach looked back to the stairs before each moving toward the iron bars of the cell. A man shuffled forward. His appearance was startling, but nothing like the rotting corpse of Drysten's father a few cells away.

"Please..."

Drysten looked on the man and saw himself from not long before that night. "Who are you?" he whispered.

"I am Gwrwst of Rheged," the man replied through a tired voice.

Drysten began to speak before Abhartach raised a hand to silence him.

"You are not the king I came for," the Gael replied. He looked to Drysten. "We go!"

As the Gaels moved through the sewer, Drysten couldn't help but look back. All he could hear were the whimpers and sobs of a man the world forgot existed.

CHAPTER NINE

Matthew knew Drysten's people were hurting by his loss. He appealed to King Uther of Powys for their asylum, but didn't realize he had no need to. Prince Ambrosius seemed to share his beliefs and granted them rooms in his villa just outside the city of Glevum, the port city in Powys' Southern territory.

The city also proved to be the kingdom's capital, as well as housing for two thousand Powysian legionaries. They were the last Roman-trained troops in Britannia, largely because the king's brother was the famed Roman general Ambrosius Aurelianus. He was the namesake of the Prince which Drysten's people grew acquainted with after the battles near Hadrian's Wall.

Matthew brought Drysten's people to Powys roughly two months after the short encounter with Abhartach's hunters. He counted fifteen dead Gaels by the time the day was through and the people were rescued. Since then, he was conducting raids on small Saxon guard posts to Powys' East, only now returning for a short respite. This hiatus wasn't brought about on a whim, however, as two men of Ebrauc followed Drysten's people with messages and a request from King Ceneus. Matthew volunteered to bring them to Glevum to address the king themselves. But first, there would be a short stop at the prince's villa.

Matthew quickly dismounted his horse and signaled for the men from Ebrauc to do the same. The three men walked by Prince Ambrosius' guards before quickly entering the villa.

Both men returned silent nods and followed Matthew through a corridor before being led into the atrium, with Matthew giving a nod to Isolde and Oana as he walked by. He wondered where the rest of Drysten's people were but knew that truly didn't matter now.

"Wait here," Matthew ordered as the three men entered an empty room. "Don't go off on your own. Stay in the room until the prince comes to see you."

He knew them from his short time aboard Drysten's ship, the Fortuna. It was then and there Matthew began journeying down the road he was now on. As he left the room, he heard one of them ask the other how long it would be until the prince chose to meet with them. It seemed they believed most monarchs to be like Ceneus. listless and disinterested.

If you only knew he was in the room next door, you may not be in such a hurry, Matthew thought with a chuckle.

He knew why they were there, especially after Prince Ambrosius' spies described how the one known as Rodric was sent to Bryneich to fetch the aid of King Garbonian. The lord over Bryneich was the king's brother, and few situations would call for them joining forces after Ceneus stole Ebrauc's crown from the man.

"Are they here?" Prince Ambrosius asked as Matthew entered the room next door to the visitors.

Matthew nodded. "They are, though I wonder why you would even entertain their presence."

"That would be because we need them." the prince stated with a sigh. "We need them now as much as they need us."

"In what way? From the rumors, it would seem Ebrauc is more divided than ever," Matthew stated.

"A man called Ethelric attacked Verulamium. He killed every man we stationed there and looted the place before Bors arrived to help," the prince explained. "They sent raiders further West than before as well. Completely overwhelmed the guard post along the road."

Matthew sighed. "War is coming…"

"War is already here," Ambrosius said as he stood. "And

many will die."

"Lord Prince!" Matthew whispered with a grin.

Ambrosius glanced down to the ground where the two young boys, Artorius and Galahad, were intently listening to the exchange. "That will be all for tonight, boys. I will have more stories to tell you tomorrow night." He grinned as he plucked each boy up and carried them under his arms like sacks of grain. Both children were madly giggling as he swung them from side to side before eventually stopping in front of Isolde.

"Which one is yours? I always forget. They all look the same to me until they get to be about ten," the prince sarcastically asked as he placed both boys on their feet.

"Cousin, I *am* ten!" Artorius answered. The boy was the prince's cousin, and heir to the throne of Powys upon King Uther's death. He had only recently begun to understand what that title meant.

Isolde ruffled Artorius' hair before she turned and extended her hand out for Galahad to grab. "I hope the prince didn't scare you with his tales of war," she whispered.

"My cousin's stories are never scary!" Artorius answered.

Prince Ambrosius' smile slowly faded. "I... explained how I owe my life, and the lives of many of my men to your husband's efforts in Caledonia."

Isolde quickly darted her eyes away, clearly unable to reconcile with the fact her husband seemed to be gone. "He isn't my husband anymore."

The prince shook his head. "He is, Lady."

Isolde quickly raised her gaze. "I am not—"

"You are the wife of a lord!" the prince interrupted. "The man is simply... lost, and it is our job to find a way to bring the man back."

Isolde lowered her head as Maebh slowly trotted up and placed his head under her palm. She produced a half-smile as he slowly stroked the beast's ears.

Artorius had taken a great liking to the dog and extended a hand to pet him. Maebh responded by swatting his hand away with his paw, with the two repeated the gesture twice before Artorius finally gave up.

"Did the short man take papa, mother?" Galahad asked.

Matthew wished there was a way to make the boy understand his father was likely gone from his life forever. As optimistic as Matthew was, not even he could believe there was a chance Drysten would return to his old self.

The prince knelt. "He did, boy. The short man took your father, but I will bring him back. I promise you." The prince winked as Galahad began to grin.

Matthew stepped forward. "Perhaps we should not—"

"Promise a child he will see his father again?" Ambrosius angrily interrupted. "Not only do we *need* to stop the Gaels but Drysten saved my life. I would've been gutted on that damn hill were it not for him. You know this too, as I recall your face being painted blue like you were one of King Garbonian's men. What a sight *that* was..."

Matthew lowered his gaze to the boys. Galahad seemed distraught, whereas Artorius seemed to have a protective and stoic gaze held over Galahad as he placed a hand on Galahad's shoulder. It was one of the many recent moments in which the boy reminded Matthew of King Uther.

"Come, Matthew. We must meet with Ceneus' people," the prince said with a sigh. He gave the back of Artorius' head a light slap before nodding to Isolde and turning around.

Matthew and the prince bid Isolde and the children goodnight before turning back to the room housing Dagonet and Cynwrig. Both men had only been waiting for a few short moments, but every second away from the task at hand always felt like forever for Matthew.

"Lord Prince," Cynwrig greeted before nodding to Matthew. Matthew thought it was strange the man greeted him twice in such a short amount of time. He wondered if Cynwrig still believed Matthew was important in saving his life from a gut wound around the time they first met. In reality, he did little. Magnus was the one who saved lives during that time.

Dagonet briefly glanced up before finally standing and nodding.

Ambrosius looked the two men over before finally gesturing a hand, silently telling them to say their piece.

Dagonet stood and took a step forward. "Lord Drysten and Abhartach disappeared after they attempted to murder the bishop."

"Too bad they didn't succeed if you ask me," Matthew whispered to the prince, receiving a grunt and nod in response.

"We all agree but they *didn't* succeed. And now Germanus is madder than ever." Cynwrig ran a hand over his head as he glanced to Dagonet.

Dagonet nodded. "Germanus knows the king offered his life to Abhartach in exchange for his own."

"And where was Drysten during all this?" the prince questioned, receiving a glance from Matthew.

Dagonet shrugged.

"The royal family?" Ambrosius pressed.

"Eidion is with the bishop in Isurium. They have mustered all the bishop's men, almost five-hundred strong, and are now patrolling the surrounding area. Gwrast was still fighting off the Gaels in the West, and Mor has begun journeying South from Hadrian's Wall. Both brothers are moving East," Dagonet explained.

Matthew glanced at the prince, seeing him rub his hand over his head. The prince looked uneasy, which was something Matthew rarely saw from the man. *Could this be the move against Germanus which Ceneus wrote to us about?*

"To fight who? The Gaels or the Christians?" Ambrosius asked as he glanced to Matthew.

"We… don't know. Whoever it is will have six hundred screaming tribesmen bearing down on them as well. King Garbonian has begun moving South, and looks to be marching to meet up with Mor somewhere near Concangis." Dagonet gave an uneasy glance to Cynwrig, who lowered his head and seemed to shake off the cold of the outside air.

"What of the king?" Ambrosius whispered.

Dagonet shot a glance to Cynwrig before continuing. "Struck down all the Christian banners in favor of the old ones. He now flies the horned snake instead of the anchor."

"I don't care what gods he worships. Tell me what he's doing," the prince ordered.

Dagonet nodded. "He has begun mustering his *own* men and remains in Eboracum."

The prince began vigorously rubbing his temples. "Every lord or cleric in Ebrauc is now mustering their own army, and we have no idea who is fighting for who."

"That would be about it, Lord Prince," Dagonet said through a heavy sigh. "Got so bad, me and Cynwrig were wondering if you could take us in along with Drysten's people. To say we would appreciate the gesture…"

The prince nodded. "What's two more mouths to feed." Both Dagonet and Cynwrig seemed to visually become more at ease at the prince's response. They looked to each other and grinned before Ambrosius managed to continue. "You will be under the command of Bors when he returns. Lost a few of his scouts fighting against the Saxons and could use you both."

Both men lost their smiles as they returned subtle nods.

"Until then?" Cynwrig wondered aloud.

The prince shrugged. "What else? Get some rest."

"There's something you should know about the bishop," a voice said from the doorway. Matthew turned to see Diocles enter the room.

"*You* were not summoned to this meeting," Matthew sarcastically put in.

Diocles chuckled before looking back to the prince. "I believe these men are nothing more than mercenaries."

Ambrosius perked an eyebrow. "What men?" he asked in obvious interest.

"Bishop Germanus' men. I don't believe they fight for Rome." Diocles shook his head. "I mean the Christians. It's hard to tell the two apart anymore," he answered.

Matthew felt a slight twinge of relief but knew there needed to be an explanation. "Go on," he stated.

Diocles nodded. "We ambushed a small band of the bastards with Lord Drysten. Titus' son came into the possession of a ring one of the men wore. It bore the insignia of *I Adiutrix*."

"How did you come to this conclusion solely based on a ring?" the prince wondered.

"They have not fought for Rome in quite some time, Lord Prince. They were either mercenaries or deserters the bishop sought out. Titus believed they fought for some barbarian king named... Theodoric, I believe he said."

The prince produced a smile. "It seems Ceneus may indeed have a chance. If we sent him aid, this could benefit us both."

Matthew nodded. "We cannot let a chance to kick Germanus from our shore pass us by."

The prince nodded and glanced to Dagonet and Cynwrig. Both men were shown to their own rooms by the prince's guards. Matthew stayed with the prince for some time before the man finally spoke. "We need to weather the Saxon storm for a little longer. Then we will push North when they have been beaten back."

Matthew scoffed. "Arthur, we have been fighting them to a stalemate ever since this new Saxon warlord arrived. Is that even possible?"

Arthur nodded. "I happen to know this Colgrin enjoys the finer things in life. My plan is to beat his armies just enough to get an audience with the man. When we do, we will pay him off until we can gather enough strength to beat him more thoroughly."

"Risky," Mathew put in. "We could just be funding his war against us. We could be killing ourselves with our own wealth."

Arthur nodded as he reclined back in his seat. "These risks will be worthwhile," he replied. "Send word to Ceneus.

The bishop can be beaten."

CHAPTER TEN

King Ceneus finally felt the freedom he longed for ever since he sold his soul for Ebrauc's crown. When he did, Bishop Germanus had quickly begun choking the life out of both Ceneus and his kingdom, but both were now free. He awoke that morning not only feeling refreshed, but almost younger.

"Heledd," the king whispered, causing his wife to stir under the furs.

His wife slowly opened her eyes and smiled as she looked on the king, "Good Morning, *Lord King*."

"Please," Ceneus started as he left the bed, "I am more to you than just your king. Husband is fine."

Heledd giggled to herself as Ceneus turned to don his embroidered tunic and boots. He did so quickly and kissed his wife's forehead before leaving their home adjoined to the Roman baths. This moment in time might have be the closest he'd ever been with his wife. She'd been good to him as queen, and even went out of her way to try and make him happy despite the dark clouds hanging over their lives. But they never really felt anything for one another until the bishop was scared off.

Hopefully, all my enemies will stay away long enough to shore up our defenses, Ceneus thought as he looked over the bathhouse.

He hated the idea of the passage to the sewers being open while the Gaels' whereabouts were still unknown, and immediately ordered it sealed following the fight against Abhartach and Drysten.

"Lord King," Jorrit greeted as Ceneus entered the baths.

Ceneus nodded. "Frisian."

"What are my orders? I was not told why I was summoned," Jorrit stated as his sleepy eyes glanced to Braxus alongside him.

"I have many enemies," Ceneus declared as he plopped down into a chair. "I suppose you could imagine I would be in need of protection with my two highest ranking officers away."

Jorrit chuckled. "Aren't we all."

Ceneus grinned and tilted his head back. "Your child-like humor never ceases to entertain me." Upon seeing a full pitcher of wine at his disposal, the king quickly reached over and poured himself a cup before downing it as quick as he once did in his youth. Once his thirst was satisfied, he cleared his throat. "Rodric and Eliwlod will become generals for the army I am assembling, and you and your Frisians will become the royal guards."

Jorrit seemed both pleased and surprised by the pleasant news. Ceneus had long wished for the moment he could show Jorrit and his people his appreciation for their service. Germanus had forbid the promotion of outsiders within his ranks, saying an apostate with power is too dangerous. But Ceneus learned from Germanus' mistakes. It was an apostate who was cast aside that nearly killed them both, and Ceneus knew he would need to be smart enough not to create another Drysten.

Jorrit finally returned a grateful nod. "My thanks, Lord King."

Ceneus grinned. "Your pay will be doubled, and you will be given homes inside the city for you and your people."

Jorrit smiled and looked to Braxus, who also showed a bright smile. "We will get our people ready for the move, Lord King."

Ceneus nodded. "You think your people would excel in this role, don't you?"

"I do. We have been roaming the coastlines for a long time. They would no doubt jump at the opportunity to serve in this way," Jorrit answered.

"Good. I will need them to train my men. Not only will they be the royal guards, but they will bring great changes to the tactics we employ in war," Ceneus began. "I will need men who not only fight as Romans, but as those who invade our lands as well."

"I will tell them, Lord King," Jorrit returned. The Frisian began to leave but hesitated before turning back. "What of... your brother, Lord King?"

Ceneus raised an eyebrow. "What of him?"

"He recently departed from Din Guayrdi and began making his way South. He hasn't attacked any city or village, but he comes straight for Eboracum. I've sent scouts to track him, and one reported back saying he will arrive within the week." Jorrit glanced to Braxus, who was also clearly interested in the king's answer.

"I have summoned him and all his men. We need to root out the Gaels, as well as shore up the defenses to the South. I plan on granting him lands South of Hadrian's Wall to call his own as thanks." Ceneus knew this was a gamble, but hopefully the Gaels would thin out King Garbonian's forces enough to where Ceneus wouldn't need to worry about another threat. If all else failed and the Guayrdians somehow proved to be too much for Abhartach's forces, the king could also offer his brother independence for his kingdom.

Jorrit nodded. "Quite the risk. What assurances do you have he won't simply retake the city and try to rule?"

King Ceneus smirked. "Bishop Germanus would never allow that to last. My brother knows this and would be foolish to try."

"Lord King..." Jorrit began, "how do we even know the bishop has the men at his disposal he claims to have? Has he ever brought anyone to the islands other than Roman deserters or mercenaries from Gaul?"

Ceneus ran a hand through his hair as he looked off to the corner of the room. He wasn't certain the bishop was simply a mad zealot who had a way with words, but he had a hunch. "Did I ever tell you what Germanus promised me when he arrived? What about what he dreamed for my people?"

Jorrit glanced to Braxus before stepping forward. "You did not, Lord King. We likely haven't spoken this much in any conversation since I began living here."

Ceneus looked the Frisian in the eye. "A new world," he whispered.

"A new world for… who?" Jorrit wondered.

"He told me what he preached to those who lived in the far reaches of the Roman territories. The ones in Gaul, Aquitania, and even Italia before he journeyed West. Everywhere he stopped, he praised his god and told of a place where the lowest man could be elevated into the hands of something greater simply by their devout service. That man would inherit a *kingdom*, but the bastard never told them this kingdom was only in their minds. The bishop knew just what to say and when to say it to the gullible fools he preached to. His following grew more and more as he made his way West. As he made his way toward Britannia." The king stood and placed a hand on the bible Bishop Germanus left behind. "The man was able to use his family's fortunes to hire mercenaries and Roman deserters to accompany him here as well," the king paused as he let out a long sigh. "The lowest of people followed him first. The ones who truly knew what having nothing meant. They leapt at the promises of wealth and happiness, only to be turned to cruel wretches when they found neither. Then came the more fortunate, the ones who knew some measure of success in some way but decided they wanted more. The greedy men, Jorrit. Those are the worst."

Jorrit's gaze seemed fixed on the king. "Which were you?"

"I was nothing until I usurped the throne," Ceneus responded, peering up from the ground. *I will not be nothing any longer.*

Braxus, looking uneasy at the sudden silence, decided to step forward. "We will go, Lord King. We have preparations to make for our people's move into the city."

The king gestured a hand towards the door, and the two Frisians began departing, passing Maewyn as they went. Jorrit gave Maewyn a strange glance, as the priest was wearing Roman armor with a black cloak.

"Lord King, I have an urgent message which you *absolutely* must hear. I told Prince Eidion I had business to the South and cannot stay here for long," Maewyn declared. He was even more jubilant than normal.

"Speak," the king commanded. "And why are you wearing—"

"Germanus has no men from the pope! The armies he employs are coming from a barbarian king. I believe you have heard of the man. King Theodoric of the Visigoths." Maewyn hesitated and looked down to the ensemble he was wearing.

Ceneus erupted from his seat. "The man tricked us into believing he had the backing of all the Christians of Rome!"

Jorrit scoffed. "From my understanding, the Christians of Rome don't even have the support of all the Christians of Rome."

Maewyn returned Jorrit with a sideways glance before turning his attention back to the king. "He tricked me as well. I saw the wealth of his family and confused it for that of the pope."

"That fucking *whoreson!*" Ceneus screamed. "The promises he made to me—! How is he communicating with this foreign king?"

Maewyn shrugged. "I would assume he sends messages along with traders who come to the city. Or at least he did before he left for Isurium."

"Lord King—" Jorrit stammered.

"Round up *every* ship's captain from the ports! Find every vagabond or wanderer and bring them to the principia," Ceneus angrily commanded. "Beat them! Threaten them with imprisonment! I don't care what you do, simply find the fucking messengers!

Jorrit nodded and quickly ran outside, bellowing the orders to his Frisian guardsmen.

Maewyn quickly put up his cloak's black hood and followed after giving the king a quick nod.

I will burn you for this, the king vowed. He furiously rubbed his hands together as the anger began to create a burning feeling in his temples. He'd known the bishop was a fraud from the very beginning, he simply never wished to face that fact. He remembered every time he begged Germanus for more men to send against the various invaders his people faced. Every time he made these requests he was denied for a different reason.

As he stared into the stone walls of the baths, King Ceneus made himself a vow. He would never place his trust in men with their own agendas ever again. On top of that, he would see Germanus killed for what he'd done.

***

Eidion was fidgeting with a loose string on the shoulder cuff of his tunic as he sat across from his bed. The woman he bought for the night was sound asleep, an inconvenience to a man wishing for a restful night. She wasn't supposed to stay once her services were rendered, but there was something unique about her. Something which made Eidion give her permission to stay with him despite knowing the sight of a whore leaving his room would invariably cause problems among the Christians.

Could toss her out the window, Eidion thought with a smirk. He knew it wasn't an option but thought the sight would be entertaining at the very least. *Only two floors up. Maybe she'd reach one of the troughs.*

Eidion glanced out the window and rose from his seat. The birds were silent, but the insects could be clearly heard outside. This place was peaceful, and Eidion wished he could stay in the small settlement west of Isurium for much longer. He had led a patrol through the area even though he knew it was unlikely the Gaels would come this way. After darkness approached, he ordered his men to the nearest town. He lamented being away from the safety of the stone walls surrounding Isurium.

But Bishop Germanus was as paranoid as ever, and here he was.

You could almost forget Ebrauc's days are coming to an end. Maybe the world will be better for it. There's not an ounce of happiness in these islands.

Eidion wondered how long Ebrauc had or how many lives it would take with it on its way to becoming nothing more than a memory. The kingdom was supposed to be the beginning of something great, but there wouldn't be any greatness here for the rest of time once the Gaels and Saxons have their way with it.

"Lord Prince," a man whispered.

Eidion turned to see the face of Maewyn staring back at

him. "You've returned."

Maewyn nodded. The priest had taken up the monotonous duty of carrying messages between Germanus and Eidion. But the man looked more tired than he should for simply riding the short distance to Isurium as he said he did. "I wish to speak a moment." As he spoke, a small abrasion on his chin became visible. One a man would normally receive for wearing a helmet of Roman make.

"I have no need of a saved soul until I'm done with that one." Eidion gestured to the room where he left his woman asleep. He glanced down to the mark on Maewyn's chin, causing the priest to lower his gaze in an all too obvious attempt to hide it. *What have you been up to?* Eidion wondered.

Maewyn offered an awkward snicker to break the silence "Your soul does not concern me." He peered through the door toward the naked woman lying on the bed. "Do you even know her name?"

Eidion glanced back and produced a shrug before returning his gaze to Maewyn.

"As is the way of a noble," the priest responded. "In any case, I wish to speak of the Gaels. That as well as your orders from the bishop."

Eidion scoffed. "Start with my instructions. As for the Gaels, they didn't seem all that dangerous from my perspective. They simply hid in the filth-ridden sewers. It was my father's fault he leaves no guards there."

"That may be so, but there are other things we need to consider," Maewyn responded.

"Such as?"

"Why would they leave when they had the momentum?" Maewyn questioned.

Eidion shrugged. "We had them outnumbered. It was likely three to one by the time they decided to flee."

"A foe such as this would be fighting in their element the moment we decided to chase them through the sewers. They would have emerged and run into the forests for cover knowing we'd never be able to pin them down. They could have ambushed us relentlessly. They could have raided anyone coming or going to Eboracum without anyone being able to stop them." Maewyn produced a bewildered shrug along with a vacant gaze. "But they didn't." The priest shook his head and sighed as he turned to stare through the window.

"They have more men...," Eidion whispered. That was the only explanation. The Gaels knew there was no need to take any risks until the main army arrived from wherever it currently was. "You're right, priest. They didn't flee to the wilderness to avoid us. They simply wished to regroup for something... bigger."

"That was what I tried to tell the bishop. I couldn't decide whether he didn't want to acknowledge the possibility, or if he simply didn't care," Maewyn replied.

Eidion scoffed as he looked to the ceiling. "Likely a bit of both, priest."

"And now for the fool's orders," Maewyn began as he unrolled a wax-sealed piece of parchment. "You are to lay an ambush along the road running South from Hadrian's Wall. Your uncle is bringing roughly six hundred fighters South to support your father."

"Support him how?" Eidion wondered.

Maewyn shrugged. "I... haven't the slightest. All I know is Germanus requires you thin them out before they can find their way behind the walls of the city. If your father has aligned himself with Drysten and your uncle both..."

"We will be forced out of Ebrauc for good," Eidion interrupted.

Maewyn nodded. Eidion noticed the priest staring into the corner of the room, carefully calculating something.

"I will be ready shortly," Eidion announced before turning back to the bedroom with a smirk. *I'll need to find out more of what you're hiding, priest. Germanus may trust you, but I certainly do not.*

"Who was that?" the woman asked from the bed.

Eidion was somewhat startled by her being awake. "What did you hear?"

"That you're a prince," she said with a giggle.

"You're rather well spoken for a common woman," Eidion returned, earning a scoff.

"Most men don't think I'm common," she returned.

Eidion surveyed the beauty of the woman's face. Her skin was unmarred and perfect, even glowing in some areas. Her eyes were a dull blue staring back at him from under her thick black hair. "What's your name?"

"What's yours?"

Maewyn knocked on the side of the door and poked his head in. "Lord Prince, we must hurry."

Eidion didn't both to look behind him. "I said I'll be ready in a moment." He looked back to the girl in his bed. "You live here?"

She nodded.

"I'll be sure to come back, and perhaps answer that question."

"I'll be waiting, Lord Prince."

The warmth of her smile made Eidion uncomfortable. It was something he wasn't used to considering most people hated him. As he threw his armor over his head and tied his sword belt around his waist, he halted for a moment, unsure why until he looked back to her. Without thinking, he knelt and kissed her forehead until she grabbed his face and kissed his lips.

"You'll come back?" she asked, a hint of worry in her voice.

Eidion nodded. "I promise." Those words held new meaning for him.

He had never made a promise he intended to keep, but this woman was different.

***

Rodric rode just in front of Bryneich's king as they made their way South from Hadrian's Wall. The ever-boisterous King Garbonian spent most of his time bragging to Rodric and Eliwlod of the many victories he held over his younger brother. For as annoying as it was, both men knew he wasn't lying. They each silently wondered whether these past victories could well indeed give him hope for more in the future. Why the king would call upon his elder brother was beyond the comprehension of both men he sent to deliver his message.

"You look damn familiar," King Garbonian yelled. "As a matter of fact, both of you do."

Rodric sighed. "And why would that be, I wonder?" He could somehow feel the king's eyes hovering over him.

King Garbonian remained silent for a moment. "You look like your king's pet from years ago. The only good man among his little following. The man nearly killed me!" Garbonian let loose a short cackle. "Good thing he didn't succeed, I'd say!"

"He's your king too," Rodric replied through a cool tone as he peered back to the king.

King Garbonian clearly heard Rodric but declined to respond. He scrunched his face before peering toward Eliwlod. His gaze was fixed on the man for some reason. Rodric wondered if the king fancied him in the odd way that some men do.

"What's your name?" Garbonian yelled just loud enough for the man to hear.

Eliwlod grumbled something under his breath as he half-turned and shouted his name back.

"Who was your mother?" the king added.

"Someone of no concern to you," Eliwlod responded.

Rodric snickered to himself as he peered back to see the king contorting his face in frustration.

The army was numbering at about six hundred, but only had two hundred real fighters worth mentioning. Those were the men who painted their faces blue like their ancestors. The rest were simply farmers or fisherman who would be wielding ancient weapons ready to fall apart. Between the old weapons and the farming equipment some chose to wield, Rodric couldn't understand why they were there at all.

The bulk of King Garbonian's army fell retaking Segedunum under Drysten's command. To make matters worse, a plague ripped through the more populated areas of his lands this past winter, further thinning out his people.

Garbonian glanced West. "Is that my nephew?"

Rodric strained his eyes to the West and nodded. "It is," he answered, acknowledging Mor was near.

"It will be good to see them again. I only met them when they were small boys and Ceneus journeyed North to help me deal with a band of Jutes who took up residence near Din Guayrdi," the king said in a joyful tone.

Rodric was somewhat confused by the happiness the king displayed. "Didn't the king take your wife as his own? Why would you be happy to see any of her children?"

The king tilted his head to the side and let out a long sigh. "Because they are hers," he whispered. "I just wish I could have brought Dyfnwal to see her as well. But I suppose someone has to stay behind and rule while I'm away."

Rodric felt exceedingly awkward as the conversation went on. It was revealed that Garbonian's son, Dyfnwal, was also Heledd son. The man was young during the war for Ebrauc, but obviously sided with King Garbonian until their defeat. The newly crowned Ceneus took Heledd as his own bride upon his victory. If he hadn't, it would have been extremely difficult to keep the peace between rival tribes of Britons. Rodric always wondered what the original royal family was like, as he only had brief memories of the times before Ceneus came to power.

"Sir," Eliwlod said as he gestured toward Mor's army. "Did Mor split his force?"

Rodric glimpsed into the distance and saw two large armies rapidly moving toward one another. "No," he whispered.

"They did not..."

Rodric turned to the king, who already knew what to do and began screaming commands in the language of the Guayrdians. There was an abrupt roar from the strange men with blue faces before an unsettling war chant began. The chant culminated in them bellowing a word which Rodric didn't understand.

All at once, the Guardians charged forward.

"I told them to aid the army with their backs to the North," Garbonian revealed as he trotted his horse toward Rodric. "They should reach them before the battle ends."

"Who is the other force being commanded by?" Eliwlod wondered.

Rodric shrugged. "If it's Germanus, then we could have a chance to kill Eidion before we even reach Eboracum. We could take care of this war here and now."

"Then go!" Garbonian commanded with a smile.

The three men turned and spurred their horses forward, keeping pace with the Guayrdians. Rodric was impressed by how easily they seemed to cover ground on foot. In addition to the foot soldiers, there were also fifty men on horseback riding behind the king. Rodric wagered they would be competent considering the dexterity they exhibited when they weaved in and out of trees. Not to mention they were outfitted not unlike Roman auxiliaries. Rodric wondered if these men were holdovers from the war between the brothers.

The army ran for longer than Rodric thought they could before they finally began hearing the sounds of war. Metal was clanking, shields were being beaten, and men were wailing in pain. Rodric had never seen a war, and it never occurred to him he would hear it before he saw it up close.

"What's wrong, boy?" King Garbonian yelled as he passed Rodric, who halted near the edge of the tree line.

"I... don't..." Rodric stammered. He was embarrassed by his timidity and felt a sense of shame from his hesitance.

King Garbonian halted as well and slowly rode close

enough to Rodric to whisper and still be heard. "You have never gone to war, have you?"

Rodric only managed to hang his head in response.

"It's alright, boy," the king whispered as he gestured for Rodric to lift his gaze.

It was strange. Rodric grew up on stories of King Garbonian's ferocity and madness. His bloodlust in war and his unquenchable thirst for women during peacetime. But in that moment, all he saw was kindness.

"You're young. Your wars will come," the king whispered. "Of that, I have no doubt."

Rodric watched as Eliwlod rode up to the king and muttered something about pressing forward. King Garbonian took his sword from his sheath, glanced to Rodric, roaring what must have been the order to attack in the language of the Guayrdians.

The king's men shrieked and chanted, with boisterous ululations erupting from their chests. Hundreds of blue-faced men rushed through the trees before disappearing toward the tree line. Garbonian and Eliwlod were in the lead, both glancing back toward Rodric one last time before disappearing. All Rodric could do at that moment was stare into the pommel of his saddle and dream of a day when he would have the courage to fight for his king.

Screams began intensifying out in the clearing. Rodric saw one of the Guayrdians running back with blood trickling from his neck. The wound didn't look all that serious, but Rodric guessed the man would die simply because he chose to run off into the wilderness.

For a brief yet tense moment, the man locked eyes with Rodric. He halted and stared with wide eyes before Rodric casually waved a hand and signaled for him to leave. The man looked to relax his shoulders as he slowly began to jog off out of view.

Doubt one man would have made a difference anyway, Rodric thought as he justified letting a deserter go unpunished.

He heard rumors the men in the North hung deserters upside down in the trees until the birds had their way with them, but didn't know for certain.

Would that be my fate had I been born in the North? Would I have been strung up by my ankles at this battles end? The thought made his stomach turn, but that feeling of shame was short lived. As his head was hanging and his eyes were shut, a low thumping noise became audible somewhere nearby.

The sounds of hooves off in the distance behind him was becoming clearer with each passing moment. He glanced back and strained his eyes, finally seeing the men in black cloaks storming through the forest. Rodric didn't understand what propelled him forward, but forward he went. Before he knew it, he erupted from the tree line and beheld the dead and dying all around him. Men in black. Men in blue. And men with painted faces writhing in agony all around him.

I need to find the king.

Rodric spurred his horse on until he found the rear of the Guayrdian lines. He could see the point off in the distance where both armies were meeting, and could just make out the sight of King Garbonian with the horsemen at the very front.

"Lord King!" Rodric screamed. "Lord King!"

But nobody could hear him. No voices could be heard over the booming sounds of war.

Rodric searched along the front of the lines until he finally noticed Prince Mor with his men. They were now being relieved by the Guayrdians, with many of the prince's men giving the Guayrdians looks of confusion as the foreigners came to rescue them.

Rodric spurred his horse down the rear of the line, screaming for the prince as he went. He peered back a handful of times but thankfully didn't see any Christians coming to from the tree line.

"Lord Prince!" Rodric shouted as he drew closer.

One man noticed him riding up and tapped the exhausted prince on his shoulder. Prince Mor turned and gave

Rodric a confused look as Rodric madly screamed for his men to form a line behind the Guayrdians. He pointed to the tree line a handful of times until Mor's eyes went wide and he finally bellowed an order to his men, all of which began sprinting their way behind the Guayrdians.

And not a moment too soon.

The shield wall facing the tree line had almost formed when Prince Eidion and his armored cavalry erupted from the darkness of the forest. He screamed and pointed his Roman blade forward as fifty horsemen charged toward Prince Mor and his men. Rodric was still mounted behind the shield wall, and immediately saw Eidion surveying the shields opposing him. He must have believed his small number of troops would have been enough to make a difference had he been looking into his enemy's back.

Once he realized his brother's men were staring him in the face, he removed his black-plumed helm from his head and gestured toward the trees. The black-clad warriors ceased their war cries and simply stared across to their enemy.

"Lord Prince!" a man from Mor's company screamed. "Fuck off back to your husband!"

"Run back to your mother's tit!"

The booming laughter of Mor's men seemed to be driving Eidion mad. The prince's eyes seemed to glaze over as he listened to the insults. Rodric had never seen anything like it. Prince Eidion was embarrassed.

"Always been weak-minded," Mor said as he slowly limped towards Rodric and rested a hand on Rodric's horse. "Never had much of a spine."

Rodric returned a nervous smirk.

"You hurt?" the prince asked as he glanced over Rodric. "You look ill."

"I… have never…" Rodric stammered.

Prince Mor interrupted him with a brimming smile as he slapped Rodric's leg and pointed off toward the trees.

Prince Eidion was hurling obscenities toward his men,

all of which stared back with blank or disinterested expressions.

Rodric finally realized his momentary cowardice had prevented the Christians from charging into the Guayrdians' backsides, but still felt ashamed for not joining the charge. He knew a better man would have.

"Good on you for coming when you did!" Mor said as he slapped Rodric's knee.

The gesture should have been met with a large smile of Rodric's own, but all he could do was stare out across the field of dead and dying men.

Mor noticed his hesitancy. "Would have likely lost a lot more men to my brother. Even if we won the battle, there wouldn't have been much of an army left."

Rodric gave a subtle nod as he looked over the front lines of the Guayrdians. Most of the enemy had been routed and the prince was ordering his horsemen back through the trees. but

They had won.

CHAPTER ELEVEN

To everyone's relief, the journey home to Petuaria was largely uneventful. The journey to the coast dawdled on for a few days before seabirds were finally heard. Drysten couldn't see them, as it was always the dark of night when the Gaels traveled, but the squawking was unmistakable. After the failed attack on Eboracum, they made their way West to the area where they moored their ships in the beginning of their invasion.

Drysten thought it was strange when Abhartach considered his little foray an invasion. While the hunters proved to be some of the fiercest fighters Drysten had ever seen, there were still only about eighty or so. A large number weren't even with Abhartach, as they were tasked with spying on neighboring kingdoms. Powys, Rheged, Ebrauc, and someplace Drysten had never heard of were all being examined by the Gaels. The last place was somewhere to the North, above Hadrian's Wall.

"Strathclyde," Abhartach had explained. "Should we ever need a place to regroup, that's where we would undoubtedly go."

It was curious to say the least. For all Abhartach's cunning and genius when it came to war, the man still seemed to think the Britons had what was necessary to repel him.

Drysten wondered how likely it was, but knew at the moment it didn't matter. He followed Abhartach toward the sea as the man grumbled his thoughts under his breath. The sight was yet another reminder the Gael was always thinking. His cruel mind was always on the move. Abhartach had recently decided it was time to venture out and summon the rest of his army.

When asked how many men Drysten could expect to see, Abhartach divulged he had roughly two thousand souls at his disposal.

Disposal, Drysten thought. *Such a strange way to speak of your people. It seems the Gaels consider them mere numbers, or pawns to be thrown away, like in some sort of game.*

Drysten peered behind him to see a hunter giving him a suspicious look. It was yet another reminder some of the Gaels believed he tried to lure them into a trap. What he wondered was if they would try and hold him accountable without proof. For all Abhartach's horrid qualities, he still seemed to be a fair-minded man, and Drysten felt the ill looks would be the end of it. Besides, Abhartach mentioned countless times how these men did not fear death.

"Great Chief!" a man greeted as the hunters neared the water. "We did not expect you for another night."

Abhartach scoffed. "In all my years, Myrddin, you are still the only one to think I age poorly."

"All men age poorly if given enough time to," the stranger returned with a chuckle. He approached from the darkness. "This is the Briton I heard of?"

Abhartach slapped Drysten's shoulder and motioned for him to step forward. "He is. Good fighter." Abhartach tilted his head to the side. "Lousy tactician," he added.

Drysten returned his king with a skeptical look before walking forward. "I am—"

"Lord Drysten of Ebrauc," Myrddin interrupted. "I know of you."

"I am not of Ebrauc any longer."

Myrddin walked close and seemed to survey Drysten's face. It seemed he had an easier time looking through the darkness than Drysten did. "When I first heard of you, you were indeed of Ebrauc."

"When was that?"

"You killed some of our people fighting along the Roman wall," Myrddin began. "There were stories of a great warrior who rallied different peoples behind him. That man shared a name with yourself."

Drysten shuffled his feet, unsure how to respond.

"My spies tell me you went on a great journey of your own. Something about a slaver taking your woman."

"Among others," Drysten muttered.

Abhartach inched forward. "This is the last of the great druids. The old ways are kept alive through him."

Myrddin chuckled to himself. "There are others who share our beliefs. Both here and across the water."

"I said the last of the great druids, Myrddin. The others simply roam from place to place while the Christians take hold in our homes," Abhartach hissed.

Drysten had no idea the Christian God had found his way into Hibernia. It began making more sense why Abhartach was in Britannia. To get to the Gaels, the Christian monks and priests would have to journey through kingdoms like Ebrauc and Powys. The ports there were the only ones in the world which still traded with Hibernians. Abhartach was in Britannia to sever that connection.

"Keep the Christians afraid of us, Briton," Abhartach commanded as he stepped passed Myrddin. He patted the druid's shoulder and pointed toward a small boat once hidden under the sand. "They must continue to fear us until my return." The Gael did not bother to make eye contact as he gave his order.

Drysten glanced to Myrddin, seeing his faint silhouette stepping beside Abhartach in the boat. The fifty hunters standing beside Drysten did not follow. "What purpose does that serve? Would it not be better for them to be lulled in believing we've left them?"

"The Christians only recognize fear," Abhartach began as he sat on the nearest rowing bench. "It runs their whole religion. If a man does mainly anything of enjoyment, he gets sent to their hell and never sees his loved ones again. That creates the fear needed to control the masses. What your job is, Briton, is to teach them to fear us more than their God."

Drysten was somewhat taken aback by Abhartach's boldness. What the beast wishes is impossible. How can a man be made to fear a mortal more than a god?

Abhartach looked to the closest hunter standing near Drysten and began speaking in an old, guttural language Drysten had never encountered. The hunter slowly nodded before taking a quick glance toward Drysten.

"What did you order him to do?" Drysten questioned. He had a brief thought the hunter would try to kill him, but that thought was short lived.

Abhartach smirked. "You will command the men I leave behind."

Drysten trained his gaze on the hunter, now standing beside him.

"They will follow you without question. They understand the language of the Britons, the Romans, and even smatterings of the Saxon language. You will find them quite useful." Abhartach gestured a hand to the men brandishing the oars of the small vessel, signaling for them to begin propelling the boat. "Use them well. And journey South to... introduce ourselves to that Colgrin fellow. They will need to learn to fear us soon enough."

May as well do that first. I hear he's somewhat mad. Fear may not come easy to him.

Drysten nodded and looked behind him. All the hunters were now approaching from the edge of the beach. Only moments ago, Drysten believed this sight would have someday signaled the time he would be sent to his father, mother, and sister. All three of which awaited his presence in the afterlife. He looked to the nearest hunter. "Do you have a name?" he asked.

The hunter nodded but Drysten knew he would never hear a word uttered from the man. "You will be called... Argyle while you are under my command."

The hunter nodded. Drysten gave the man the same name he used to address Abhartach's bastard son in the prisons under Eboracum. As he looked on the masked faces of the hunters around him, he almost felt a sense of pity for what he would do to them. He knew he would order them to their deaths. It was his job to make their deaths useful.

"There is a cave where we have made our home! The hunters will show you where," Abhartach yelled from his boat now moving out to sea.

Drysten nodded and returned him with a casual wave. *Show me every place you left these beasts. I will no doubt need to return to each one to route them out.*

Drysten turned to Argyle and gestured for him to lead him to the cave Abhartach spoke of. The man briefly mentioned the place once before, saying it was about thirty Roman miles East from where they laid some sort of trap months before.

They marched for a few nights, resting during the day, and staying out of sight of villagers or farmers. When they finally reached the cave, Drysten barely noticed it until Argyle disappeared into the ground.

Drysten slowly walked up to see torchlight emanating from a hole in the ground. As he stood, a pair of hunters picked up a rope and descended one at a time. *Another night sleeping underground. How wonderful.*

Drysten slowly picked up the rope and carefully lowered himself down the shaft. He was surprised once he realized the hunters had constructed a crude ladder right below the opening, meaning the rope was just to aid someone before their foot found the rungs.

"Please!" a woman shrieked from below.

Drysten quickened his pace until he reached the bottom. He glanced up and guessed he was roughly thirty feet below the surface as he watched a pair of hunters calmly descending behind him.

"Why are you doing this?" the woman shrieked from further inside. "We've done nothing to you!"

Drysten turned and moved toward the torchlight coming from a narrow passage. He had to crawl through before he came out into a space he could barely squat in, bumping his head when he tried to stand taller.

After a wail of pain the pleading stopped. Drysten emerged from the narrow space to see the beginnings of six hunters preparing their meal. A woman and a man were their prey. Drysten paused for a moment, unable to process the sight in his mind. All he could do was stare at the dainty wrist of the woman, seeing a beaded bracelet being spattered with blood. A hunter noticed the beads and ripped them from her wrist as he tossed them aside, landing right at Drysten's feet.

With no conscious thought to it, Drysten knelt and plucked the beaded bracelet from the ground and placed them under his belt.

The sight and smell in the confines of the underground passage was overwhelming. Drysten dry-heaved before hastily turning to venture back to the nighttime air. The two hunters who journeyed behind him bumped into him as he moved back through the passage toward the entrance to the cave. Before he knew it, he was already up the ladder and breathing in the fresh nighttime air

He stumbled his way to a cluster of trees where he vomited profusely at their base. Stealing a glance back to the hole in the ground, he saw Argyle emerge and begin shuffling toward him with a torch.

I need to get these men killed before more innocents get slaughtered, Drysten concluded as he heaved once more. Slaughtered was more literal than Drysten realized. How can a man... eat another person?

The base of the tree was coated in chunks of jerky he ate earlier that day. Thankfully, he slaughtered a wolf a couple of days prior. If he hadn't, he'd likely be eating some poor villager to stave off the stomach pains he grew so accustomed to. He was the only person in Abhartach's scouting party who struggled to find food, a strange thought that crossed his mind ever so often.

Drysten glanced back to Argyle, who had a surprising look of concern in his eyes. He held out the torch and viewed the base of the tree, producing a sigh as he began fishing around in a pouch at his waist.

"No!" Drysten whispered. "I don't want any of that filth."

Argyle shook his head as he produced some kind of dried plant from a pouch at his waist and extended his hand. He made a gesture around his stomach and nodded more emphatically when Drysten still hesitated to take it.

"For my belly?" Drysten asked.

Argyle nodded.

Drysten sighed and nodded as he carefully took the offering and began chewing it. The taste was strange, as the plant largely had no taste at all. Drysten struggled to swallow it before turning back to his temporary second in command. "Which way are the Saxons? How far from us are they?"

Argyle peered around before finally looking back and gesturing in what must have been Southeast. He then held up three fingers in the torchlight before pointing back in the same direction.

"Three days… or nights rather," Drysten concluded as Argyle nodded. "Get them ready to march. Let them have their… fill."

Argyle nodded and began marching back to the hole in the ground, disappearing down into the darkness.

They need to die, Drysten thought. *Now.*

***

King Ceneus was fidgeting with his father's ring as he stood in front of the main gate to Eboracum. The ring was given to his brother upon their father's death but taken after the war for Ebrauc's crown ended with Ceneus' victory. It was the ring of a king and belonged on the finger of the person ruling Ebrauc. He stood under the morning sunlight, wondering how his brother would react to seeing it upon the finger of the man who usurped his crown and took his wife.

"Lord King," Jorrit said as his horse trotted up. "The Guayrdians have almost arrived. They will be here shortly."

King Ceneus nodded. "And my brother?"

"Their scout told me he's with them, but he will do no fighting while he is here."

"Why not? He's likely one of their best, even given his age."

Jorrit couldn't help but let loose a heavy sigh. It was obvious he admired King Garbonian given the fact they fought side by side in the past. "He is not well."

"In… what way?" King Ceneus stammered. He remembered his younger years when he used to greatly admire his older brother. The man was a beast on the battlefield but had one of the softest hearts and fairest minds of any man he met. When Ceneus took the crown of Ebrauc, he justified his actions by claiming the man was too cruel to rule the kingdom. He now remembered this was further from the truth than he liked to admit. Being away from Bishop Germanus brought many of these realizations.

"Your oldest attacked them on the road," Jorrit explained. "The Guayrdians were ambushed and the king wounded."

"Damnit," King Ceneus whispered to himself.

"Your son as well," Jorrit added.

King Ceneus' heart dropped to his feet as he gazed to his captain. "Is Mor—?"

Jorrit shook his head. "He rides in the front with Rodric

and the king. Merely a flesh wound on his leg, I believe."

"Lead them here," he commanded.

Jorrit nodded and turned his horse back the way he'd come.

King Ceneus let out a sigh of relief as he nodded and began moving toward the small church Maewyn had once tried to construct before he fled with the bishop.

Shoddy looking place.

He slowly walked over to the beams stacked near the road, and ran his hand over an old hammer resting on top of the pile.

"Could I 'elp you?" a man asked as he came around the corner of the incomplete church.

King Ceneus shook his head. "Merely waiting until my people arrive."

His people. The king thought the idea his brother could ever again be part of his family was laughable. He saw to that when he stole the crown.

"Well, don't go about touching anything. The man'oo runs all this is rather particular," the man whispered.

Ceneus smirked as he looked over the aged individual now standing in front of him. His hair was gone at its top but gathered around the sides of his head. It was a strange sight. His eyes were narrow and there was a cluster of scars near his chin.

"Do you have everything you need for this place?" Ceneus asked.

The man finally began to understand that he was speaking to someone holding high rank as he uncomfortably rung his hands together and looked around. "Fink so. Maewyn provides for us rather well."

Ceneus nodded. "He's a good man."

The man nodded and opened his mouth to speak until glancing over the king's shoulder and moving back a pace.

They're here, Ceneus concluded. He turned to see the faces of bloodied men riding their horses behind one of his best scouts serving under Mor's command. Gawain was his name, and he rode alongside Jorrit in the very front of the army. Mor, Rodric, and Eliwlod followed behind before the king finally spotted Garbonian. It had been so long since Ceneus had seen his older brother.

"You've aged," Ceneus yelled as Garbonian rode ahead.

Garbonian nodded. "People tend to do that."

The two awkwardly stared at each other for some time until Jorrit walked up besides the king.

"Frisian!" Garbonian happily yelled as he quickly dismounted.

"Lord Ki—," Jorrit awkwardly responded as two big arms wrapped around him.

I wish I could show how happy it makes me to see you, brother. How sorry I am for it all.

Garbonian finally released Jorrit and took a step toward Ceneus, furrowing his brow and glancing toward the building. After another awkward silence, he finally gestured a hand toward the old man silently standing near the stack of beams. "New homes?"

Ceneus shook his head. It's going to be… a—"

"Don't say it," Garbonian interrupted with a grimace.

Ceneus knew any other man would get scolded for cutting him off mid-sentence, but decided it was best to let it go. He watched his brother look over the city with sad eyes. It was apparent he held the same opinions of its state that Ceneus did. Fewer people and less happiness than in its prime, though neither man was alive to see the bulk of those years.

Rodric slowly began sauntering up, snatching Garbonian from his daze. Garbonian turned and rested a hand on his shoulder before looking to Ceneus. "This one did well."

Ceneus grinned as he looked over Rodric, who sported a confused, or even ill look. Ceneus found it hard to decide. "Fought well?" Rodric shook his head but neglected to say anything before Garbonian began ushering the small group toward the city.

"Where are my other nephews?" Garbonian asked.

Ceneus gestured for Jorrit to follow before turning back. "Gwrast is nearly here. You already know where Eidion likely is."

Mor caught up once he heard the exchange. "Should have killed him when we had the chance. Told you his whole routine, and you still wouldn't send anyone to cut him in his sleep."

Ceneus sighed. "It was a mistake." He looked to his brother. "One of many."

Garbonian seemed somewhat pleased by the comment. "We all learn. Just takes some men a little longer."

"And what of Lord Drysten and the one-eyed Greek?" Garbonian asked. "Where is that man? I mean to marry him to one of my daughters!"

Ceneus' heart sank to his stomach. He clumsily glanced to Jorrit and Mor, but he could see neither man wished to save him from having to answer. Even Rodric looked at him with a hint of curiosity in his eyes.

"Little brother?" Garbonian insisted while taking a step forward. "Did that bastard Germanus kill him somehow?"

"Bishop Germanus had him imprisoned when he returned from Segedunum," Ceneus finally blurted out. *How could he not know? That was five fucking years ago.*

Garbonian threw his hands into the air and looked to Jorrit, receiving a sad nod. "Are you not king here? Why was this allowed? The man fought for you, Keneu!"

Ceneus felt a twinge of shame as he was addressed by his birth name. Flashbacks to the times his family was happy and unified began running through his mind.

"Brother! Answer me!" Garbonian firmly pressed. "Where are his people?"

Rodric took a step closer. "Lord, the king—"

"Not a word!" Garbonian yelled as he raised a finger to Rodric. "I would speak to my brother alone."

"Give the Guayrdians empty homes. I would speak with

my brother." Ceneus nodded for the men to continue on without him.

Garbonian waited until his men had all filed into the city. Once they did, he turned to Ceneus and beckoned for him to follow.

"You took everything from me. You robbed my wife of her husband and my son of his mother. I have chosen to forgive you for this considering you seek to rectify it all in some way. What you will do, right now, is explain to me what you have allowed to happen to my people." Garbonian's voice went low and hoarse as he tried to hide his anger.

"Germanus lied to me. He lied to everyone. We thought if we went against him, he would take the crown and place it on the head of someone more loyal to him. It seems all the man has done is make hollow threats and hire mercenaries," Ceneus explained. "Before we figured this out it had been many years since he took up residence here. Many years, brother. When Lord Drysten came back, he showed himself to be a threat to the bishop. So Germanus had the man imprisoned."

Garbonian grunted in disgust as he turned away. "I had looked forward to seeing all of them again. They were good people, Keneu." Again, Ceneus felt the sting. "Where are they now?"

Ceneus sighed. "I tried to let Drysten go. I tried to bring him back into the fold, but five years of torture and seclusion broke him. He now leads a band of Gaels through my kingdom. Hunting."

"Hunting? You said hunting?" Garbonian began to turn back around and face his brother. It was uncommon for the man to display his nerves. "Why did you use the word 'hunting'?"

"You know why," Ceneus whispered.

"We... need more men," Garbonian declared through a weak voice. "I know the man he fights for. He wished for me to join him in an attack on Ebrauc. He wanted to fight alongside the Saxons. The bastard has nearly two thousand men at his back."

"How do we fight that many?" Ceneus wondered aloud.

The king's brother scratched his bearded chin before shaking his head. "We can't. Not with what we have."

Ceneus let out a long sigh and glanced to the horizon. He didn't like admitting it, but his brother was right.

CHAPTER TWELVE

Matthew was leading the marching column East toward the war against the Saxons. It was odd how different his life had become. But the greatest oddity was how similar his life had become to what he was always told he was supposed to be. Being the bastard grandson of Emperor Constantine III, the usurper, meant he moved more than most children. There were always whispers of an heir to the throne of the Roman Empire, but thankfully most believed them to be just that. Rumors.

"Where are we?" Cynwrig asked as he glanced around.

Matthew did the same before turning to the Briton. "See those mounds?" he asked as he pointed off to the right. Cynwrig nodded. "Those are the graves of the old people. The ones who lived here when Rome was still nothing but a field near some hills."

"So, where are we?" Cynwrig asked once more.

"Close to an outpost. We should be coming up to it soon." Matthew glanced ahead and saw smoke rising into the sky. *Too small and light in color to be burning buildings. The place must be close.*

They were marching to an old Roman government compound once responsible for with supervising trade movements throughout the area. The Saxons raided it two nights prior, and any wealth was likely lost. Matthew remembered traveling through the surrounding village once he was rescued from Bishop Germanus' servitude a few years ago.

Most of those poor villagers are probably slaves, Matthew thought. He turned his gaze toward the five hundred men under his command and wondered if they could prevent the same thing from happening to the residents of Glevum.

"Sir!" a voice yelled from up ahead.

Matthew looked forward to see Dagonet riding up with a handful of scouts behind him.

"Prince Ambrosius needs you. The Saxons have been moving against us off and on for the last day or so. Never a full-scale attack, just enough to keep us from sleeping," the scout explained as he waved a hand toward the smoke.

Matthew quickly turned to his men. "Break formation! Reinforce the compound!"

The men in front heard him first and broke out into a sprint. Matthew rode down the line of men and relayed the order to those who were too far back to hear him the first time. It didn't take long before the whole column was on the move, with the wagons now being left behind in a cluster of trees. Only a handful of men would remain with them.

"Keep moving!" Matthew yelled. His lorica segmentata began chafing the skin of his arm as he waved for the men to run. Satisfied all his men were now on the move, he turned to Cynwrig. "With me."

Cynwrig nodded and clicked his tongue to spur his horse beside Matthew. The two quickly caught up to Dagonet and his scouts when the compound finally came into view. The fires were indeed only campfires, and silhouettes of men running back and forth could be seen in the twilight. They quickly arrived at Prince Ambrosius' camp to see him riding back and forth behind his men, bellowing the order to form a shield wall on the Eastern side of a ditch bordering the small village.

"Lord Prince," Matthew greeted as he brought his horse to a stop.

Ambrosius smirked. "Took you long enough."

Matthew smiled and nodded his head toward the darkness to the East. "How many guests are we expecting?"

The prince shrugged. “Anywhere from five hundred to a thousand. They’re Ethelric’s band that sacked Verulamium.”

“It’ll be good to get rid of that bastard,” Mathew declared with a sneer.

Dagonet straightened his back as he glanced East. “Saw cavalry with them. Likely about a hundred.”

“This isn’t another raid.” The prince cursed under his breath before turning back to his scouts and officers. “Use the ditches to our advantage. Matthew, your men will take the right.” He turned to his captain approaching from the rear of the shield wall. “Bedwyr, you take the left flank.”

Bedwyr nodded and turned away.

“Dagonet, take the scouts and let us know if they try to circle around back,” the prince added.

Before long, the men were all lined up facing East, with Dagonet and his scouting party of about twenty hidden in the darkness somewhere behind the army. No more commands were issued. There was only silence.

Matthew always got antsy in the moments before a battle. If he weren’t taught how to lead at such a young age, he believed he’d be a terrible officer. He spent years being tutored by former Roman generals and statesmen on the topics of war and diplomacy. He always thought those sessions wouldn’t amount to anything, as the Romans had already forgotten about Britannia. But here he was, plumed helmet and all.

Matthew glanced to his left and saw Cynwrig sitting atop his horse right beside him. “Ready?”

Cynwrig nodded. “Been a long while since I killed any Saxons.”

Matthew smirked as he looked back into the darkness ahead. He was impressed by Cynwrig. The last time he saw the man he was no more a soldier than the children who used to run through Petuaria. Now he was an armored warrior proudly sitting atop one of the Powysians formidable war horses. “Where’d you get that fancy piece around your neck?”

“Lord Drysten’s woman gave it to me shortly after we all

thought he'd been executed," Cynwrig answered.

Matthew sighed. "Too bad about that one."

"Much too bad. Could use someone who hears the gods fighting with us," Cynwrig responded.

"Those rumors were actually true?" Matthew wondered.

Cynwrig raised an eyebrow at the comment. "You've seen what he's capable of and you don't believe them?"

The two remained silent for some time before the sounds of war began. A drum off in the distance began to sound, its booming melody growing as war cries began to sound alongside it.

"Testudo!" Ambrosius screamed as he dismounted his horse.

The testudo was the Roman formation used to repel scores of arrows. The men were tightly packed together, with those in the middle lifting their shields over the heads of those around them. When done correctly, the testudo was quite effective.

The Powysians were well trained as evidenced by the proud gaze of Prince Ambrosius as he looked over his men.

Matthew watched as the prince turned and hefted his shield from the young man carrying his gear. The shield bore the likeness of a red wagon wheel with eight spokes in red. All the prince's men bore the insignia. It was one of the few which the Saxons had grown to fear in recent times.

Matthew followed his prince, but preferred not to fight with a shield, apparently much like Cynwrig. Both men simply walked close enough to the back of the nearest testudo to be protected by the rear line of shields.

The drumming continued for some time before finally ceasing. The silence was eerie to Matthew. He couldn't make heads or tails of why the Saxons would simply call off their attack when they clearly held an advantage.

"Lord Prince!" Dagonet screamed as he hastily rode up. "They've circled around us. Their horsemen rode right past us toward the wagons. Their footmen are moving back East."

Matthew watched the prince hand his shield off and glance toward the East. He slowly unstrapped his helmet and gazed into the darkness.

There was a tense moment in which every man remained silent. The prince stared into his hands, and Matthew would have given anything to peer inside him mind.

"We will not pursue," the prince declared with a dissatisfied shake of his head. "It's likely what they want."

Dagonet nodded. His relief was obvious. "What of the wagons?"

"We have no choice. Leave them to the Saxons." Prince Ambrosius turned to Matthew. "Half watch through the night. Douse the fires and torches." His stern tone showed his displeasure with his commander's decision to leave the wagons.

Or was it the fact I left men behind with them to be slaughtered? Matthew wondered. Either way, he knew his mistake had just cost the souls of those he was entrusted to lead.

Ambrosius turned and calmly made his way toward the main building of the compound.

Matthew felt Dagonet's gaze hovering over him. "What is it?" he asked, believing Dagonet wanted was second guessing his decision as the prince had done.

"It was surprising, is all," Dagonet whispered. "Refreshing, even."

"What was?" Mathew asked.

"Not being ordered into a massacre," Dagonet answered through a sigh of relief.

***

Drysten led his hunters to the edge of the clearing. They had been marching for the three nights predicted by Argyle, and Drysten was fairly impressed to see his second's prediction was spot on. There seemed to be a large Saxon force getting ready to encircle a party of Britons encamped in a small village. There were few lights to be seen, with most coming from the Britons' campfires. It was just bright enough for Drysten to discern the shapes moving around in both armies. As he surveyed the camp, he noticed the fires were being doused.

Must be preparing for an attack.

"But who will be attacking who, son?" Hall put in.

Drysten cocked his head to the side before turning toward Argyle. "Find the weakest point of the Saxon lines and wait for my order. The Britons still worship our ways and should not be harmed. Not unless I say otherwise," Drysten whispered to Argyle, who nodded and moved back to the rest of the men.

The purple cloaks could mean they're Powysian. Either that, or Rome came back without us knowing, Drysten thought with a scoff.

Argyle quickly returned and tapped Drysten's shoulder, nodding to say the order was carried out.

"We wait until we—." Drysten paused as he saw a small party of Saxons on horseback converging on another cluster of trees just inside the range of his hunter's bows. They were to the rear of the Briton's strange looking shield formation, with a handful of their own cavalry waiting between the two groups.

"They will die first," Drysten stated as he pointed to the mounted Saxons.

Argyle nodded and made a hissing noise. All the hunters strung their bows and plucked their arrows from the bags at their waist. It was disturbing how quiet they could be.

"Poisons as well. Abhartach wanted these men to fear, and fear they will." Drysten slowly crept closer to the Saxons now riding in and out of the trees. He heard them hollering to one another and laughing as they killed a small group of men left to guard what Drysten guessed to be a wagon train belonging to the Britons.

"Get ready," Drysten ordered.

Argyle turned and made another strange hissing noise before raising a hand and turning back to Drysten.

Drysten knelt and found a small grouping of dead grass and plucked it up, scrunching it into a little ball. "Lure them in," Drysten said as he handed the ball of grass to Argyle.

Argyle nodded and turned, quickly fashioning a small torch before handing it back to Drysten and grabbing his flint from his waist. The torch was quickly lit, and Drysten took two steps toward the rampaging Saxons, brandishing it high over his head.

"Put it out!" Drysten yelled at the top of his lungs. He guessed if he sounded like he was trying to hide, the Saxons would more carelessly charge to their deaths. Five or six horsemen immediately stopped, with Drysten faintly seeing one point in his direction.

Argyle chuckled as Drysten threw down the torch and stamped it out.

"I know," Drysten agreed with a laugh. "Get them ready. Saxons are careless when they smell blood."

Argyle nodded and raised his hand. The sound of the hunters stringing their bows was barely audible for anyone who didn't know to listen for it.

They have no idea what's coming to them, Drysten thought with a smile.

***

Strange things were happening that night. Dagonet stood with Matthew, Cynwrig, and Prince Ambrosius as they listened to the wagon train getting overwhelmed. Matthew looked guilty, as the handful of men left behind were his. But Dagonet knew to expect this. He warned the prince of how this Saxon liked to fight, but nobody listened to him.

He heard the reports of how Verulamium was sacked, as well as the handful of raids led by Ethelric. It only took Dagonet a moment before he understood the man. Whereas Colgrin was a brute and fought as such, this Ethelric was anything but. He was clever, and fought like a seasoned warrior.

"I think there's someone else out there," the prince whispered.

Dagonet nodded. "Saw a torch lit briefly at that tree line." He pointed off to the right. "The Saxons must have too, as they're lining up for a charge."

Dagonet saw Matthew perk his head.

"You can see all that? In this darkness?" the priest asked.

Dagonet nodded before looking to Prince Ambrosius. "Did you have any men coming after the priest?"

"I'm not a priest," Matthew uttered to no one.

Prince Ambrosius chuckled at Matthew before shaking his head. "I ordered Bors back to Glevum a day ago. Whoever's out there isn't with us."

Dagonet shuddered at the thought of another army randomly showing up without knowing who they fought for.

The Saxon horsemen off in the distance seemed ready to charge into the tree line. A roar sounded, with the Britons behind Dagonet giving each other uneasy glances to one another. The horses could be heard ferociously rampaging through the empty space. The three Britons glanced to one another as a handful more walked over and stood nearby.

"Who's that?" Bedwyr asked of the prince as he approached.

Ambrosius shrugged. "The Saxons. No idea who they're fighting."

"Hm," Bedwyr responded.

Cynwrig glanced to Dagonet. "You know who this is. Don't you?" he whispered.

Dagonet nodded.

"So do I," Cynwrig muttered, his tone noticeably uneasy.

The roar of the Saxon cavalry was loud enough for

Dagonet to wonder if they were actually charging toward the Powysians instead of whoever else was out there. But those roars soon turned to wails of pain, and all too familiar gurgles. The shrieks and thuds of bodies hitting the ground was loud enough for most of the Powysians to stop staring toward the main Saxon force. Almost all the men were now standing behind Ambrosius, staring toward whatever battle was taking place.

"Sounds like someone's losing," the prince observed in interest.

Dagonet nodded. "Badly."

"But who," Ambrosius wondered aloud.

Cynwrig and Dagonet gave each other a knowing glance before looking back to the prince.

"Arthur..." Matthew whispered. "We need to form a line."

The prince nodded. "Testudo! Look to the rear!"

The Powysians quickly assembled behind the prince, with most of the officers remaining still as they stared into the darkness. The battle seemed to be coming closer, but Dagonet was having trouble hearing if it was the Gaels retreating or if the Saxons were being forced their way.

"Look!" Bedwyr whispered as he pointed into the darkness.

Dagonet turned to see a handful of Saxon horses riding past without their riders, with a handful of men stumbling toward them clutching at arrows protruding from their legs or chests.

"Grab them!" the prince commanded.

Bedwyr began rushing forward until Cynwrig yelled for the man to stop.

Dagonet shook his head and looked to the prince. "You won't be taking any of these men as prisoners."

The prince gave him a strange look as he peered back to the shambling Saxons. One began wheezing before he seemed to fall to his knees. Dagonet could just make out the man clutching a hand to his throat and began trying to remove his armor. It seemed the Saxon believed the armor to be the cause of his choking on air.

The prince looked back to Dagonet. "Is it the ones from the West?" he asked, referencing the Gaels. The ghost stories of Britannia.

Dagonet nodded, still faintly seeing the dying Saxons stumbling from the darkness toward the last fire the Powysians hadn't put out.

"What drives a man to seek comfort with their enemy?" Bedwyr wondered.

Dagonet chuckled to himself. "A worse enemy, I'd expect."

Just then, a shape slowly emerged from the darkness behind another Saxon clumsily shuffling toward the Powysians. The Saxon glanced behind him and saw the Gael in slow pursuit. He fell to his knees and began wheezing while trying to crawl forward. He locked eyes with the prince and extended a hand in a last bid for aid.

The Gael dropped his bow and drew his blade, a Roman blade, and slowly followed the Saxon trying desperately to elude him. More screams were heard from the darkness as the sounds of battle began to dissipate. The Gael still followed the Saxon, toying with him as he moved. His prey attempted to rise from the ground but tripped and turned over onto his back, with the Gael stopping and standing over him. But he did not kill the man, he simply stood. Waiting.

Bedwyr glanced to Cynwrig. "Why's he just standing there?"

"Poor bastard's already gone," Cynwrig whispered back. "He's likely just figured that out."

Right when the Briton answered, the Saxon's choking turned more violent. He began clawing at his throat before finally convulsing until he stopped everything altogether. Dagonet knew the Saxon was doomed the moment the arrow touched the man's skin.

"God..." Bedwyr whispered.

Just when the majority of the Powysians were forced silent from shock, the prince sheathed his blade and began carefully walking toward the Gael.

"What are you doing?" Bedwyr yelled.

"Lord Prince!" Matthew added.

Dagonet scoffed as he gazed over the sinister looking man staring at the prince. "He won't hurt him," he declared. "He knows him."

The men all stared as the prince had nearly reached him. Most of the Powysians were doing a poor job of hiding their uneasiness. But Dagonet looked to Cynwrig, and both men slowly followed the prince's lead.

"And where the fuck are you off to?" Bedwyr demanded, causing the prince to turn back.

"I know you aren't addressing me, Bedwyr," Ambrosius hissed.

Bedwyr's eyes went wide as he looked between the prince and Dagonet. "No, Lord Prince... I was merely speaking to the two scouts who—"

"Have a piss somewhere else," Cynwrig answered to the amusement of Dagonet.

"I outrank both of you! Now come back!" Bedwyr ordered. He was hushed once he looked across to the prince, and immediately noticed the Gael was now glaring at him with an unnatural intensity directed only at him.

This should be interesting, Dagonet mused.

Cynwrig followed him toward the prince, with both men only stopping when they stood directly beside him.

"Arthur," Drysten said as he greeted the prince with a nod. He glanced to Dagonet and Cynwrig and offered them a nod as well.

Arthur glanced back to his men and gently removed his plumed Roman helmet, allowing his blonde hair to fall freely to his shoulders. "Your wife and child are safe," he began. "My uncle allowed them to live in my villa until they find their own path."

"You Romans and your villas," Drysten joked as he slowly lifted a bloodied hand to his mask and yanked it from his face. "How's my son?"

Arthur clicked his tongue and looked to the sky. "Misses his father. It's not fair what you've done to him. To your wife for that matter."

Drysten tried to conceal his emotions but failed, with Dagonet seeing a twinge of guilt wash over his face.

I suppose there's still a good man in there somewhere, Dagonet noted.

Arthur sighed when he didn't receive any response and looked behind Drysten, seeing the rest of the Gaels slowly waft out of the darkness like puffs of smoke. It was Dagonet's second time seeing them, but it was Arthur's first. The prince took an uneasy step back as the men began to creep closer.

"They will not harm you," Drysten explained. "They follow my commands. If I don't tell them to do something, they simply don't do it."

"That's... useful," Cynwrig awkwardly put in.

Drysten nodded as he stepped closer to the prince. "More are coming," he whispered. "Abhartach has gone to bring the rest of his people here. They seek to kill the Christians and the Saxons."

Arthur glanced to Dagonet before returning Drysten's gaze. "Perhaps we should let them."

Drysten shook his head. "Who do you think they'll go after once both those groups have gone? The man believes he's bringing the old ways back, but I've seen them preying on anyone they come across. The man doesn't care who he kills. He just does so because he wants to. He's simply another madman using his faith to do what he wishes."

Arthur gave Dagonet a worried glance. "When will they be here?"

"For all I know, they already are. They are on the small island to the West of Ebrauc. I remember someone calling it

Mevania once," Drysten whispered.

"Mevania?" Arthur whispered to himself. "Where the—"

"The island halfway between Ebrauc and Hibernia," Dagonet explained. "Went there once after Lord Drysten—" Dagonet glanced to Drysten. "When we thought you were dead. Nothing there but traders and a small hillfort from what I saw."

"They're there," Drysten said as one of his hunters shuffled up beside him. "How many losses?" he asked as he turned to the man.

The hunter returned a nonchalant shrug, leading Dagonet to believe there likely weren't many dead Gaels to find in the morning.

The prince glanced to the hunter before taking a small step toward Drysten. "If you could do but one more thing for me."

Drysten perked an eyebrow. "You're sheltering my family," he whispered. "Anything."

The prince turned and pointed to where the rest of the Saxons were lined up and ready to charge into the Powysians. "Kill that fucking Saxon."

Dagonet looked back to Drysten to see him offer a half-smile as he raised his mask back up over his nose. "With me," he whispered as he turned to the Gaels.

The hunter turned and produced a strange whistling noise towards the rest of the men as Drysten lifted his mask over his smile and began leading his men back into the darkness.

CHAPTER THIRTEEN

Drysten was pleased to hear his family was being taken care of. The only thing he wished he asked was how Diocles was faring. He guessed there was a small chance he could see for himself someday but squelched the thoughts for a later time. He was currently leading the hunters through the trees toward the area the Saxon army had gathered. He could still turn back and see the Powysian lines off in the distance, but knew the Saxons were much closer to him than they were.

"Argyle," Drysten whispered. He waved the Gael forward from the thigh-high grasses around them.

The Gael approached, holding a large ear in his hand that must have been taken from a dead Saxon. Drysten couldn't help but wonder whether it was taken as a trophy or as a snack.

"Scout the camp and find their leader," Drysten ordered as he glimpsed down to the ear.

Argyle nodded and whistled to a handful of hunters, ordering them to join him.

Drysten made himself as flat as possible on the ground as his men slowly moved off toward the Saxons. *If I get enough of them killed right now, I could be rid of them altogether by sunup.* He glanced behind him to see the rest of the Gael's silhouettes gathered close by.

The small band of men were still until Argyle's return sometime later. Drysten guessed the morning hours were nearly there and knew if he was going to make a move it had to be soon.

"Follow," he commanded the Gaels before turning to Argyle. "Is he there?"

Argyle nodded.

"Within range?"

Again, the Gael nodded.

"Lead me to him," Drysten whispered. "It will be me who kills the man."

Argyle turned and crept low towards a patch of grass by an abandoned farmhouse. Figures were casually roaming about just ahead. Judging by the size of their shoulders, Drysten knew them to be Saxons wearing furs from large beasts across the sea. Argyle looked back and waved Drysten over, pointing to a small fire with four men seated around it. He placed a hand on Drysten's shoulder and leaned closer to show him exactly which Saxon he was pointing to.

The one with no beard? What kind Saxon has no beard? Drysten wondered with a scoff. Drysten nodded and strung his bow, with the rest of the Gaels following suit. He took an arrow from the pouch at his waist and carefully removed the covering on its head. The covering was the only thing which kept a man from being pricked by the poison on the arrow's point. He carefully knocked the arrow and raised it toward the fire, slowly drawing it back as he did so.

Argyle went down to a knee and did the same. The sound from Argyle's bow being drawn back was louder than Drysten's, leading him to believe that bow may have more force to it than his own.

"On my arrow, loose the rest and run back to the Powysians," Drysten whispered to Argyle, who nodded.

The force required to pull the arrow back to his ear would have been too much for Drysten only a couple months before. But now he was strong. He closed one eye as he aimed toward the neck of the Saxon commander, steadily monitoring his breathing and heartbeat. With each breath and beat of his heart his arm moved ever so slightly, meaning he would have to time the shot in between them.

He did, and the arrow began to sing through the air. The Gaels followed Drysten's command and turned after firing their own volley. The men were all sprinting away while Drysten stayed to watch if he hit his mark.

He did.

The Saxon screamed as the arrow embedded itself just below his left shoulder. The man let loose a shocked grunt as his shiny armor became visible from under his cloak. Satisfied by the sight, Drysten began his mad dash to safety.

"Form a line!" the Saxon screamed at the top of his lungs.

You won't be alive to see them do it, Drysten thought with a chuckle.

After a quick moment Drysten and the Gaels finally reached the halfway point between the Saxon and Powysian camps. Thundering footsteps were beginning to sound out from behind him, and Drysten knew them to be a handful or horses mixed with a huge number of Saxon footmen on their heels.

"Turn and fire! Then keep moving!" Drysten commanded as he quickly knocked another arrow and turned. He fired it toward the only large silhouette he could see through the darkness but was unsure if he hit anything.

The Gaels did so as well, with a handful of screams coming from behind him.

"Arthur!" Drysten bellowed. "Arthur! Shields!" He was unsure anyone heard him as the Saxon war drums began sounding into the night.

Those drums should get the Powysians moving, Drysten concluded. *I wonder who gave the command to begin the charge.* He had a brief moment of panic as the idea of the Saxon somehow surviving crept to the forefront of his mind.

That fear was forgotten as a massive force slammed itself into Drysten's shoulder, toppling him to the ground. The pain was agonizing as he glanced behind him to see the faint shapes of Saxons drawing closer at a rapid pace. He looked forward to seeing Argyle spinning and firing an arrow before racing toward him and scooping him from the dirt. Drysten slowly glimpsed down, and noticed a familiar arrowhead jutting from the front of his shoulder.

"Gods, no!" Drysten shouted.

The panic stung its way through his chest as he stared at the arrowhead. It was the first shot he fired into the chest of the Saxon commander.

"Argyle...," Drysten whispered.

It was all he could manage as his head began to burn and his lungs began feeling as though the gods themselves held a grip over his chest. He collapsed to his feet, and the darkness of the night gave way.

***

Rodric and Eliwlod walked from the barracks to the Roman baths to see a handful of Christian priests gathered in front of the doorway. Green banners bearing a horned snake were waving above either side of the doorway. Both men glanced to one another before halting just behind the group to listen in on what was being said.

"These filthy apostates rampage through our city!"

"The bishop will burn you for this!"

"Think of your soul, Lord King!"

Many more of the angry priests were screaming insults into the face of the royal guard barring their entrance. Rodric noticed as he got closer the man was Braxus, who recognized Rodric and Eliwlod through the crowd and casually waved a hand for them to enter. Rodric gently nudged a priest aside to receive a plethora of insults from the rest of them until he finally made it through the entrance.

"Bastards have some spirit. I'll give 'em that," Eliwlod stated as he glanced over his shoulder.

Rodric nodded. "I wonder what set them off."

King Ceneus waved the two men into the baths where Rodric immediately noticed King Garbonian sitting as well. "I told them they could worship how they wished, but those who worship differently were not to be driven out."

Garbonian chuckled. "They took one look at me and nearly shat their robes."

Rodric smirked at the thought. The men from Bryneich were a stark contrast to the Christians, with most speaking an unfamiliar language and covered in blue markings. "What drove them to this madness?"

"They wish to be the only religion in the isles. Can't say I blame them when they hear of ghosts in the night who want to steal their souls," Ceneus answered. "In any case, no religion will be above the other while I rule."

Garbonian nodded. "Incites conflict to favor one over the other."

Strange to see them acting as though they're friendly with one another. I wonder how long this will last, Rodric thought.

Garbonian looked to Eliwlod and produced a puzzled stare. One which King Ceneus noted.

"Brother," Ceneus began as he stood, snatching his brother's attention. "We need to move on the bishop soon."

Garbonian let out a hollow grunt as he lifted his wounded leg out of the water. "Who will lead them? I'm useless at the moment, and Lord Drysten is off with yet another enemy from what I've heard."

Ceneus sighed. "I will," he answered. "When Gwrast returns, he will be second." He looked to Rodric. "With you third," he stated with a reassuring nod.

Rodric glanced to his feet.

"Brother, he's still got much to learn. Perhaps I could send for my son," Garbonian suggested.

Ceneus shook his head. "It would take much too long. Not to mention he'd likely be ambushed in the same way Mor was."

"Where is he?" Rodric wondered.

Ceneus shrugged. "He's been spending time with the Guayrdians. Apparently, they like him."

Garbonian snorted in amusement. "They appreciate a gifted warrior. Your boy certainly fits the mold of one."

Rodric saw Ceneus emanate a proud smile as he looked up toward the ceiling.

"How many men do we have?" Rodric found himself wondering. He wasn't sure why he even asked considering he already knew the answer.

"Not enough. Not anymore," Ceneus replied. "When I ordered the traders imprisoned, one fed us enough information to get a clearer picture of the bishop's plans. The man said more Visigothic mercenaries should have arrived in the North two nights ago. There's more on the way as well. He mentioned this Theodoric wishes to expand his empire and is testing us to see if we can be conquered."

Garbonian stared toward the ceiling. "If he knew anything about Britannia, he would've just come right away. Hardly anyone would be able to stop him."

Rodric stepped toward the baths. "Maybe the Saxons?"

Garbonian shook his head. "They've already been beating the Saxons bloody for years. Why do you think the bastards wanted to come here in the first place? Colgrin may have wished to be king, but many of the ones who fight for him do so because they lost their homes to other tribes."

"This Theodoric leads one of the tribes?" Rodric wondered.

Both Ceneus and Garbonian shook their heads.

"He actually leads many," Ceneus added. "The traders were very forthcoming."

All the men were silenced by the entrance of Jorrit and his son, Lanzo, by his side. Braxus followed as well but elected to remain in the doorway after giving Ceneus a casual wave, Jorrit must not have expected for there to be so many people, as his eyes seemed to widen as he surveyed the room.

"Enter," Ceneus stated as he waved the Frisian in. He was surprised by the strange sense of hesitation from his officer.

"Lord King," Jorrit greeted. "I wished to introduce my son to King… Lord… Garbonian."

Ceneus smiled as Garbonian stood and began wandering over to the small boy.

"This one is yours?" He asked with his usual jovial tone. "He looks much too strong!" He plucked the boy from the ground and hefted him up to his side. "What's your name, boy?"

"Lanzo," the child whispered through a small voice.

Jorrit smiled at his son's uneasiness. "My wife also wished to meet you, if that would be permitted." He looked to Ceneus, who nodded.

"Go," Ceneus instructed his brother and Jorrit. "We can discuss these matters later."

Jorrit returned an uneasy smile, with Garbonian doing

the same as he was led out of the baths. Braxus followed, and the three men departed.

"You trust them?" Rodric asked of the king.

Ceneus perked an eyebrow and shifted in the water. "My brother or the Frisians?"

"The Frisians. Your brother seemed much different than we were all led to believe."

Ceneus chuckled to himself. "I would expect that shouldn't be a surprise." He rose from the bath and wandered toward a nearby table, pouring himself a cup of diluted wine. "As for the Frisians… I trust if I treat them well, they will serve me in kind."

"Fair enough, Lord King, but I will have them watched."

Ceneus turned and smiled toward Rodric and Eliwlod. "Fair enough, Lord King."

***

Ceneus led Garbonian and his officers from the baths, quickly making their way toward the principia. It was nice being able to use the old building now that Bishop Germanus had fled with Eidion to Isurium. But that wasn't why this meeting was being called. A Powysian messenger had ridden East with a disturbing message.

The Gaels are coming back.

"Send word out. All able-bodied men are to join us at Glanoventa," Ceneus ordered. A handful of riders were awaiting such instructions near the principia's entrance.

The roughly dozen men nodded and began marching back to their horses near the main gate of the fortress.

Garbonian tapped Ceneus' shoulder. "How many can we expect to meet us there?" Ceneus heard the man's awkward tone toward him. He'd had it ever since he met Jorrit's family, and the king wondered what conversation may have taken place.

"Expect?" Ceneus pondered. "I expect nobody to arrive. We've burned many bridges due to Germanus' cruel ways. I could hope for about five hundred."

"Out of how many?" Garbonian asked.

After a sigh, Ceneus shrugged. "If all were to show up, the Gaels would be routed, and we could even pursue them to their own homes if we wanted to. I rule over the most populated kingdom in Britannia."

"The messenger told us the beast has two-thousand men...," Garbonian stated in surprise.

Ceneus nodded as they passed through the principia's doorway. "We would have many more. In any case, I'm hoping for a thousand in total when counting the Powysians."

The group found their way to the main hallway and quickly passed through toward the basilica. The open-aired courtyard was the meeting area for the king and his officers who were getting ready to receive the news of their enemy's arrival. It was a strange sight for the king.

There were a handful of men who nearly looked like Romans. They wore strange fish-scale armor purchased from traders who frequented the lands still under the Empire's control. Ceneus overheard one mention the armor was known as lorica squamata, but couldn't be certain he heard correctly. Beside them stood the blue-faced men of Din Guayrdi, and standing in the corner was Gaius and his captain, Citrio.

"Thank you all for coming on such short notice," Ceneus announced.

The Guayrdians glanced to one another, clearly not understanding the Roman language still in use by Ceneus and his men.

"Abhartach will soon return with his main army, and the bishop still holds Isurium," Ceneus explained. "Our job is to defeat them both."

"Who will aid us?" Gaius asked as he slowly sauntered out of his corner.

Ceneus shook his head. "Aside from a small Powysian field army, the men in this room and the ones who follow them are all we have."

Gaius cursed under his breath before raising his gaze back to the king. "It won't be enough."

Gwrast stepped forward. "But it's what we have."

Ceneus nodded. "So we'll have to make the most of it."

The king looked to his feet for a moment, searching for the right words of encouragement. He knew he wouldn't be able to, but still held out hope he could perform one last bit of encouragement as king before being slaughtered by the Gaels.

"If I may, brother," Garbonian whispered as he stepped passed the king, who nodded. "We have an advantage over them they won't expect us to use."

The group stared at the king's imposing brother. A small feeling of jealousy crept up inside Ceneus, but he managed to stifle it quickly enough to ignore the thoughts of sending the man away for being a better leader than himself.

"They are masters of the wilds. They live to hunt, and

fight with the element of surprise. Their scouts are beyond any of ours, and their tactics of hitting hard and running back to regroup are nearly impossible to fight against."

Gwrast scoffed. "How is that an advantage?"

"We simply need to fight them the moment they arrive. We still have time to garrison Glanoventa with enough men to halt them. All we have to do is beat them there," Garbonian said with a smile.

Gwrast looked on his uncle in admiration. "That's not a bad idea. They have to weather the currents before they arrive."

Ceneus took a pace forward. "There have been easterly winds of late as well."

Gwrast smiled at the thought of victory. "We simply need to march along the road."

Garbonian nodded. "We should be able to not only arrive before they do but fortify the town as well."

There was a rumble of approval from most of the men in the room besides Gaius and the Guayrdians. Gaius because he likely didn't wish to face the Gaels a third time, and the Guayrdians because they most certainly couldn't understand a word that was being said. Ceneus took notice and made a mental note of keeping Gaius a bit further from any fighting to be done.

Gwrast whispered something to Mor before raising a hand to gain his father's attention. "How do we avoid Eidion?"

The room went silent as all eyes moved to the king. Ceneus noticed Gaius taking this moment to quickly duck out of the room but chose to think nothing of it.

"Brother," Ceneus began, "You will harass the bishop and his men."

Garbonian shook his head. "You need every man you can muster for the Gaels."

"No, I simply need enough." Ceneus glanced to Jorrit and beckoned him over. "You will go to the Saxons and promise them whatever you need to make them fight."

"No!" a man yelled from the back. "Those men are treacherous—"

"They are the most able warriors in Britannia not currently fighting for us, Powys, or Bishop Germanus!" Ceneus roared, silencing the man immediately. I'll have to find out who that was.

Jorrit nodded but gave Garbonian a subtle glance. "Octha will likely fight if we offer him more land. Ebissa..."

"Whatever it is he can have it. How many exactly would I be able to expect?" Ceneus questioned.

Jorrit lifted his head toward the ceiling as he searched for the answer. "I would say... four-hundred of them in total."

Gwrast nodded. "Octha's fought beside me before. Four-hundred of these men will... help at least."

Ceneus gestured a hand toward the door. "Convince them to fight." He turned to the rest of the men. "The Saxons will be the last line of defense against attackers while we are away."

The room erupted. Every officer not related to Ceneus was screaming over the idea of Saxons protecting their loved ones. Most believed they would simply kill the Britons in Eboracum and take the city for their own. A few thought they would just burn everything and sort through the ashes later.

"I have spoken," Ceneus bellowed. "If you don't trust them to fight, why would you want them on either side of you?"

That simple statement seemed to satisfy the grumblings for the moment as Ceneus looked back to Jorrit.

"I will hurry to them," the Frisian replied.

The room was silent until Jorrit's exit. The men began murmuring amongst themselves until King Garbonian walked toward Ceneus, placing a hand on his shoulder, and pulling him aside.

"Brother," Garbonian whispered. "I know this is not the best time, but I have a favor to ask."

Ceneus perked an eyebrow and looked on his brother's

solemn face. His features were stiff, and his eyes hinted at a small amount of ambivalence. "Is there a problem?"

Garbonian shook his head. "This is more of a family matter than a conversation of war."

Ceneus knew immediately what his brother request was going to be. "You wish to speak to her," he whispered.

Garbonian nodded.

Ceneus released a long sigh as he gestured for his brother to follow. The two men turned until Ceneus halted and called for his two sons to join them. Gwrast and Mor both glanced to one another before following.

"I have no intentions of—"

"They are not joining you as protection. They should hear of their older brother," Ceneus returned.

Garbonian returned a subtle nod and followed Ceneus as they roamed toward the Roman baths.

Heledd would never forgive me if she weren't able to learn of how her oldest son was fairing, Ceneus concluded. He remembered the day of their wedding, and the tears his wife shed when she was told Dyfnwal would be banished from Ebrauc with Garbonian. In truth, Ceneus saved the boy's life, despite a nasty wound his nephew gave him during the war for the crown.

Bishop Germanus wanted Dyfnwal and Garbonian executed, but Ceneus decreed this wasn't an option. He went to war with them both, but he never once hated them. This lack of hate was likely why Dyfnwal even had the chance to wound him in the first place.

"Do you believe she will speak to me?" Garbonian whispered.

Ceneus nodded. "She thought of you often, brother. It was only somewhat recently when she looked on me with any kind of affection in her eyes."

The answer seemed to bring a hint of satisfaction to Garbonian, but the man was smart enough to try and hide it. He did a poor job, but Ceneus appreciated the gesture all the same.

They finally made it into the baths where Heledd and a handful of women were sewing cloaks for the officers on their way to war. She produced a smile as she saw Ceneus, then noticed Garbonian and began turning red in the face.

"Wife," Ceneus greeted through an awkward tone.

Heledd nodded, her eyes fixed on the large man standing beside him.

"It has been a long time," Garbonian murmured.

Heledd nodded and placed the cloak she had been working on onto the table in front of her. She rose and looked to both her sons with a smile before looking back to Ceneus. "Why—"

"You need to hear of Dyfnwal," Ceneus interrupted. He didn't mean to, but his nerves had made him antsy. The silence as everyone watched the woman move from the table toward them was torture for the man.

Heledd glanced to Garbonian. "Is… he well?"

Garbonian nodded. "He is. Took a wife a few years ago. You're a grandmother."

Heledd smiled, but it was clear to Ceneus she wasn't sure how much happiness she should display in front of him.

Ceneus patted Garbonian on the arm before looking to his wife. "I will leave you for a short time." He turned to his sons. "You need to hear of your older brother. There is a decent chance you will inherit this kingdom in the coming days. It would be irresponsible if you did so without knowing of the future king to the North."

Both Ceneus' boys nodded as he left the room. Eliwlod was milling about outside with Rodric and two others Ceneus didn't know, all of which gave him a polite bow as the king leaned against the doorway. He was somewhat surprised by how brief the conversation was, as Heledd exited the baths with the other women only a few moments later. She was clearly happy judging by the beaming smile on her face.

"Thank you, husband," she whispered. Her eyes were becoming watery as she embraced Ceneus and walked toward the city.

Ceneus returned to the baths to see Garbonian speaking with his nephews as he entered.

Gwrast and Mor returned their father an awkward glance before Gwrast stepped forward. "Uncle," he began. "You have another son as well."

Garbonian turned back in surprise. "If you're going to try and pin that fucking Eidion on me—"

"His name is Eliwlod," Gwrast interrupted. "I just assumed Eidion spawned from dirt." Everyone in the room chuckled before Gwrast turned to the door. "Enter!"

Eliwlod did so, looking uncomfortable as he shuffled toward Gwrast. "Am I needed?" He noticed the way Garbonian looked over him as he approached, and looked to Ceneus through the side of his eye.

Ceneus turned to his brother. "I saw to it he was kept away from Germanus. There are only a few who know he is yours?"

"Fucking what?" Eliwlod exclaimed.

"You're a prince," Ceneus returned with a smirk. He expected confusion, but the sudden outburst from his nephew proved to be more entertaining. "Though I am happy you're finally meeting him," he turned to Gwrast, "I would have done this at another time, son."

Gwrast shrugged. "Mother is gone. Figured this was as good a time as any. Doubt she'd want to know what our esteemed uncle was up to before he..." Gwrast gave an awkward glance to Garbonian. "Before he left."

Garbonian chuckled as he approached Eliwlod. "Your mother was beautiful. I remember her well." He produced a warm smile toward his newfound son.

"Not beautiful enough to take her with you?" Eliwlod hissed. The sharpness in his tone caught everyone off guard. "She would tell me stories of my father when I was young. She never named him, but she told me how great he was." He stepped closer. "She loved you even when the fevers took her.

She told me she'd dream of you as they got worse and caused her to sleep for hours during the day."

Garbonian's face was turning white as he seemed to shrink where he stood. "I… loved—"

"You loved visiting her in the tavern when my grandfather would close up for the night. You loved meeting her out of view." Eliwlod's cracking voice betrayed his sadness. "You never cared for her."

"I did, El—"

"No! You simply viewed her as a secret plaything!" Eliwlod screamed. "I don't care to know you any more than you cared to know her." He turned to leave but halted as he faced his father one last time. "Perhaps if you took us with you, she would have lived. Perhaps if she had the comfort of a queen, she wouldn't have died from the cold in her sleep." He turned and stormed out, leaving everyone with gaping mouths.

Ceneus stepped toward his brother, only to be halted by a gently raised hand as Garbonian hung his head. "The boy is right. I had the opportunity to take her with me. I chose not to."

The men went silent.

CHAPTER FOURTEEN

Hall led Drysten through the densely packed forest, occasionally glancing back to check if he was still there. Both men were silent until Drysten thought he felt a twinge in his shoulder and produced a hollow gasp.

"Everything alright, son?" Hall asked as he turned. He reached down and picked up a small twig, turning it over in his hand before walking toward his son.

A brief flash seemed to turn Hall's face into that of another, less familiar figure. But Drysten blinked and the figure left him.

"My shoulder," Drysten said as he glanced down. "Something... I feel as though I shouldn't be here."

Hall chuckled through a warm smile. "We all feel that at first." He snapped the twig and dropped it at his feet. "You learn to live with it."

"Where are we?"

Drysten's father knelt and scooped up a small handful of snow, slowly running it through his fingers before rising back to Drysten's level. "You know where we are," he stated as he gestured to the forest around them.

Lord!

Put him on the table!

What's that muck he spread all over his shoulder?

"What was that?" Drysten wondered as he glanced through the trees. The wind seemed to make the branches gently dance above him, but he couldn't feel it on his face.

Hall slowly walked over and put a hand on Drysten's shoulder. "You won't be here for long."

"But where exactly is *here*?"

Get away from him!

Lord Prince, find the Gaels!

Watch out for the point of it!

Hall leaned in toward Drysten, only stopping a hair's breadth away from Drysten's ear. "The small ones turn into big ones, Lord. Much easier to kill them before then," he whispered. A wicked grin crossed his face as he leaned back. A dark, rotten smelling liquid began oozing from between his teeth.

"Father?" Drysten whimpered as he stole a step back.

His heel knocked into something, and Drysten looked down. The sight was all too familiar to him. The boy he saw murdered during his attack on a raider's encampment laid at his feet. It happened so long ago near Burdigala, but Drysten recognized the boy immediately.

"What..." Drysten stuttered in a panic.

Shields!

How many are there?

The fucking Saxons...

Drysten looked up from the boy and saw an uncountable number of funeral pyres behind his father. Each one held an equally uncountable amount of men, some of which Drysten knew. Their faces were familiar to him, but he couldn't find their names no matter how hard he searched his mind.

"You betrayed them," Hall stated as he outstretched his arms toward the fires. "*All* of them."

"And now I'm here," Drysten responded as he glared into Hall's eyes and stepped forward. "But *you* are not. My father voice and image were one of the gods' favorite instruments to bring me torment. I remember the funeral in Petuaria. You tried the same thing there. I will *not* fall for this again."

It was at that moment Drysten realized he had no feeling in his body but a dull throbbing in his shoulder. He glanced down once more and the image of two bloody hands gripping his arms went by like lightning before there was nothing.

"You're not going to be okay," Hall declared. "Not even *if* you survive."

"Survive what?"

I've almost got it out!

Hurry up!

They won't fight without Drysten!

"Poison..." Drysten whispered.

"No. *Truth,*" Hall answered as he lifted a finger. "The only truth is there isn't one. And if there isn't truth then everyone is lying. I'm lying right now!" Hall began to cackle to himself as his head began tilting back further and further until all Drysten could see was a rotting hole in his father's neck.

"What the fuck?" Drysten whispered as he glanced back down to his feet. The boy was gone, but Drysten stood staring into his own eyes. Or he believed them to be. But everything was wrong. The world began to spin and the blazes atop the pyres grew until the whole forest was up in flames.

"Now, Kill!" a voice yelled from above.

"Oh, yes!" Hall screamed, his head snapping back down to show his mangled and decayed face.

Drysten fell to his knees as he looked to the sky. "Who said that?"

"The one you believe in," the voice whispered. It repeated the statement over and over, quicker and louder each time before the voice became deafening. All Drysten could do was stare in the madly cackling image of his father as the man began to slowly crumble down into dust before his very eyes.

I think he's waking up, Lord!

The lines are barely holding, Arthur!

"I want to go home," Drysten began to cry.

"You... have... no... home," the voice growled.

"Lord, he's awake!" a familiar voice screamed as Drysten felt his eyes burst open. His shoulder burned, and stank when he turned his head to look at it. He saw Argyle rubbing a strange, muddy substance over it before looking back to see Dagonet and Cynwrig. Both men were covered in blood, and Drysten tried to speak before being shushed quiet by Argyle.

"We think he saved you, Lord," Cynwrig explained in a pained whisper.

Dagonet nodded. "The Gaels have done fuck all while you were asleep."

Drysten struggled to move but was helped to the edge of the table by Argyle. "How did you save me?"

Argyle pointed to Dagonet and Cynwrig before lowering his mask to reveal a strangely warm smile. He gestured to a pouch containing the foul-smelling substance now coating the wound in Drysten's shoulder.

"Of course," Drysten realized. "It would be too dangerous to use these poisons if you didn't have a way to stop them."

Argyle nodded and began applying a bandage to Drysten's shoulder.

"Get the rest of the hunters into whatever fight's going on outside," Drysten commanded through a hoarse voice.

Argyle nodded and gave Dagonet a strange look as he sauntered by.

"He knows you," Drysten stated.

Dagonet's eyes widened. "What the fuck does that mean?"

"Likely was with Abhartach when he ambushed you some time ago. The Gael told me all about it," Drysten answered.

"Your decision to work with them is confusing to say the least," Dagonet stammered. "Not to mention it's too bad the bastard didn't mention who rode out to grab you when you went under."

"I'm guessing it was you two," Drysten murmured. His placed a hand on his chest and looked between them both. "Thank you." Drysten waited a moment before he finally pressed his feet down to the ground, carefully checking to make sure he could hold his balance. Considering the strange ordeal he just endured, he was surprised to find his strength hadn't quite faded as he originally thought. "My sword?" he asked of the two men as he glanced to his side, noticing it was missing.

Cynwrig walked to the corner behind Drysten and plucked up his sword belt and quiver, dangling the arrows far in front of him.

"Careful with those. Don't want you seeing the same things I just did," Drysten whispered as he grabbed his belongings. He found it hard to look Cynwrig in the eyes as the strange vision from moments before played out in his memory.

"What did you see?" Cynwrig wondered.

Drysten shook his head. "Nothing I wish to speak."

The three men walked out of the room and down a wide corridor of stone before making their way outside. The screams of war became ever louder as they moved. Drysten peered around and immediately saw Prince Arthur on horseback with a handful of others, bellowing orders to his men fighting a large number of screaming Saxons.

"How many are there?" Drysten yelled to Dagonet.

Dagonet shrugged. "More than us. The only thing we have going for us is they madly charged into us once you did whatever you did."

Cynwrig nodded. "They're disorganized."

Drysten nodded and looked to his right, seeing Argyle and the hunters casually walking toward the right flank with their blades drawn. Drysten glimpsed toward his two friends and offered a nod before moving to join the Gaels. The hunters moved around the Powysian line, with the legionnaires giving them worried glances.

"They're with me," Drysten assured the strangers, as two men looked as though they were about to attack.

"You!" a voice screamed from behind Drysten. He turned to see a stout man wearing a plumed helmet sauntering toward him. "Get those filthy pricks into it!"

Poor wording, Drysten thought with a chuckle. For some reason, he also felt a twinge of anger toward the man when he addressed the hunters in that way. He simply scoffed and turned to Argyle. "Show them who the best fighters here really are.

Argyle nodded, and Drysten could see a smile form beneath the man's mask.

The Gaels shoved the Powysians aside as they worked their way through the back ranks of the shield wall. The first hunter to enter the fight caught a Saxon off guard, killing him easily with a quick swipe of the blade as he leapt over a Powysian legionnaire. The blade easily dug into the man's neck, sending him to the ground. More hunters followed him, their speed proving too much for most of the men who attacked them. Drysten finally found his way through and burst toward the first Saxons he saw. A big man with a bushy red beard, and an old helmet with rusted cheek plates.

The man silently took Drysten's challenge, rushing forward and swinging his sword from over his head. Drysten nimbly stepped out of the way, parrying the Saxon blade to the ground. The Saxon thrust his shield toward Drysten, missing narrowly overhead when Drysten quickly struck the man in the belly. He drove his blade into the man's stomach, causing a shriek of pain as the man fell aside. In that moment, a horn sounded behind the Saxons and they ceased their attack.

"Stay," Drysten commanded as he glanced to a pair of hunters moving to pursue. He looked back to the enemy and noticed they weren't retreating; they were simply forming a shield wall a few yards off from the Powysians.

"Gave 'em a good fight, eh?" a strange, muffled voice whispered.

Drysten turned and only saw hunters before he noticed Argyle step closer. "You?" he asked.

"Never thought of who he spoke to before you came around?" Argyle whispered.

"You could speak all this time?" Drysten asked with a chuckle.

Argyle nodded. "Had your job before you did! The king needs at least *one* person to speak with," he said in a happy tone.

"Suppose I got you demoted."

Argyle dismissively waved a hand. "We can speak more of this after these fuckers piss off back to Londinium."

"What's your given name?"

"You gave it to me. It's Argyle for some such reason."

"No," Drysten returned through a snort of amusement. "I mean the name you had before I gave you one."

Argyle smirked and returned him with a shrug as he turned away to address the hunters.

Drysten nodded and looked behind him. The Powysians were dragging their dead and wounded behind their lines before filling gaps with fresh troops.

"Where do you want us?" Argyle asked.

"Grab your bows. We've done enough for these men already," Drysten answered. "We'll stay in the back and shoot who we can. If they get overwhelmed, we'll move off back West."

"You would abandon your people?" Argyle asked in surprise.

Drysten shook his head. "They likely have more men on the way. This prince knows what he's doing."

Argyle nodded and motioned toward the stone building Drysten had woken up in.

After traversing a small ditch, Drysten found a black bow and hoisted it from the ground. After gazing over the hunters, he guessed he still had about thirty of them left. Even with Argyle's cheerful demeanor, Drysten knew he still needed to rid himself of them as soon as he could. "Find angles to hit the Saxons without risking the Powysians," Drysten commanded.

It was clear the hunters didn't care for Prince Arthur's men, as only Argyle bothered to return him with a nod. The rest gave each other subtle glances, further hinting Drysten's time with them needed to end. And soon.

"Fire when ready," Drysten shouted.

The Gaels lined up directly behind the Powysians, with Prince Arthur looking rather worried at the sight. Drysten hoped the man understood that he didn't like working alongside the Gaels either, but guessed that wasn't so. Arrows would fire every so often toward the Saxons, with a handful meeting their mark. Drysten wagered the sights of the poisons working on their comrades gave the Saxons pause. How could it not? Men changing color and choking on nothing would disturb anyone.

Anyone except Colgrin.

The sun began to illuminate more of the carnage left behind after the first Saxon charge. It seemed the added light was also making it easier for the Gaels to do their deadliest work of the whole battle. Something the Saxons noticed as well. They began to draw back and raise their shields in defiance of the oncoming Gaelic arrows.

Drysten glanced off behind the Saxon shield wall, seeing many Saxons now moving to reinforce the front line. "Aim over the shields!" he commanded. The Gaels followed the order with deadly efficiency. Saxons trying to reach the shield wall were being halted roughly thirty yards behind it, with more Saxons tripping over those felled by the Gael's arrows.

"Arthur!" Drysten yelled.

The prince turned from orientating the alignment of his men.

"More on the horizon!" Drysten shouted as he pointed to the East.

Arthur seemed to curse under his breath as he looked back and nodded.

The Powysians were banging their swords into their shields and bellowing insults toward the Saxons, but Drysten noticed they sounded more like fearful screams than those of defiance. The Saxons would likely outnumber them once the rest of their people made it into the battle.

"Argyle," Drysten whispered.

The Gael turned. "Aye, Lord?"

"Fire off the last of the arrows and move West. Go to the place Abhartach will return," Drysten commanded.

Argyle nodded. "You're makin this sound like you'll be leavin us."

Drysten nodded. "I will, but I intend to return. Abhartach will need allies if he's to return the Britons to the old ways. These Powysians are a good start."

Argyle nodded once more. "I'll let'm know, Lord. Go where we ambushed those two friends of yers when yer done here."

Drysten nodded. Piss off back to Abhartach so I can kill you all at once.

The Gaels fired every arrow they had into the Saxons before turning tail and heading back toward the wagon train. The Powysians noticed this as well, with many screaming insults into their backs as they ran off.

"They aren't fleeing," Drysten shouted. "They have other orders."

"Damn your orders!" a man screamed.

Drysten chuckled to himself before turning and making his way toward the prince.

"Drysten!" Arthur yelled. "Where are your Gaels off to?"

"Northwest, Lord Prince," Drysten explained. "Once their arrows were gone, they outlived their usefulness." Drysten lied, but knew it was better to lie for the moment then tell him the truth during the battle's aftermath. He wanted the prince totally focused on the Saxons rather than worrying about a band of Gaels who may or may not become an issue.

Arthur dismounted from his horse and approached Drysten. "We can't win. Not against this number."

Both men turned to see a long line of shields being interrupted by a break in the middle. After many shouts in a language Drysten couldn't understand, a massive man with a blood red beard walked through a gap. He raised his hands, both wielding blades of Roman-make, and began a rambunctious chant which was soon echoed by the rest of his men. It seemed the whole field was vibrating under Drysten's feet as the gloomful chorus rang out.

"God...," Arthur muttered as his eyes scanned the Saxon shields from end to end.

"No, he's not." Drysten shook his head as he turned to the prince and smiled. "I'd be able to tell."

The prince returned a perplexed glance as Drysten brought his last arrow from his bag and carefully removed the covering from its head.

"Hard to kill a man with an arrow when you have no way to fire it," Arthur noted.

Drysten smirked as he drew his father's dagger from his sword belt. "It's not the arrow I need." He carefully rubbed the arrowhead over the dagger's edge, doing his utmost to smear as much of the Gael's poison onto the blade as he could. Once satisfied he could get no more from the arrow, he thrust the tip into the ground so it could do no harm and sheathed his father's dagger.

Drysten drew in a deep breath and began to stride forward. The pain in his shoulder was beginning to come back. He felt the dull throbbing start to erupt into something more but was able to ignore it as he reached the back of the Powysian shield wall.

"Move," Drysten commanded as he nudged each man aside.

The Powysians only returned him with awkward stare as he finally made his way to the front, with Colgrin seeing him immediately.

The Saxon pointed and shouted something in his native tongue, with the rest of the Saxon shield wall erupting into laughter. To the delight of those nearby, one man even lifted his furs and began urinating into Drysten's direction.

If there's a battle, I hope we win just so I can piss on your corpse, Drysten mused. After a brief pause, he began to march toward the Saxon shield wall, head held as high as he could manage.

Colgrin nodded and gave a sarcastic bow as he thrust the point of his sword into the ground and ripped a shield away from the man beside him.

Again, the Saxon line erupted.

"Lord Drysten!" a familiar voice screamed from behind.

Drysten let out a heavy sigh as he fought the urge to turn around. He knew it was Matthew. It was too easy to pick out the man's voice. *I have wronged my people too much to cower behind your shields. I have to kill this man and save the prince who protected all of you.*

"Ah! This Briton filth wishes dance with me!" Colgrin screamed. "We will make dance for all to see!"

Who the fuck taught you the Roman tongue? Drysten thought as he shot a glare toward his enemy. Whoever it was did a horrible job.

Drysten glanced over his shoulder toward the cowering Powysians before looking back to Colgrin. His shoulder began to burn with more intensity. "We will settle it the old ways. The way of your people and of mine."

"Ha!" Colgrin screamed. "*You* kill me? You are skinny little prick. How does skinny prick kill anyone?"

Drysten smirked. "I remember the things your wife used to say about you!" he yelled until Colgrin's jovial attitude began to wane. "If anyone could recognize a skinny prick, it would certainly be you."

Colgrin's face began to contort as he placed his jeweled helmet atop his head. It was an impressive piece. Small jewels and fine metals adorned its top, with long cheek plates reaching below his jawline. His face was also covered by a mask connected on the helmet's front. It was the helmet of a king.

The enraged Saxon screamed an insult toward Drysten, though his voice was muffled by his extravagant helm. He lumbered forward. "Speak of whore again and I… I…"

"You'll stutter like a beaten child?" Drysten turned around and glanced to Arthur.

Thankfully, the prince was smart enough to understand

what Drysten needed. After Drysten turned back, he was relieved to hear the Powysians erupt into laughter of their own. Fake laughter to anyone who had just seen their scared faces, but all too real to a man who was having his manhood questioned.

"I'll rip your guts from your belly and feed them to those fucking Gaels!" Colgrin screamed as he began to rush forward.

Finally, Drysten thought as he too broke into a sprint.

"Gut him slow!" the voice commanded. It was the unmistakable speech from the god which tormented Drysten for the better part of his life. He'd learned to live with it, and this time he even agreed.

The two men quickly met in the center between the Saxon and Powysian shields. Colgrin opened the fight with a massive upward swing of his blade, narrowly missing Drysten as he eased back and returned one of his own, glancing off the Saxon shield.

I need to wear him out, Drysten thought. *I'll never beat the brute with one arm.*

Colgrin hefted his shield and slammed it into Drysten's left side, knocking the Briton to the ground with ease. Drysten sprang up to hear laughter from both Colgrin and the Saxon shield wall. Nothing could be heard from the men behind him.

You always hated to fight with a shield, Hall whispered.

Drysten took a step forward, feigning low before bringing his blade high into Colgrin's shield. The force of it surprised the Saxon, who stumbled back a pace as small splinters flew from the wood and metal.

"You are *stronger* than most Briton," Colgrin said with a laugh. He pointed his Roman blade toward Drysten. "Not strong enough!"

"Care to make this interesting?" Drysten replied through a smile.

Colgrin lowered his blade and cocked his head to the side. "What way?"

His Roman is painful to listen to. Drysten glanced to the

Powysians before lowering his blade as well. "Why are you here?" he knowingly asked.

"To conquer! To create kingdom to rival great Rome!" Colgrin screamed to his men, who roared with approval.

Drysten stepped closer. "What if I could give you Powys, right here, if you beat me?"

Colgrin slowly turned back with obvious interest. "How would a pup do this?"

Drysten smirked as he gestured a hand toward the Powysian shield wall. "I am Prince Ambrosius Aurelianus. I am the heir to the throne, and if you beat me, I will swear my allegiance to you. I will fight your wars and help you create a rival to Rome."

"All I do is win? I win and you did this?" Colgrin whispered in obvious interest.

Drysten nodded. "I simply ask your people go back to Londinium if *I* win. They leave here and don't return for... one year." It was Drysten's hope he could quell the threat posed by both Germanus and Abhartach within a year. Either way, it wouldn't matter if he could not.

Colgrin released the most riotous, howling laugh Drysten had ever heard.

"The deal is off unless you turn to your men and tell them my terms," Drysten insisted.

Colgrin finally finished displaying his amusement and returned a polite bow before turning and screaming the agreement to his people. The first unintelligible statement was received with the Saxons screaming at the top of their lungs while slamming their axes and swords into their shields. Colgrin gave a brief glance to Drysten and gestured a hand before the second statement, which received howling laughter as Colgrin turned back to face his opponent.

They won't be laughing when they see my poison do its work, Drysten thought with a smile.

"After you," Colgrin said with a bow.

Drysten nodded and raised his blade, now unsheathing

his father's dagger as well. He stole a quick glance to the dagger to make certain it had the strange poison coating its edge. It did, and Drysten couldn't help but smile when he saw it.

Colgrin let out a roar as he rushed forward, swinging both his shield and sword with a mad rage. The fervor was undoubtedly brought on by Drysten's empty promise, but Drysten couldn't have cared any less. He knew he just needed to break the man's skin and let the poison do its work.

Drysten parried Colgrin's sword and sidestepped away from the lumbering swing of the Saxon's shield. The heaviness of his own blade was becoming more apparent from the hole in his opposite shoulder. Colgrin wheeled around and brought down another overhead swing, only for Drysten to step back a pace before lunging forward with a swing of his own. Colgrin raised his blade in defiance, and that was when Drysten struck. The Saxon's skin on his sword arm only showed for a moment, but it was all Drysten needed. With a short stroke of the dagger, a small trickle of blood began running down Colgrin's arm.

"Ha!" Colgrin yelled. "Your little tooth does nothing to me!" he yelled as he looked to the small stream of blood oozing from his wrist.

Drysten smirked and took two slow paces backward. "It was all which was needed," he replied through a cool tone.

Colgrin paused and tilted his head to the side as he slowly glanced down to his arm. That was when Drysten knew the Saxon understood what had just been done to him.

Drysten jabbed forward, only seeking to prevent the man from giving his men new commands to begin an assault on the Powysians. The blow was deflected away with Colgrin's shield. Drysten could see the man's gaze darting between himself and the Saxon shield wall. He began to speak once more before being halted by Drysten swiping low with his sword, clipping the man's ankle.

It's already working, Drysten guessed. *He's becoming slow.*

Colgrin stumbled back and collected himself for a moment. He released a bloodcurdling roar toward Drysten and attempted to rush forward but tripped over nothing and landed on his knees. Drysten kicked the Saxon's shield away and exposed his off hand to the air as he lunged forward with the dagger. It sliced Colgrin's arm, cutting its way up from his elbow to his shoulder.

Colgrin began to gurgle and wheeze, but Drysten knew he needed to kill him in a way which would satisfy the Saxons. They could never know he had cheated the man, or they would no doubt rape their way through Powys.

"You… fuck—"

Drysten brought his sword down into the Saxon's neck, sending Colgrin to the ground.

The field was silent.

"Go back to Londinium!" Drysten shouted to the Saxons. "The Morrigan required a king! And a king she has *taken!*" He kneeled beside the corpse at his feet and swiped his blade into the man's neck until it separated the head from the body. He slowly brought the fine crown away and lifted Colgrin's head toward the Saxons, all of which were looking to one another for guidance. He tossed it forward, landing just at the feet of the closest man standing opposite him. All that was left for him to do was wait and see what response this would garner.

A horn sounded, and another break was created in the middle of the Saxons. Drysten glanced back to Arthur to see him ordering the spacing between the Powysian shields tightened. He looked back and watched three men walking toward him, none armed. To his surprise, one was the man he thought he'd sent to the Saxon afterlife.

Drysten hid his shock and stuck his sword and dagger into the ground before approaching. "Do you speak the Roman Language? The language of the Britons?"

One burly looking man with a golden chain showing under his pitch-black beard returned a nod. All three men looked furious.

"The deal was struck. Now leave us!" Drysten shouted.

"Lord Drysten," a familiar voice whispered as it approached from behind.

Matthew settled in at Drysten's side. "Poison?"

Drysten nodded, but did not return Matthew's stare.

The three Saxons stopped about ten yards off. The man with the golden chain stepped forward after saying something in his native language to the one Drysten guessed to be Ethelric.

"He said to keep them in formation," Matthew whispered.

Drysten nodded.

"You fought well, Briton," the Saxon began. "What's your name?"

"Prince Ambrosius Aurelianus. Of Powys," Drysten answered. He was pleased Matthew didn't do any more than glance to him.

The Saxon grumbled something under his breath. "Well, Prince Ambrosius Aurelianus of Powys, it seems my father made you a deal."

"A deal you are honor bound to uphold," Drysten replied in earnest. "You have my name. What's yours?"

After a pause in which the Saxon glared into Drysten's eyes, he finally turned to the other two men behind him. "We are the three sons of Colgrin."

Drysten looked over the three. The one who spoke was clearly younger judging by the lack of wear on his face. Then there was the one with no beard, and another with a huge red beard mirroring his father. "Your name."

The Saxon nodded. "My name is Cenred." He stepped closer and eyed Matthew before turning his attention back to Drysten. "We will honor the agreement," he stated before turning away. "For a time."

Matthew's eyes went wide as he turned and waved to Arthur. "How long is a time?" the priest questioned.

Cenred glanced over his shoulder. "We will have peace until the spring rains arrive."

"The deal was for a year," Drysten insisted. "Your father —"

"Is dead and can no longer be king. Isn't there something about three kings you Britons like to speak of?" Cenred asked with a smile.

Drysten didn't understand what the Saxon was trying to get at and peered to Matthew.

The priest nodded. "You speak of something the Christians believe. Not all Britons are Christians."

Cenred shrugged. "I care so little there are no words for it." He stepped forward and jabbed a finger into Drysten's chest. "We will give you until spring. No longer."

Drysten glanced to Matthew before returning his gaze to that of Cenred's. "Deal," he muttered under his breath.

Cenred returned a polite bow and looked to his two brothers before waving for the Saxons shield wall to disperse.

"One more thing," Drysten began. "Which one is Ethelric?"

The man with no beard began to smile as he turned to face the two Britons. "I am Ethelric."

Drysten smiled as he began to turn away. "The Morrigan came remarkably close to meeting you. You are marked for her now," he whispered. "We will be meeting again."

Ethelric seemed somewhat distraught at the idea, but Drysten really had no idea what he was saying. He simply wanted to play some sort of mind game with the Saxons before he would face them in the future.

The Saxons all turned and began moving back East as Drysten faced the Powysians alongside Matthew.

And with that, the Saxons were defeated.

***

Ceneus led Garbonian and his officers from the baths, quickly making their way toward Eboracum's principia. It was nice being able to use the old building now that Germanus had fled with Eidion. Scouts reported they reached the nearby Vicus of Isurium.

But that wasn't why this meeting was being called. A Powysian messenger had ridden East with a disturbing message.

"Send word out. All able-bodied men are to join us at Glanoventa," Ceneus ordered. A handful of riders were waiting for such instructions just outside of the Principia.

The Dozen men nodded in purposeful unison and began to march back to their horses near the main gate of the inner fortress.

Garbonian tapped Ceneus' shoulder. "How many can we expect to meet us there?"

"Expect?" Ceneus asked, considering his answer for a moment. "I expect nobody to arrive. We've burned many bridges due to Germanus' cruel ways. I could hope for about five hundred."

"Out of how many?"

"If all were to show up, we could not only mount a defense, but chase them back into the deepest parts of Hibernia," Ceneus flatly answered. "You forget that I rule over the most populated bits of Britannia, brother."

Garbonian shot him a disbelieving stare. "The messenger spoke of Abhartach having two-thousand men..."

"I have much more, though most will not be reluctant to join us. In any case, I would like to see a thousand trickling into that area around the time of the battle."

The group moved into the building, quickly finding the crowded main hallway and passed by the men awaiting their orders. It was an odd mix, with Guayrdian, Saxon, Frisian, and Briton men under Ceneus' command. But nobody would be able to question their fighting abilities, however diverse their backgrounds.

The entered the open-aired where they were met by yet more men. But these men were different. They were the king's and his alone. They nearly looked like Romans, and were possibly the best fighters in the North. That is, if there were no Powysians roaming the northern wilds too.

"Thank you all for arriving so promptly," Ceneus began, turning to face the small crowd. "I know this was short notice."

He noticed the Guayrdians peered at one another awkwardly, likely because they didn't understand the Roman tongue; the most commonly spoken language of Ceneus' commanders.

"Abhartach will soon return with the main body of his army at his back. In addition to that rather inconvenient truth, the bishop now holds Isurium. Our job is to defeat them both."

"Who will aid us?" Gaius asked as he slowly sauntered out from a dimly lit corner. "What help do we have?"

Aside from who is already here, the Powysians will field an army of their own. But so far as I can see it, what we have, is what we have."

Gaius cursed under his breath before raising his eyeline back to the king. "It won't be enough," he snapped, earning an awkward glance from some of the other officers.

"It will have to be," Ceneus shot back.

He looked away and tried his damndest to find the right words of encouragement, but his mind seemed to be failing him. All he was mustering was an awkward silence couped with a similarly vacant look which he wondered mimicked Drysten's.

I wonder where he fits into all this...?

"If I may, brother," Garbonian said, stepping forward but waiting for Ceneus' approval to fully speak. He nodded in gratitude before turning to the crowd. "We have an advantage over them, which they do not see. Or maybe they *do* see it, and expect us not to use it."

The men all eagerly stared at Garbonian's imposing figure as he let his words hang in the air.

"They are masters of the hunt. They are above all in fighting in the wilderness. It is their existence, after all. They know no other way of combat, but they are so empowered by the shadows of trees and tall grasses that we have no hope of winning by fighting them in their places of strength."

"How the fuck is that an advantage?" Gaius hissed. "You Guayrdians are no better than —"

"Silence!" Ceneus boomed. He felt the veins in his neck throbbing from the intensity. "I will have no more of it."

Garbonian grumbled something under his breath, likely a curse from the Old Ways if the king knew his brother, and continued speaking. "We simply don't fight them there. We meet them where they make landfall."

"Do we have time to garrison Glanoventa?" Gwrast wondered.

Garbonian nodded. "There have been rather nasty easterly winds of late." His face contorted into that same jovial smile Ceneus remembered form his youth. "We have enough men to meet them there and possibly strengthen the vicus' defenses beforehand as well."

There was a murmur of assent which made Ceneus' heart nearly stall from relief. These men could simply march part of the way and slip out of the marching column in the night if they felt strongly enough about the prospect of defeat. But he saw no reluctance in their eyes.

Yet.

"That's the best way to go about it, then," Gwrast said, turning to the men. "Ready your men for a Western march!" he barked, causing the warriors to turn and begin shuffling their way out.

The rumble of approval faded out as the men departed. The only man who looked reluctant was Gaius, who likely didn't want to have to face the Gaels for a third time. Nobody could blame him, really, and Ceneus made the quiet decision to keep him in the rearguard, to keep him from having to face them.

"Brother," the king began, turning to Garbonian. "I have a separate set of instructions for you."

"That is…?"

"You will harass the bishop and his men," Ceneus explained. "I will not have father's only two surviving sons at risk in this war."

"That's the most foolish thing —"

"I don't care," Ceneus cut in. "I owe you everything."

Garbonian went silent for a moment before suddenly taking a step closer. "You will need every man you can get…"

"Jorrit!" the king called out.

The Frisian entered and bowed, silently waiting for his orders.

"I need you to find Octha and Ebissa. Promise those two Saxon bastards they can have whatever they want if they join us."

"I don't know that they will…"

"I don't care what it costs. You tell them that, and I'm sure you will have no issues."

Jorrit bowed and made his way outside.

"I have a request, brother," Garbonian suddenly blurted out. "I know this is not the time, but may I see… her…"

Ceneus felt a pit form in his stomach. He knew his features had gone stiff and he likely looked a bit more pale than usual. But he knew the right thing to do, was allow his brother to see the wife he almost had. He nodded, but said nothing.

"I have no intentions of —"

"I know," Ceneus assured him. "I know."

Ceneus released a long sigh as he gestured for his brother to follow. The two men turned until Ceneus halted and called for his two sons to join them. Gwrast and Mor both glanced at one another before following.

"They should hear of their older brother," Ceneus explained.

Garbonian returned a subtle nod and followed Ceneus as

they roamed toward the Roman baths.

"Heledd would never forgive me if she weren't able to learn of how her oldest son was fairing," Ceneus concluded.

He remembered the day of their wedding, and the tears his wife shed when she was told Dyfnwal would be banished from Ebrauc along with Garbonian. In truth, Ceneus saved the boy's life, despite a nasty wound his nephew gave him during the war for the crown. He simply never mustered the nerve to point that fact out. It always felt like if he had, then it would be him seeking her devotion as some sort of reward. It would cheapen what feelings he hoped she would naturally come to feel for him, even if it was hopeless to dream of them. And by some miracle, it actually happened, even if it took kicking out a Christian bishop to do so.

Bishop Germanus wanted Dyfnwal and Garbonian executed, but Ceneus decreed this wasn't an option. He went to war with them both, but he never once hated them. This lack of hate was likely why Dyfnwal even had the chance to wound him in the first place.

"Do you believe she will speak to me?" Garbonian whispered.

Ceneus nodded. "She thought of you often. It was only somewhat recently when she looked at me with any kind of affection in her eyes."

The answer seemed to bring a hint of satisfaction to Garbonian, but the man was smart enough to hide it. He did a poor job, but Ceneus appreciated the gesture all the same.

They finally made it into the baths where Heledd and a handful of women were sewing cloaks for the officers on their way to war. She produced a smile as she saw Ceneus, then noticed Garbonian and began turning red in the face.

"Wife," Ceneus greeted through an awkward tone.

Heledd nodded, her eyes fixed on the large man standing beside him.

"It has been a long time," Garbonian murmured.

Heledd nodded and placed the cloak she had been patch-ing onto the table in front of her. She rose and looked at both her sons with a smile before looking back to Ceneus. "Why—?"

"You need to hear of Dyfnwal," Ceneus interrupted. He didn't mean to, but his nerves had made him antsy. The silence as everyone watched the woman move from the table toward them was torture for the man.

Heledd glanced to Garbonian. "Is... he well?"

Garbonian nodded. "He is. Took a wife a few years ago. You're a grandmother."

Heledd smiled, but it was clear to Ceneus she wasn't sure how much happiness she should display in front of him.

Ceneus patted Garbonian on the arm before looking at his wife. "I will leave you for a short time." He turned to his sons. "You need to hear of your older brother. There is a decent chance you will inherit this kingdom in the coming days. It would be irresponsible if you did so without knowing of the future king to the North."

Both of Ceneus' boys nodded as he left the room. Eliwlod was milling about outside with Rodric and two others Ceneus didn't know, all of which gave him a dutiful bow as the king leaned against the doorway.

He was somewhat surprised by how brief the conversation was, as Heledd exited the baths with the other women only a few moments later. She was clearly happy, judging by the beaming smile on her face.

"Thank you, husband," she whispered. Her eyes were becoming watery as she embraced Ceneus and walked toward the city.

Ceneus returned to the baths to see Garbonian speaking with his nephews as he entered.

Gwrast and Mor returned their father an awkward glance before Gwrast stepped forward. "Uncle," he began. "You have another son as well."

Garbonian turned back in surprise. "If you're going to try to pin that fucking *Eidion* on me—"

"His name is Eliwlod," Gwrast interrupted. "I just assumed Eidion spawned from dirt." Everyone in the room shared a laugh before Gwrast turned to the door. "Enter!"

Eliwlod did so, looking uncomfortable as he shuffled toward Gwrast. "Am I needed?" He noticed the way Garbonian looked over him as he approached and peered to Ceneus through the side of his eye.

Ceneus turned to his brother. "He was kept far from Germanus. There are only a few who know he is yours."

"Fucking what?" Eliwlod exclaimed.

"You're a prince," Ceneus returned with a smirk. He expected confusion, but the sudden outburst from his nephew proved to be more entertaining. "I am happy you're finally meeting him," he turned to Gwrast, "though I would have done this at another time, son."

Gwrast shrugged. "Mother is gone. Figured this was as good a time as any. Doubt she'd want to know what our *esteemed* uncle was up to before he..." Gwrast gave an awkward glance to Garbonian. "Before he left."

Garbonian chuckled as he approached Eliwlod. "Your mother was beautiful. I remember her well." He produced a warm smile toward his newfound son.

"Not beautiful enough to take her with you?" Eliwlod hissed. The sharpness in his tone caught everyone off guard. "She would tell me stories of my father when I was young. She never named him, but she told me how *great* he was." He stepped closer and spit at Garbonian's feet. "She loved you even when the fevers took her. She told me she'd *dream* of you as they got worse and caused her to sleep for hours during the day."

Garbonian's face was turning white as he seemed to shrink where he stood. "I... loved—"

"You loved visiting her in the tavern when my grandfather would close up for the night. You loved meeting her out of view." Eliwlod's cracking voice betrayed his sadness. "You *never* cared for her."

"I did, El—"

"No! You simply viewed her as a secret plaything!" Eliwlod screamed. "I don't care to know you any more than you cared to know her." He turned to leave, but halted as he faced his father one last time. "Perhaps if you took us with you, she would have lived. Perhaps if she had the comfort of a queen, she wouldn't have died from the cold in her sleep." He turned and stormed out, leaving everyone with gaping mouths.

Ceneus stepped toward his brother, only to be halted by a gently raised hand as Garbonian hung his head. "The boy is right. I had the opportunity to take her with me. I chose not to."

The men went silent as the thuds of Eliwlod's stomping feet disappeared into the night.

CHAPTER FIFTEEN

Drysten wiped his brow as he glanced behind him. It was a beautiful, late-summer's day in the Southern portions of Powys. Prince Aurelianus left most of his men under the command of Matthew and elected to bring Drysten back to his family a few days after Colgrin had been dealt with.

"Looking forward to seeing them all?" Arthur asked. He rode beside Drysten with Dagonet and Cynwrig behind them.

Drysten glanced out to the surrounding grassland but neglected to speak. The irony of it all was how much he spoke while he was once surrounded by men who couldn't carry a conversation with him. Now that he was around those who could, he struggled.

"You did them proud. Not at first," Arthur whispered. "But you did."

"Let's hope they agree," Drysten returned.

Arthur chuckled. "Galahad already worships you. I saw to that while I was home last. Made sure to tell of your bravery and—"

"That's enough," Drysten interrupted. The idea his son would ever worship him after the things he'd done to his own people was absurd. He knew it would be foolish to let himself think that was even possible.

Arthur opened his mouth to speak but simply responded with a nod.

"What about you? You mentioned having a wife," Drysten asked. The awkward silence was nagging on him. He knew he wasn't going to be able to get away with not speaking at all.

Arthur produced a warm smile and looked to the sky.

"She truly is a marvelous woman."

Drysten smiled, seeing the same look in Arthur's eyes people said Drysten had when he'd look on Isolde. "Tell me of her."

Arthur nodded. "You may have met her before. She's King Ceneus' daughter."

Drysten let out a gasp he hadn't intended to as he quickly turned toward the Powysian. "You married into that family? Don't you know of their—"

"I know full well," Arthur interrupted as he returned a reassuring nod. "I know what the family took from you. I understand that fully. But you cannot possibly think they're all like their father. Or Eidion for that matter."

"I never said that. What I mean is you inherited more problems than you may realize." Drysten ran a hand over his chin, feeling the stubble rub against his thumb. "I mean no disrespect, but I can't imagine any woman would be worth that."

Arthur chuckled to himself as he tilted his head to the side. "I may be mad, but I'd say she's worth it. Wouldn't you feel the same if it were Isolde? I seem to remember you being rather proud of fishing her out of the sea."

"You make it sound like I rescued her from Neptune's bed. I merely sailed to Frisia."

"You would think Isolde worth the trouble. You won't be able to change my mind of that," Arthur declared with a wink.

Drysten felt a strange mix of guilt at the thought of not knowing how he was about to feel when he saw his wife again. He loved her from the bottom of his heart but knew doing what was best for her may be to stay away.

"Villa's right this way. See the small crowd?" Arthur asked. His tone was happier than Drysten expected.

Drysten nodded suspiciously as he peered between the strangers and the prince.

Arthur's smile turned more serious. "Those people are there for you, Drysten. Or should I say, Lord Drysten."

Drysten returned the prince a look of confusion, and yet

more awkward silence.

"I sent messengers ahead. These people wish to see the Saxon killer. The one who ripped the crown from Colgrin's head," Arthur whispered.

"I didn't even keep the crown. Threw the damned thing to the ground beside the bastard's head," Drysten replied as he glanced back to Dagonet and Cynwrig.

Arthur nodded and reached into one of the large sacks tied to the side of his horse. After a moment, he produced the helmet which once rested on the heads of Saxon kings. He eyed it briefly before tossing it to Drysten, who caught it.

"Lord Prince..." Drysten began. The crown had clearly been polished and shined before given to him. The cheek plates nearly looked reforged, and the jewels likely hadn't sparkled in this way for an exceptionally long time.

"What's the matter? Afraid to lead again?" Arthur asked with a scoff. "You'll get no pity out of me on that account."

Drysten hadn't thought of it, but that was exactly what he was afraid of. Those he led ended up living in squalor after his imprisonment. Two men who helped raise him had dangled at the edge of a rope, and a third who followed him faithfully was tortured and drowned for carrying on Drysten's fight. Not only that, but his wife looked as though she aged twenty years, and he ended up offering one of his friends up for slaughter.

As far as Drysten was concerned, he was a horrible leader.

"You're a lord of Powys now, Drysten. You seem to forget I owed you for saving my life some time ago. Not to mention I now owe you for possibly saving me again. "Arthur produced a warm smile and gestured for Drysten to lead the four men toward the small crowd.

Drysten didn't know why, but he nodded and spurred his horse forward. What drove him to the crowd was a mystery, as every fiber of his being wanted to turn tail and run back to the Gaels. He trotted on toward the onlookers. To Drysten's dismay, more could be seen rounding the corner of a sprawling villa off to his left.

Why so many? he wondered.

He could see banners over the heads of the crowd, with the people in the back making room for someone to pass through. As Drysten got a better look, he saw the depiction of a wheel, with eight red spokes connecting to a red center, resting over a golden background.

"Our sigil," Arthur explained. "Taken from the men my father led for Rome."

Drysten glanced back and nodded. "Does that mean your father is here as well? Is he who I swear allegiance to?"

Arthur shook his head. "He is here, but you'll swear to Uther. My uncle."

Drysten nodded once more and looked back to the crowd. His heart skipped, as there stood Isolde right in front, holding the hand of his jubilant son.

A voice whispered into Drysten's mind the moment he saw them both. "You'll disappoint them all. You always find a way."

Drysten shrugged off the whispers and halted his horse. He dismounted about twenty yards off from the smiling faces. He looked on his wife and saw a hint of happiness but didn't understand why. He grabbed his horse's bridle and began leading him the rest of the way. Galahad immediately broke away from Isolde and ran up to him, clamping onto Drysten's leg.

"Father!" Galahad screamed.

Drysten couldn't help but smile. "You've grown since I last saw you!

"Mama said you'd notice!" Galahad happily replied with a beaming gaze.

"What else did she say about my return?" Drysten wondered. He glanced up to see Isolde walking forward with a very Roman-looking man standing in front of one of the Powysian banners.

Drysten glanced to the man before standing and looking on his wife. "I've... missed you," he whispered. His voice sounded hoarse, likely from his nerves.

Isolde produced a half-smile. "Are you back for good?"

Drysten glanced to Arthur, standing behind him. Arthur nodded and smiled before gesturing back to Isolde. "I believe I am."

Isolde slowly walked over and embraced him. Drysten could hear her sobbing lightly into his chest as he returned her embrace. "You're... bigger than you were the last time I saw you," she said as she looked over Drysten's chest and arms.

Drysten nodded. "I had help regaining my strength."

"From the Gael's?" Isolde whispered.

Drysten nodded.

"Surely you didn't eat—"

"No!" Drysten interrupted with wide eyes. "Those filthy beasts... no I didn't. They know the old ways, and gave me strange herbs. I hunted my own food while they... hunted theirs..."

Isolde glanced to Arthur before looking back and nodding.

"My lady," the Roman who walked with Isolde whispered. "I don't mean to interrupt, but I really must speak with your husband.

"May I join you?" Isolde questioned.

The man nodded. "I'm sure Lord Drysten would enjoy that very much." The man smiled before turning his gaze toward Arthur. "What's this? You're too old to hug your damned uncle?" he roared.

Drysten glanced to Isolde before looking back to the Roman. "Uncle? So you're Lord Uther?" he asked in a timid voice.

"This newcomer insults me already!" Uther roared through a laughing and boisterous tone. "The man calls me a lord!" he yelled to the crowd, who quietly chuckled. "I am not a lord any longer, newcomer! I was given the crown of Powys once my father died and that bastard Ceneus was deemed unfit to rule Britannia himself."

"My apologies, Lord King," Drysten stammered.

Uther smiled. "I was merely toying with you. I miss the days of being a humble lord." He turned his attention to Arthur. "Your father and my son will be returning from Rome within the week. Hopefully, they'll be bringing some form of aid along with them."

Arthur smiled before looking back to Drysten. "We should take this discussion inside," he said as he gestured for two Powysian guards to come forward and lead the horses to the villa. "That may be the best news we could have hoped for!"

"One can only hope!" Uther said as he clapped a hand to Arthur's shoulder.

Drysten and Isolde held hands during the short walk, with Drysten occasionally having to wave toward the crowd as strangers shouted his name and demanded he display Colgrin's helmet. He awkwardly raised the fine piece up over his head, receiving joyous shouts from the people.

"How'd you manage killing him?" Uther questioned as they entered the walls of the villa. "Only saw the man once, but even I wouldn't have fought him in single combat."

Drysten chuckled. "I cheated."

"How so?"

"Gaelic poison coated on my father's dagger." Drysten patted the dagger at his waist. "Pricked his arm and merely had to wait until his strength began to leave him."

Uther scoffed and thumped a hand onto Drysten's shoulder, causing the throbbing of the arrow wound to begin again. "Must have been a sight."

"It was for the Saxons. His sons apparently won't be an issue until the spring."

Uther clicked his tongue and glanced toward Arthur. "They tend to break their word."

The group wandered their way into the courtyard of an elaborate villa. The main doorway was adorned with more Powysian banners on either side, with heavily armed soldiers in Roman armor wandering through the enclosed area. It was the closest thing to a real Roman villa Drysten had seen in roughly twenty years.

"Impressive, isn't it?" Uther said as he nodded his head and gestured toward the scenery.

Drysten nodded as he examined the finely trimmed trees and bushes. Servants were roaming from one area to another, all carrying on with their day to day tasks. "It is, Lord King. I never thought I would see anything like it outside the Empire."

Uther smiled. "We have been fortunate. We only had the Saxons to deal with these past few years, and even they wouldn't dare stray too far into Powys. We have the strongest army they'll likely face here."

"And what role am I to play in all of this?" Drysten wondered.

"That remains to be seen," Uther responded in a reassuring tone. "There are some here who would follow you, but others who would need a little coaxing."

"I find it hard to believe any of my men would return to my service," Drysten returned. The idea Diocles would ever serve under his command was wishful thinking at best. The Greek's last words were one of the many things which played over and over in his mind.

"I may," a familiar voice stated from behind.

Drysten turned to see his old friend, clad in fine Roman mail and a plumed helmet under his arm, marching toward him. Diocles' one eye was uncovered, while the one which was taken now had a cloth wrapped over and around his head. Drysten's heart leapt as he noticed the other familiar faces from Drysten's past stepping up from behind him. His oldest friend, Bors the Younger, as well as the Cretans and Magnus were all looking back at him.

Bors let out a snort as he stepped toward Drysten. "You look like an ass' backside."

"You're beginning to look much like your father," Drysten quipped with a grin.

Bors scrunched his massive face. "I'll kill you."

Magnus smiled and nudged his way past Bors. "It's good to have you back, Lord."

Drysten shook Magnus' hand and looked on both the Cretans. "You're here as well?"

Paulus nodded. "Just arrived. Matthew sent a message to Maewyn saying where you were. I'd assume that means others know as well, Lord."

"Doesn't seem like Germanus will be able to reach me here," Drysten responded as he eyed a small band of Powysians marching past the villa's entrance in formation.

Diocles stepped forward and looked to Magnus and the Cretans. "Get the ship ready. We have work to do," then looked to Drysten, "You're needed North. We need to fix a mistake which was made."

"Mine," Drysten agreed.

Diocles nodded before looking to Uther. "Lord King, I mean no disrespect, but we may need to forgo the pleasantries and get the men moving."

Lord Uther scoffed. "You will wait. Our ships haven't seen any of Abhartach's vessels near Britannia. All remain docked where they were."

Drysten let out a heavy sigh. "No, he's right. We need to leave as soon as we can manage."

Uther tilted his head to the side and glanced toward Diocles. "You know… I have half a mind to let Ebrauc burn." Arthur's mouth fell agape as took an urgent pace forward. "The fools brought the Christians in. Not to mention the many deals they've made with those damned Saxons who once fought for Colgrin."

Diocles placed a hand onto Arthur's forearm and shuffled in front of the king. "Lord King, the Saxons Octha and Ebissa are trustworthy. Believe it or not, they hated Colgrin just as much as you did. Their people were massacred by a slaver on the orders of him." Diocles looked to Drysten. "Do you remember Servius?"

Drysten nodded. "Hard not to." He glanced to Isolde and immediately saw her eyes go a little wider as she ran a hand over the slave brand on her forearm.

"He fought for Colgrin. He holds some form of leadership among the Saxons, but nobody has been able to explain it to me," Diocles added.

Lord Uther rubbed a hand to his chin. "Brings light to the recent reports I've been given. Slaves were seen in Northern Cantia fighting for the Saxons. Men with tribal markings from across the water."

Arthur sighed. "There were a handful fighting against us as well. The markings are from the Veneti tribe of Armorica."

King Uther scoffed. "My brother's people?"

Arthur nodded with a saddened grimace.

Diocles leaned in toward Drysten and began to whisper. "King Uther is the brother to King Aldrien of Armorica. They've had their differences regarding Rome for quite some time."

"Differences?" Drysten muttered.

Diocles nodded. "Aldrien's been in open rebellion against Rome for years. Started not long after Constantine was killed. Aldrien supported him and refused to swear loyalty to Honorius. Been fighting ever since."

Drysten nodded. "Hard to blame him when you hear some stories of the boy-emperor."

Lord Uther glanced to Drysten from the corner of his eye. "He swore to fight for Rome. Now he fights against her. To break one's oath isn't honorable. Especially when it puts your people in danger."

"How has it?" Drysten wondered.

"If Rome was protecting his people instead of fighting them, then maybe this slaver wouldn't be able to take my brother's tribesmen and throw them against us." Uther pointed a finger into his own chest as he looked to Arthur. "Your grandfather would have been rather displeased by what's been happening since his passing."

Drysten turned a quizzical glance to Diocles.

"Constantine," the Greek whispered. "The usurper."

Drysten had never considered the fact that Constantine left behind family to rule in his stead while he made his move on the Roman Empire. The idea that he was standing in the presence of people who truly had the blood of kings flowing through their veins was strange. These people carried themselves in ways King Ceneus never could.

"What was he like?" Drysten blurted out. "What was Constantine like?"

Uther smiled. "What stories have you heard of him?"

Drysten wasn't sure he should say, but Uther didn't seem like he was ill-tempered. "My father fought for him." He gestured a hand toward Bors. "His too. They both would tell me of times he would drink himself under a table then go out and swat around the Romans Honorius sent against him. They both said he was fierce. But they also told me how he died."

"The stories are true," Uther replied. "He died wearing a priest's robe in a city which never wished for him to be there."

Drysten saw the sadness in Uther's eyes.

"He enjoyed his drink, as you've said. He enjoyed many things of that nature. But he was brave and taught his boys to rule well." Uther tilted his head to the side. "I just wish Aldrien paid him more attention," he muttered.

Drysten sighed. "Lord King, I went across the water five years ago and saw Rome's strength. That strength lies in the places they still call home. I was then forced to return and saw the areas they had left behind and were forced to flee from. The strength people speak of only exists in memories and stories now. They have kept up the appearance of a great empire spanning countless kingdoms, but that is all it is now."

"Just an appearance?" Uther wondered.

Drysten nodded. "Your brother may have seen their weakness and understood the Romans could no longer protect them. He saw that Rome's time is likely coming to an end."

Lord Uther's smile faded as he glanced to his feet. "Doesn't mean we have to help it along."

***

Gaius glanced down to his father's armor, freshly mended from its long years buried in a vacant grave. He was pleased with the job the local blacksmith of Petuaria had done in restoring it. It was no longer encrusted with muck and dirt. The sun was able to glint off the brass bull placed into the center of his chest. The leather was a darker color than it had once been, but now looked worn instead of ancient.

Gaius lifted his gaze and watched Bishop Germanus shuffle from one side of the dimly lit room to the other, rubbing his chin and grumbling to himself as he moved. The man was a terror in Gaius' eyes, but he could prove useful.

"The Guayrdians have how many?" Germanus asked as he perked his head up.

Gaius glanced to Citrio at his side before stepping forward. "Likely two hundred. Your people did well in the ambush."

"Gah! That's two hundred failures," Germanus shouted toward Eidion, standing in the corner. "In any case, we can rectify those failures soon. When will they be here?"

"They will not be here, Your Excellency," Gaius returned as he pointed a finger toward the ground. "They will merely begin harassing your patrols near here. Their only aim is to keep you occupied while Ceneus marches past," he explained.

"When will that be?"

"He will be doing so soon."

"How many men did you bring with you?"

Gaius smirked. "I have fifty men. My father's mixed with a handful of former soldiers of Rheged."

"How did you get those fools to fight for you?" Germanus asked in shock.

Gaius smirked. "Mentioned something about their king being freed if they helped you. There could be more on the way, as messengers were sent out to the Southern portions of Rheged as well."

"Hm," Germanus muttered as he shifted his gaze onto

Eidion. "You remember the war with Rheged?"

Eidion shrugged and shook his head.

"Figured as much. You were merely a child when your father beat them into submission," Germanus stated. "They were able warriors. We only won because of those damned Powysians."

Eidion rolled his eyes and scoffed as he glanced to Gaius.

"Your Excellency, I don't believe the Powysians will be joining Ceneus anywhere near Eboracum. Before I left, I heard the king mention they would be meeting them," Gaius divulged.

Germanus looked back to Eidion. "Get the men ready to move. You'll kill every last one of Garbonian's people, but leave him alive. You'll make an example of him to the rest of the fools."

Eidion smiled and nodded and turned to leave.

Strange the man didn't speak a word. If it weren't so odd, I'd consider it a blessing, Gaius thought. He looked to Citrio. "We'll be going with him. Get the men ready."

"Yes, Lord," he replied.

After both Eidion and Citrio left the room, Gaius slowly strolled toward the bishop. "What of Maewyn?"

Germanus sighed and pointed toward a door at the opposite end of the room. "Threw him down below. Of all the people to spy for Ceneus..."

Gaius nodded. "It seems he holds a soft spot for the ones who worship the old ways."

Germanus neglected to respond. It seemed to Gaius the bishop actually felt a significant amount of sadness for Maewyn.

"Do you remember the day you baptized me, Your Excellency?" Gaius questioned, changing the subject.

Germanus adopted a quizzical, yet pleased gaze. "I... do, yes."

"Good," Gaius replied. "I just wanted to be certain you remembered we are of the same people."

"I can hardly blame you. What with all this treachery going around," Germanus said with a chuckle. "You will have a place high up on the ladder once we secure our position here. Ceneus is a fool, but I will be surrounding myself with those who prove not to be."

"Perfect," Gaius replied.

Bishop Germanus extended his hand bearing the ring signifying his position in the Christian Church. Gaius knelt and kissed the ring, knowing he just swore himself to a man who his father had hated. But it was not Germanus who killed his father, it was Drysten.

And Drysten must die.

CHAPTER SIXTEEN

Drysten spent a day getting himself cleaned up and ready to join the rest of his men. He hadn't realized it at the time, but Diocles had mentioned a ship in one of their previous discussions. This would prove to be the very ship Drysten had grown up on while it sailed under the command of his father.

"How does she look?" Diocles asked as the men stared over the Fortuna's hull. "Just as you remember?"

Drysten found it hard to contain his excitement. This was the one place that always felt like home whenever he stepped aboard. "She looks like her captain has been taking very good care of her."

"Amiram wouldn't let anyone else near her until Bors took charge of her," Diocles said with a laugh. "He nearly chased Arthur off with an oar when the prince suggested someone else step in."

Drysten nodded. "Well, it was his home too after all."

"That it is," Diocles agreed.

"Where's the mute now?"

Diocles shrugged. "Either finishing up a mug of whatever they drink in Powys or finding more provisions. Can never tell with him.

"Anything I should know about him since I last saw him?"

Diocles chuckled and glanced over his shoulder. "Married with a few children. Tiny golden-haired woman. No idea how she pushed out so many little ones for him."

Drysten smiled. Since he'd been in Powys, he was happy to hear not all his people lived under the oppression of King

Ceneus and the Christians. Though happy, he thought it was strange his life was now pushing him toward protecting the people of Ebrauc instead of waging war against them.

"Lord," Diocles whispered as he pointed off in the distance. "A ship?"

Drysten strained his eyes to the Southwest, indeed noticing sails. Roman sails at that. "I wonder if the Empire actually did send help," he wondered.

Diocles shrugged and glanced behind him, telling the nearest rower from the Fortuna to find Prince Arthur and summon him to the docks.

"The river leading into Glevum doesn't go anywhere else important?" Drysten asked.

Diocles thought for a moment before returning another shrug.

"We'll wait and see who this is."

The two waited for some time before Arthur finally showed. Most of his family were in tow, with Drysten finally getting a look at Arthur's pregnant wife, Ystradwel. She noticed Drysten immediately and awkwardly shuffled toward him.

"I... feel I should... apologize for—"

"There's no need," Drysten interrupted. "I've learned how little control your father has had over Ebrauc since Germanus arrived. I know it wasn't him who sent me to their prisons."

Ystradwel sighed and produced an uncomfortable smile.

"I meant no disrespect, Lady," Drysten assured her.

Ystradwel nodded and looked behind her, with Drysten seeing Isolde walking up with Galahad. She looked back and produced a more genuine smile. "I asked her to come and work for me!"

Drysten glanced to Isolde and saw her beaming back at him. "Did you now?" he asked. He finally noticed how young the girl was, maybe being nineteen. She was a woman, no doubt, but still finding her way in life. An innocence which he once saw in Isolde so many years ago.

Isolde approached, with Drysten noticing she seemed younger than before. Almost like a weight was lifted from her shoulders. "Drysten, you really must see the forum here. We will be moving across the way from the king! The king of all people!"

Drysten smiled. "I'm happy," he whispered as he kissed her cheek."

"Ah!" a voice screamed from behind the crowd.

That must be Amiram, Drysten concluded. And indeed it was.

The man who had had his tongue ripped out by Frisians long ago sauntered over with an unmatched jubilance, wrapping Drysten and Isolde in the tightest hug the man had ever received from anyone. "Orh!" the man yelled. It was assumed Amiram had tried to say 'lord' but failed due to his lack of a tongue.

"I'm assuming Drysten was too hard to say?" Drysten asked with a laugh.

The man from Judea laughed and patted Drysten's shoulder before turning and yelling "Ara!"

A short but beautiful woman walked through the crowd leading a small tribe of children. Drysten glanced to Amiram, who nudged him with an elbow and whispered "wife."

"That's... your wife," Drysten whispered. He felt as though he'd fallen in love for a second time before glancing to Diocles and seeing the same look in his eyes as well.

The short mother of four walked with grace as she turned and smiled toward Drysten and Isolde. "Lord and Lady!" she greeted.

"I... hello," Drysten muttered.

Isolde gave him a dissatisfied glare as she heard the timidity in his voice.

Drysten shrugged it off and looked back to Ara, "A pleasure to meet you."

"You as well. Alda's my name. Not whatever that one

said." She gave Amiram a playful look, with Drysten turning to see the mute staring back at her the same way he saw the Gaels staring at who they wished to eat.

Diocles pulled Drysten and Isolde away from the strange unspoken conversation between the two. "Alright... well."

The Roman ship was moments away from docking, with Prince Arthur and King Uther now moving in front of Drysten and his men. The Powysians looked as though they were hoping to receive a Roman dignitary, but Drysten thought that would be highly unlikely.

"Is it him?" King Uther whispered.

Arthur nodded. "You know it is."

Uther nodded. "We'll have him leading our people North then. Good thing he arrived... early."

"Always seems to," Arthur added.

Drysten glanced to Diocles for clarity, with the Greek simply shrugging in response before glancing behind him and waving for Bors to come forward.

"What is it?" Bors asked.

Drysten pointed to the ship now making port. "Who's this?" he whispered.

"Prince Aurelianus' father. The first Ambrosius Aurelianus who fought for the Empire and secured the Powysian borders after the Romans left. The man is a genius on the battlefield," Bors explained. "We're lucky he arrived when he did. Those fucking Gaels of yours don't stand a chance."

Drysten was impressed by the reputation of the prince's father. He nodded and looked back to see the loading ramp plopping down onto the pier, and the most regal man imaginable stepping off. He wore a strange looking armor which looked to be made of metal fish scales, and had a strong jaw with pitch black hair. Whereas King Uther had a big, braided beard, this man's face was clean much like a typical Roman's.

"Brother!" the man shouted as he walked toward the king. The two shared a brief embrace before Arthur strolled toward him with a beaming gaze.

"Father," Arthur greeted.

Strangely, the prince didn't receive quite the warm reception the king had. Ambrosius glanced to his son, and though still smiling, whispered something which seemed to dampen the happy mood of Arthur. Ambrosius whispered something else before looking toward the crowd and settling his gaze on Ystradwel.

"You," Ambrosius shouted as he gestured for her to approach.

Ystradwel gave an awkward glance to Isolde, who chose to follow her forward.

"You're Ceneus' girl?" Ambrosius questioned as he looked her head to toe.

"I... am," Ystradwel whispered uncomfortably as she looked to her husband.

"Well, the stories I've heard are true. You are indeed beautiful," Ambrosius declared.

Ystradwel began to smile until she realized Arthur's father was not.

Don't torture the poor girl, Drysten thought as he glanced at his own wife, also looking uncomfortable.

Arthur shuffled closer to Ystradwel and wrapped an arm around her. "She's expecting your grandchild, father."

"I can see that," Ambrosius flatly replied. "*Why* is this?"

Arthur looked behind him toward Uther before looking back to his father. "Because I took her to be my wife, and that is what married couples do. They create children."

"We will speak more of this later, son. I fear you don't understand what you've done," Ambrosius declared. He began to walk by them both until Ystradwel clasped a hand onto his arm. She did so gently, but hard enough to gain the tired man's attention.

"I love my father, but he is weak," she began, her gaze stern. "I am not. I am giving you Ebrauc. Take it before the Gaels or Christians do."

Drysten stood in shock as Ambrosius began to produce

a strangely warm smile. He slowly lifted a hand to Ystradwel's and unclasped her fingers, both of them holding the other's gaze. "I suppose I certainly should." He removed her arm and gave Arthur a warmer look than he had when he first arrived.

Diocles leaned to Drysten. "Families in Britannia are... strange."

Drysten nodded.

***

Drysten was accompanied by Diocles, Bors and Amiram into the Roman forum of Glevum. Drysten wondered if this was likely the last truly Roman-looking city in all of Britannia. Walking through the streets, he gazed over everything he once saw in Rome and Ostia during his brief journey to the cities. Guards, markets, walls, and even concrete apartments seemed to be a common enough sight to the locals. The forum still had all the various statues to the gods and was being kept up by the local authorities. It even seemed there were worshippers of the Roman faith still dwelling in Glevum, as flowers and small offerings were seen at the base of a handful of statues.

"King Uther takes care of civic duties while his brother keeps the Saxons in line," Bors explained as they entered the open aired forum. "Until now, the Saxons were all that we worried about."

Drysten nodded as they approached King Uther, his brother, and Prince Arthur gathered near a small podium. Dagonet was waiting with them as well, but had no real role to play until Drysten began speaking of the Gaels.

"You're early," Ambrosius noticed.

Drysten nodded. "Never a bad thing."

Ambrosius looked to Arthur. "That's the one?"

Arthur nodded.

Ambrosius rose from his seat and walked with a straight back toward Drysten. "It would have been a sad day if I'd returned home to learn I'd lost my son," he began, finally reaching Drysten and shaking his hand. "And now I've been told it was you who came to his rescue at Segedunum."

Drysten gave an awkward glance to Arthur, who nodded. "I did what was necessary."

"You saved my boy twice. You will also prove useful against Abhartach," Ambrosius declared. "I will be in charge of this voyage North, but you will be accompanying me."

Drysten nodded. *Thought I already was.*

"Now," Ambrosius added as he returned to his seat, "tell

me everything I need to know to kill these bastards."

Drysten accidentally scoffed, drawing a strange look from King Uther.

"What was funny," the king asked.

Drysten glanced to Diocles. "How much have you heard of them?" Causing Uther and Ambrosius to shrug as they gazed back at him. "Fair enough," Drysten muttered with a sigh. "For a start, these men don't know fear."

Uther scoffed. "So did the Saxons but we killed them anyway."

Drysten shook his head. "The bulk of his army will be no different than the Saxons. That's true." Drysten felt a throb in his shoulder before continuing. "But… the others are another matter."

"The ones you roamed with," Ambrosius questioned.

Drysten nodded. "They are the cannibals you've heard stories of. They truly cannot fear anything. I've seen it."

Ambrosius smiled. "All men fear something."

"Not them!" Drysten emphasized. "Not Abhartach's hunters."

"I agree," Dagonet said with his head hanging. "I've seen how they move. How they fight. We will not be able to route them out if there's even a hundred to worry about."

Ambrosius peered back to King Uther before looking to Bors. "Get the Fortuna ready. We sail at dawn."

Drysten felt a pang of guilt that he wasn't the man in charge of the ship which had given him so much, but silently held out hope he someday would be.

"Lord Drysten," Prince Arthur said as he walked beside his father. "If you're going to fight with us, you really should look the part as well."

Drysten glanced to the king and noticed him produce a quick grin before glancing away.

"We'll get you looking like a Powysian," Arthur said as he patted the back of Drysten's shoulder, ushering him forward.

The prince led Drysten and Amiram, who also needed

armor, toward a back room further into the Glevum's basilica. He glanced back to the two men before briefly smirking and opening the door, revealing what must have been the Powysian armory. There were scores of weapons stacked on tables along with different types of Roman mail scattered around in chests.

"Pick what fits," Arthur said as he gestured toward the boxes. "There should be something here you'd want."

"Thank you, Lord Prince," Drysten returned with a nod.

The prince smiled and walked out, leaving the two to look over the old Roman armor stacked around them.

"They have more equipment in this room than Ceneus had in all of Ebrauc," Drysten said with a scoff. "I remember my father telling of the shoddily repaired rungs in the mail of his men when he first met them. Said they barely held together."

Amiram nodded and walked toward more of the strange armor resembling fish scales, picking it up and turning the armor over in his hand. He looked mildly impressed but confused at the same time.

"Think it'll stop an arrow?" Drysten wondered as he extended a hand and fidgeted with one of the scales."

Amiram shrugged and glanced around before pointing to a bow hung on a far wall. There was also a small bag of arrows dangling below it.

"May as well try it out," Drysten said as he walked over and plucked the bow from its resting place. He turned back and saw Amiram beginning to don the armor. "Amiram, no… we'll just…" he gestured to a vacant armor stand constructed in the rough shape of a man.

"Ah!" Amiram said with a bright smile. He marched over and placed the armor over the wooden man before walking back to Drysten and gesturing directly across to the door.

"Probably right. Not too many people would try to fire an arrow from a few arm's length away," Drysten answered with a nod. He led Amiram through the door and moved back a handful of paces before looking back to the mute. "If it stops an arrow from this distance then it can likely stop anything."

Amiram nodded and urged Drysten to fire before standing behind him.

Drysten lifted the bow, immediately noticing the heavier weight than that of the Gaelic bow he had grown accustomed to. After nocking an arrow, he carefully aimed. He heard faint footsteps behind him, but fired anyway.

"What are you—?" the voice asked before being cut off by the tink of the arrow bouncing off the armor and wobbling in the air.

Drysten glanced back to see King Uther and Lord Aurelianus standing behind them, with Amiram awkwardly glancing between the two.

"Lord King… we were—" Drysten stammered.

"It's quite alright," Uther said with a smile. "Had my doubts about it as well. To this day, I've never seen an arrow pierce one of those." He smiled and glanced to his brother. "Well, never fully anyway."

"How many do we have?" Drysten asked.

"Roughly a hundred not in use. Give or take a few," Uther answered as he glanced to Lord Aurelianus, who nodded.

"We will need them all," Drysten assured him. "The hunters prefer to work from afar If we take that advantage away…"

King Uther nodded. "Then they are yours."

With that, Drysten knew he'd found the advantage he needed over the Gaels.

CHAPTER SEVENTEEN

Ceneus led the army's march into the West. He spent much of that time riding alongside his two younger sons and King Garbonian. It was an uneventful ride, with them only seeing a handful of people until they reached a small town the Romans once called Olenacum. The plan was to reach the Western coastline of Britannia and continue North until they finally reached Glanoventa.

Something that stuck out was how few people were still living in the Roman cities. Ceneus remembered his father taking him and his brother West when they were small, with them marching through bustling town centers along the way. This time, however, Ceneus passed through the decrepit ruins of one of those towns to see buildings collapsing unto themselves and wildlife roaming the streets.

"Almost a graveyard," Gwrast had mentioned.

Ceneus couldn't have agreed more. He always feared his kingdom was going to fade into nothingness, but always held out hope he could stave it off. It seemed his dealings with Germanus hurried everything along. No Christian pilgrims were arriving to replace the nonbelievers, as the bishop had once promised.

"Everything alright, brother?" Garbonian asked as he leaned toward Ceneus.

Ceneus clicked his tongue and looked to the sky. "I ruined our father's legacy. Aside from that, I suppose so."

Garbonian returned an awkward nod. "You already know my thoughts on the matter. I may agree, but this would have eventually been Ebrauc, anyway. The Romans left and took the civilized people with them."

"Even so, I think I played a greater role in the decay of this place than anyone," Ceneus muttered.

"Maybe," Garbonian answered. "Maybe not. Your God will decide when you eventually meet him."

Not sure if he was ever really my God to begin with.

The men marched on.

Ceneus glanced back to the seven-hundred men at his back. The diversity was extremely surprising. A handful of months back, he would never have expected such a strange assortment of tribes coming to his aid. The irony of it all was how his father, the great Coel Hen, and last High King of Britannia, never managed it. The tribes barely ever saw eye to eye on anything under his father's reign.

Strange how all it would have taken was a smattering of incompetence, Ceneus thought with a chuckle.

Ceneus turned around to address his men. "We'll rest for the night near a village up ahead," he yelled. After a handful of nods he looked to his brother. "You remember the plan?"

"I do," Garbonian answered. "With the gates of Eboracum closed, the bishop won't have a chance at reclaiming it. Once he figures that out, he'll likely try to attack us from behind. I will set up scouting posts and watch for him. When we see him coming up on us, we'll begin harassing him til the fucker leaves."

Ceneus nodded. "And?"

Garbonian sighed. "And I'll do no fighting, Lord King."

The king smiled and stared ahead. "That's a good liege," he jokingly whispered, causing a grumble from his brother.

The army stopped in an abandoned village near the Western coast of Britannia. There were no villagers around, and no signs there had been for quite some time. The buildings had almost all collapsed under the weight of winter snow or wind, and the well had run dry. It was likely the worst spot the army could stop, but Ceneus knew the men would need rest. He ordered everyone to make camp and light fires to cook what little food they still had for the rest of the journey.

"Should reach the city tomorrow night," Garbonian observed. "You remember when father took us this way when we were children?"

Ceneus was pleased with the memory and felt himself showing a bright smile. "I do. Saw my first set of tits when in a village not far from here."

"Ha!" Garbonian roared as he slapped his good leg. "I remember that well! You looked terrified when you came back to camp! Mother thought you'd eaten bad meat by how white in the face you were!" Garbonian's tumultuous laughter brought smiles to both of Ceneus' sons, who were also sitting around the fire.

"I was all of eight years old!" Ceneus explained as he felt his cheeks becoming red. "Didn't know what to do."

"That is still one of my happiest memories!" Garbonian added. His laughter slowly began to fade. "You remember when we came back this way a few years later. Back when the Gaels and Picts had decided to attack."

Ceneus glanced down to the cooked bird in his hands. "I do," he whispered.

"There were no smiling faces then..." Garbonian said as he stared into the fire. "You think he was there?"

"Who?" Ceneus wondered.

"Abhartach."

Ceneus shrugged. "I know extraordinarily little of the man. I know what Maewyn and some of my spies have told me, but not much else from those years."

Garbonian sighed. "My own spies have a little more. When I was first... given charge of Bryneich, they told me of certain threats to look out for. Abhartach was not one of them."

"How does that help us?" Gwrast wondered.

"All he did was lose battles against other tribes in Hibernia. The man isn't a good commander in a real fight," Garbonian explained. "He's simply lethal if you give him the chance to hide."

"Failure taught him much. War is more about thought than anything else," Gwrast put in, prompting Garbonian to nod with an impressed look on his face.

The men sat near the fires for a while longer, with Ceneus occasionally rising to walk amongst his men. He'd heard tales of Prince Ambrosius doing so when the Powysians had last fought on the side of Ebrauc at Segedunum, earning ample praise from those in Ebrauc's army.

He glanced toward the officer's tents belonging to tribal chieftains accompanying him to Glanoventa. Ebrauc's royal family had rarely called upon many of these men, with Germanus seeing them as untrustworthy apostates who would soon be replaced. However, now that Ceneus was the sole power of Ebrauc, he endeavored to change the ways his lords and chieftains would be treated. He immediately found his attention drawn toward one man who erupted from his tent and began storming toward a small group of men nearby.

"How can I sleep while you rabble are right outside my fucking tent," the man roared.

Ceneus became infuriated at the tone of the man. "You!" he called. "What's your name?"

"What's it to you?" the grey-haired man answered.

"I like to know the names of those fighting for me," Ceneus returned. He glanced to the men who had been yelled at and saw a couple of smirks and rumbling whispers. He looked back to the officer and saw him go white in the face.

"Lord King, my apologies. I didn't know who—"

"Does your ignorance excuse your actions toward your men?" Ceneus asked as he approached. "For all I care, you can sleep with the wolves in the hills." He stopped barely an arm's length away. "You ever speak to your men… my men like that again and you will."

The man stammered something the king couldn't hear before nodding and giving a long-winded apology the king didn't care to listen to.

Ceneus nodded. "Your name."

"I'm Amalech, Lord King," the man answered.

"Where are you from?"

"Rheged, Lord King," Amalech explained through a shy tone.

"Right, I remember you now. You swore allegiance to me almost immediately. You betrayed your King Lledlwrn right before we crushed him that day in the forests.

Amalech's mouth fell open as during his visible struggle to find a response.

Ceneus inched closer. "Did you not?"

Amalech's eyes went wide as he gave a slow nod.

"I will have my eye on you, Lord Amalech. Pray I have no need to speak with you further." Ceneus couldn't help but grin. He was proud for scolding the man, something he rarely had the backbone to do in the past.

"Lord King," one soldier bid as Ceneus began walking away.

Ceneus turned back and smiled to the man. "You're *my* men before you're his. You should all be treated with honor."

The small band of men nodded and returned to their conversation, leaving Ceneus to roam a while longer. There were no more ego-driven officers to scold, just more soldiers trying to stave off the cold of the nighttime air. Ceneus found himself doing the same by wrapping his warm fur cloak tighter around his chest.

The winter storms will be here soon, Ceneus concluded. Best take care of this business before then.

***

Drysten looked over the Fortuna's starboard side as he leaned onto the wooden railing. They had been sailing at a leisurely pace for a day after quickly rowing downstream until finally reaching the sea between Hibernia and Britannia. It seemed colder than the waters to Britannia's East, but Drysten wasn't sure if that was due to weather or the knowledge of an impending fight.

Lord Aurelianus was technically the man in charge, but Amiram and most of the other rowers had sailed under Drysten and his father since the ship was claimed in Gaul. They would routinely look to Drysten to affirm the captain's orders, with Drysten feeling awkward and caught in the middle.

Aside from the rowers, there were others who once sailed under Hall aboard the ship. Namely Bors the Younger and a handful of men once paid as guards under Drysten's father. Those men were now Powysian legionnaires serving under Bors, who served directly under Lord Aurelianus' command.

"Got promoted right before you came back," Bors previously told Drysten. "Only outranked by the prince now. Well the prince and you for some odd reason."

Drysten was proud of his childhood friend, and knew he was likely one of the best warriors in Britannia. He was a big brute of a man, much like his father who died fighting for Hall. He was huge in the chest, with arms the size of small tree trunks. The only one more terrifying than Bors, was possibly Abhartach. The truth was, Drysten didn't know who would win in a fair fight between the two.

"The Greek's been spewing his guts into the sea since we began moving along the coastline," Bors observed with a chuckle.

Drysten fidgeted with the collar of his Roman fish scale armor as he turned and saw Diocles hunched over the port side directly across from him. The Greek was staring into nothing until he violently lurched forward and began vomiting into the water. He wretched once more, drawing amused glances from Aurelianus and a handful of men he was speaking with before Diocles finally stood straight and glanced around. The embarrassment on his face was obvious. He produced an awkward smile and muttered something before seeing Drysten across from him and sauntering over.

Drysten couldn't help by grin. "Don't want any of that here. You throw up at my feet—"

"It's all out of me now," Diocles stated as he waved a dismissive hand through the air. "Haven't been on a boat since... well since I was taken back to Petuaria when I lost my eye," Diocles explained. "Always hated the damned things."

Bors chuckled. "Me and this one were practically raised on them. This very one as a matter of fact," he said as he gestured to around to the Fortuna.

Drysten nodded. "Hard to remember a time when I went longer than a month without stepping foot onto this boat."

Bors agreed. "What was her first name? The one Amiram suggested before your father named her for your mother."

Drysten glanced away as he tried to remember. "The... Amnestia, I believe. Father said he was giving local tribesmen a way to prevent being run through by Roman swords. Said it was a form of amnesty."

Bors smiled and nodded. "Good man, your father. Exceptionally good man."

Drysten showed a proud smile. "He was."

"Shame the apple fell so far from the tree," a voice whispered.

Drysten shook off the voice and looked back to the coastline. For all of Britannia's struggles, she was certainly more beautiful than most places he'd seen. Luscious green as far as the eye could see. Rolling hills further than that. Drysten deeply missed this place while his people were in Burdigala. He didn't know it at the time, but he missed his first home greatly.

"How much longer are we aboard this cursed..." Diocles hissed before noticing his tone angered a rower passing by, "the Fortuna. How much longer are we aboard the Fortuna?"

Drysten looked to Bors, who glanced toward the shore.

"Only been to Glanoventa once," Bors stated. "I think a half day. Maybe a little more."

"Too long if you ask me," Diocles quipped.

Drysten again pulled at the collar of his Roman armor. It was significantly heavier than he expected when he shot an arrow into it, but knew the weight meant it was much sturdier than what his father wore when he fought for Rome. "How'd someone think crafting armor after a fish would be useful."

Bors shrugged. "No idea. All I know is I've seen more arrows bounce off it than get through it."

"Suppose it'll be worth the torture of lugging it around then," Drysten said with a sigh.

Bors nodded and gave Drysten a light punch in the chest, causing a low gasp followed by a raspy cough.

"Already tested it out, Bors," Drysten responded.

Bors grinned. "I know. I just wanted to show you how much I appreciate you bringing the Gaels into all this."

"That reminds me," Diocles added. "Gaius swore to kill you, as I'm sure you remember."

Drysten returned a heavy sigh. "As is his right."

"He'll try. He'll try soon," Diocles whispered.

"Why warn me? Aren't you married to his sister?" Drysten wondered.

"I… was," the Greek explained. "She left me right after you did what you did to her father."

Drysten's heart sank. He knew the agony he felt when he thought he cost himself Isolde, but never considered he could have caused others that same pain. "I don't know what to say…"

Diocles shrugged. "She didn't leave me when I told her I would be going to Powys."

Bors and Drysten glanced to one another, both confused.

"She made up some excuse about me following you at all. She must have been speaking of Segedunum. Fairly certain she'd made her mind up before then."

"Even so..." Drysten whispered.

"Don't worry. She's not my concern anymore," Diocles added with a nod.

"Could have been her brother speaking through her. Perhaps she fears him and told you this to drive you off," Bors put in.

Diocles shrugged and glanced out to sea.

The three men stood in silence near the starboard side of the Fortuna. Drysten simply couldn't find the words to convey how sorry he was for all the pain he'd caused those close to him. Diocles may have been his greatest friend, and he had known Bors longer than anyone except Cynwrig. He hated the idea he not only let them down, but put them in more danger.

I won't make those same mistakes again, Drysten declared as he fidgeted with his father's ring. *And I will make things right if it kills me.* He suddenly found himself thinking of his son and the world he would need to help build for him. Drysten knew the Romans were gone forever, but that there was also hope for a future where Britons came together to rule over themselves as they had before Rome's invasions.

"Lord?" Diocles whispered, snapping Drysten from his thoughts. "Smoke over the hills."

Drysten turned and saw the faint outline of black smoke far off in the distance. "Glanoventa?" he wondered aloud as he turned to Bors.

Bors nodded and began stomping toward Lord Ambrosius.

"Another thing," Diocles stated in a panicked tone. "They look all too familiar."

Drysten turned his attention from the smoke to the direction Diocles was pointing toward. He didn't see anything clear but knew he could just barely make out a handful of familiar silhouettes huddled near a cluster of trees.

"Is it—?"

"Yes. They're here," Drysten's voice cracked as he took a

step toward the side of the ship. "Not the whole army."

"Lord Drysten, how likely is it that they were able to sail through the night and make it before us?" Ambrosius roared as he too stared toward the trees.

Drysten shook his head. "Doubtful. The ones who may have attacked Glanoventa were what's left of mine."

"How many?"

"Thirty in number. Maybe a handful more if they called their scouts back. Even then, I doubt those extra few men would all make it here in time to help," Drysten explained.

Lord Ambrosius grimaced as he settled in at Drysten's side.

"I have a plan," Drysten declared as he turned to Diocles. "Remember how we captured Servius?" he asked, referencing the slaver who stole Isolde from him long ago.

Diocles peered toward the shoreline before returning a doubtful nod. "Not sure they're quite as full of themselves as that fat bastard was."

Drysten shook his head. "They aren't, but they follow orders well."

Drysten raced toward the entrance to the Fortuna's middle deck and bellowed the order to bring the ship closer to the shoreline. He caught a faint gasp from a sleepy-eyed Amiram before turning and moving back to the starboard side near Diocles.

Lord Ambrosius was clearly not impressed by Drysten taking command judging by his glare of intent. "What —"

"Argyle!" Drysten screamed at the top of his lungs. He continued screaming in the hopes the Gael was one of the men watching from the shore.

"Lord Drysten, be quiet!" Ambrosius hissed. "You want them to—"

And a man stepped forward.

"The Powysians are with us, brother!" Drysten roared. "When will our king return to us?"

Argyle glanced behind him before stepping closer to sea

and cupping his hands over his mouth. “Two nights.”

Drysten turned back to Lord Ambrosius. “We will need to send Abhartach a message to ensure we can draw him in.”

Diocles let out a heavy sigh. “The same message as the ambush...”

Drysten nodded.

Lord Ambrosius contorted his face as he looked to Bors, who shrugged. “How do we send this message then?”

Drysten let a small grin cross his face before turning to fetch Colgrin’s helmet.

CHAPTER EIGHTEEN

The Powysians docked at Glanoventa just after nightfall. Of the two docks to choose from, Lord Ambrosius and Drysten both thought it best to stop at the one leading directly into the town. They decided it was likely the closest place to the majority of the hunters.

"Best we kill them all while they think we're here to help them," Drysten explained. "If any of them get away..."

"We'll take care of them here," Lord Ambrosius affirmed with a nod. "Now."

The two were the first to disembark, with Bors and Diocles walking right behind them. Argyle and the thirty hunters were awaiting them across the long, narrow pier. The long walk ended with Drysten seeing Argyle pull down his facemask to reveal his proud smile through the light of his torch.

"One of the great lords of Powys has come!" Argyle greeted. "It is a pleasure to know your people are with us."

"I'm sure it is," Lord Aurelianus returned with a scoff, peering to Drysten.

The heavy stench in the air betrayed the Gaels had killed everyone they could. Probably driving the rest into the nearby forests.

Drysten glanced around to see bloody corpses littering the ground near homes as well as in the middle of the street. Most had arrows jutting from their backs, with their vacant eyes still showing the fear from the victim's last moments. "How many?"

"How many of *us* or how many of *them?*" Argyle inquired

as he gestured a hand toward the bodies littering the ground behind him.

"How many men do *you* still have?" Drysten whispered. He found it hard to conceal his hate for the man. He was also wondering if Argyle picked up on Drysten insinuating the two were no longer on the same side.

Argyle glanced behind him. "Forty-seven. We brought together all the scouts after the fight with the Saxons. Nobody's off on their own any longer."

Drysten nodded. "Good."

"What's the plan?" Argyle wondered as he stepped closer.

Drysten looked to the hunters and saw the first hints of fatigue in their eyes. The whole time he'd roamed with them, he never noticed it. But now, they looked tired. "The Morrigan spoke to me in a dream," Drysten whispered. "She demands a sacrifice."

Argyle smiled as he glanced to Lord Ambrosius. "Is that what *their* purpose is?" He nodded toward the Powysians quickly disembarking. Most were doing a decent enough job at conveying they weren't looking for a battle, but there were a handful with their hands close to their weapons and shields.

Drysten looked behind him to see the Cretans had strung their bows, and Dagonet was leading the rowers off with Amiram at his side. "They will serve a… *higher* purpose."

"That is?" Argyle asked as he tilted his head to the side.

Drysten peered behind him once more and was happy to see the Powysians and his crew forming a shield wall, causing Argyle and the Gaels to step back a pace as they began to understand what was about to happen. "The Morrigan requires another king," he whispered as he looked back, slowly placing Colgrin's helmet over his head. "And a king she will have."

Lord Ambrosius quickly hefted his shield and drew back a pace, connecting himself with the center of the shield wall. "Now!" he screamed.

Drysten followed suit and slunk behind Lord Ambrosius'

shield as the first arrows began to fly from the Gaels. One hammered into Drysten's chest right before he was concealed by the shield, causing a stinging panic until he noticed it harmlessly thump off the scales and bounce away.

"Told you!" Bors quipped from Drysten's right.

Drysten nodded and ripped his blade from its sheath.

"Forward!" Ambrosius commanded.

The shield wall began creeping forward when Drysten noticed the Gaels weren't trying to keep their distance. Argyle was ordering them to charge. *They must have taken their time in recovering their arrows,* he concluded.

A Gael slammed into Lord Ambrosius' shield, wrenching it aside and fully exposing Drysten. Drysten grabbed the neck of the pale-faced man and plunged his blade into the man's stomach, only earning a grunt from his kill. One more began to charge from Drysten's right but was tripped by Bors swinging his blade into the man's leg before Drysten stuck his sword point into the second man's neck.

Argyle screamed a challenge to Drysten, who gladly accepted as he broke away from the shields in a full sprint.

"Lord!" Bors yelled before an arrow plunked into his shield.

Drysten could only make out the faint shape of two men bearing down on him until they were both dropped by arrows erupting from behind him. *The Cretans are still in good form.*

Argyle threw his torch to the ground and swiped his crudely fashioned blade toward Drysten's head but missed without Drysten even having to move more than an inch to his left. After letting out a brief chuckle, Drysten awaited the Gael's next move. Argyle attempted to bring his blade down onto the top of Drysten's head but was parried aside before the Gael was shoved to the dirt where Drysten immediately unleashed a brutal kick with the heel of his foot. It landed square into the side of Argyle's temple. The Gael went limp as Drysten pointed to Bors.

"Take that one! We need him alive!" Drysten ordered.

"Bind him and put him on the ship."

Bors nodded, grabbed Argyle by his matted hair, and began dragging him behind the Powysian shield wall.

Drysten turned back to see two Gaels coming toward him with their blades drawn. *The ones from the cave,* he instantly recognized. One even wore the beaded bracelet of the woman who they slaughtered and consumed, with Drysten seeing it tightly wrapped around the man's wrist.

The closer of the two jabbed his blade forward to no avail as it glanced off Drysten's fine Roman armor. Drysten returned a jab of his own, planting his sword into the man's chest and letting it fall with his kill. The second of the two swiped toward Drysten's head, missing as Drysten ducked out of the way before tackling the man to the ground. He stole a brief glimpse from side to side and immediately noticed this was one of the last Gaels still fighting.

You'll die slow, Drysten thought as he glanced down to the bloodstained beads on the man's wrist.

Drysten began pummeling his fists into the Gael's face, with his prey able to do little to stop him. He started slow, working his knuckles unto the crevices of the man's face. But after a short moment, the hate for the Gaels began to pour out of Drysten through the thundering claps of his hands. Up and down, up and down. He wasn't sure how many it took before the man had stopped breathing, but Drysten didn't care. He was the reason these beasts were able to kill his people and threaten his loved ones, and Drysten was about to punish them for his own mistakes.

"Lord!" Diocles yelled from nearby.

Drysten peered around until he saw the Greek being attacked by the last pair of Gaels right across from him. He rose and grabbed his sword before breaking out to a full sprint and crashing into the backside of the one nearest to him, sending him hurtling to the dirt.

Drysten glanced toward Diocles, who parried a swing off to the side and slammed the edge of his shield into the neck of the last Gael still standing. The Gael dropped his sword and fell to his knees, both hands clawing to his throat.

"Didn't see that second fucker..." Diocles whispered through panting.

"That'll happen when you lose an eye," Drysten responded as he jabbed his sword point into the stomach of the Gael he'd knocked down.

"I wonder whose fault *that* was," Diocles returned with a smirk.

Drysten scoffed. "Talk to King Ceneus about that. Fool should arrive soon enough."

The battle ended as quick as it began. The Gaels were slaughtered, meaning it was now time to prepare for the rest to arrive. Drysten and Diocles helped a small group of Powysians collect their fallen as the rest of the men began digging small pits along the beach. Argyle was tied up and placed under guard at the pier next to Amiram. The mute took a great deal of pleasure in displaying his own lack of a tongue, with Argyle returning a confused grimace.

"Were you once one of us?" Drysten overheard Argyle wondering.

Amiram smiled and leaned in close before blaring a scream into the man's face.

Drysten smirked at the sight. "Stop playing with your food," he quipped.

Argyle didn't enjoy the thought of being eaten, as he peered into Amiram's eyes, moving his gaze between him and Drysten. "You *were* one of us..."

The heads of the dead Gaels were all taken on Drysten's order before their bodies were thrown into a pile right across from the Fortuna. Drysten made a point to stare Argyle in the eye before every head was removed from the body. As the blood pooled beneath the stack of death, Argyle produced a slight grin, chilling those who saw it.

"Lord Drysten," Lord Aurelianus beckoned.

Drysten glanced to Argyle once more before walking to

his commander. "Lord?"

"Is this really necessary? Is desecrating the enemy dead going to help us or are you simply doing this for your own satisfaction," the Powysian lord questioned.

"Can't it be both?" Drysten returned.

Ambrosius frowned as he looked toward the bodies. "I will assume that was a bad attempt at humor."

"You'll get used to it," Drysten answered with a slight chuckle. "The heads are needed for a ritual Abhartach deemed sacred. He is compelled to answer to it if he sees or hears of it."

"Why is that?"

He believes it to mean The Morrigan is summoning him. That she is acting through us."

"Ah," Aurelianus replied. "I heard you mention that god with him." He gestured toward Argyle. "Thought I didn't hear you right."

Drysten sighed and glanced toward Argyle. "Sadly, Lord, you heard correctly."

"I would assume these men are the last who worship her."

Drysten shrugged. "I don't care if they are or not. I just hope they are the last who worship her by eating their enemies and slaughtering helpless villagers."

"What else is needed for this ritual?" the Powysian wondered as he stole another look toward the pile of heads.

Drysten turned toward the forest still containing a handful of dead civilians sprawled out in front of the tree line. "I'll be needing wood. More wood than will be needed for the spikes."

***

Ceneus saw the smoke the moment the sun came up. He was the first to spot it once he emerged from his tent and looked Northwest toward Glanoventa. Garbonian noticed it as well, with him concluding the only chance the army had at defeating Abhartach was to remain united instead of splitting to protect the rear from Bishop Germanus.

Ceneus reluctantly agreed and ordered the Guayrdians to continue marching forward.

That was few hours ago, and the army was nearly over the hills leading to the town.

"If there's really two-thousand…" Gwrast stated from behind the king.

Ceneus glanced behind him. "We have to give them a fight."

Garbonian sighed heavily from beside Ceneus. "This is true, but if they've had a chance to gain a foothold…"

"I'll hear no more of it. We fight them here," Ceneus commanded. He didn't bother to look at either man, as he already knew what expressions he'd see. It was strange to be the only man not afraid of something, but Ceneus couldn't understand why that was.

"Lord King!" a voice yelled from ahead.

Why does that voice sound so… familiar? Ceneus wondered as he spurred his horse forward a few paces, looking toward the town.

"Lord King!" the man screamed again, now closer.

The sound of hooves beating the ground just ahead became clearer and clearer until Ceneus finally saw the purple-cloaked men approaching.

"Who are—Dagonet?" Ceneus returned in surprise.

The scout looked rather uncomfortable as he approached with Cynwrig and a Saxon wearing an extremely ornate headpiece.

"Lord King, the Gael's killed everyone before we arrived," Dagonet explained. "It was the hunters."

Ceneus glanced to the Saxon before looking to his brother. "Judging by the fact the Powysians are still here, I'd say you can continue with the original plans."

Garbonian returned a skeptical glance before looking to Dagonet. "Your lot killed them, boy?"

Dagonet nodded. "The hunters are all dead. We've been preparing for Abhartach's ships since."

"The villagers?" Ceneus wondered through a heavy tone.

Dagonet shook his head. "A handful survived by running off to the woodlands. We buried the rest as good as we could manage before we had to focus on the preparations."

Ceneus nodded and trained his gaze toward the Saxon. "Who are you?"

It was hard to tell through his ornate faceplate, but the Saxon seemed slightly amused before turning his horse back toward the town.

Odd one, Ceneus thought with a grunt.

"We need help digging, Lord King," Dagonet urged as the men from Ebrauc were spurred forward by Mor and Gwrast. "There's work to be done."

"Fair enough," the king replied. "We'll also have to... catch up."

Dagonet grimaced before nodding and turning back toward Glanoventa.

The ride into the town was peculiar. Fresh graves lined the side of the road, with about a hundred crows circling overhead. Ceneus eyed the graves and noticed a small handful of purple cloaks draped over the freshly packed mounds. A Powysian soldier was holding his Roman helmet under his arm as he stared down to one in particular, with two men just behind him on either side. The man slowly raised his gaze to the king and produced the most abhorrent glare Ceneus could have imagined.

He shook off the stranger's hatred and continued until he finally entered the section of Glanoventa which had no walls. It was the main Vicus of the area and was gradually constructed on the Northern side of the Roman fort as people began settling into the area generations ago. The homes all looked about how Ceneus remembered from his childhood. The only thing missing was people.

Ceneus was the first man from Ebrauc to dismount. He glanced around toward the strangers conducting short funeral rites or digging holes on the beach just outside the town. One man stuck out above the rest and didn't look like he belonged with either the Powysians or the Gaels.

Garbonian had followed until the king made it safely into the town's fort. It was then he turned to make his way back to his fellow Guayrdians. "We'll be a few miles back," he declared. "Keep an eye on that one," he suggested as he craned his head toward the Saxon.

Ceneus nodded. "I will. I have no desire to make any more enemies."

Garbonian snorted before patting his brother's shoulder and riding off.

"Father," Gwrast said as he strolled up. "The Powysians are digging pits along the beach and lining them with spikes. I ordered some of our men to find more wood to be sharpened."

Ceneus nodded. "Go supervise them. Take your men with you."

Gwrast shook his head. "Not wise considering that." The prince let out a heavy breath as he pointed to the sea.

Ceneus didn't wish to look, as he already guessed what he would spot. A slow turn of his head revealed a massive grouping of ships all lined up and approaching Glanoventa. "Abhartach is here," he whispered.

Gwrast cursed under his breath as he surveyed the enemy fleet assembled offshore. "I'm going to order my men to form a line between the Gaels and the traps being created. If we obstruct their view in time, they may still fall into those spikes."

Ceneus nodded and gestured for Gwrast to do so. "Seems this man is as dangerous as we thought," he muttered under his breath.

"That he is," a regal voice replied from behind him. Ceneus instantly recognized the voice. It belonged to the man Germanus always said he owed his crown to.

"Lord Ambrosius," Ceneus greeted.

The Powysian nodded. "Keneu," he returned. The man didn't use Ceneus' birth name to be defiant or condescending as Germanus liked to do. He simply used it because that was how he had addressed the man during their previous encounters fighting in their fathers' wars. "You look like you have a new lease on life," the man observed as he extended his hand.

Ceneus nodded as he grasped Ambrosius' hand. "Tends to happen when you cut out an infection."

Ambrosius grinned. "I did warn you about him."

"I know," Ceneus remembered. "Where's your boy? I looked forward to asking him about my daughter."

"He's home patrolling around Glevum," Ambrosius explained. "Your brother?"

Ceneus pointed a thumb over his shoulder. "Protecting the rear from Germanus or the Gaels should they try to come around us. He won't halt them forever, but he'll be able to slow them before warning us."

Ambrosius nodded. "Always liked him. Good man."

"He is," Ceneus muttered. He hated being the reason his brother wasn't king of Ebrauc. Even his enemies admired his brother more than himself. "You mentioned your boy patrolling around Glevum. I thought I'd heard you stopped the Saxon advance?"

"They have been stopped." The Powysian lord smiled and pointed to the Saxon. "It wasn't me who did it thought. Lord Drysten killed the madman who led them. Even tricked his sons into swearing off attacking us until spring."

Ceneus felt shock ripple through his body. "Drysten did this? How?"

"Well he originally wanted a full year without their attacks." Ambrosius chuckled and nodded his head toward Drysten. "Go ask him yourself." He pointed to the man still peering into the sky toward the flock of ravens hovering overhead.

Ceneus nodded as he drew in a deep breath and began shuffling over. Drysten was only a few feet away from him, but each step felt like it took years before the king finally arrived within earshot. "Drysten," he whispered.

The former lord of Ebrauc slowly brought his gaze from the hovering birds down to the king. Ceneus could hardly see his eyes through the small openings in his Saxon crown. "Lord King," he hissed.

Despite Drysten's tone, Ceneus felt a strange sense of relief in the man's presence. "Why did you save my life? That moment has brought me nothing but confusion since."

"I may hate you… but we had a deal," he said as he removed the crown and showed Ceneus his scarred face.

"But you vowed to kill me…," Ceneus returned.

"What does it matter? You're alive." Drysten sneered as he looked over the king. The weight of the man's gaze made Ceneus extremely uncomfortable.

"I suppose I shouldn't complain," the king replied with a nervous laugh.

Drysten shook his head. "I took you to be the man behind my suffering. As it turned out, Maewyn was correct in explaining you were merely a pawn."

"Maewyn… said that?" Ceneus wondered.

Drysten smirked. "Not in so many words."

"I am… sorry, Drysten," Ceneus whispered. He gazed up at the birds dancing overhead and shut his eyes as he thought of the pain he'd caused so many people. "I'm sorry for everything. I'm sorry for the years I stole from you. I'm sorry for the pain I caused your wife by not preventing your imprisonment. I'm sorry for the five years your boy had no idea you were alive." Ceneus felt the tears welling up in his eyes as his voice began to go hoarse. "I'm the king that will forever be remembered for killing and abandoning those who served me the best."

"Then don't be king," Drysten quipped. "Maybe you're not suited for it."

Ceneus felt his skin going white as all the doubts he had in himself began to manifest and rush through his mind. He remembered every man he ordered executed, every woman he loved before having to take Heledd's hand, and every man who died because of a decision he made.

Drysten noticed this as well and seemed a bit uncomfortable by the internal pain he'd caused. That by itself seemed out of character for a man who had been tortured in Ceneus' name. Drysten looked away and shuffled his feet before shrugging. "What do I know? Maybe I'm wrong," he muttered before stepping away.

When there were no people in earshot, Ceneus spun the ring of Ebrauc's kings around his finger. "No, you aren't," he whispered.

Ceneus now understood what he must do to keep his people safe.

CHAPTER NINETEEN

Gaius watched as Eidion crept toward the tree line. It was the middle of the night, and there had been no signs of Ebrauc's army until moments before. A small fire was seen for a moment before being stifled or thrown into a hole in the ground to prevent its light from being seen.

"Must not be the whole army," Citrio suggested.

Gaius nodded. "Likely the rearguard. Get the men from Rheged ready. They'll go in with us."

Citrio nodded and crept away.

Gaius watched Eidion whisper something to the man next to him before creeping back through the darkness.

The man began the low crawl over before he settled next to Gaius, leaning in close to whisper. "The prince wants to make certain you remember the plan."

Gaius let out a sigh as he glanced to his right. "I'm the one that *thought* of the fucking plan."

"I follow orders. Are you ready or not?" the man demanded.

"We split our forces and find both kings. Garbonian will be killed immediately in a place his people can see him. Ceneus will be taken to Isurium to be brought in front of the bishop," Gaius whispered. He saw the man return a faint nod before he skulked back toward Eidion.

I hate these people, Gaius thought to himself.

The darkness came with a stinging chill which embedded itself into Gaius' bones. He shivered the whole time they were huddled in tall grasses a few miles East of Glanoventa. He worried the Powysians and Ebrauc's men would lose the fight for the town, giving the Gaels easy access to where they were located. But he also considered the possibility of killing the retreating Britons, and knew this was worth the gamble.

"Everyone's set and ready, Lord," Citrio announced with his return. "The Rhegedians seem like they'll do anything to get their king back."

Gaius returned a snort of amusement. "Most weren't more than five when the man was taken prisoner. Doubt they hold any personal attachment to the man."

"Even so, a king is still a king," Citrio responded.

Gaius never held any loyalty to anyone other than his family. He never knew what it was like to devote himself to anyone other than a blood relative, and wondered whether this was more or less the same feeling. It really didn't matter in the grand scheme of things, as Gaius preferred the reward he would receive from Bishop Germanus for King Ceneus' capture rather than some strange sense of duty.

"Roman," a man hissed.

Gaius turned and saw Prince Eidion's unmistakable silhouette staring back at him through the darkness.

"We move," Eidion ordered.

Gaius nodded and patted Citrio's shoulder, signaling for him to get their men moving. He heard the sounds of roughly a hundred warriors standing and moving left to the edge of the tree line, while roughly a hundred more under Eidion's command moved right.

Let's kill the fuckers, Gaius mused with a smile. *All of them.* He hoisted his shield bearing the Christian cross freshly painted onto his front and quietly pulled his blade from its sheath. After peering behind him, he ordered the men to move, whispering the command in a barely audible voice.

A hundred souls began creeping out of the trees, all being careful not to startle whoever it was they would soon be slaughtering. Gaius found himself wondering if Drysten was in the group but knew it was unlikely. The bastard was likely off with the Gaels getting ready to spearhead the attack against the Britons. Gaius hoped for the day he would return the favor for what he did to his father.

The men were now a hundred yards away from the opposing tree line. Gaius stole a glance to his right to see faint outlines of Eidion's men creeping toward the opposing side. His heart began to race as it always did before a fight.

"Lord," Citrio whispered before Gaius quieted him. Citrio nodded and pointed toward the spot where the fire was briefly seen moments before.

Gaius strained his eyes and immediately recognized a familiar outline huddled over a fire placed in a shallow hole in the ground. *Good. King Garbonian is here…*

Gaius looked to the men to his left and whispered to the closest man to move in the king's direction. "Take him alive."

The men obeyed in silence.

Everyone was now moving toward the Guayrdian king. A hundred souls against one man almost seemed unfair to Gaius, but so was the way his father was killed. Anyone who was close to Drysten was now his enemy, and King Garbonian was on the list.

"Now!" the king suddenly roared.

Torches were lit and tossed from the trees, revealing Eidion and Gaius' Christians. Screaming men with blue faces all stood in defiance just their opposite. They were chanting something Gaius couldn't understand, but Gaius didn't need to. "Kill them all! Take the king!" he ordered.

His men from Rheged were the first to meet the Caledonians. Armored men always had an easier time against the men from the North. Garbonian's people preferred to fight without armor for some odd reason, with the only ones wearing any being his personal guardsmen. The men who followed him North when he lost the war against his brother so long ago.

A screaming man barreled into Citrio, but only succeeded in making the man stumble a bit before swiping his blade into the Guayrdian's chest. The furious attackers screamed as he tried to swing his small axe into Citrio's head. Citrio blocked it with his shield and slammed the man's head with the pommel of his Roman spatha before jabbing it as far as he could into the man's stomach. Gaius always wondered where the man was trained to fight before he'd been recruited by his father. He turned to see King Garbonian splitting the head of a Visigothic mercenary under Eidion's command before turning to his attackers and bellowing what Gaius assumed was the Guayrdian order to show no mercy.

Gaius was happy to return the favor.

He ran as hard as he could to close the gap between him and the king, with Eidion appearing from Garbonian's other side with the same intentions. Both Gaius and Eidion met the man at the same time, with Garbonian swinging wildly between the two.

"Fuck the both of you!" the king screamed as he swung his axe with a crazed rage.

Gaius got close enough to parry the axe with his shield, but the force of the swing knocked him onto his back. He was sprawled out and looking up as the king leapt over the top of him and raised his axe high above his head. Gaius couldn't help but shut his eyes as he waited for his death. But a scream, followed by the weight of an axe falling to his side was all that followed. He opened his eyes to see Eidion bringing his blade down into the hands of Garbonian, with the king wailing in pain.

"Fuck you too, uncle," Eidion whispered with a smile. The prince lowered his blade as the king's blood began pouring from two stumps at the bottom of his forearms. Both his hands were now dangling by threads of skin Eidion had failed to slice through. The giant of a man, fell to his knees, whimpering like a beaten puppy. Eidion seemed to take great pleasure in the sight as he gestured for Garbonian to look around.

Gaius stood and peered through the dim torchlight to see Guayrdians being slaughtered by Eidion's men and his own. "No Prisoners!" Gaius roared. "Not a single fucking one is to walk away from here!"

After a few short moments of fighting, the battle turned to an execution. Guayrdians were trying to flee into the darkness only to be caught by those who were waiting for them on either side of the trees.

Gaius began to smile as he glanced down to the beaten king. "Not a bad start, wouldn't you say?"

All Garbonian could manage, was another whimper.

***

Drysten watched Ceneus' sons each holding one of Argyle's arms in a tight grip as they led him to the Fortuna. The men from Ebrauc would form a shield wall at the top deck of the ship during the battle, with both princes commanding it. There wasn't time to sail the vessel back to safer waters, so Drysten reluctantly agreed to keep her there even though Abhartach would likely ram her with one of his own vessels.

Gwrast nodded to Drysten as they approached and silently wrenched the Gael up the loading ramp. Argyle knew his death was about to find him and apparently wanted to meet it with grace. He didn't struggle or spew insults toward his captors. All he did was give Drysten a brief glare before being thrown to his knees right in front of him.

"The heads?" Drysten asked of Prince Gwrast while still holding Argyle's gaze.

The prince returned an uncomfortable gaze. "All placed inside those wretched looking wooden things you ordered made. Men with torches stand at the ready."

Drysten nodded. "Good. We'll light them when they get close enough to see them in the night. If Abhartach still doesn't take the bait, we'll dangle this one in front of him as well." Drysten pointed to Argyle, who sneered in response.

Mor slapped the back of Argyle's head. "True what they say? They eat those they capture?"

Drysten nodded. "They do," he acknowledged as he hefted his circular shield. There was no insignia emblazoned on it yet, as Drysten hadn't found the time to pick one.

Gwrast eyed his brother before nodding and pacing back to the starboard side of the ship. Both men looked tired. Or possibly antsy, Drysten couldn't decide which. He heard rumblings both of Ebrauc's princes had been fighting the Gaels off and on for a few years but knew no more than that.

At least some of the men here understand what Abhartach's people are capable of.

Abhartach's ships were all lined up about a mile offshore,

with the biggest one in the center presumably their king's. It was a Roman vessel not much different than the Fortuna. It was long, narrow, and likely old when considering how few of the ships had ever been to this part of the world. Drysten could tell the Gaels would outnumber them judging by the number of torches dancing over the waves. He wasn't sure Abhartach really had two-thousand men, but knew it wasn't impossible as he gazed from side to side of the fleet.

"The fuck are they waiting for?" Diocles whispered as he approached. It was clear he was nervous. His eyes were glazed over, and he was wringing his hands together as if he were trying to keep the cold at bay.

"You okay, brother?" Drysten asked as he gave the Greek's shoulder a light tap.

Diocles' gaze snapped from the ships to Drysten as he began stammering something about him feeling ill.

"Go," Drysten whispered as he nodded his head East.

"What?"

"You can leave, and nobody will stop you. I'll say you were going on my order. I gave you a message to take to the Guayrdians," Drysten whispered as he leaned closer and pulled Colgrin's mask over his head.

"I can't leave my people," Diocles explained with wide eyes. "I can't do that again."

Drysten shook his head. "You're not deserting anyone. Not this time. You're not leaving a failed legion of Rome. You're going back to Garbonian and explaining we may need him to come and help us." Drysten gestured a hand toward the oncoming Gaels.

The two hadn't noticed but the ships had begun pressing forward while they were speaking. One by one, their torches were being doused to conceal their exact location.

"Go!" Drysten commanded.

Diocles' face went white as he nodded and moved back out of the town.

"Lord Ambrosius!" Drysten yelled. "Light the fires!"

The wickermen Drysten ordered built were now being set ablaze. The smell of cooked meat soon followed the heat from each fire. He gazed off in the distance to see the few ships with torches still lit all turning and pointing themselves directly at the pier outside the vicus. Right toward the fire lined behind where the Fortuna was docked.

"Shield wall on the beach!" Bors screamed.

"Shut the gate to the fortress," Drysten ordered Amiram. "Make sure Diocles made it out of the city then keep the Gaels out of the fortress."

Amiram nodded and raced off.

Drysten ran behind him a few paces before turning and finding Bors. "Abhartach will try to send some of his men behind us. Likely a job for his hunters." Drysten glanced over his shoulder and saw Petras and Paulus trying to peer into the darkness. "Hard to hit anything when you can't see them. Go with Amiram," he commanded.

The Cretans nodded and unstrung their bows before moving to the Eastern gate of the town.

Drysten eyed the approaching Gaels as he covered his head with the Saxon crown and gave his armor a slight tug to make sure it was all in place. After a moment, he made his way toward the Powysian shield wall which now held Lord Ambrosius and Bors at its center.

"Lord Drysten," Ceneus greeted as he began moving toward the Fortuna.

Drysten nodded as they passed one another and kept moving toward the Powysians. For some odd reason, he plucked the beaded bracelet he took from the cave the Gaels inhabited when he served Abhartach. He looked down, with the torchlight illuminating the dried blood of the innocent woman.

I'm so sorry, Drysten thought. His eyes began watering as he remembered the frightened face of the woman the moment after she was killed. It was strange to be able to see her fear when there was no life in her eyes. It somehow made the image even worse. He approached the Powysian shields and began making his way toward the center, placing the beaded bracelet into his belt.

The men were nervous judging by their silence. The stench of the rotting heads set ablaze filled everyone's nostrils and was likely one of the causes of the tension in the air. That scent seemed to grab at the back of Drysten's throat. Voices began ringing out in his mind with each passing moment. He stifled them away as he approached Ambrosius.

"Traps are set," the Powysian revealed. "First fifty or so to come ashore will find them easy enough."

"It's the ones who come after I'm worried about," Drysten answered.

Ambrosius returned a slow nod as he looked toward his men.

An eerie silence had fallen over the beach. Not a single man dared to speak but the highest ranking among them, and even then, they preferred to whisper. Drysten thought it was funny. The men were afraid of an enemy who hadn't yet set foot on their shores.

Suppose the stories of these beasts would scare most men, Drysten concluded.

"You're not most men, son," Hall whispered. "Don't disappoint them."

"I won't," Drysten whispered as he peered from side to side.

"Look!" a voice yelled from behind the shields.

The fires aboard Abhartach's ships were all put out, signaling to everyone within miles of Glanoventa the battle was about to begin.

Drysten could make out the scant, nervous breaths of those on either side of him. The Powysians were likely the best fighters in Britannia, but even they were having trouble hiding their fear. These men had been hearing stories of invisible ghosts stealing the souls of those they hunted. And now the men of Ebrauc and Powys would be fighting those ghosts.

Even though the noises from the men at his side were audible, the only thing Drysten heard from in front of him was water. The waves were crashing into the shoreline, causing many of the men to grunt each time.

Must think that's the sound of men coming ashore, Drysten guessed.

And so it was.

The first few arrows sailed over the Powysians. The rest found their marks. Men were now screaming in pain on either side of Drysten and Lord Ambrosius. Sloshing noises began sounding from the beach.

"Shields!" Lord Ambrosius roared.

I wonder how long it will be until they find the spikes...

The torchlight from behind the Powysians illuminated shapes of men racing toward them. Arrows came with them, but so did the sounds of Gaels screaming in pain. They had stepped in the shallow pits dug along the beach, and others were no doubt trying to pull their brothers away from them.

Good luck, Drysten thought with a chuckle. He remembered how the Powysians had dug the traps. They were clever, much like the Romans once were. They pointed the sharpened pieces of wood downward. This meant the Gaels could try to pull their people to safety as much as they pleased, but all they would succeed in doing was ripping more flesh from their brother's bones.

Drysten hefted his shield and tightened his grip on the leather straps as he heard the thundering beats of the Gaels approaching. The first finally showed himself in the torchlight but looked nothing as Drysten was expecting. The man yelled something in Abhartach's language as he neared the Powysians, his long hair and scraggly beard swaying with each step. The man's eyes were set deep into his head, and he looked half emaciated.

Must be sending in the least fit of his men to try and soften us up, Drysten concluded.

The Gael leapt into Drysten's shield followed by about

a hundred more on either side of him. The man's weight was negligible compared to that of the Saxons Drysten had encountered. The attacker bounced off and fell to the sand where Drysten kicked his marred face. There were strange spots along his mouth, some of which looked to have bled before the man had ever set foot on the shore.

The fuck sort of disease does he have?

Drysten's blade found its mark as it sliced open the Gael's neck, pouring blood at Drysten's feet. The man looked ill. Deathly ill.

Another man took the place of the fallen Gael, leaping forward and clamping his ragged fingers at the brim of Drysten's shield. Drysten thrust his blade forward, feeling it tear into skin and bone, but the man still didn't let go. The shield was ripped aside, with the torchlight illuminating just enough of his decrepit face. His eyes had black circles, and his teeth seemed to have been filed into short spikes.

The man screamed something into Drysten's face, his eyes wide and pupils narrow. Blood was gushing the spot in his chest where Drysten's blade was still implanted, turning it. The Gael let out a roar, but not of pain, a roar of defiance. Whatever illness the man suffered from seemed to be spurring him forward. Forward until Drysten finally removed his blade and quickly pushed it once again, landing into the man's neck. He felt his foe's brittle spine crumble under the force, and the Gael went still, slumping to the sand of the beach.

A woman's scream alerted Drysten to another group heading from the water. He turned to see a similarly ill woman charging him, wearing nearly nothing. She was skinny, and it was at that moment Drysten realized he would have to kill a woman for the first time of his life.

Drysten stepped back as the Gaelic woman with dark black hair greeted him with a weak swing of a crude sword, connecting with Drysten's shield before bouncing away out of her grasp. That was supposed to be the end of it, as no man Drysten ever met would wish to fight a heavily armed foe without a weapon.

This woman was different.

She didn't seem to care she now lacked a blade. It seemed she believed her fingernails were long enough to be capable talons, much like a bird. She jumped up to Drysten and wrapped her arms around his neck, not unlike a child embracing a parent in a loving hug. Drysten had a hard time seeing her limbs through the narrow eye slits of his crown as the woman screamed and clawed into his exposed neck. She was even more bloodthirsty than the hunters had been.

"Get the fuck off me!" Drysten wailed. He didn't understand why, but he was afraid of her.

A high-pitched scream reverberated through Drysten's helmet as the woman forced her mouth by his ear. After a sudden impact which sent them both to the ground, the woman began to snivel and bleat as she crawled away. Drysten ripped his helmet off and hefted his blade before standing and staring down toward his attacker.

"Kill the fuckers!" Bors screamed.

Drysten peered to either side of him while the woman rested at his feet. She believed her end was near, but Drysten knew he couldn't do it. How could he ever hurt a woman? That was something he prided himself on. Even when men had told him at a young age a woman should be struck to keep her obedient, he knew he would never be able to field the cruelty to do it.

Drysten looked down to the crying, pathetic being staring back at him with wide eyes, simply whispering, "No," even though he doubted she could understand the Roman language.

Drysten glanced away to see men trying to jump up and wrench Bors' shield away, only to be tossed aside and run through by the neighboring man to Bors' left. Only a handful managed to kill any of the Powysians when the first wave had been slaughtered. A large group of men could be heard screaming or grunting along the spike pits, but no man would dare journey through the darkness to end them.

Silence was what followed. A heavy silence that seemed to grab at Drysten's nerves. He looked back to the woman. "What's your name?" he whispered as gently as he could manage.

She simply stared up from her back as a small trickle of blood pooled beside her head. Her wound was not going to be fatal, but it certainly looked like it hurt.

Bors settled in beside Drysten. "Women?" He seemed as uncomfortable as Drysten. "I… killed one," he whispered as he looked behind him to the body.

The woman who attacked Drysten noticed as well, beginning to sob as she meekly crawled over to the other's corpse.

Drysten looked at his friend. "These people must have been slaves."

"How does he make them fight for him? How does he make them crazed like this?" Bors muttered.

"He has druids. They know how to work with herbs to create poisons. It would make sense he can create something to make people obedient as well," Drysten answered.

"The druids and their magics…" Lord Ambrosius said with a scoff as he marched over.

"Magic has nothing to do with, Lord," Drysten responded as he glanced toward the shield wall.

A handful of Powysians began dragging their dead or wounded brothers behind the shields while Drysten strained his eyes, staring into the darkness along the beach. He could scarcely make out the faint outline of the enemy ships, but none were drawing closer to the beach.

Suddenly, King Ceneus screamed for his men to raise their shields. The order was followed by a loud crash coming from the Fortuna. Wood smashing into wood, causing a boom that reverberated like a score of trees falling in a forest. Drysten knew this could only be one thing, the Gaels had rammed a ship into the Fortuna to create their foothold there.

"Go see to the king. I will have this one bound and…

clothed," Lord Ambrosius ordered as he gestured to the Gaelic woman. Bors tapped Drysten's shoulder and gestured for him to follow.

Drysten nodded and followed his childhood friend towards the sounds of battle. Ebrauc's men were holding firm, but clearly faced a more seasoned foe than what was sent against Powys. *The first wave was sent to find our traps,* he concluded.

Drysten knew Abhartach must have seen what the Powysians were planning. The man's eyesight was certainly good enough despite the distance between his ship and the beach. The idea he deliberately sent people into the spikes was chilling. It signaled he had men to spare.

The two pressed on with a handful of others now trailing them. Drysten peered behind him to see both Dagonet and Cynwrig leading about twenty Powysians from Bors' cohort.

The men finally reached the rear of Ebrauc's shield wall to see Princes Gwrast and Mor in the front and King Ceneus holding a flesh wound at his side while being led back by two others.

"Lord King," Drysten greeted as he passed.

The king could only return a grunt and nod before being set down onto a crate on the pier next to the Fortuna's port side.

Drysten saw Bors halting to speak with Ceneus as he pushed forward through the rearmost ranks of Ebrauc's shield wall. The men in the front were fighting well, but those in the back didn't look to be in a hurry to do much of anything.

"Out of the way!" Drysten demanded. He pushed and shoved until he finally caught a glimpse of the Gaels attempting to board the Fortuna.

Hunters, Drysten noticed. *Hunters wearing Roman mail?*

And so they were. The armor was old and worn, likely seeing battles as long ago as the war Drysten's father once fought in. The protection was rusted and repaired in a shoddy or makeshift manner, but the hunters clearly didn't care. They knew they were going to be the chosen few who would bring Abhartach a king in the opening moments of the battle.

Drysten finally reached the front rank and shoved a wounded man of Ebrauc behind him before deflecting a sword with his shield. “Get to the back,” he told the wounded man.

The stranger nodded before being shot through the eye with an arrow, falling limp to the ground.

The noises seemed to fade from notice as Drysten turned back. Screams and wails of pain vanished, leaving a strange silence only heard by Drysten.

“Kill!” the voice commanded.

Drysten felt a rush to his temples as he found the first man he’d face. The Gael’s worn mail and brown facemask was stained with blood as he locked eyes with Drysten and charged. He raised a shield with the likeness of a raven emblazoned at its center and drew his sword arm back for a swing.

Drysten saw it immediately. You’re nothing without your arrows.

Drysten cleaved down with his own blade, which was parried aside as the Gael stepped to Drysten’s left. The two became linked in a brief skirmish of their own, both men swinging and striking into each other’s shields. The Gael was about the same height as Drysten, but his reach couldn’t match.

He swung low toward Drysten’s unarmored legs only to be halted by a man standing behind Drysten, while Drysten himself jabbed his sword point forward into the man’s uncovered shoulder. The Gael dropped his blade and let out a hollow curse in his native language as Drysten’s shield slammed into his face.

As Drysten was about to finish him off, Prince Gwrast stepped forward and did the deed for him, jabbing his own blade through the Gael’s neck and withdrawing it in one swift motion.

“*That* one’s killed five or six of my men,” Gwrast hissed as he watched the body fall.

“He’ll kill no more.” Drysten glanced back before turning

his attention to his next foe, this one without a shield. The Gael tried to keep his distance after witnessing the fate of the last man who couldn't match Drysten's reach but was pushed forward by the Gael standing behind him. The shove staggered the malnourished looking man right into Drysten's shield before Drysten stabbed him in the belly.

"Reform the wall!" Drysten heard Bors yelling.

The men from Ebrauc and the handful of Powysians created a strange looking wall comprising differently designed shields scattered throughout.

As Drysten drew back, he caught a glimpse of a man brandishing a shield with the image of the horned snake of Ebrauc, while standing next to him was a man whose shield bore the likeness of the Christian cross.

Ironic, Drysten thought with a snort.

The rest of the Gaels' second attack turned out to be a disaster. One more wave of men tried to attack from the beach, while another handful of ships did their best to take the Fortuna's top deck. All attacks failed. Drysten guessed the dead or dying Gaels on the ground likely outnumbered the dead Britons twenty to one.

"These are the men we feared?" Ceneus whispered as he stepped beside Drysten.

Drysten shrugged. "I know a man who fears sailing. That fear seems about as rational as emaciated foreigners."

The king scoffed. "How can someone be afraid of sailing?"

Drysten shrugged as he removed his helmet and placed it under his arm.

"There's still more coming," Ceneus began, "and I'm willing to bet the first couple hundred men he's thrown at us held no real importance to him."

"Likely not. We fought women on our side."

Ceneus gave Drysten a disgusted look before peering toward the beach.

Amiram had returned to the battle moments before its

end, but only now had found the time to join back with Drysten.

"Diocles made it out?"

Amiram nodded as he wiped the blood from his sword with the facemask of a dead hunter.

"Good." Drysten looked behind him toward the Cretans and waved them over.

"Lord?" Petras asked.

"Remember how we won Segedunum?"

Both Cretans smiled and nodded. They had wounded the leader of the Picts who had taken the fortress. With their leader unable to command them, the Picts thought it was best to surrender the fort and leave with their lives. The Pictish leader was held as a hostage, while Drysten's father went with the enemy for the same purpose.

Typically, the hostages would be returned in good faith at a later time, but Hall had succumbed to a mortal wound to his chest. The man's body was hung naked from a tree by the Picts. This brutal action drove Drysten and his men to kill the leader of the Picts and display him in the same manner. Drysten was told by Bors that the tribe they fought had never attacked Ebrauc or Bryneich since.

"You will have the same orders now. Look for a bald man with pale skin. He's short, you won't miss him," Drysten explained.

"We never do!" Paulus answered as he turned to fetch his bow.

"That's all you had to do?" Ceneus asked in surprise. "You just killed their commander, and they left?"

Drysten smirked. "There was a bit more to it than that, but yes."

"I suppose it makes sense. People won't risk their lives if the man who pays them is dead." Ceneus adopted a fascinated expression. "I always wondered how you managed—"

"Drysten!" Bors screamed from behind. "To the East!"

Drysten felt a sudden dread come over him for some unknown reason. He gave a quick look out to sea, but didn't notice any of the Gaels' ships moving off to attack from another direction. *The Gaels are moving behind us?*

"Hurry up!" Bors yelled. His frantic tone signaled something else was happening.

Drysten donned his helmet and gestured for Bors' Powysians to follow. King Ceneus also instructed Prince Gwrast to accompany him. As Drysten glanced toward Lord Ambrosius' men, he noticed they were also moving into the town, leaving only a small force at the beach.

"Where are they going?" Drysten shouted.

"Movement spotted outside the town," Bors panted as he struggled to keep up. "Dagonet and Cynwrig..."

"Just go with the Powysians!" Drysten chuckled to himself he journeyed on. But the feeling of dread persisted.

He rarely gambled in all his years but knew a betting man would assume Bishop Germanus was here.

***

The sounds of the battle began to fade from notice as Gaius and Eidion stood silently behind a nearby tree line. Glanoventa was either taken by the Gaels or remained under control of the Britons. Gaius found himself wondering if Drysten was lying dead under a pile of corpses but hoped his luck would win out.

"We'll wait," Eidion whispered. "I want to see who holds the town."

Gaius nodded.

"The armor suits you."

"Thank you, Lord Prince," Gaius muttered.

"You wear it as a Roman should. Head held high. Can't even fathom what the Gael-lover looked like in it," Eidion added with a scoff.

"Why my father ever gave it to him is beyond me." Gaius looked down to the refurbished chest plate, running a finger over the bull at its center. He remembered exactly why his father had given the exquisitely crafted armor to Drysten, he simply didn't want to face it. Drysten had once saved the lives of everyone Gaius ever cared about, then gave them a home.

"Mind if I ask you something?" Eidion blurted out.

Gaius thought it was strange for Eidion to ask permission to do anything. "I suppose."

"Your woman…" Eidion began, awkwardly.

"Don't even think of it," Gaius interrupted.

Eidion shook his head. "That's not what I… just wait a moment. Why do you love her?"

Gaius peered toward the prince. If he had asked that question out of some sort of malice, he hid it well. "I don't know. I've never had a reason. I just feel that I do."

Eidion seemed satisfied by the answer, his silhouette showing the man nod and glance away.

"Why?" Gaius wondered through a sigh. He couldn't help himself.

"I met a woman I can't get out of my fucking mind," Eidion shot back, somewhat harsher than expected. He seemed angered, or inconvenienced by the fact. "She's the most beautiful thing I've ever seen."

"A woman shows you her tits and you fall in love that easily?"

Eidion grumbled to himself.

"What's her name?" Gaius wondered. "Where'd you find her?" The idea Eidion found anyone who could love him back was laughable, yet here he was speaking of her.

"I found her near Isurium. Led a patrol and stayed the night in the town she lived in."

"Her name?"

"I don't know..."

Gaius snickered to himself. "Can't love her that much if you don't even know her—"

"She doesn't know mine either. I don't want her to."

"Everything alright, Lord?" Citrio wondered as he stepped beside both men.

Gaius nodded. "It is." He looked back to see Eidion shrink away. It seemed their short, and strangely friendly conversation was over. "Look," he whispered as he pointed toward the town.

A pair of Britons in purple cloaks shuffled around the corner of Glanoventa's fortress and settled down at the base of the wall. One handed the other a skin of water while they both wore expressions of relief.

"Seems we know who won," Eidion grumbled as he peered behind him. He snapped his fingers and his men rose to their feet.

Gaius knew what needed to be done. "Bring them both forward," he commanded.

Citrio returned an uncomfortable stare, showing no signs of movement. "Both—?"

"Bring both!" Gaius raged.

Citrio gave a dejected look to his feet as he shuffled to the rear of Eidion's war-band.

Gaius looked back to Glanoventa's walls and saw both

Britons had stood and were now staring in their direction. One gave the other a gentle pat on the arm and pointed a thumb over his shoulder, with the other nodding and racing away into the town.

"Wonderful," Eidion whispered. "You couldn't have simply blown a horn and really let them know we were here?"

Gaius felt the blood rush to his cheeks, but knew the fact the Britons heard him didn't actually matter. That was their intention from the start. Gaius was to cause a distraction while Eidion moved around to the Northern side of the town to flank what men the town's defenders had left. Yet another of Gaius' plans.

"Get the rest of the men up," Gaius ordered Citrio, who just returned with his two captives in tow.

Citrio nodded and gave Diocles a sorrowful look, returned by a vacant stare from a blood-covered face.

Gaius took a moment to survey his captive's face. He looked worn out to say the least. That was understandable considering the fact he was venturing to King Garbonian's men and found himself a prisoner instead.

There was a small cut where Gaius had held the knife to his brother-in-law's empty eye socket. The bandage once covering the gaping hole was torn away when the man was caught. Aside from the cut near the hollow opening, there were numerous others along his cheeks from the quick beatings of Eidion's Visigothic mercenaries. The sight betrayed they enjoyed every ounce of pain they inflicted.

The men under Gaius' command waited until Eidion's people were far out of view and passed a tree line on the other side of the open field. A small host of Britons was assembling on top of the fort's walls, with a handful of torches being lit within their ranks. No activity was seen throughout the dimly lit, unwalled vicus of Glanoventa.

Only a handful must be alive, Gaius assumed. He gestured for his men to form a line and follow. The captives were bound and led forward behind him.

They marched forward toward the gateway, now closed and under guard of the defenders. Gaius noted a mix of Powysian shields mixed in with those of Ebrauc's. It was a strange sight, as Gaius knew the two kingdoms were often at odds with one another in recent years.

"You'll never win," Diocles hissed as he was shoved in front of Gaius. "Your father would be ashamed to call you his son. Siding with Germanus and his pawns will only—"

Gaius struck him hard, widening a gash across his cheek. "What do you know of my father? You're nothing, and you will die as nothing."

Diocles stumbled over his own feet as the blood began to run down the side of his face. The man was about to die, and Gaius had an odd feeling of satisfaction in knowing he was the one to kill him. He chose to follow his father's killer into battle, and even did so despite his wife being pregnant.

"Did you know?" Gaius asked as he knelt beside brother-in-law.

"Know what?

Gaius smirked. "Oana."

Diocles' eyes began to widen. "What... happened?"

"She forced you away on my instructions. The women of a family are always bound to the will of the patriarch," Gaius answered.

Diocles' head tilted to the side as he watched a man light a torch and hand it to Gaius. "One man thought that was possible. I, however, thought you weren't capable of sinking to those depths."

Gaius nodded. "It's those depths that will someday find my hands around your lord's throat. Until then, there are no depths," he explained as he jabbed a finger onto Diocles' temple.

Gaius turned and waved the torch overhead. He saw one familiar shape on top of the fort's wall, but couldn't tell who exactly it was. The stranger erupted away from the stonework, likely to fetch his commander like a good dog always should.

After a moment of waiting, the gates bean to creak open, with a Saxon and Prince Gwrast stepping through.

Diocles began to cackle in defiance. "You're... fucked!" He coughed and smiled wide as he slapped the ground beneath him. "You have no idea. These men won't just kill you—" Gaius struck him again, this time feeling a crack under the weight of his fist. Still, Diocles proved defiant. "You have nothing to take from me!"

"Lord Gaius," Prince Gwrast yelled before he could do further harm to Diocles. "That's quite enough."

Gaius turned and stepped toward the prince, lowering the torch before dropping it to the ground. "I will speak with your king."

Prince Gwrast smiled. "My king was killed defending our people from the Gaels."

Gaius scoffed. "So then Prince Eidion is king?"

"That miserable twat will never rule over me," Gwrast answered with an amused smirk as he stepped forward.

The Saxon had his eyes fixed on Diocles as he ran a hand over the hilt of his sword. There was something strange and familiar about the man and his worn looking cloak, but Gaius couldn't understand what it was.

"Release him," Gwrast ordered. "Release him and go."

"And what of the other one?" Gaius challenged as he gestured for the second prisoner to step forward.

Gwrast betrayed a twinge of pain as he saw his uncle slammed down to his knees. King Garbonian was the only survivor from the battle against the men from the North. Eidion and Gaius saw to that personally.

"What do you want for him?" Gwrast demanded as he glanced North. The sounds of a battle became clear in the distance. "Coin? The kingdom?"

Gaius peered over his shoulder toward the trees, wondering if Eidion had made it inside the town. He believed the noises to be loud enough for the two men opposing them to notice as well, but neither man was showing any interest.

That's curious... Gaius wondered as he looked back to Gwrast. "What I want... is for you to find me Drysten. You will find his corpse if you've killed him... or you will find him alive and turn the traitorous wretch over to me."

The noises of a skirmish intensified. Gaius saw two faint silhouettes approaching the clearing before stopping. One looked to place a hand on the other's shoulder and mutter something before both men raced North.

Eidion must be winning, Gaius concluded, betraying a smile as he looked on the Saxon and prince.

Gwrast adopted a confused expression as he glanced to the Saxon. "Lord Drysten is not mine to give."

"Oh?"

"He is a lord of Powys now. You can take that up with Lord Ambrosius Aurelianus," Gwrast muttered with a smile.

Gaius let out a long sigh. "And where would this Ambrosius Aurelianus be?"

The Saxon peered over his shoulder before stepping forward. He locked eyes with Gaius, his intense glare showing two sparkles through the narrow eyeholes of his facemask. With a gradual lift of his arm, he pointed a finger North.

It was at that moment Gaius knew the plan had failed.

"Give me them both and leave with your lives, Gaius," the Saxon demanded with an outstretched hand.

Diocles had become silent as Gaius glanced between the two. He now understood where Drysten was, and why the Saxon held an air which felt so familiar.

"No," Gaius whispered. In one motion he drew his blade and stabbed it into Diocles' neck, causing a brief wail of pain before the edge found its way into the man's windpipe. At that moment, Diocles could do no more than writhe around on the ground in agony. "Now you can have him, Lord."

King Garbonian released a hollow gasp as he fell to his knees and crawled to Diocles, completely unable to help him without his hands. All he could do was stare into the eyes of a dying man and whisper something Gaius could not hear.

"Gaius, run!" Eidion shrieked from the tree line. He burst from the darkness with about twenty blood-soaked men on either side. They were being pursued by Powysians led by Bors and a Roman who Gaius didn't know.

"Withdraw!" Gaius screamed.

King Garbonian met Gaius' eyes as the Roman turned to run.

"I won't waste my strength ending you. You're already dead," Gaius whispered as he looked over the pale-faced man with a grin. He then turned and began running.

"Gaius!" Drysten screamed, weapon now drawn. Gaius turned back. "You... cannot hide... from me," he croaked, pointing a finger toward his chest.

"Good!" Gaius returned with a smile. He turned toward the tree line, and ran for his life.

CHAPTER TWENTY

The sun rose, but nobody cheered. Men from Ebrauc found out one of their most beloved commanders, Gaius, was now their enemy. Men from Powys dug more graves for many of their brothers, who had died for another kingdom's war. The Fortuna's men were mourning the loss of Diocles and Garbonian in silence. They were two men who made great impressions on the crew. But for as gracious and boisterous as they remembered Garbonian to be, no man was greater than Diocles.

The horror of the night settled in quick for those in Glanoventa. The Gaels had been repelled, but many Powysians died fighting Prince Eidion before the man escaped. There were now only three hundred men in total to repel the rest of Abhartach's forces, and everyone knew it would not be enough.

Drysten brushed a hand through his hair as he remembered the carnage. Diocles was killed by Gaius right in front of him, and Garbonian only lived long enough to say a brief farewell to Ceneus and his nephews before joining Diocles in the afterlife. Drysten was there for their goodbye and found a small amount of comfort in the sight of the two brothers parting on good terms.

"You would have been a better king than me," Ceneus had told his brother. Drysten remembered Garbonian's smile at the comment.

"I know," the king of Bryneich whispered back, earning a chuckle from Ceneus. It was then the man handed a ring to Ceneus and ordered him to give it to someone Drysten didn't know. A son the man apparently never knew he had.

That was the moment the light faded from Garbonian's eyes, and Ceneus and his sons went quiet. All three men simply stood over the body until this moment.

"He told me once," Bors whispered, speaking of Diocles. "He told me where he thought we'd go once we passed."

Drysten stared down at the mound containing the greatest friend he'd ever had. "Where?"

"Elysium."

"Where's that?"

Bors shrugged. "Only brave men go there. Wherever it is, I'd say he's waiting for us."

Drysten felt the tears welling as he remembered how he'd sent Diocles away to try and keep him safe. No matter what decision he made since he became a leader, he got those closest to him hurt. "He was a good man," he whispered.

Bors nodded. "He was."

He may have been afraid, but he was no coward. He would have faced the Gaels if I would have just let him... Drysten peered a few feet away to King Ceneus and his two sons, all three doing their best not to show their pain.

Ceneus met Drysten's gaze. "Wherever Elysium is, I'd assume they're both there now."

"With Aosten," Gwrast put in, referencing one of the few good men Drysten had men while serving Ceneus. Aosten was a captain who served under Drysten's father. He ended up being murdered by Prince Eidion.

All Drysten could do was nod and peer back to the dirt. Diocles was buried with a sword and a handful of coins, as none of the men really knew his religion. Either way, it was the best they could have done without the time to build a funeral pyre.

Abhartach's ships were still sitting far off the coast. There were a few scattered along the beach as well. The largest one Drysten assumed to belong to Abhartach had disappeared sometime in the night, but all others remained. Drysten could just barely make out the silhouettes of the men crewing them, and he found himself wondering how many were slaves rather than hunters.

"Where's the girl?" Drysten asked of Bors. "The Gael."

Bors shrugged. "Lord Ambrosius had her placed under guard inside the fort."

"Probably best to keep her apart from the men. Who is watching her?"

Bors shrugged once again but remained silent.

"And Argyle?" Drysten questioned.

"Scurried off when we weren't looking. Jumped in the water."

"Waters cold and the ships are far," Drysten returned as he rubbed his thumb over the space between his eyes. "Likely died."

The men remained silent. Dagonet and Cynwrig led Amiram and a handful of the Fortuna's rowers toward the grave. But still, no one said a word. It was eerie, but Drysten felt more at home in this heavy silence than anywhere. King Ceneus and Prince Gwrast paced over from King Garbonian's grave and provided a nod to those near Drysten before finally speaking.

"He was a good man," Ceneus whispered. "I remember him during my visits to Titus."

"Titus..." Drysten muttered as the painful memories returned.

Gwrast patted Bors' arm, earning a scowl until the giant felt he had no more angst to give to the prince. He simply began sobbing as he looked to the grave once more.

Drysten glanced toward Gwrast and gave a nod of thanks as Bors began to shuffle away. "Take no offense, Lord Prince. The man deals with grief in his own way."

Prince Gwrast nodded. "Many do."

Ceneus looked from the funeral mounds to the sea. "Where did their king run off to?"

Drysten shrugged. "If he knew better, he'd piss off back home. Nothing for him here but more of his people dying on our swords."

"Your optimism is rather impressive," Ceneus quipped.

"Hopefully, it's not misplaced," Drysten answered. "I know our numbers have dwindled."

Drysten turned and plucked up his helm before moving back toward the beach. Lord Aurelianus was now speaking with a loud-mouthed officer serving under Ceneus when he finally arrived.

"I don't care about your losses," Ambrosius explained through a stern tone. "Nobody leaves until they're either dead or back in Hibernia where they belong."

The officer with the armor fashioned in the same way as Drysten's scrunched his face in disgust before storming off back to his own men. Drysten looked them over, finding them rummaging through the dead Gaels piled next to the pier.

"Lord Drysten," the Powysian greeted, "How are your men? I know Diocles was rather loved among their ranks."

"He was."

"After we're done here, I'll allow Dagonet and Cynwrig to join you in your pursuit."

"I won't need them," Drysten answered. "I'll find them on my own. You forget," Drysten whispered as he began to smile, "Hunting is not new to me."

Lord Ambrosius returned an uncomfortable, yet somewhat impressed glance before nodding and walking back to the Powysians lined up along the beach. "Then what are you waiting for?" he yelled over his shoulder. "I just ask you send my son here in your stead."

With that, Drysten was released to find his prey.

***

The horses found in Glanoventa's stables once belonged to Dagonet's scouting party. Drysten learned they were attacked not long after the Gaels had made their presence known to the townspeople of Glanoventa. He wondered what these innocents must have done to provoke such repeated ire from Abhartach and his people. The area didn't seem special in his eyes, but he wondered if there was another motive.

The horses were apparently raised to be warhorses by a farmer in Petuaria, one Drysten was even familiar with. The man's name was Conway, and he had a nephew who apparently took over the farm when the man died a few years past. They were of Roman stock and performed better than the weak and sickly-looking beasts in the rest of Britannia.

"Not much further now," Drysten whispered into the ear of his horse.

He had ridden through the night and guessed he was about a third of the way to Glevum. It would be there he would explain to King Uther his nephew was needed to the North. Then, his own hunt would begin.

"You!" Drysten called to the closest man on the road. "What city is that?"

The old man lifted his grayed head and gazed upon Drysten, not wearing his Saxon crown for fear of frightening the locals. "Mamucium," the stranger rustled. His voice betrayed the long years of living in squalor which followed the Romans leaving this area.

Drysten nodded and tossed him a coin from the pouch given to him by Lord Ambrosius before departing Glanoventa. "Thank you, old man. Get some food in your belly."

The man hobbled over and scooped the coin from the ground, biting the edge and nodding in thanks as Drysten carried on.

I'm already in Rheged, Drysten thought in surprise. He knew he'd made good time, but was still impressed by the speed of his horse. *Conway would have been proud, my boy.* He leaned forward in his saddle and gave the side of his steed a quick pat before clicking his tongue and pressing on.

Mamucium wasn't unfamiliar to him either. His father once spoke of a battle taking place outside the city to the East. Gaels and Picts had thought to take it in the night until the great Roman general, Stilicho, caught wind of it. He sent Hall's men along with a handful of other tribes from Gaul to route them out. The defense held, and Drysten remembered his father speaking proudly of how their people fought.

"They sought to kill everyone and loot the area," Hall had explained with a smile. "They didn't succeed in either." Drysten remembered the proud tone of voice his father had spoken through. The man was widely known to hate war and was largely peaceful. But it was at that moment when Drysten figured out how a war could be necessary if defending villagers was its only aim. In a sad turn of events, it was also that memory which convinced Drysten to pursue a band of raiders into the forests of his previous home of Burdigala. He wanted so much to have a memory of protecting innocents, but only created one of a massacre instead.

As Drysten got closer to the city, he noticed the lack of life on its Northwestern side. Most of the homes were in disrepair, with only a handful looking to be inhabited. The roads were taken care of well enough, which meant the area was likely heavy in foot traffic from traveling merchants or locals. Two guards wearing leather tunics were milling about in the middle of the road, with one giving Drysten a cautious stare.

"What are your intentions here?" the guard yelled. "Are you passing through or are you staying the night."

Drysten peered to the East, seeing the sun beginning to disappear behind some far-off hills. "I suppose I'll be staying until morning."

"No trouble out of you and you'll be getting no trouble from us. Same deal as the one we gave the men from Gwynedd," the guard assured him.

"What are men from Gwynedd doing here?

The guard shrugged. They moved off a few hours ago. Only stayed the one night," he explained. "The tavern is that way. *Haggard Pict,* they call it."

Drysten chuckled to himself and returned a slight nod. "Thank you. I'll be on my way then."

The guard nodded and turned to his subordinate as Drysten passed.

It wasn't hard to find the tavern. It was the only place Drysten could overhear a happy crowd in the midst of their drink, or any sort of chatter for that matter. Located right outside the abandoned Roman fort, it must have seen considerable patronage in its heyday.

Drysten dismounted his horse as a young boy with long hair sauntered up. He tossed the boy a small coin and handed the reins off as the child looked at him in surprise before leading his horse toward a small stable conjoined with the tavern.

"Feed him and water him," Drysten ordered. "Do it well enough and you'll get more tomorrow morning." He jingled the pouch of coins at his waist, with the child's eyes immediately being drawn toward it. He turned and made his way inside.

"What'll be?" a stout innkeeper with kind eyes and a boisterous laugh asked.

Drysten glanced around as he spotted a table on the far side of the room. "Just staying for the night."

"We'll have a room made up for you!" the man returned with a reassuring nod.

Drysten nodded and reached into his pouch, handing the man three silver coins which looked freshly minted. He gave a brief glance down to one, noticing it held the depiction of a Roman he didn't recognize.

"Is there… anything else you'd require?" the innkeeper wondered as he eyed the pouch.

Drysten returned him with a suspicious glance. "No. The room will be all."

The innkeeper's smile faded as he nodded and walked to

a back room. Drysten eyed the other patrons, seeing the usual mix of whores and local farmers he'd expect in an establishment like this. The dim candlelight only revealed the most noticeable features of those around him. The whores were rather uncomely, with pox-ridden faces and matted hair. The farmers looked much like the livestock Drysten guess they tended.

After a short wait, the innkeeper journeyed back into the main area of the tavern and waved him over. "Room is ready," he declared from across the way.

Drysten nodded and rose from his seat before walking through the blank stares of the locals. He guessed they were startled by his Roman mail he still chose to wear along his journey. He knew it was either that, or someone had caught a glimpse of Colgrin's crown dangling from the back of his belt.

"Finest one's up this way. Should serve its purpose right enough." The innkeeper's tone hinted at an added nervousness. Drysten nodded and waited until the man turned around before clutching a hand to his sword hilt in response.

The two rounded a corner down a short hallway where Drysten was greeted by three women staring back at him.

"Finest you'll find in all of Rheged! Have your pick," the innkeeper whispered as he nudged Drysten with an elbow.

Drysten scoffed as he looked over the three women in a similar state as those he saw in the main room. "My wife is the finest I'll find. Move. I'm tired and need some rest."

One of the women stepped forward and produced a toothless smile." Come now, Lord. I think we can 'elp you—"

"No," Drysten interrupted. "No, you cannot." He pushed open the door as he blocked out the protests from the women and the innkeeper and closed it behind him. *Maybe in another life, he thought with a chuckle. A much bleaker one.*

He unbuckled his sword belt and laid it on a small table by the bed of straw before beginning to undo his fish scale armor. A hollow, scarcely audible thump came from under the bed, halting him as he was about to untie a leather lace at his side.

"Who's there?" Drysten hissed.

A shuffling noise moved further away under the bed. Drysten guessed it to be a rat as he, in silence, bent down to one knee and began peering into the darkness below the straw.

"I'm sorry!" a young voice screamed Drysten looked closer.

By instinct, Drysten thrust a hand under the bed and found his grasp clutching onto someone's collar. He pulled as hard as he could and ripped what he thought was a young girl from under the bed. A scream and a kick to Drysten's head followed, with Drysten tossing the child to the ground beside his sword.

The child rose. "I'm... sorry..."

Drysten looked over the face of a young boy with exceedingly long, matted hair. The very same child who led his horse to the nearby stable. The golden-red hair was almost plastered to the sides of his head as his bright green eyes looked back at him in sheer terror. "What's your name?" he menacingly growled, though he had no intentions of actually threatening the boy.

The child looked from side to side until his gaze met Drysten's sword belt. He leapt toward the blade and fumbled with it until he finally drew it from its resting place.

Drysten knew the boy posed no real threat to him and allowed him to find some sense of security. "Bad luck to kill a man with his own sword, boy," he responded with a smile.

The child began to tear up as he struggled to heft the blade and point it toward Drysten.

"Your name."

"L... Lucan, Lord," the boy whispered.

Drysten smirked. "First person here to rightly address me as a lord!"

The boy stared back with a blank gaze.

"How old are you?"

"I don't know," Lucan muttered as he looked to the door.

"Your father? Your mother?"

Lucan's tears began dropping down his cheeks. "I promise I didn't want to, Lord."

"Didn't want to do what, boy?" Drysten demanded as he saw the boy look to the door.

"He wanted me to steal, Lord. I didn't want to do it. He said to wait until you slept and take your coin from you," Lucan divulged.

Drysten sighed as he extended a calm hand and gestured for Lucan to return his sword. "There's no need to be afraid," he whispered in a reassuring tone. "If you need food, I'll get you something before I leave."

Lucan tried to lower the blade in one slow motion, but his strength gave way, slamming the point into the packed earth below his feet. He looked embarrassed as he raised his gaze to meet Drysten's "Thank you, Lord," he muttered.

Drysten stepped forward and took the sword from the boy, placing it in its sheath. He noticed Lucan's eyes fixed on his dagger hanging from the other end of the sword belt. "You want to see it?"

Lucan returned a cautious smile. "Yes, Lord."

Drysten smiled as he pulled the dagger free and spun it through his fingers, turning it over in his hand to give the boy the hilt. "On one condition," he stated. "You answer my questions."

The boy nodded.

"Where are your parents?"

"Dead, Lord. The Gaels..." Lucan dropped his gaze.

Drysten felt the guilt ripple through him as he extended his hand and let the boy grasp the dagger. Lucan took it and stared into the artfully crafted hilt, letting the scant light from the twilight hours illuminate the metal. "So why are you here?"

"It's my home."

"Was it always?"

Lucan shook his head.

"Where was home before here?"

"In the same place it always was."

Drysten chuckled to himself. "What was the name of you home?"

"Calunium, but Torin says I shouldn't go back there."

Drysten nodded as he glanced to the door. He heard a faint whisper between a man and a woman. Looking to Lucan, he shushed the boy quiet before taking a handful of subtle steps toward the door. He drew in a breath and ripped it open to see the startled innkeeper and who Drysten guessed to be his wife. "I'm to assume you are Torin?"

"I'm sorry, Lord! We were only... we," Torin began to stammer.

All I wanted to do was sleep and these fuckers won't even allow me to remove my armor.

The woman slapped Torin's arm and looked back to Drysten. "I told him it was foolish to think the child could steal from a member of the legion, Lord. He puts too much faith in that boy, stupid as he is."

Drysten grimaced in disgust as he peered back to Lucan, now staring down to his feet. "The boy will no longer be your concern."

Torin "What—"

"I am in need of slaves, and the boy will suffice. If you have issues with this, take it up with Lord Ambrosius Aurelianus of Powys. I'll be sure to explain how it was I came by the boy in the first place," Drysten said with a grin.

The man and woman both went silent as they stared at one another.

"Bring me and Lucan food and drink. We will both be dining as lords tonight," Drysten ordered, receiving no response from neither the innkeeper nor his wife. "Now!" he yelled.

"Yes, Lord," Torin returned as he walked off. His wife stared Drysten in the eye for a quick moment before joining him.

As he shut the door, Lucan crept up beside Drysten and peered up in his eyes. "I'm... a slave?" he asked with teary eyes.

Drysten smiled and shook his head. “No. I detest slavery. My father always did, and he taught me to as well.”

“Then…”

“Then you’re free to do as you please. I’d recommend coming with me to Powys, but it’s your decision to make.”

Lucan glanced toward the sword belt and returned Drysten with a smile.

CHAPTER TWENTY-ONE

It took two more days' riding to reach Glevum. The sun seemed to shine brighter over Powys than it did the rest of Britannia. But as welcoming as it was, Drysten knew he'd be delivering a message that would no doubt demand more Powysian blood in response.

Lucan seemed excited at the new life Drysten wanted to give him. He asked endless questions about Isolde, Galahad, and the Fortuna. All of which Drysten was happy to answer. He knew he owed the boy that much. Lucan never explained how his parents died, but Drysten knew he could've had an indirect hand in it.

"How far away have you been?" Lucan wondered as they reached the Northern gate to the city.

Drysten nodded to a purple cloaked guard as he entered before turning to face Lucan, sitting behind him atop the horse. "I've been to Gaul and Frisia. Do you know where they are?"

"I've never heard of *Gaul'n'frisia,*" Lucan answered in confusion.

Drysten chuckled. "What about Caledonia?"

"I know that one! You've been there?"

"I have. Fought there beside a king from those parts." Drysten glanced at his saddle's pommel as he remembered watching Garbonian die.

The rest of the ride to the Roman fortress was silent, brief as it was. Lucan must have been staring into the small crowds of people on either side of them while Drysten peered ahead toward the fort's gate.

I hope Isolde doesn't think I fathered this one, Drysten found himself thinking as he glanced behind him. Too old to be mine anyway.

"Lord!" a voice yelled in surprise. Drysten turned and allowed a Powysian guardsman to bring Lucan down from his saddle before joining him on the ground. "Fed and watered, if you please," he ordered the guard.

The Powysian nodded and took the horses reigns, leading it away.

"Lord, this is a surprise," Matthew stated as he sauntered over.

Drysten nodded and poked Lucan's shoulder, gesturing for him to follow. "Glanoventa needs more men. Abhartach has arrived, but so did Germanus. We can't stop them both with what we have."

Mathew's gaze betrayed a hint of confusion. "You... haven't heard?"

Drysten shook his head. "Abhartach is no longer interested in Glanoventa..."

"I know that place too!" Lucan added.

Drysten shushed the boy quiet and looked back to Matthew. "Where—?"

"Here," Matthew answered. "That's what his messenger told us."

Drysten peered toward Lucan, staring back at him with wide eyes as he finally began to understand the people who took his parents were now about to find him once more.

Matthew led the two toward Prince Ambrosius' small residence inside the fort. The prince was due to return from patrolling against the Saxons by the end of the day, but his wife and her handmaidens were still there. Isolde being one of them.

Drysten looked over the pair of guards stationed by the door, and immediately caught the familiar voice of his son. He was crying over the punishment for misbehaving in some such way but stopped when Drysten entered the room.

"Father!" Galahad screamed with joy. The boy ran up and wrapped his arms around Drysten's waist, taking all fears or concerns of the Gaels away for a swift moment.

Isolde poked her head in from a side room with a similar reaction, but then produced one of confusion as Lucan stepped around Drysten and Galahad. "Something you wish to tell me?" she asked in suspicion. She had the brief thought Drysten had been unfaithful, but it was clear she noticed that wouldn't have been possible considering his age.

"This one will be a slave!" Drysten announced to the room, earning a worried expression from Lucan. Drysten winked and patted the boy's head in a joking manner. "He needed a home. The Gaels took his parents..."

Isolde understood as a wave of pity and sorrow flooded her gaze. "Then he needs a new one."

Drysten nodded.

"Isolde!" a woman called before entering the room.

Ystradwel smiled toward Drysten, still weathering the embrace of his son. "Arthur should be returning soon. He'll be happy to see you."

Drysten smiled. "I look forward to it." He turned to Matthew. "Have you told them?"

Matthew nodded. "Whole city knows. Everyone's just under the belief the Gaels cannot reach us here."

"They don't understand who they are. What they're capable of."

Matthew sighed as he looked to Lucan, now showing great concern as he had overheard most of their conversation. "You'll be fine, boy," Matthew said with a smile. "I've never seen the men from Powys lose!"

Lucan smiled as he looked up to Drysten. "Is that true,

Lord?"

Drysten nodded with a fake smile before turning to Isolde. "Someone should get him washed. He's been more a guttersnipe than anything else for quite some time."

Isolde smiled and nodded before taking Lucan to an adjoining room, with Ystradwel waddling her pregnant self behind.

"Take me to the king," Drysten ordered Matthew, who nodded and pointed toward the door.

The walk to the other end of the Roman fort was short, with Drysten barely having enough time to scrape a crusty object from his eye before finally seeing King Uther seated next to Prince Ambrosius.

"Lord Drysten," the king greeted.

Drysten returned a slight nod before looking to Prince Ambrosius. "Your wife thought you'd be seeing her the moment you arrived."

The prince smirked. "She's been a terror since getting pregnant. With feet the size of roasted hams and a temper like a feral dog, I'll spend a little more time here."

King Uther released a jovial laugh and slapped the prince on the arm.

Drysten smirked and remembered Isolde when she was getting ready to have Galahad. He felt he was lucky she displayed none of those qualities. "Heard of the Gaels?"

The prince nodded. "That's why I'm here. My father sent a messenger back saying he will be joining us in a couple of days." The prince raised a small piece of parchment before gently setting it down in front of the king.

Drysten released a long sigh. "Abhartach will come after me. If I leave here, there's a chance he'll follow."

King Uther glanced to his nephew before looking back. "Why would I allow you to run off and die by yourself. You're a lord—"

"A lord who brought them all here in the first place," Drysten interrupted.

King Uther scrunched his face in annoyance at being interrupted. He looked to Matthew. “Bring the prisoner.”

Matthew nodded and marched out of the room, disappearing down a stairwell across the forum.

“Had a prison built beneath the Roman stonework,” King Uther explained. “Only holds about a dozen people but seeing as there’s not much crime in Glevum it does the job well enough.”

Drysten nodded. “And what do the prisoners think of sharing the space with a Gael?”

“Apparently, the Gael sits on one side of the cell while the others clamor for space beside the opposite wall,” Uther explained through a laugh. “They’re terrified of him!”

“Maybe they should be,” a familiar voice said from the doorway.

Drysten clasped his eyes shut and pursed his lips as the voice tore through the air. “How are you alive?” he hissed.

Argyle, being led by Matthew, was forced in front of the king. “The Morrigan has a use for me. She will not allow my death until that purpose is fulfilled.”

Drysten scoffed as he looked to King Uther. The king had a peculiar expression as he stared into the Gael’s hollow eyes. It was at that moment, Drysten understood the king was a worshipper of the old ways. No Christian would put stock in the murmurs of ancient gods.

Argyle noticed this as well. “Give us the traitor, Lord King. Give us Drysten and we will never harm your people.”

King Uther looked to the desk in front of him, running a hand over the message from his brother. “I want to know what will happen if I don’t.”

Argyle scoffed. “Look to Ebrauc and the vacant towns which now fill our bellies,” he responded while running a hand over his stomach. His smile wicked as Drysten had ever seen.

Uther scowled as he looked to Drysten. “We would beat them in a war,” he began, “but how many innocents would suffer before it was won?”

Drysten understood what was about to happen as he lowered his gaze. “Many.”

King Uther nodded and looked back to Argyle. “I will do what you ask. My people believe this place is impregnable, but you’ve shown that term holds no meaning to you. I heard what you did to Eboracum,” which caused a proud smile to cross Argyle’s lips.

Prince Ambrosius stepped forward. “Uncle, no!”

The king raised a hand to silence the prince. “We will speak of this no more. It is my decision to make.”

Ambrosius understood he could do nothing and stepped back a pace while looking to Drysten.

“So… I will do what you ask,” Uther whispered. “But not how you demand it.”

Argyle’s smiled faded as he cocked his head to the side. “Your meaning?”

King Uther stood and walked around the table. “I will allow Drysten to leave my kingdom peacefully. His family is going to be taken care of and his son will always have a place under my roof.”

“Sons,” Matthew whispered.

The prince and king both looked at the priest in surprise.

“He’s adopted one,” Matthew explained.

The king looked to Drysten, who gave a hesitant nod. Uther grimaced before looking back to Argyle. “He will leave peacefully. You can try and take him somewhere else.”

Argyle paused and looked away before finally giving a nod and raising his chained hands toward the king. “I’ll be needing a key.”

***

It didn't take Drysten long to understand the king's intentions. Once Argyle was released to meet with Abhartach, Uther summoned all the lords and officers in Glevum to explain his actions.

"I lied," the king said with a scoff. "Once your men return, you will lead the Gaels through Rheged and move them back toward Germanus."

"You had no intention of handing me over, did you?" Drysten wondered.

Uther chuckled and slapped a hand to Drysten's shoulder, causing a slight throb from the arrow wound which hadn't quite healed yet. "No, boy. You're a lord of Powys. Not to mention, I know all about the other times you've placed your faith in kings only to be cast aside."

Drysten glanced to Prince Ambrosius, watching him step forward.

"Uncle's ships should arrive within a week." Arthur's uneasy tone hinted at his discomfort. "They will help fend off the Saxons while we turn our attention to the Gaels and Germanus."

"I knew I would rue the day I asked that fucking traitor for aid," Uther seethed.

"Blood is blood. He was compelled to help," the prince responded, matter-of-factly.

Traitor? Drysten wondered. *A traitor with ships, no less.*

"So long as they hate Saxons and Gaels then they should prove useful," Hall answered.

Uther nodded and looked to Drysten. "Your main duty is to buy us time for the rest of the men to arrive." He stepped toward the prince. "When the Armoricans are protecting our Eastern flanks, we will be able to send more aid…" He turned back to Drysten. "Until that point, I need you to lead Abhartach's bastards on a chase back to Ebrauc."

Drysten glanced between the king and prince, noticing Arthur had adopted an awkward stance as if waiting for the king to add something.

"Oh," Uther muttered as he glanced to the ceiling. "I'd forgotten nobody told you. My brother is married," the king added.

"So am I. What does that—"

"To Bishop Germanus' sister."

Drysten felt his eyes go wide and his jaw fall open. For a split second, he believed all kings to be fools. "He will surely come to Germanus' rescue, Lord King!" Drysten found it hard to remain respectful.

Uther gave a sympathetic gaze. "He detests the bishop. Of that, I can assure you."

Drysten sighed and chose to trust King Uther. Arthur, in the least, had yet to show he was a fool in the way Ceneus had been. If he deemed Aldrien's men friends, Drysten knew he would have to do so as well. He glanced to the prince. "I will need a new second," he muttered.

Arthur stepped closer. "What has happened to Diocles?"

Drysten couldn't bring himself to answer.

"I... Matthew will go," Arthur whispered in a solemn breath. "The Greek was a good man."

Drysten nodded. "I know."

King Uther placed a hand on Drysten's shoulder. "For only having the one eye, he was rather insightful."

Drysten couldn't help but grin, but still felt the words catch in his throat.

The rest of the day mainly consisted of Drysten trying to figure out where his family lived. He knew Ystradwel had them sleeping close to her chambers, but no more than that. He dawdled around the courtyard of the forum while he waited for his wife to show herself, which she eventually did when the sun began to sink behind the Eastern hills.

"Love!" Isolde greeted as she sauntered up with Galahad and Lucan.

Drysten turned, producing a warm smile as he saw his wife. "I was hoping you'd turn up soon."

"Spent five years hoping the same for you," Isolde quipped. "Lucan has had little problem showing his excitement at becoming the son of a lord." Isolde placed a hand on the back of Lucan's head and ruffled his hair. "You could've simply told me you wanted another one."

Drysten's smile widened. "We will have a large family one day." He looked to Lucan. "Even if that family doesn't totally share my blood."

Lucan began to smile until he saw Argyle being led from the prisons toward the Northern gate of Glevum's vicus. The man saw Drysten and Isolde, and gave an evil wink while raising his hands to show they were no longer in chains.

"Be seeing you, Lord!" Argyle hissed.

Drysten turned and returned a smirk of his own. "You're making a mistake," he answered.

"How could that possibly be?"

"You think you'll be hunting me..."

Argyle scoffed and looked to Isolde. "You'll be needing another husband soon," as he was pushed forward by a Powysian guardsman. "I'll make sure to return here and find you myself."

The guard snickered and pointed toward the gate before shaking his head with a smile.

Drysten turned back to his wife and saw the worry in her eyes.

"What did he mean by that?"

Drysten scoffed. "There's always going to be someone who hates me. Now, Abhartach and Gaius seem to be the two most dangerous men in that group."

Isolde looked to Galahad and Lucan. "You're forgetting someone."

"Who?"

"Marhaus still fights for Colgrin," Isolde murmured, referencing the son of the slaver who once held her captive in Frisia. "Or he did. I can't imagine who he fights for now."

"Likely one of his sons," Drysten guessed. "That Ethelric

seemed to be the most dangerous of the three."

"Why?"

"He wasn't simply another brute. He fights with his mind as well as anyone I've seen. He will no doubt be an issue sometime in the future."

The pair watched Argyle disappear through the gate before walking hand in hand toward their temporary home. Drysten was a touch embarrassed, as it was the same room he'd first seen her in upon his return.

Could've just found the nearest bed and fallen in, Drysten thought with a sigh.

"Prince Ambrosius told us we're to have a new home once the Gaels are defeated. King Uther means to create a new kingdom from Rheged," Isolde explained. "Until then, this is what we have."

"Oh no, a palace," Drysten sarcastically exclaimed, earning a nudge from Isolde's elbow. He grinned before remembering he was about to leave her once more. "I have to tell you something..."

"I know," Isolde responded. "The only thing I didn't know about was Lucan, but that's hardly a problem for me. King Uther brought me in with Matthew and they both explained his plan to me before you arrived. It was odd, as they actually asked for my permission before settling on anything."

"They are good men." Drysten was shocked, but pleased the king saved him another disappointing conversation with his wife. That, and the manner of respect they showed was more than surprising in and of itself. "I promise I'll come back."

Isolde offered a weak smile. "I know." She stood taller and kissed Drysten before looking back into his eyes. "I can't imagine two kings would double-cross you," she whispered with a hollow chuckle.

Drysten nodded and looked over her shoulder. *A new kingdom, he thought. I wonder what role we'd play there.*

As Drysten watched his wife and two sons scurrying off

toward a pair of servants preparing their meals, he spied the image of his father marching up. He seemed to be conjured up out of nothing, stepping forward out of a wisp of air.

"What did I tell you?" Hall demanded of his son.

Drysten turned and unbuckled his sword belt, leaning the blade against the doorway before leading his father's ghost into the vacant courtyard.

"Well?" Hall demanded.

Drysten turned, but didn't see the vacant eyes Hall once had in Drysten's dreams. He didn't look emaciated or deceased. He looked like Hall ap Lugurix, Drysten's loving father. "I... don't know. You told me many things..."

"Such as?"

"Such as how I would disappoint my people and bring them nothing but—"

"That was not me!" Hall interrupted as he pointed an angry finger toward his son.

Drysten cocked his head to the side. "Then who was it, father?"

Hall sighed. "The one you believe in."

Drysten scoffed and looked around, content in knowing nobody was close enough to hear the exchange between him and a man long dead. "The one I believe in?"

Hall nodded.

"Who might that be?"

"You should know," Hall replied. "You were a worshipper of her for a short while."

"The Morrigan..." Drysten whispered.

Hall nodded. "She has plans for these people, son. Plans you've ruined."

Drysten scoffed. "Why the fuck should I care?"

"Because now the only plan she has, is to make sure you join me and your mother. All she wishes now, is for us to be reunited."

Drysten turned and saw a faint wisp of thick air in the shape of a woman walk from behind his father. "Mother...?"

A hand slowly rose from the smoke as the woman's silhouette returned a faint nod.

Tears began welling up in Drysten's eyes as he tried his best to remember the face of his mother. The closer he got, the more the fog began to turn to someone he could vaguely recognize. "I... can't remember your face, mother..." he stammered. "I'm so sorry." A tear began to fall down his cheek as the fog was whisked away as if by the wind, with Drysten extending a hand as though he believed he could have caught it.

Hall stepped closer. "She loves you in case you didn't know. She knows you've done your best."

Drysten remained silent.

"Love," Isolde called from inside. "We have food waiting!"

Hall smiled and placed a hand on Drysten's shoulder, with Drysten feeling no weight from his father's hand "Go be with my grandchild."

"How do I know?"

Hall adopted a perplexed expression. "How—?"

"How do I know you're even real," Drysten pleaded.

"One would think, after you've spent so much time near holy men and believers of ancient religions you would have developed the ability to have a little faith." Hall removed his hand and produced a warm smile. "But I suppose until the point that you do, you simply don't know."

Drysten sighed as he glanced to his feet. He looked back to his father, but the man had vanished.

CHAPTER TWENTY-TWO

So, it would be another hunt. Abhartach loved a good hunt. It had been so long since he had one which led him into the wilds; he wondered if their caretaker would even recognize him.

"Ready for a hunt, Argyle?" Abhartach asked with a snicker. His second in command had hated the fact Lord Drysten dubbed him by the name of Abhartach's bastard, grimacing every time Abhartach used the name to address him. Though he knew his place and would never object. "Cernunnos will be pleased with the display, no doubt," Abhartach murmured to himself as he rose from his seat. He had taken up residence in a cave the Gaels frequented over the past few months. He knew Drysten would no doubt remember the place, so he understood he wouldn't be able to stay for more than a couple of nights.

Argyle settled in beside him, freshly returned from his foray into Powys. "We go when night falls?"

Abhartach nodded. "We go when night falls."

"What of Drysten?" Argyle questioned as he pulled down his facemask. "The man has the idea he can kill us using our own ways."

Abhartach would typically discount any threats made by the Britons or Romans, but Drysten was different. He was the first outsider who had the voices of the gods whispering into his ears. Abhartach knew he would need certain assurances the man would fail in any effort against him. "There will be a sacrifice," he ordered. "One of great importance." He placed a hand on Argyle's shoulder.

Argyle's eyes went wide until he stifled the fear from his mind. "I would be honored, Great Chief."

Abhartach smiled wide and looked to the dimly lit path leading from the cave. The smell of cooked meat emanated from the next chamber over, bringing a pleasant and relaxing sensation to the king. "You will feast," he assured Argyle. "You will be permitted any meats you could desire. Then the deed will be done. The Morrigan will have her sacrifice."

"You're certain she will whisper to Cernunnos on our behalf? He will bring us a great hunt?"

Abhartach nodded. "You are the most important man I have brought with me. The souls of the great weigh heavy on her scales."

Argyle produced a smile as he leaned his head back and shut his eyes.

Abhartach looked back and rose, creeping toward the chamber holding his meal. The man would no doubt have the tougher meat. The woman would be soft. The fires were bright and warm, causing the king's head to throb. "We will have a sacrifice!" he announced.

The dozen Gaels rose in the cramped space, whooping and hollering with approval.

One man stayed silent.

"Myrddin!" Abhartach called. "Why don't you join us?"

The man stood, giving Abhartach a clear view of his greying beard. He shuffled over, the Gaels moving aside for fear of touching the man's raggedy clothes. "I do not rejoice because I have seen the outcome."

"Why don't you enlighten us as to what you've seen?"

Myrddin shook his head. "It is forbidden. All will be revealed in time."

Abhartach grimaced before seeing Argyle stepping up beside him.

Myrddin scoffed. "This is the one?"

Abhartach nodded. He couldn't understand why Myrddin didn't seem to think highly of the best hunter Abhartach had. "It is."

Argyle stepped forward. "I look forward to dining with my ancestors. I cannot think of a more honorable—"

"That is the problem with you!" Myrddin shouted as he jabbed a finger toward Argyle. "None of you can think!" The man threw his hands in the air and trudged toward the ladder. The hunters watched him disappear up into the daylight, most wondering what issues he had toward Argyle's noble wishes.

"Prepare a feast," Abhartach commanded.

Two hunters nodded as they followed Myrddin up the ladder, presumably for more firewood. The rest huddled against the edges of the rock walls of the cave. Abhartach wondered how long the men would be able to stomach the overabundance of light, but knew they would never voice their concerns.

Voice, Abhartach thought with a snicker. *Some men waste such a gift.*

A short while later, Myrddin began moving back down the ladder, the two hunters in tow.

"He returns!" Abhartach announced.

"I do," Myrddin replied with a grunt as his feet settled down onto the stone base of the cave. "And I believe I have an answer for your little sacrifice."

Abhartach stood and perked an eyebrow. "Explain."

"You place too much importance in that… man," Myrddin hissed as he pointed to Abhartach's left.

Argyle stood straighter and folded his arms as he glared back to Myrddin. Abhartach felt the man's gaze shift from Myrddin to himself.

"You will give The Morrigan a bounty. A bounty instead of one measly—"

"Measly!" Argyle roared.

Abhartach raised a hand, silencing Argyle and preventing another one of Myrddin's insults. "That is not an option. I will not sacrifice—"

“The hardest sacrifices are the ones which grant the most favor from the gods,” Myrddin interrupted. “Did you not say those exact words yourself?”

Abhartach felt his brow furrow. “How many of my men would you think would sate The Morrigan’s thirst?”

“The most you can spare,” Myrddin responded. “How else will The Morrigan know you wish her favor?”

Abhartach glanced to the layer of dirt covering the stone below his feet. He knew the druid was correct in assuming the larger the offering, the greater the reward. But the hint of persistence in Myrddin’s voice could have signaled an ulterior motive. One which Abhartach would lament giving in to. In any case, Abhartach knew he couldn’t risk the chance the man’s intentions weren’t aligned with his own. “As you wish,” he muttered. “Choose them and be done with it. There is work to do.”

Myrddin nodded and began condemning hunters to death.

***

The Powysians under Lord Aurelianus returned two mornings after Argyle departed. Drysten had already regained his strength from his own journey South, feeling almost new as he woke up the following morning. Galahad and Lucan looked as though they were becoming closer, with both children giggling to themselves during their meals together.

"Boy must be about ten," Isolde observed.

Drysten shrugged. "Likely looked younger before he had steady meals. He told me Torin never fed him much."

"I'll see he gets more food in his belly," Isolde returned.

Drysten nodded and rose from the finely crafted bed of Glevum's royal estate. He outstretched his arms and turned to speak before Maebh sauntered in from the courtyard. "Put that down!" he shouted in surprise.

The dog gave a playful bounce toward Drysten as he dropped the large rat he held in his mouth. The rat hissed at its captor, with Maebh bopping it on the top of the head with his paw.

"Drysten, get it out!" Isolde shrieked.

Maebh heard his master's order and plucked the rodent up into his mouth before sprinting out into the morning air.

Drysten smirked before looking to his wife. "Suppose his morning meal is taken care of."

Isolde shivered from disgust before slamming her head back down onto a pillow.

After a quick kiss on Isolde's forehead, he donned a tunic along with his sandals and walked outside. He stepped around Maebh in the middle of his meal and moving toward the grouping of men toward the forum's main entrance.

"Lord Drysten!" Matthew greeted with a wave.

Bors glanced over and offered a wave of his own. "Almost ready, Lord."

"Good," Drysten whispered. Originally, he was in no rush to leave Glevum on account of his next task. However, now he was somewhat joyed by the idea he could rid the world of

Abhartach and his hunters. He knew the task was dangerous, but so were many of the other feats he had accomplished. "Who will be joining us?"

Matthew pointed a finger to himself before craning his neck toward Bors. "Me and this one will lead. The Fortuna's men and a handful of others will follow as well."

"That should come to roughly two hundred souls," Drysten guessed, adding a satisfied nod.

Bors nodded. "After you departed Glanoventa, they tried the beaches one more time. One wave of hunters led more slaves. We killed every one of them."

"Were there more women?"

Bors nodded through a heavy sigh.

Matthew grimaced as well. "We must have killed fifty in total..."

Drysten felt a pang of guilt at women being harmed in that way. "Where's the one we captured?"

Bors pointed toward the prison under the forum. "She's alone. Lord Ambrosius was incredibly detailed in describing what would happen should someone try to touch her."

Drysten was surprised others shared his views on harming women but knew the Powysians had shown themselves to be better souls than the Romans. They seemed to show much of what Rome's values should have been. What they were always rumored to be, but never were. Another ting that surprised him about Powys was how few slaves Drysten saw.

"Lord Drysten," Uther yelled from behind.

Drysten turned and gestured for Matthew and Bors to follow as he approached.

"King Ceneus was just describing the best areas to make a stand against Abhartach if you get cornered," Uther said as he pointed a thumb behind him.

King Ceneus exited the king's study, carrying a small piece of parchment before stepping toward Drysten and handing it to him. "There are hillforts between here and Ebrauc. The only ones you could easily fend off an attack in—"

"I have no intention of running," Drysten said with a shake of the head. "Abhartach will assume I'll run. I simply don't intend to."

Both kings glanced at one another before Ceneus finally spoke. "In any case, take this with you. You never know if you'll need it."

Drysten shrugged and took the parchment before handing it to Bors.

"You look much like Constantine with the way you wear that purple cloak," Ceneus observed.

Drysten looked up to see the king of Ebrauc looking to Matthew, who took on an uncomfortable gaze as he peered toward Uther.

"I... well, thank you, Lord King," Matthew whispered before looking to Drysten. "I'll see to it our people are ready to move by noon." He nodded to both kings and ducked away toward the city.

"Odd one," Bors muttered with a chuckle.

The only one who seemed unfazed by Matthew's awkwardness was, in fact, King Uther. The king placed a hand on Ceneus' shoulder and gestured for him to follow back to his study.

"I will be leading a siege against Isurium while you weather the storm further East," Ceneus explained. "I hope to see you all soon." Ceneus bid Drysten and his men farewell and turned to follow Uther back inside.

"Did you notice that as well?" Bors whispered.

Drysten nodded as he looked back to Matthew, seeing the priest give an awkward glance over his shoulder before he disappeared into the city. "Likely nothing but the awkwardness of a priest. You know how they can be," he whispered. He found himself remembering Maewyn and hoping the man had found a way to separate himself from the bishop. *Germanus would never allow that. He's likely dead already,* he thought with a sigh.

Bors accompanied Drysten back to Isolde, who was having her morning meal with both children as well as Prince Ambrosius and Ystradwel. The group spoke for a short while before Drysten finally began donning his equipment, and altogether readying himself to leave. Galahad and Lucan both sauntered up and shared a farewell, with Lucan almost looking more worried for Drysten than his actual son.

"Don't worry, father will come back," Galahad explained. "Everyone's tried to kill him, but they never do!"

Drysten gave an awkward glance to Isolde before hugging his son and looking to Lucan. "The boy speaks the truth," he said with a wink. "I'll be back before you know it."

Lucan returned an awkward smile before hugging Drysten and walking back to the table. Prince Arthur noticed the uneasiness in the boy and immediately brought him over, whispering something into his ear which seemed to make the boy laugh away some of his worries.

"Arthur," Drysten said, "when I return, we'll have to speak of this new kingdom of yours."

"That we will, brother. I'll have much to say," Arthur replied with a warm smile.

Drysten nodded and shared a moment alone with his wife before finally moving back toward the city's Northern gate. Isolde accompanied him most of the way, with Bors and Maebh trailing close behind.

"Hard to guess which one is more dangerous," Drysten whispered.

Isolde laughed as she peered behind her. Maebh seemed alert and ready to defend her to the death, while Bors seemed as though he hadn't slept in days. "I'd place my bets on the pup."

"Which one is that?"

Bors seemed to become curious when both Isolde and Drysten glimpsed behind them after hearing him clear his throat with a slight growl.

Isolde eventually halted and kissed Drysten farewell, journeying off to fulfill some mundane errand for Ystradwel.

Drysten watched her leave, somehow knowing this wasn't the last time he was going to see her.

"You should always treat each time leaving your family as though they'll never see you again, son," Hall whispered. "If the last five years haven't taught you that, I don't know what will."

Drysten froze and perked his head up, turning slow to look behind him. "Isolde," he called.

Isolde turned back, curious.

"I love you," Drysten whispered. He knew she couldn't hear him. She was much too far away.

Isolde produced that same warm smile that had always seemed to melt Drysten's mind into mush. She whispered back the same, and both turned away.

The walk out the city's gate led Drysten and Bors to the rest of the men still milling about. Amiram was just off to the side with his own wife when the mute spotted him. Amiram seemed pleased to see Drysten, waving him over and pointing to a small child of roughly six or seven years.

"You'll love this," Bors muttered as he rolled his eyes.

Drysten shuffled over to see Alda being ushered forward by Amiram.

"Wouldn't let me leave without introducing you to him," Amiram's wife stated. "This one's name is Tristan. I figured you'd know why if you had half a mind."

Drysten felt himself going red in the face. The idea he was important enough to anyone for them to name a child after him was strange. "I… thank you…"

Amiram chuckled and ushered the boy forward. "Go!"

The boy sighed and walked toward Drysten before meeting his gaze. "I was named after you," the child whispered.

"Now we can go?" Alda asked with a smile.

Amiram paused, staring up for a moment before slapping his wife's backside and pointing toward the city.

"You're a horse's ass," Alda whispered in frustration. She nodded to Drysten before taking Tristan's hand and leading him away, stealing one look over her shoulder to blow a kiss back to her husband.

"You're an odd one," Drysten whispered to Amiram, who nodded with a bright smile.

Drysten turned and saw Matthew sauntering up with the few Powysians Lord Aurelianus chose to send along. Their presence brought an added comfort to those who hadn't yet faced the Gaels, as these Roman-looking men were all present at Glanoventa.

Drysten nodded toward Matthew and turned to look upon the freshly painted shields of those were now oath sworn to follow him. He chose black ravens like those used by the Gaels, but three in number over a white background. The crows signified each powerful man he had defeated or was to kill in the coming days. The first was Colgrin, the man responsible for raping and burning his way through Londinium and Powys. The second represented Gaius, the man who cut the throat of his closest friend right in front of him. The third, was Germanus. He thought long and hard over adding a fourth for Abhartach, but chose against it. He knew enough about the man not to underestimate him. Not to be too overconfident.

"Looks like a fucking *chicken*," a man yelled as his wife handed him his shield, drawing a grin from Matthew as he passed by.

Drysten scoffed as he looked it over from afar. The black ravens indeed looked like burned chickens.

After slight protesting from a handful of men, Drysten ordered the war-band North. The men in question were not cowards, they simply didn't understand why they couldn't use the Fortuna's speed and safety to get to the Eastern reaches of Rheged.

"We won't be stopping until we reach Petuaria," Drysten explained to Matthew, Bors, and Amiram.

Bors released a heavy sigh. "Why on earth do you want to go back there of all places?"

"I intend to lead Abhartach around Ebrauc to root out

Germanus' men. We will lead them both right into each other." Drysten looked behind him, hearing the faint whisper of an old Roman war chant beginning to come together.

"Hard to expect a couple hundred men to fight two armies," Bors replied.

"I don't expect them to. I simply expect them to fight what's left."

CHAPTER TWENTY-THREE

Drysten's war-band crossed into Rheged on the third night after departing Glevum. They'd marched East over the border into Linnuis, one of the two neighboring kingdoms to Powys' East. It was after walking along the Northern border of Linnuis when they began seeing seabirds hovering overhead. At that point, they turned North and finally crossed in the still war-torn Rheged.

"Should reach Petuaria in another day," Matthew guessed as he huddled near a small fire. "Can't say I'm excited about all this fucking rain."

Drysten nodded as he looked up from the fire. "Better than our tracks going uncovered. Hunters will have trouble following us through the swamps we've passed."

Bors nodded and took a small morsel of meat from Amiram. The mute had journeyed out with Dagonet and the Cretans to make certain nobody was trailing them and managed to do a little hunting along the way.

"Didn't see signs of anyone following," Dagonet had said. "Nothing but wild dogs."

The scout had returned from speaking with a handful of men huddled by another fire. He settled in next to Drysten and wrapped his cloak around his shoulders and legs.

"How's your sister?" Drysten wondered. She had been

the wife of the man who took Isolde as a slave five years ago, likely marrying the man against her will. She still bore the scars from her years of abuse and torment.

Dagonet shrugged. "Haven't seen much of her for a couple years. She's married a butcher in Petuaria."

"It'll be good for you to see her again," Drysten added.

Dagonet glanced off to the side. "Doubt it."

"Why do you say that?"

"She's become one of Germanus' true believers. The bastard baptized her right in front of me about two years after you were taken prisoner."

Matthew raised his gaze from the fire. "Just because she's Christian doesn't mean she stopped being family."

"I barely knew her anyway," Dagonet answered with a shrug.

The men sat in silence until each decided it was time to retire for the night. Drysten and the other high-ranking officers brought their own small tents from Glevum. Each was pitched in a circle, with the rest of the men encamped around them. Drysten hated the idea he was using his men as shields while he slept, but Bors assured him it was nothing other commanders wouldn't do.

The night was quiet and peaceful. Drysten managed to fall asleep fairly quick, with no disturbing dreams coming to him for the first time in a while. But what he awoke to the next morning, was anything but peaceful.

"Lord!" Bors yelled as he burst into Drysten's small tent. "We need you outside."

Drysten sighed and threw his worn blue tunic over his head before following. There was a group of men huddled around his tent, all wearing disturbed expressions as they began to trail behind Drysten and Bors.

"They were found this morning," Bors explained. "Sent Dagonet and Matthew out straight away to find their trail."

Drysten let out a heavy sigh, knowing what he was about to find.

The group walked to the edge of the camp, only halting when Drysten saw a disheveled man under his charge sitting on a small crate near the wagon train. He had his head in his hands as he sobbed with two others kneeling beside him. They were consoling the man through his hysteria, though neither one knew how to do so.

"He woke up with them on either side of him," Bors whispered.

Drysten fought off a cold shiver and nodded as he followed Bors to a small tent with a pool of blood seeping out from the entrance.

Magnus, the healer of the war-band stepped away from the tent. "I'll do no good for these ones, Lord," he muttered with a sad shake of his head.

"That will be all, Magnus," Drysten uttered as he approached. The healer nodded and moved off toward the survivor.

After peeling back the flap, Drysten saw what looked to be the handiwork of the Gaels at first glance. Two men with space in between for a third were lying on their backs. Their heads were gone. They had slept with their heads to the entrance, while the rags used for the middle man's pillow showed he had slept with his head near their feet.

Drysten crept in near the men still draped in the furs they had slept under. The tent was the furthest one from the center of camp. A fact which brought a certain amount of confusion. "If this was Abhartach, he wouldn't have stopped with one tent."

Bors scoffed. "Who else would it be?"

Drysten looked up from the bodies. "Bury them deep. The wild dogs will go hungry tonight," he ordered before walking back outside. He peered to the survivor, seeing the man's vacant eyes staring back. "We'll end this for good," he said with a nod.

"I know, Lord," the man whispered.

"I need to know what you saw," Drysten whispered as

he approached the man. "I need to be certain I'm right in my hunch." As he got closer, Drysten detected the unmistakable smell of wine coming from the man's breath. Along with the scent, the man's eyes were tired and sunken in.

"I did'n see 'em—"

"What were you drinking?"

Magnus approached from Drysten's left and leaned toward his ear. "I don't know how this is relevant, Lord. Perhaps we should ease the man's—"

"I'll have an answer," Drysten declared, eyes still fixed on those of the survivor.

"I brung some'n to help my sleep'n, Lord..." the man stammered, his bloodshot eyes going ever wider.

Magnus cursed under his breath and waved Bors over before moving back toward the officer's tents.

Drysten hadn't realized he was holding his breath until he finally released it a slow huff. "You simply didn't wake up because you couldn't. There were no ghosts here. Simply those of the Bishop."

Bors looked as though he wanted to scold the survivor but elected to simply wave him off with his two comrades. "That shouldn't put my mind at ease, but it certainly does."

Drysten looked to the remaining men now assembling in front of him. "Call back the scouts," he ordered. He pointed North. "We go!"

The men dispersed to break camp, with Bors hurrying them as they packed up their belongings. Dagonet, Amiram, and the Cretans returned when the tents had all been placed back onto the horses. All sporting looks of confusion in their eyes.

"That wasn't Abhartach," the scout explained.

Drysten nodded. "I know. I'm guessing the tracks you found belonged to armored men trudging along through the darkness."

Dagonet nodded. "Small group seemed to approach the camp before removing their armor. Four men kept going and killed the two while they slept. The third…" Dagonet shrugged.

"Was too sloshed up to tell which end of the tent his head was supposed to be," Drysten added with a scoff.

Bors snickered to himself. "Saved his own life."

Drysten nodded. "It wasn't the Gaels, but someone trying to make us think so. The only reason the third man lives is because his head was at their feet. This wasn't a message, simply incompetence," he whispered.

"How do we respond to this?"

"Don't tell a soul what you've found. We can use this to our advantage."

Dagonet raised an eyebrow. "How so? The men all know already."

"I mean the locals must believe we are being chased by the Gaels. Word will get out to Abhartach's scouts, and that is how we will end the Christians who are chasing us."

Bors and Dagonet glanced to one another, clearly not understanding.

Drysten produced a smirk. "Eidion or Gaius did this. The Gaels will certainly follow when they hear of it. "Who do you think will get caught in the middle once Abhartach and his men come within arm's length of us?"

Bors and Dagonet gave a skeptical glance to one another. "Drysten…"

"It'll work," Drysten returned.

Dagonet tilted his head to the side. "It fits with the tracks, but this is still a risk."

"A risk worth taking," Drysten assured them.

The men began marching North once the two bodies were buried. Drysten rode in front with Bors and Amiram on either side of him. From Dagonet's best estimates, Drysten wagered his war-band was now about fifty miles South of Petuaria. The skies were clear, and the ground had little mud, making the march through Rheged last only a day and a half before the men first set their eyes on the shore across from their destination. They came within sight of Titus' villa, but no souls looked to have been there for quite some time.

Off in the distance, Drysten could make out the familiar sight of Conway's farm, now looking overgrown and neglected. The familiar smells of the pottery kilns wafted into Drysten's nose, reminding him of the last happy moments he had in the town. The last time he saw his father.

"Lord?" Cynwrig whispered from the brush beside Drysten.

The two men had been scouting the river to see if the old ferry was still in working order. It was, and that would be how Drysten and his first group of warriors would cross.

"Are the men ready?" Drysten asked of his scout.

Cynwrig nodded. "All are lined up along the shore. Dagonet's leading the rest around to the bridge a few miles away."

Drysten nodded. "We move at nightfall."

Cynwrig nodded, and the two crept off.

The stars began showing themselves not long after. The peculiar thing about it all was the lack of noise or light coming from across the river. Even though Drysten only spent a handful of nights in the town, he always remembered the abundance of noise coming from the tavern or from various buildings by the pier.

"We move," Drysten whispered.

Cynwrig nodded and waved the men forward.

Drysten donned his Saxon crown and moved to the small ferry. Upon closer inspection, it was recently repaired, and seemed able to hold about six men at a time without much cause for concern. "Five or six at a time depending on who's heaviest. Stay in the tall grass of the farm across the way until everyone is ashore." He looked to Bors. "Stay here until the last group is across."

Bors returned a silent nod. He had plastered mud all over the right side of his face, into his beard, and over his arms. He looked fearsome indeed, but somewhat strange all at once.

Drysten looked back and joined Cynwrig on the ferry.

Four others of a smaller build than Drysten huddled behind him, two of which were using the long poles to push the ferry across the river. The lack of noise coming from across the way meant the noise of the poles wading through the current was even more audible.

"Why isn't there anyone here?" Cynwrig wondered.

Drysten shrugged but knew Cynwrig likely couldn't see him.

"I spent more than my share of nights by the river. I could always hear the villagers," Cynwrig whispered.

"What were you doing by the river?"

"Conway's daughter," Cynwrig explained with a slight chuckle.

"Think she's still around?"

Cynwrig went silent for a moment. "She died."

"Of?"

"Same… as your mother," Cynwrig whispered back.

Drysten felt the weight on his friend's shoulders. "Childbirth…"

Both men went silent for the remainder of the journey to the other side of the river. Drysten wished to tell Cynwrig his woman and child were simply awaiting him in the Otherworld, but wasn't sure whether that was even true.

Watch over them, father, Drysten thought. *Make sure they're—*

"There's no need. I wager they'll be reunited soon enough," Hall whispered back.

Drysten glanced to the faint silhouette of his friend crouched beside him, wondering if Hall's words spoke any truth.

The ferry finally stopped at the opposite bank of the river, with all men clamoring out before two remained to bring the rest of the men. Drysten hoped nobody knew they were there, as the size of the force that was with him currently numbered himself, Cynwrig, and two others.

"It'll take far too long to bring the rest," Cynwrig whispered.

Drysten shook his head. "We wait," he whispered back. "Dagonet's men should be approaching from the Northern side of the town by now. We'll have most of our people on this side of the river soon enough," he assured his friend. "Be patient."

Cynwrig mumbled something to himself and crouched down into the tall grass. It was clear he disapproved, but likely knew better than to question his commander in front of others. Even if his commander was his friend.

Most of the men had ferried their way across the river when Dagonet crept up out of the darkness.

"Drysten," the scout whispered.

"Here."

"No movement inside the village. Everything's dark. No candlelight in the windows or anything," Dagonet whispered.

Drysten turned to Cynwrig. "How many men do we have with us?"

"Only a small handful are on the other side."

Drysten nodded. "We move. "He turned to Dagonet as he slowly drew his sword. "I'll give you a moment before moving into the village."

Dagonet must have nodded but Drysten couldn't see it in the darkness. The man stayed low as he moved around the outside of the village and back to his men.

The eerie silence seemed to hang over the shoulders of the men until Drysten finally rose and gave the order to begin skulking forward. All that could be heard was the slight rustling of the grass. Drysten knew the village was unlikely to be abandoned and wondered what group could be lying in wait for them across from Conway's farm.

"Lord!" a man screamed. "Shield wall near the villa!"

Drysten trained his eyes and saw the faint light from a torch inside the villa's walls. "Good," he whispered before turning to the men. "Sheath your swords. There will be no fighting these men." Drysten rose, walking taller until he finally approached the enemy shields.

"You'll go no further, Saxon," a familiar voice bellowed from the shields. "Go back to Colgrin—"

"Colgrin is dead," Drysten shouted. "You'll find no threats from us."

A murmur began behind the shields. A torch was lit and brought to the front of the shield wall, illuminating the bear on the red background. There were also men carrying images of fishes or trees, and in the center was a small group carrying the horned snake of Ebrauc.

"Who are you?" the voice demanded.

The man sounded older than Drysten remembered from their last meeting. Drysten felt himself smiling under his helmet as he lowered his head and removed it. "Dagonet!" he yelled as loud as he could. "These men are not our enemy."

Dagonet's men began creeping from behind the presumed enemy, coming from behind wooden buildings. How they managed to get through the town's stone gate was beyond Drysten, but the sight of the shield wall becoming confused and turning every which way was comical to say the least.

"Good to know!" Dagonet shot back.

"Who are you?" the man bellowed in hysteria. It seemed he didn't share Drysten's sense of humor.

Drysten began stepping forward until a lone man took a few steps forward to meet him, shield and sword raised in defiance. "Jorrit, put that down before you hurt yourself."

Jorrit glanced behind him and lowered his weapon. "Who the fuck—"

"Drysten."

Jorrit cast a faint smile as he stepped forward. "Haven't come to stab me again, have you?" he asked with a laugh.

Drysten shook his head and looked behind him. "I was under the assumption Eidion's men held Petuaria. I came for him and the Roman."

"You'll find no Romans here. Just us filthy Frisians," Jorrit responded as he gestured over his shoulder.

"And Saxons, Lord," a big bearded man added as he led

another behind him. The Saxon who spoke carried a shield bearing the likeness of a bear on a red background, while the other had one depicting a fish.

"The Saxons, Octha and Ebissa," Drysten declared as he extended a hand. "It's been too long," he added as he shook each man's hand.

Jorrit stepped forward. "Since you're alive, I'm guessing Abhartach isn't."

Drysten paused a moment before shaking his head. "He's hunting me, as are the Christians."

"So you chose to bring them here?" Jorrit asked in surprise. "Drysten, our families are here..."

"I know. I wasn't planning on staying."

***

Gaius crept forward through the brush. Eidion was right behind him, but both men knew it was too late. They had arrived just soon enough to see the faint shapes of Drysten's last few men reaching the opposite bank.

"Too late," Eidion whispered in an unimpressed tone.

Gaius didn't bother to look the prince in the eye. "I noticed. They seemed to quicken their pace after our little raid."

"You were right," Eidion begrudgingly noted. "It was a bad idea."

Gaius scoffed. He noticed a huge change in the prince since their alliance began. *This woman he loves must be a damned goddess to cause this.*

"We go back to Isurium," the prince commanded. "There's no victory for us here. The Frisians will likely join Drysten and outnumber us more than they already do."

"I'd imagine we'll be seeing them rather soon then," Gaius added as he rubbed the space between his eyes. He wanted Drysten dead more than anything, but a short stay in Isurium would be a welcome respite. His wife had joined him there with their son, and he hadn't had a chance to see either of them for more than a moment since his father's death. "You'll be seeing your woman?"

Eidion nodded, a smile showing through the scant light of the moon. "I'd hope so."

"Yet you just told me you still don't know her name."

"No names. Safer for her if I don't know it."

"Because of the bishop?"

Eidion nodded. "Because of the bishop."

"Citrio," Gaius whispered, waving him over.

Gaius' second in command stayed low as he approached.

"We'll cross the same way they did, we'll simply go further West before we do. Wait until no more of his men are —" Gaius knew he heard something coming from behind his men. He had never been more certain of anything in all his life. When he looked, however, all he saw were the lights of his men's eyes staring back at him.

"Lord?" Citrio urged in a hushed tone.

Gaius rose and patted Eidion's shoulder.

"What is it?" the prince hissed.

"Someone's out there..."

The three men turned about and stared into the darkness. Nothing could be seen, but Gaius felt someone staring back. Every fiber of his being screamed for him to turn tail and run as hard as he could in any direction but that one.

"Fucking hell," Gaius whispered as he turned to Eidion, "they've been our trail this whole time." He felt his eyes go wider as the terror began to drag at the hairs on his neck. "That fucking bastard was leading them to us!"

Eidion glanced around, still confused. "Who—?"

A chorus of shrieks erupted from the darkness as malevolent shapes burst forward.

"Behind!" Gaius screamed. His men stood tall and ripped their blades from their sheaths as they turned to face their attackers.

The men furthest in the back of the group never had a chance to face their attackers. The backs of their skulls were caved in by dark silhouettes bursting from the wilderness. A handful more were able to put up a fight until being overwhelmed by the tide of Gaels erupting toward them.

After he trained his eyes through the darkness, Gaius then saw the number of blurs racing at them. It was then he understood their end was near.

***

Jorrit had introduced his son to Drysten and Matthew when the screaming began. It was far off and barely audible, but was growing in ferocity at an uncomfortably fast pace.

"Get your people inside the villa," Drysten ordered of Jorrit, who nodded. "It was a pleasure to meet you, Lanzo," he said with a wink. The dark-haired boy smiled as Drysten looked back to his men. "Shield wall in front of the villa!"

Matthew led the Britons as they formed a wall behind Jorrit's people while Drysten donned his Saxon crown. He glanced over the heads of the bearded men, seeing Matthew barking his orders to the shields assembling in front of him as the screams intensified across the river.

"The Christians," Dagonet explained as he walked away from a heated argument with his sister. "They must be fighting with someone."

Drysten nodded. "We know who that someone likely is."

"What are my orders?" Dagonet asked in an antsy tone. Drysten wondered if he was anxious about the argument or the possibility of his impending death.

"Families are tricky things in Britannia," Hall whispered.

"You will take fifty men through the Northern gate of Petuaria and creep behind them," Drysten returned as a muffled war cry rang out near the river. "You'll attack them from behind when the majority of their men make it to our shields."

"How will I know when that'll be?"

Drysten shrugged. "Use your best judgment."

Dagonet returned a hesitant nod. "I'll see to it," he muttered as he walked toward the Northern gate.

Drysten nodded and turned back toward the ferry, the location he knew the Gaels would soon erupt from. The men stood silent as the howls of a massacre unfolding intensified. Whoever had been attacked was clearly defeated, and Drysten knew who the Gaels would turn on next. Splashing soon became audible, and figures began running out of the darkness.

Drysten glanced from side to side to make sure the men were mostly prepared to repel the first wave. I suppose it would be too much to hope for Bishop Germanus to be present for that slaughter across the way.

Two drenched and staggering men were faintly illuminated by the torches Drysten had ordered placed on either side of the street. The closer of the two was shrieking as an arrow protruded from his chest, only to become wobbly and fall over from the poison of the Gaels. The second man began to yell something to Drysten's shield wall until he was hit in the back of the head by an arrow of his own.

"Hold!" Drysten ordered his men as he glanced behind him. Dagonet had just made it out of the town's gates and would only need moments before he was in position to attack Abhartach from behind.

After looking back, Drysten now saw more men staggering toward him. Most were unarmed, but all were bloodied and beaten. A few paused when they saw Drysten's shields staring back at them, but all eventually kept moving, sobbing as they ran.

Drysten gestured for a Frisian on the right side of the shield wall to stop one of the men from running past. The presumed Christian was wrestled to the ground and brought forward by the scruff of his beard. At first glance, he looked no different than most Britons Drysten had seen. But then he saw the tribal markings.

"You're not from here. Are you?" Drysten demanded.

The man tried to answer but couldn't take his eyes away from the river. "They're coming, Lord..."

Matthew gave Drysten a frantic look. "He's right, Lord!"

Drysten waved a dismissive hand toward Matthew and looked back to his captive. "I know they're coming, and if you want to outrun them, you'll answer my questions," he hissed. "Now, speak."

"I am from Narbo, Lord," the stranger yelled as he tried to wrench himself free from the Frisian's grasp.

"How did you come to this place?"

"The bishop..." the man stammered. "He paid our king for men."

"To fight who?"

The foreigner looked back to the river. "Not them... not men like that," he said as he pointed to the darkness.

"Shields!" Drysten bellowed. He looked back to the mercenary. "Run for your life."

The man nodded as the Frisian released his arm. "There were hundreds, Lord..."

"Then stay and help," Drysten suggested with a sarcastic scoff. He turned back to the river as the mercenary began making his way through the shield wall. More silhouettes were appearing. But these were armed and crazed men chanting ancient war cries of their forefathers.

Drysten hefted his shield and moved to the center of the shield wall. "Brace!"

The first of the Gaels crashed into a man just to Drysten's left. Dagonet and Bors were that way, with Matthew, Cynwrig, and Jorrit to his right. More erupted from the darkness and raced toward the flanks of the shields. Drysten remembered Titus' teachings and knew what they were trying.

"Don't let them collapse inward!" Drysten shouted. "Keep them steady!"

A massive weight banged into Drysten's shield, bringing with it a soreness in his opposite shoulder. He pushed the man away and stole a brief second to look past him. There was at least a hundred more bearing down on them.

Drysten knew Abhartach couldn't be far behind. He jabbed his blade into the fallen man's belly and brought it back to ready himself for the next. To his horror, the Gael rose from the ground despite his entrails poking out from the small wound on his belly.

Amiram appeared from behind Drysten and swung his sword down into the Gael's skull, sending him to the dirt like a dead fish thrown from a barrel. Drysten and Amiram quickly glanced into the corpse, each wondering whether he would stand. After peering to one another, they both turned back to the oncoming enemy.

The battle raged for some time, with most of the losses being incurred on the Gaels. Drysten knew Abhartach was holding his main force back for the moment the Britons began to tire. He kept glancing toward the river crossing, but only saw faint shapes lurking in the darkness. He couldn't tell whether they were real people awaiting the command to charge, or ghosts from his own mind hovering between the plains of the Otherworld and that of the living.

"Keep the formation!" Bors commanded over the war cries.

And so, they did. A handful of Saxons were serving as the rear guard near the gate leading to Eboracum. Octha and Ebissa had more than enough men to hold a line from attack while simultaneously sending word if there was one. Drysten glanced behind him and was pleased to see they had followed his command, sending a sizeable force along with Dagonet. He knew if anyone were to fight the Gaels without fear, it would likely be the Saxons. They were brought here by Colgrin to root out anyone who would resist them on the islands, and everyone knew they were the most seasoned fighters outside of Powys.

He looked back to see one of the last Gaels to make the charge coming straight toward him. He blocked a mad swing of an axe with his shield and thrust his blade forward. The red-haired Gael was sent to the dirt atop the pile of others who made the pointless charge into the armored Britons. The first wave was much like the one in Glanoventa, no armor and sickly looking.

Thankfully, there didn't seem to be any women this time.

"Hold!" Drysten yelled as he surveyed the shield wall. It was standing firm, with only a handful of men being killed or wounded.

The attack ceased for the time being. Bors was helping move the wounded Britons or Frisians away from the front line of the fighting, with Cynwrig speaking to him as he went. Drysten looked over his men and saw Amiram wipe a small spatter of blood from his face, and Paulus clutching a hand to his side.

"Check him," Drysten ordered Amiram as he nodded toward Paulus.

The mute shuffled over to the Cretan as Drysten turned toward the river. He could still make out faint silhouettes lurking in the darkness. The second group looked to be larger than the first.

Much Larger.

Drysten was about to warn Bors and Jorrit when a horn sounded. "Shields up!" he ordered as the arrows began pelting into the men beside him. He found himself wondering whether Abhartach purposefully meant to miss him directly, as the men on either side of him were now wounded.

You must have plans for me then.

Another volley followed, less effective than the first. About twenty men were writhing in agony while a few more were picking arrow shafts from their shields or sturdy armor.

The pair of wounded men to Drysten's left and right were now making the all too familiar gurgles witnessed by many of the Britons who had opposed the Gaels in recent years.

"They have those fucking demons fighting for them!" A man shrieked.

"No!" Drysten roared. "They aren't demons! Merely madmen with poisons."

A man who was unknown to Drysten took the spot to his right. "How... do you know that, Lord? How—"

"Because I was one of those madmen," Drysten whispered. "Only for a time." He didn't bother to look for the stranger's reaction. He guessed the man was either displaying fear or confusion. Either one would have made sense.

"Lord Drysten!" a familiar, wicked voice shouted over

the arrows. "My king would have a word with you!"

The shield wall went silent.

Drysten scanned from side to side and immediately noticed the eyes of his men peering back at him. He knew he had no choice. To show his fear or ambivalence could demoralize his men into believing the Britons had no chance of surviving. The ideas of ghosts and people who don't die of normal wounds already chilled their souls.

"Bring the fucker forward!" Drysten returned. "Bring him forward and I will meet him!"

A horn sounded, and another king presented himself for Drysten to kill.

***

The smell of the bodies was overwhelming. Abhartach had thrown the small handful of prisoners near the piles of corpses stacked at the bank of the river. They were being watched over by those damned masked men who were the first to attack Ebrauc a few years ago.

"Roman?" a voice whispered from behind Gaius. He turned to see Eidion's bloodied face staring back. His hair was matted down by dirt and blood from the short skirmish with the Gaels. Gaius had watched the man completely overwhelmed by about a half dozen of the frenzied slaves Abhartach had sent against them.

"What is it?" Gaius muttered.

Eidion chuckled. "Tough spot, eh?"

"Fuck off."

The two were silent as the battle raged across the water. Abhartach had lined up the first wave some time ago, with most of them failing to make it through the river's current. Gaius heard Abhartach and one of the hunters snicker to themselves as scores of men were whisked away toward the sea.

"Must be a tough swim," the king had jokingly put in.

Gaius knew those were just the men sent to test the mettle of the Britons. A test the men under Eidion and Gaius had failed miserably. He guessed there were a small number of Ceneus' own men with them but couldn't figure whom.

There were about ten prisoners from the first skirmish the Gaels found themselves in. The two men in the lead, being Eidion and Gaius, and a small host of others who were stupid enough to throw down their weapons when the first hunters began appearing during the battle. Gaius didn't know their names. He didn't even care to.

Citrio was beheaded right in front of him by Abhartach himself, and Gaius couldn't help but stare into the lifeless eyes of one of his closest friends.

I scolded him. I yelled at him, Gaius thought. *The last thing I said to him was in anger.*

"Great Chief!" an older man said as he approached Abhartach, standing near the prisoners. "The Britons are mighty, and we have few warriors. I fear it was a mistake to hold so many back. They will do us no good in Dal Riata."

"We have warriors enough, Myrddin," Abhartach hissed back. "The others I sent away will be called back to fight off the Roman-lovers. We simply needed to finish this errand before that could happen."

"You should have marched the entire force here together," Myrddin returned in anger. "You believe these men to be more capable than they are."

Abhartach returned a dismissive wave as he walked closer to his second in command.

Gaius thought the exchange between the king and the old man was peculiar to say the least. The man he assumed to be in complete control of the Gaels seemed to have an equal.

But what is equal to a king?

"Their lines are holding," Myrddin insisted, stepping closer. "You send the common rabble in place of the real warriors. The herbs will only prevent pain, not death."

Abhartach tilted his head to the side in clear frustration. He seemed to find it hard to look the man in the eye regardless of the fact he was being talked down to by an old man.

"We think that one is their prince, Great Chief." The hunter pointed to Eidion, who was somehow managing to hide his fear despite Gaius being certain he could hear the man's heartbeat. Its thunderous beat sounded over the battle across the way.

Abhartach trained his eyes onto Eidion as the prince looked to the blood-soaked dirt at his feet. "Are you the man Drysten wishes to kill?"

"I am." Eidion whispered as he glanced to Gaius. "Though he'd likely wish us both dead."

That fucking twat...

Abhartach raised an eyebrow as he shuffled toward Gaius. "And why would that be?"

Gaius stayed silent.

"You... look familiar..." Abhartach whispered as he grabbed a torch from the nearest Gael and held it closer to Gaius' face.

"I should."

Abhartach's lips curled into a wicked smile. His teeth were even more yellow than Gaius thought possible. They were almost rotten. If it weren't for the man's sunken eyes, he'd find it hard to look away from the creature. "Your father now walks with The Morrigan..." He moved his patchy cloak to the side to reveal a skull hanging from his waist. The leather cording was hooked near another skull hung in the same manner, as well as a spot for a third where the cording was vacant.

"Fuck you," Gaius seethed.

"Ha!" Abhartach screamed, bringing Titus' skull up from his belt to his eyes. He stared into the vacant eye sockets and made a mocking noise from deep in his chest while sticking his tongue toward it. "That explains why you should hate the great Lord Drysten, but why would he hate you," he asked as he returned the skull to his waist.

"I returned the favor."

Abhartach's smile grew as he turned to who seemed to be his second in command. "The hunters will fire two volleys of our poisons. Then we will have words with our foe."

The hunter nodded and moved toward the river.

Abhartach looked back to Gaius. "The two of you could prove to be quite useful should things not go our way."

There was a noticeable lull in the fighting across the river. Abhartach looked over toward the men lining themselves up along the bank and waved a hand, sending them forward into the frigid waters. The Gael smirked once again as he watched a man disappear below the waves and turned back to Gaius.

"Get those two up," the king commanded.

One of the malnourished Gaels fortunate enough to not be sent across the river walked up and wrapped his emaciated fingers around Gaius' arm. He tugged him up and ushered him forward, with Eidion being led by one of the hunters. The men followed the king as he walked toward the ferry Gaius had overseen the reconstruction of. He remembered the moment he came to the conclusion following his father's death. It was obvious he'd need to traverse the space from his villa and Eboracum quicker than ever to outrun the Gaels.

The short trip over the waves proved less fearsome for the people on the ferry. A handful of men had drowned and floated back near the spot it was docked. Once the bodies were pushed away, they began their short trip across the water. That was the only hindrance the party faced. They were quickly across the river with what Gaius deduced would be half of Abhartach's forces.

Men were lying on their backs, screaming up toward the stars. This was a normal sight during a battle. Men could always be seen begging for whatever god they worshipped to come and usher the pain away.

Abhartach approached his lead hunter, tapping his shoulder and giving the man a knowing look.

The man smiled and turned toward the carnage. He blew a horn, which produced a strange tone Gaius only heard in the past when the Gaels were near. The hunters fired two volleys of arrows and looked back toward their leader as men were limping back from the battle.

Seems Drysten beat them back better than we did. It was another reason Gaius found to hate the man. His own people had killed a decent amount of the crazed men who attacked them, but it still wasn't enough for a victory. The Gaels simply pulled back and fired volley after volley into Gaius and Eidion's men. At that point, their short-lived defense was over.

The lead hunter marched a few steps before slowly raising both hands to his lips, cupping them around his mouth. "Lord Drysten!" he yelled. "My king would have a word with you!"

Eidion was pushed down beside Gaius, already on his

knees beside Abhartach. "What use could two dead men be?" Eidion wondered.

Gaius shook his head as a scarcely audible response was shouted back from the Britons. He turned to the prince and finally saw the worry in his eyes. "I don't know that he intends to kill us."

There was a long wait before anyone showed themselves. When they finally did, it was only a small group led by Drysten, adorned in his Saxon crown. Bors the Younger was beside him, as was the mute who Gaius knew to be a close friend to Drysten.

"Lord Drysten," Abhartach hissed in a long, sarcastic tone. "A pleasure to see you again!"

Gaius peered over his shoulder and noticed the hunters were silently beginning to gather behind him. He looked down to his hands and wondered if he still had the strength and will to fight them off for his escape. As he raised his gaze, he saw Drysten looking back at him before finally pointing with a slow raise of his arm.

"That one," Drysten muttered from underneath his helm. "Give him to me and leave."

"Aha!" Abhartach screamed before walking toward Eidion and placing his hands on the man's cheeks. "You weren't joking! He truly does hate the man!" He turned back to Drysten and ran a hand over his chin, sauntering between Gaius and Eidion with a playful step. "No!" he announced as he turned back. "I will not."

"Oh?"

"I captured these men. I did the hard work while you were fleeing for your lives. Running in fright to this wretched place. I think it is only fair to be compensated in some manner."

Drysten took a step forward, causing the hunters to lift their bows before Abhartach raised a hand to cease them from firing. "I don't so much care what you do to the other one anymore. But you will give me him." He thrust a finger toward

Gaius, who couldn't help but roll his eyes and look away.

"I will make you a deal," Abhartach declared. "I will give you one of the men."

"How is that a deal when I could just kill you and take them both?"

"Because I will set the other free. If you survive, you can hunt him yourself!"

Gaius glanced to Eidion as he realized he may survive. He wondered if Drysten hated the man who tortured him for five years more than the one who executed his greatest friend.

Abhartach slapped the back of Eidion's head and continued sauntering between his prisoners. "Did you believe I would make things easy for you?"

Drysten relaxed his shoulders and took a step forward. He brought his hands to his helm and removed it, revealing a strange smile of his own. The man peered off in the distance, out across the river for a time, before finally beginning to speak. "Who am I?" he asked.

Abhartach looked at his second in command, both taken aback by the strange request.

"I asked you a question. Now, who am I?" Drysten insisted.

"You are… Drysten. Or rather, Lord Drysten of—"

"No. No, I'm not."

Abhartach seemed to be frustrated by whatever game Drysten was playing. A game which Gaius figured out almost immediately.

What are you stalling for? Gaius wondered as he stole a peek over his shoulder.

Drysten stepped closer and looked to the lead hunter. "Do you know, Argyle?"

The Gael could only return a confused glance as he watched Drysten and his two friends both begin to smile.

Gaius stole another look behind him and thought he saw faint movements in the taller grasses nearby.

"When I was underground, with your son…," Drysten

began. He spoke slow and deliberate. Each word seemed to stall off his tongue, and anyone who could hear him was now hanging off his every word. "I was called many things by those in power. I was called a murderer. I was called an apostate. But above all, I was called something else. Something my father was accused of being. Now, what am I?" He glanced off into nothing, almost as though he was listening to some unknown man speak.

Abhartach produced an uneasy gaze into that same direction, clearly wondering who may be whispering into his enemy's ear.

"He was called a usurper, you fucking dullards," Eidion blurted out. As he spoke, he must have opened a wound inside his mouth, as he spit a wad of blood onto the dirt in front of him.

Abhartach and Argyle both snapped their attention to Eidion, who seemed to shrink down under the weight of their gaze.

Bors seemed entertained by the sight. "Sad day when that one is the smart one," he put in, earning a scowl from Abhartach.

"And what does a usurper do?" Drysten asked as he faced the Gaels, slowly donning his helm. His eyes disappeared, replaced by the vacant darkness of the slits in his mask as he stepped back a handful of paces.

Gaius saw Abhartach draw a blade as he glanced to Argyle. "They kill kings," he whispered as he looked back to Drysten. "What game are you playing, boy?"

"The one you taught me."

A gasp from behind told Gaius what was happening. He saw the enraged face of Dagonet plunging his sword through the back of a hunter just behind him.

"Now!" Drysten yelled.

A roar was heard as every man under Drysten's command charged forward from the shield wall. The screams from the Britons were ferocious, with Abhartach drawing back a pace as he frantically glanced to the two groups of men cutting their way toward him.

"Fight!" Abhartach screamed as Drysten closed the gap between them. The hunters had been taken by surprise but still managed to form a quick line near their king. The rest of the more feral of Abhartach's warriors were proving to be nothing more than fodder for whichever group of Britons they ran to face.

Gaius met Dagonet's eyes as the scout pressed forward through the rear of the Gaels. Abhartach's forces were taken completely by surprise.

Gaius couldn't see his eyes, but somehow felt the hate emanating off Drysten. It was gratifying to see the king of the Gaels displaying a small semblance of fear when he looked on Powys' new lord. But that happiness quickly passed as Gaius saw his father's skull dangling from the man's belt.

"Get up, Roman!" Eidion whispered in haste. "This is our chance to—" Dagonet kicked the side of Eidion's head so hard his back nearly folded over from the force.

"Move and you'll join your father," Dagonet hissed.

Gaius slunk back to the dirt. He gritted his teeth and nodded as Dagonet and his men cut their way deeper through the sporadic line of unprepared Gaels. As more of Drysten's flanking force moved through them, Gaius was able to figure out exactly who they were.

Those stinking Saxons, he thought.

It made sense from his perspective. The Saxons were the only fighters in Ebrauc who hadn't had more than a handful of small skirmishes with Abhartach's men. They had no reason to fear their poisons or their supposed druids.

It also made Drysten that much more dangerous, as they were known to be loyal to him sometime in the past.

***

Drysten knew what would happen to his people should he lose this battle. He knew it in his bones as he stalled just long enough to allow Dagonet to move his men behind Abhartach's force. It was an advantage essential to the hope of victory. He was now facing down the worst man he had ever laid eyes on, and the spirits of those he'd lost were also in attendance.

Just over Abhartach's shoulder, Diocles was standing stoically beside Hall and the woman Drysten witnessed butchered in the cave. Drysten caught the faint glint of torchlight coming from the beads on the woman's wrist, remembering he still had it under his belt.

There were many more with them. Men and women showed themselves as the same faceless shape his mother had taken the appearance of in Powys. But one's presence drove Drysten forward more than any of them. Titus stood beside his weary son, still kneeling on the ground beside Prince Eidion.

"Come here, Lord Drysten," Abhartach yelled as he raced forward.

Drysten remained silent as the fight began with a heavy swing from the Gaelic king landing into Drysten's freshly painted shield. The impact sent a shock-wave through Drysten's left side as he feigned a counterattack before taking a pace backwards. He glanced down to his shield and noticed it had splintered at the brim, right near his head.

Hits hard, Drysten observed. He glanced to his father to see Hall give a reassuring nod before stepping forward.

Swinging his blade from the side, Drysten attempted to cleave into his foe's legs. He missed as Abhartach danced out of the way and returned him with another heavy blow, this one parried to the side by Drysten's sword. Again, the shock went through his body and caused Drysten to almost lose the grip on his blade. Abhartach's strength didn't seem human, and Drysten found himself wondering if he actually was a supernatural being.

Argyle seemed delighted in the exchange between his

king and a traitor. “Once we have our fill of you, the crows will get what’s left!” he yelled as he cut the throat of a Briton who couldn’t best him. The Saxon crown weighed heavy upon his head. He struggled to see through the narrow eye slits, and finally ripped it off. The air felt frigid and bitter on his ears, much how he expected death to feel.

Abhartach grinned as he advanced for another strike, swinging low toward Drysten’s leg in the same manor Drysten had done. Drysten swung his blade into Abhartach’s, the impact producing a loud clang which gained the attention of those fighting closest to the pair.

“Argyle tells me your boy looks much like you!” Abhartach shouted as he stepped back, parrying a blow from Drysten’s sword. “Without those glamorous scars painted across your face!”

Drysten knew the man was goading him and neglected to respond.

“Perhaps we will see about changing that!”

Drysten hefted his shield to block a quick stab before returning one of his own. The two were locked in a battle for longer than Drysten had ever fought a single opponent. He quickly began to feel the strength in his arms and legs begin to leave him, while Abhartach looked just as formidable as ever.

“You Romans are a weak stock, aren’t you?” Abhartach announced with a laugh.

Hall’s ghost showed himself right behind the Gael. “Lie to him! Trick him the same way you tricked Maurianus!” he bellowed. He referenced a man Drysten put to death by convincing those who followed him to turn against him.

Abhartach was observant enough to see Drysten peering off into vacant air behind him. “Who speaks to you?” he wondered. There was a hint of reluctance in his voice.

Drysten smirked as he turned his gaze back to the Gael. “The one you believe in,” he whispered.

Abhartach’s brow twitched as he stepped back. “The Morrigan cannot speak through you. She has spoken through me for nearly a decade."

"She says she is pleased."

Abhartach's lips began to curl into a devilish smile. "As she should—"

"With me," Drysten added.

Abhartach scrunched his face in annoyance. He jabbed his blade toward Drysten's neck, with Drysten brushing the attack aside with his shield.

"You have been a great disappointment, Lord King," Drysten hissed as he slammed the edge of his shield into Abhartach's shoulder, drawing a grunt as the Gael stepped back.

"I am a devout follower. Only I—"

"Can fail her in the way you have."

"Liar!" Abhartach swiped low once more. His overly aggressive movements would be his undoing.

Drysten moved out of the way with a pirouette before drawing first blood from Abhartach's chest. The Gael released a squeal as he slapped his free hand to the blood trickling from his leather tunic.

"Finish him now, son!" Hall screamed.

Drysten nodded and lunged forward, clipping Abhartach's leg with his blade before slamming the edge of his shield into the man's neck. Abhartach fell to the ground from the force. The impact of the man hitting the dirt gave the hunters still standing a startling moment's pause. A familiar skull fell from his belt, rolling a few feet away before resting at a Roman's feet. Drysten raised his gaze from the man's ankles.

"I hope this will begin to make things right," Drysten whispered.

Titus' eyes met Drysten's as he peered up from his own skull. He produced that familiar smile Drysten grew accustomed to during his weeks in the man's care. After a nod, Titus finally looked to Gaius and began fading from view.

"Lord," a man yelled over the fighting. Dagonet had joined him. "We've nearly won, but there's still more to do."

Drysten peered around and watched a handful of Gaels being completely overwhelmed by a larger force of Saxons. One was thrown over a Saxon shield, his head cracked open with a swing from another man before the Gael had even hit the ground. "Where is Argyle?" Drysten muttered as he watched the carnage.

"He picked up the prince and fled," Dagonet answered.

Drysten nodded as he watched the Gaels being massacred all around him. "We'll find them eventually."

An old man began creeping from the darkness of the river. The same one Drysten had met at the beach near Glanoventa the night Abhartach left to fetch his army. "As you should," he declared. "They are indeed dangerous, though that prince seemed… softer than yourselves."

Drysten turned and pointed his blade to the old man's chest. "That's close enough." A scream caused by Amiram stabbing a hunter in the stomach rang out before the mute withdrew his blade and moved beside Dagonet. "Tell me why you shouldn't join the rest of your people," Drysten ordered.

The old man seemed somewhat taken aback by the demand. He stood straighter as he looked over Drysten. "I am an Arch Druid, Lord. One of great importance to Abhartach." He looked to the Gaelic king unconscious on the ground near Drysten's feet. "I was willing to provide my knowledge of the old ways in exchange for the lives of my people."

"I'm guessing your deal with him didn't last."

"He took me from my people before he massacred them."

Drysten flashed a glance to Dagonet. "What knowledge do you possess that was so important for him?"

"I would expect you may have wondered where he received his herbal remedies from. His poisons."

"I did," Drysten acknowledged with a nod. He turned toward Amiram. "Bind his hands. He may prove useful."

Amiram shuffled over as Drysten began stepping toward Abhartach's motionless body. The man still gave off an air of ferocity despite being unconscious. Two Gaels were trying to hobble toward him until a Saxon slammed the edge of his shield into one's jaw and stabbed his blade through the gut of the other.

The ruckus caused Abhartach to stir, flipping himself onto his back. The madness in his eyes was ever present. Even with the loss of his army. "You learned our ways," he murmured as Drysten now stood over him.

Drysten nodded.

Dagonet and Amiram both settled in beside Drysten, with Myrddin's arm being in the tight grasp of Amiram. "What should we do with him?" the scout asked.

Drysten plucked his Saxon crown from the ground, wiping off a small amount dirt before placing it onto his head. "He will watch the rest of his people killed. Then I will end him."

Dagonet nodded and ordered the men to line up along the river where the last of the Gaels were making the futile effort to save their king. The fighting took mere moments, as many of the Gaels were swept away by the current of the river before even posing any kind of threat.

"This was the army we were afraid of," Drysten observed with a scoff.

Bors was standing next to Drysten with a hand on Abhartach's shoulder, keeping the king on his knees. "Besides the hunters I haven't seen any real warriors to speak of."

"Where were the hunters?" Drysten wondered as he looked down to Abhartach.

Myrddin tried to step forward but was halted by Amiram. The druid pursed his lips and looked to the river. "I gave some as an offering. The rest likely left when that one cut them off from crossing," he replied as he pointed toward Dagonet.

"Traitor..." Abhartach seethed, though Myrddin did not seem to pay him much attention.

Drysten wondered if the surviving Gaels would attempt to return home, or if they would try and mount some kind of resistance as their ancestors had done against the Romans.

"How many are there, and where is the rest of your army?"

Abhartach shrugged. "Why would I tell you anything? If you were meant to know, The Morrigan would tell you herself."

Myrddin again stepped forward, this time allowed to by Amiram. "They will go to Dal Riata, far into the North and a little West. They will pose no threat for a time."

"How long?" Drysten wondered.

Myrddin shrugged.

Abhartach released a sad whimper as he lowered his gaze. His eyes hovered over his blade lying close by. Any hopes of using it were dashed as Dagonet kicked it off out of reach. "I failed her…" the king whispered.

"You did."

"I expect you'll be adding another crown to your collection then, Lord," the king rasped.

Drysten nodded as he thrust his sword forward, puncturing a hole in Abhartach's neck.

CHAPTER TWENTY-FOUR

The fight was over. The sun rose to illuminate the massacre of the Gaels as the townspeople of Petuaria shuffled out from the protection of the villa. Drysten watched each of them step from the noble home while running the beaded bracelet through his fingers. The last thing he saw before moving toward his officers outside the main gate of the villa was Gaius being led with Myrddin to the old cellar. The very same one that had once housed Jorrit when the Frisian had been captured by Drysten. Myrddin gave him an understanding nod, while Gaius refused to look him in the eye.

"Thank you, Lord," an old man whispered in a hardened voice. He looked like he had been formidable in his day, with a strong brow and arms that once held muscle.

Drysten nodded but couldn't find the will to say anything. Many people approached him after the battle's end, all receiving the same response from him. He knew it was from the guilt of bringing the might of the Gaels into Britannia. He also knew he was lucky to have repelled it the way he did.

"Everything alright, Lord?" Matthew asked as he sauntered up alongside Jorrit and Dagonet. All three men looked exhausted and were covered with spatters of blood. Jorrit even had part of his beard caked to his leather jerkin.

Drysten nodded. "I expect we should turn our attention to our second enemy."

Jorrit produced a warm smile. "One victory wasn't

enough for you?"

"No," Drysten answered. "No, it wasn't."

"Isurium is only a day's ride from here, Lord," Dagonet replied. "We could be there about the same time as Ceneus."

"Assuming they didn't leave until well after us," Drysten replied. "For all we know, Germanus has already killed them."

Matthew tilted his head to the side. "Or Ceneus could have won."

Drysten shook his head. "I'll take Visigothic warriors over a rabble of random tribes any day. I remember hearing how ferocious they were when they fought against my father." He paused and looked toward the old storehouse now in use as a prison for Gaius and Myrddin. "Have either of them caused problems?" Nobody spoke, signaling the answer was no.

Dagonet did, however, adopt an awkward stare as he looked to his lord. "Why are either of them alive?"

"The Gael could prove useful," Drysten responded. "As for Gaius, I intend on killing him in front of the Christians. They need to understand what will happen to all who follow Germanus."

Bors and Cynwrig approached from the villa, both looking just as haggard and fatigued as the rest of the officers. "The men need rest," Bors observed.

Drysten nodded. "They will have it."

"You could use some yourself."

"You're the ugliest wife I have, Bors."

The men all grinned at Bors' expense before going their own ways in search of rest. Drysten told them to stay in the villa, but none wished to. They each believed the place to emanate misfortune to anyone who dwelled there.

"Look what happened last time you stayed here…" Cynwrig exclaimed.

Drysten didn't care for the idea of luck. He never believed it was luck that got his father killed or him thrown into a cell. He knew it was simply a combination of incompetence from Ceneus and cruelty from Germanus. The Gaels being brought into Britannia was his own fault. Nothing that has ever happened to him, happened because of good or bad luck, merely bad decisions.

Drysten entered the villa and looked over the familiar mosaics on the floors and walls. He was just as impressed as he was in the past. For as dreary as Petuaria looked when he first rose from Eboracum's prison, it now seemed somewhat pleasant.

Suppose that would happen if people aren't currently out to kill you, Drysten thought.

"There will always be men who wish to kill a lord," Hall explained. "Some for your wealth, some for what you did to gain it."

Drysten shrugged off his father's words and found his way to the old room, which once housed himself and his pregnant wife so long ago. The bed hadn't been made since the last occupant used it. Drysten guessed it was one of the rooms which provided the locals some semblance of safety while the fight against Abhartach raged outside.

"Drysten," a voice rumbled from behind him.

"What is it, Jorrit?"

The Frisian stepped into Drysten's view. "What is... Powys like?"

Drysten turned. "Nicer than here," he answered as he waved a hand through the air.

"Suppose that wouldn't take much," Jorrit responded, his voice sounding heavy and awkward. He slowly made his way to the other side of the room before turning back to Drysten. "This kingdom is dying."

Drysten nodded.

"So you know what I have to ask of you?"

"You and your family will be welcomed in with open arms. The Powysians treat things like loyalty very seriously, and you have shown me nothing but loyalty since I've known you."

Jorrit seemed to relax his shoulders at the response,

looking to the door. "Those two will be happy to hear it."

Drysten turned to see Inka and Lanzo standing in the doorway. "You'll both be treated well. I assure you." Drysten knew he didn't have the heart to turn away a friend in need. His recent mistakes taught him well. He turned back to Jorrit. "Were you planning on using them to guilt me into letting you accompany me home?"

Jorrit smiled and tilted his head to the side.

"Suppose I would as well," Drysten added, looking back to Jorrit's wife and child. "You will all be welcomed with open arms."

"Thank you, Lord," Inka responded. She held a tight grip on Lanzo's hand.

Drysten looked back to Jorrit. "Didn't you tell me you were one of Ceneus' highest ranking men?"

Jorrit nodded. "We thought Garbonian was going to kill him and reclaim the crown to this place. Braxus and myself even pulled the man aside and pledged our support for him before Ceneus left to go West."

Drysten couldn't help but hang his head. "Garbonian'll do no usurping now..."

"No, he won't."

Both men stood quietly until Jorrit bid Drysten farewell and led his family to one of the neighboring rooms of the villa. Drysten wondered how alone he really was. His father and the others who whispered to him seemed to have left him for the time being.

As he unbuckled his sword belt, removed his armor, and lowered himself onto the bed, he finally found himself able to rest.

***

Ceneus and Gwrast were overseeing the construction of a temporary camp just outside Isurium's walls. There was no fighting to that point, but a siege could spell ruin for Ceneus' men, and everyone knew it.

Germanus had spent the better part of the afternoon hurling insults into the faces of Ceneus' army, with nobody choosing to respond. The one thing on everyone's minds was the idea they could only hope to keep their current footing so long as more mercenaries didn't show up to remove them.

"How long would you say we can hold this area?" Mor asked as he led a handful of men toward the king.

Ceneus shrugged before running a hand over his head. "Not until winter. Not that long."

Mor nodded and looked to his brother. "Have your men found any sewers entrances? Abhartach's people showed us how effective they can be."

Gwrast shook his head. "The one we've found was blocked up. Looked like it had been that way for a while. We would attract too much attention if we tried to open it up."

The men all paused as Germanus' voice rang out from the city's walls. Nobody could understand him, but all craned their heads to the side to try.

"I hate that man," Ceneus grumbled. The opinion was echoed by everyone.

"Lord King!" a man called from behind.

Ceneus turned to see Lord Amalech rushing up with a handful of his fellow Rhegedians. "We've found an entrance. We'll end the whoreson tonight!" he happily exclaimed as he patted Gwrast's arm.

Ceneus grinned wide as he looked toward the city's walls. "Then we wait until darkness." He looked to the man from Rheged. "Show me when the sun begins to sink low."

Lord Amalech nodded and shuffled away, presumably to find a last-minute meal.

"I don't trust him," Gwrast muttered as he wiped the

arm Amalech touched. “Something off about him and his men.”

Ceneus looked toward the Rhegedians all huddling by a fire. “They seem like they mean well,” he put in, harkening back to the smiles on their faces from the night before the battle at Glanoventa.

“They’re much too quiet...” Gwrast shook his head and moved away toward his own grouping of men milling about nearby.

The wait until sunset seemed to drone on forever. Ceneus wanted nothing more than to throw Germanus into the deepest, darkest prison in Ebrauc. He even considered offering him to the Gaels as a tribute. That outcome was unlikely considering he had no idea where they were.

“You think Lord Drysten beat them back?” Ceneus asked of Gwrast, who tilted his head to the side and looked toward the coming night.

“I would guess he’d have quite a fight on his hands.”

“But do you think it’s a fight he could have won?”

Gwrast let out a heavy sigh and shrugged as he pointed toward Lord Amalech and his men approaching.

“Lord King,” the lord announced. “Let me show you this entrance.”

Ceneus nodded and gestured for Gwrast to follow. Mor wished to as well, but the king understood it would have been foolish to take the three most important people of the kingdom into the same area without knowing who may be waiting.

“This way,” Amalech beckoned.

Ceneus and Gwrast were accompanied by a half dozen of their own personal guardsmen from the camp. They moved through a sparse woodland on the outside of Isurium’s walls until they found a ditch once used as protection by the Romans. Ceneus peered up to the top of the wall, noting how strange it was there weren’t any sentries posted to the area.

“Nearly there, Lord King,” Amalech whispered.

Ceneus looked over his shoulder toward the camp, seeing a handful of men now standing and donning their armor. *Seems Mor is getting them ready.*

Gwrast noticed as well. "How many men can fit through this opening?"

Amalech turned about as the group began making their way around the wall and out of view of the camp. "Only a handful at a time."

"A handful could be enough if we do this right," Gwrast acknowledged. He seemed uneasy as he glanced behind him once more.

The trees became thicker on the edge of the ditch. The men were nearly within view of one of the smaller gates of the other side of the city when Amalech finally turned.

"Here we are, Lord King," the lord from Rheged announced.

Ceneus cocked his head to the side and looked up toward the wall. "What exactly am I supposed to be looking for?"

Gwrast did the same as Amalech pointed toward the Roman stonework. "There's no entrance—"

"Father," a voice hissed from the tree line.

Ceneus knew what was happening. He slowly turned and looked on the bloodied face of his eldest son and what looked to be about fifty mercenaries creeping from the trees.

"You never were the smartest," Eidion hissed to Gwrast, who had drawn his blade in defiance. "There's no need for that. Our orders are not to harm you."

Ceneus felt his heart sink. He glanced to the small bodyguard with him and gestured for them to lower their blades. Everyone knew they weren't going to be winning this fight. He looked back to Eidion. "What exactly were your orders?"

"They were actually quite simple. You will secure our passage back to Gaul," Eidion divulged. "But they have no importance to me."

Ceneus glanced to his men, all of which raced to pluck their weapons from the ground. The reaction from the Visigothic mercenaries was to race into the ditch and begin slaughtering them relentlessly. A handful of the Britons managed to form a small shield wall, killing one mercenary before becoming victims themselves.

"No! Run!" Gwrast screamed in panic.

One of the Britons tried to until he was shot in the back by a black arrow which erupted from the trees.

Census looked in the direction of the shot and saw a handful of hooded men slowly stand and walk forward. "Gaels!" he exclaimed as he looked to Eidion. "How did you—?"

"We have an uneasy alliance with them for the moment. Not all of them, just these few," Eidion answered. "They needed assurance they could pass through with no trouble from the bishop."

"But why—"

Eidion held up a hand, silencing his father. "Their job is now to harass men in other kingdoms. They will trouble Ebrauc no longer."

One Gael stepped forward and stood beside Eidion, lowering his mask from his nose until his yellowed smile was shown. "Lord King," the man sarcastically greeted.

"Seems your people got swatted well enough," Gwrast jeered.

The Gael turned to the prince and gestured for his men to bind his hands along with the king's. "Thank your Lord Drysten for that," he muttered. His gaze drifted to his feet, showing the men from Hibernia had indeed been beaten and likely scattered at the hands of Drysten.

So he did win, Ceneus thought. He made sure to cast a smile toward his new enemy before being shoved forward by one of the Visigoths. Eidion showed little to no satisfaction by the exchange. Something odd which Gwrast noticed as well.

"Hurry up," Eidion ordered. He pointed toward the nearest gate at the other end of the ditch before dabbing a hand to his forehead, checking for blood.

Ceneus scoffed at the sight. "Seems to me you were forced into a truce with those beasts, son. Your lot must be truly desperate."

"It won't be your concern for much longer, father," Eidion returned.

Lord Amalech quickly stepped up in the front of the silent group, whispering something in Eidion's ear to which Eidion shook his head.

"My deal was with him!" Amalech announced. "We haven't forgotten what your bishop did to our people. We will have our king, or you'll find yourself sending fewer men against the Powysians when they get here."

How will they manage to rescue King Lledlwrn? Ceneus wondered. He was thrown down into the same place as Drysten.

Eidion sighed and simply returned a nod before pointing toward the gate. "All will be well. We've sent for him. Should be here soon."

Amalech peered behind him and smiled to one of the other Rhegedians following closely behind him. Ceneus and Gwrast glanced to one another, both unsure who Germanus could have possibly sent to rescue Rheged's king.

The strange group finally made their way into Isurium, with Ceneus finally getting a chance to see how life for the common folk in the vicus was fairing under Germanus' rule.

"Father..." Gwrast whispered, nudging his head toward a small Roman apartment building in disrepair. From a window on the highest floor hung six men and a woman. All of which had brands of the Christian cross burned into their foreheads before they were executed.

Ceneus wrenched his arm away from the man leading him. "Eidion, how can you support such barbarity!"

His son turned. The king was somewhat caught off guard by the look in Eidion's eyes. He showed remorse, and even pity for those who were executed. There was something about those few individuals which was different to him.

"How can you allow this...?"

Eidion's tear-filled eyes looked on the face of the woman.

Birds had gotten to her. "Her eyes had been blue..." he murmured.

Ceneus now understood. "You loved that one?" he asked as he looked on the woman's corpse. She had indeed been beautiful in life. Now, however, she lacked eyes from the crows, and bits of skin along her cheek had also been ripped away along with them.

"Eidion, why...?" Gwrast demanded, also showing surprise at his brother's demeanor. "Why were they executed?"

"They held importance to the people here. They were all important to someone and would have caused problems for us if we were forced to remain here." Eidion brought his gaze from the woman and pointed toward the largest building of the city.

"But that girl... that one gave you a reason to remain," Ceneus muttered as he pointed toward the dangling corpse. The Visigoth who oversaw marching him toward the city's fort even allowed him to take a short step away from him.

"She did," Eidion finally stated. He waved a hand toward the fort, and the men kept moving.

It was an old Roman fort built in the same fashion as many others, but with a large, black cross shoddily painted over the main archway. The paint of the cross beams had run, giving it a misshapen and malicious look.

The men trudged on under the weight of the stares from terrified locals. The normal sounds of a city were nowhere to be seen, replaced by a thick silence. No children played; no market stalls held patrons. Dark clouds seemed to form overhead as the last rays of the sun were disappearing to the West.

"Keneu!" Germanus announces with outstretched arms. The man waddled out from underneath the painted cross with a beaming smile. His normally ornate and well fashioned robes were now tattered and torn. The man was trying to portray an air of authority and elegance as he did before he fled Eboracum. To Ceneus, all he looked like was a beaten man in desperation.

Eidion gave the bishop a quick glance before continuing

toward the fortress. His usual brashness was no replaced with a solemn, glazed over stare.

"You know you can't win," Ceneus grumbled to the bishop.

Germanus nodded, shocking the king and prince. "I've no intention of trying to fight. I would surely lose that battle regardless of the prowess of my men." He stepped closer and leaned in toward the king's ear. "There are other ways to do God's will. Ways the brutes of war cannot fight against, nor understand." He moved aside and pointed toward the fortress. "You will see."

CHAPTER TWENTY-FIVE

Matthew and Bors were leading the marching column northwest from Petuaria. After the battle against Abhartach, Drysten ordered his men to rest for two days while they prepared for what was hoped to be their final fight until the following spring. Once winter was through, the Saxons would be their next enemy. While winter had not yet arrived, it still sent forth a frigid breeze to chill the bones of Drysten's men.

"Almost there," Drysten explained to Amiram, who had never marched this way before.

The mute had done most of his fighting at sea, and the constant walking was beginning to greatly annoy the man. He returned a surly grunt in response.

"You'll be able to rest soon, you child."

Amiram sighed before straining his gaze ahead of the column, pointing forward.

A small group of men was walking far in front of them. Drysten looked to Dagonet, riding just behind him. "Find out who they are."

"Yes, Lord," the scout replied. He rode off and halted beside the small group of strangers a couple hundred yards ahead. Drysten saw him give the men a faint nod and spur his horse back toward the marching column, drawing stares from the strangers. "Traders taking their father home, Lord. They live just outside Isurium," he explained. "The old man is ill and wished to see his childhood home one more time."

"Strange for the men to be so well armed, wouldn't you say?" Drysten returned.

Matthew turned around and echoed his observation. "They're lying," he said flatly. "They could be scouts serving the bishop."

Drysten nodded and looked to Dagonet. "How many are there?"

"Eight when counting the old man," he answered.

"Take twenty riders and circle through the trees. Cut them off and keep them there," Drysten commanded.

Dagonet nodded and relayed the order to Cynwrig. The group waited until a bend in the road which cut off the view of the presumed traders. Once there, the riders quickly moved through the trees and disappeared out of view.

"What if they are telling the truth?" Bors asked of Drysten.

"Then I suppose we'll be scaring them for no good reason other than the priest seems to be paranoid," Drysten replied with a chuckle.

Matthew took exception to the comment and returned a glimpse of annoyance. "You did agree with me," he muttered.

Drysten smiled and looked behind him. "Swords," he ordered the nearest group of men. About fifteen souls tugged their swords free and looped their arms through the straps of their shields as Drysten dismounted.

A handful of shouts were heard just ahead.

"Let's go have a word with them!" Drysten shouted. He and his men broke formation and rushed toward the area where a brief scuffle seemed to have taken place. When they turned the bend of the road, they saw Dagonet and the rest of Drysten's riders circling who Drysten guessed to be the traders. There were two bodies on the ground between Drysten's group and Dagonet's, with six men on their knees in the middle of the riders.

"I'm guessing they weren't traders!" Drysten shouted as he neared.

Dagonet turned with wide eyes and shook his head.

Is he... worried? Drysten wondered. He eventually reached Dagonet and his men, with the riders creating a gap for Drysten to walk through and speak with the new prisoners.

"Who the fuck do you think you are?" an old man shouted, his tone more towards inconvenience than fright. "Taking a king as your prisoner? Haven't you fucking Northerners done enough to my people?"

Drysten immediately recognized the man. He was Gwrwst Lledlwrn, the king of Rheged who was deposed once Ceneus and the Christians went to war with the neighboring kingdom to their south. "I thought you were simply a madman when I last saw you," Drysten stated with a smile. He referred to the moment he led the Gaels back down through the sewers, crossing in front of the man's cell and having a brief conversation with him before leaving. "Seems you're important enough to someone to bring you back." He turned to a man with his hands in the air and gold chain with a cross draped around his neck. "Are you in charge?"

The man shook his head. "The king is in charge."

"I mean did you lead his rescue?"

The man nodded.

"Who are you?"

"Tybion ap Cunedda," the man snarled with gritted teeth.

"Are these men bound to you by money or oaths?"

"The two dead ones and one other were paid in Mamucium. The rest are mine."

"Well, Tybion, it seems your rescue attempt hit an unfortunate barrier." Drysten knelt down to the man's level and glanced back to Dagonet. "Did they try to fight?"

Dagonet nodded and pointed to the two corpses. "Those two did. The rest simply stared at us."

"Odd." Drysten looked back to his captive. "Why did you

rescue him?" He waved a hand to the king.

"I was told we would receive relief from the raiders if we did."

"Where is this relief needed?" Drysten began, understanding this man was high-ranking officer. Whether in Rheged or somewhere else, he couldn't tell. "If you mean the Gaels, I already relieved you," he proudly added.

Tybion shook his head. It was clear he had conflicting feelings over what his job entailed. "These raiders come north from Dyfed, Lord."

Drysten looked to Matthew. "Smaller kingdom bordering Powys' Eastern border," the priest explained. "Mainly Hibernian tribes in that area."

"I guess we know why they left for Britannia. Too bad nobody thought to ask them for help against Abhartach." Drysten looked back to Tybion. "Explain your dealings with the bishop."

"Germanus needed this man saved for some odd reason. In return, he would send a force to protect us" Tybion glanced to his two dead men lying behind him. "Job wasn't too difficult until this point. There were no guards in the sewers." The dark-haired man sighed and looked back to Drysten, who had been studying his face intently. "You'll kill us?"

"No, but you're a damned fool, so I should."

Tybion raised an eyebrow at the statement. "Why is that?"

"Because Germanus has no intentions of helping you. The man can't even help himself anymore."

Tybion lowered his eyes as two men on either side of him began grumbling to themselves.

"In any case, you'll be joining us on our march." Drysten peered to the two bodies and looked to Matthew, who had caught up with the rest of the marching column. "See that they're buried. We have no enemies here." He looked to the king. "Your hands will stay unbound until you give me a reason to change that. Is that clear, Lord King?"

The king nodded and looked to Tybion before he stood.

The two bodies were buried and given some strange Christian rites which Drysten didn't understand. Matthew did, however, and it seemed Tybion was rather appreciative of the gesture. Once that matter was settled, the men marched on.

Isurium's walls finally showed themselves not long after. It was somewhat funny to Drysten how close the king of Rheged had gotten to his destination before the man once again became a prisoner, albeit a prisoner who was being afforded the rights a man of his stature was entitled to.

"Make camp alongside the Britons," Drysten ordered. He scanned over the sullen faces of King Ceneus' men and wondered what had happened. It seemed they felt defeated judging by their aimless stares.

"Lord Drysten," a man yelled from the largest tent in the camp. Prince Mor and another man quickly approached the new arrivals. "They took my father and brother," he explained in a frantic tone. "We cannot risk them killing either of them with an attack."

Drysten sighed and dismounted, glancing over his shoulder to his prisoners. "Do you have an explanation?"

Tybion gave Rheged's king an uncomfortable glance before shaking his head. "I was only told to retrieve this one from the sewers." He pointed toward King Lledlwrn, who also showed no knowledge of Germanus' intentions. "I have no idea what he's planning."

Drysten looked back to Mor. "Has the bishop approached you yet?"

"Not even to insult us as he had been."

"Matthew! Bors!" Drysten called. "With me." Drysten beckoned for Mor to follow and began making his way toward the main gate to the city. There were only a handful of men atop its walls, but Drysten wagered there were many more inside and an attack could quite possibly fail. Even if they did change their minds and attack, the cloud cover overhead signaled rain. No army would have an easy time keeping its footing on siege ladders.

Always easier to defend a city than to take one, Hall affirmed.

"When were they taken?" Drysten asked.

Mor stepped a little quicker to catch up to Drysten. "Last night."

"And they stormed the camp and took them both? I didn't see any bodies when I arrived."

Mor adopted an uncomfortable, glazed over expression. "They… walked off with a handful of Rhegedians. They were supposed to be examining an opening we could exploit to enter the city. The few bodies were burned outside the camp."

Drysten's jaw fell open. "Your father's stupidity never ceases to amaze me," to which Mor turned red in the face and looked away. Drysten couldn't gather whether the man was angered or embarrassed. Both emotions would have been understandable.

The small group approached the gate, with Drysten making certain the men around him had their shields ready in the case of any arrows being shot at them.

"You!" Drysten called to the nearest man atop the wall. "Bring your bishop. I would have words with him."

The stranger in the black cloak nodded and disappeared. Drysten and his small company waited a short while before Germanus finally showed himself in place of the sentry.

"Lord Drysten!" the bishop yelled, a hint of surprise in his voice. "I believed I would be dealing with that dullard of a prince alongside you." He pointed a finger at Mor, who shrank a little under the man's gaze. "A pleasure indeed! Your wounds have healed nicely!"

"Why did you want the king of Rheged released?" Drysten demanded, not wanting to indulge the bishop with more conversation than necessary. Out of the corner of his eye, Drysten noticed Mor turn toward Bors, who muttered an explanation.

Germanus was far off above Drysten, but still failed to

hide the displeasure as it crossed his face. "I suppose you would want to see Keneu?" he returned in defiance, acting as though he hadn't heard him. "Give me a moment and I will—"

"We'll get to that in a moment. Speak of Rheged's king!" Drysten noticed a man step alongside the bishop and peer off toward the temporary camp.

Germanus scrunched his face and looked behind him, whispering something to the man. He seemed annoyed by whatever response he garnered, turning back. "Bring him forward," he grumbled. "We will do our dealings at the gate."

Drysten was about to decline the offer but the bishop had already disappeared from his line of sight.

"I don't like this," Matthew whispered. "If he's not planning to fight us..."

"What else could he be doing?" Bors wondered.

Drysten shrugged. "I'd wager he was trying to dig his claws into Rheged. Likely thought Ebrauc was lost to him and wished to start anew."

"Start anew?" Bors wondered.

"He was moving to take over Rheged the same way as he did Ebrauc," Drysten explained. "Smart plan. Rheged's king is a haggard old fool and probably wouldn't have been able to resist him."

Mor shook his head. "These Christians and their tricks..."

"He wants to make a deal with us now that we've thwarted those plans." Drysten turned and pointed to King Lledlwrn, with Dagonet nodding and ushering both him and Tybion forward, unarmed.

Both men were silent as Amiram and Dagonet led them toward the gate, stopping just behind Drysten. After a short wait, Isurium's entrance began to creak open, with Germanus and a bloodied Eidion approaching once there was enough space to walk through the giant wooden doors.

"Now will you explain yourself?" Drysten asked through a drawn-out sigh.

Germanus wrinkled his brow before eyeing the men opposing him. "The kings will be exchanged upon the guarantee of safe passage," he hissed. "Not a moment before."

"Safe passage to where?"

"I had sent for men to arrive in Petuaria before you… joined forces." Germanus looked to Mor with a disdainful glare. "Instead of bringing me more men, they will take me and the rest of my people away from here."

Drysten glanced behind him. "Why would I allow that?"

"Because if you don't, Keneu and his heir will be executed."

Drysten scoffed. "We already have an heir for Ebrauc right here," he responded, gesturing a thumb over his shoulder at Mor. "What's one more corpse to bury?"

Germanus smirked. "There are others as well." He looked behind him toward the gate where two other men were being led forward, sacks over their heads. The shorter man wore the robes of a priest, while the taller was quite obviously Gwrast judging by the ornate golden chain draped around his neck. The priest was forced to his knees by a Visigoth in a black cloak, the bag quickly ripped away.

Drysten gritted his teeth as he stared into Maewyn's eyes. *I can't repay his kindness by allowing his death.*

"Do we have a deal?" Germanus hissed, sensing Drysten's sudden shift in demeanor.

"Maewyn," Drysten called. "How have they treated you?"

Maewyn peered toward the mercenary whose hand was tightly gripping his shoulder. "If you saw the way they've been treating the townspeople, you'd say I've been treated like royalty," to which Gwrast seemed to snicker from under the sack on his head.

"We will make a deal," Drysten declared. "You will leave Britannia with all your men and never return."

Germanus nodded, reluctantly. "Fine. Have it your way, filthy—"

"And to show that fact you will give me the priest now."

"I will not—!"

"You will," Drysten hissed, locking eyes with the bishop. "You will because if you don't, I will kill every man inside this city as slow as I can manage. I will save you for last, and you will endure more than you thought possible." Drysten took a short step forward. "Your people taught me various ways to inflict pain on a man. I'd imagine I can recall most of them quite clearly."

A man in a drabby brown cloak appeared from behind Germanus. He quickly stepped to Germanus' side and whispered something in his ear. The bishop took a moment and peered off behind Drysten, returning a slight nod as he looked back. "He is yours on one condition," he muttered. "You have Titus' son with you?"

"I do," Drysten confirmed. Good thing I didn't kill the fucker.

"I will take him now," Germanus declared. "We will exchange both of the kings and princes once we reach the coast."

Drysten peered to Matthew, receiving a surprising nod of approval. "Get your men moving. We will march behind you." Germanus began to turn away until Drysten raised a finger toward him. "You will march unarmed."

Germanus looked as though he was about to mount a fervent protest, but simply shook his head. "I will instruct my men to lay down their weapons. I will not, however, travel without a small detachment of my personal guards carrying their weapons in case your treacherous ilk decides to betray me."

"Fine," Drysten conceded, ignoring the insult.

Gaius was brought forward and placed under Eidion's care. It seemed some of Drysten's men hadn't forgotten what the man had done to Diocles and had beat him to the point he could barely stand. Drysten hated seeing the man get away but knew he would soon become useless to Germanus and would likely be cast aside. That would be when Drysten would get his revenge. All he would have to do is wait.

Bors and Amiram glared toward the Roman as Eidion helped him away. The two seemed dissatisfied with the deal being struck. "How can you let the man get away with what he's done?" Bors demanded. "Never mind Gaius. What about Germanus simply being allowed to leave?"

Drysten waited until all his enemies were out of earshot before turning back to his men. "His new plan is easy to spot. He believes he can return and rule over Rheged in the same manner he ruled Ebrauc. He wants King Lledlwrn as another puppet."

Bors sighed as he glanced to Amiram. "Then this whole mess starts over?"

"No," Drysten returned with a scoff. "He's weakened Rheged with all the raids on the non-Christians. Those who could have helped him now fight for Powys or Linnuis." He turned back and watched the Visigoths begrudgingly throwing their swords and cross-painted shields into piles by the gate. "If we decide to try and kill him, we can simply go looking for him in Gaul or Germania."

At that, Bors and Amiram were satisfied for the moment.

Drysten watched the Christians slowly exiting the city, unarmed. The moment they began their march, a small number of haggard looking men exited through the opposite gate on the Western side of the city.

"Looked to be beggars," Dagonet had explained. Drysten had sent him and Cynwrig to the other gate to make sure Germanus wouldn't play any tricks. "Most wore rags. None looked strong enough to fight if they were once warriors."

Cynwrig nodded in agreement. "One rider, with the rest on foot. They were hobbling north. Likely came from villages Germanus wiped out when he took Isurium."

"There were many," Tybion put in. It was the first time he had spoken since the deal was struck, with all men looking at him in slight shock. "We rode by them on our way to Eboracum."

Matthew stepped forward and shot a glance toward

Drysten. "I oversaw scouting through Rheged before all this. The Powysian scouts I sent explained he mainly raided to the south of the city."

Something had rung a bell in Drysten's man's mind. "Where exactly are you from?" he asked Tybion with a glance over his shoulder.

"Gwynedd."

"And why were you charged with retrieving the king?" Matthew wondered.

"I... am important?"

Drysten glanced behind him to see the reluctance showing over Tybion's face. "Princes..." he whispered before looking to Matthew. "Germanus said he would exchange the kings and princes. Meaning we had one as well." He looked to Matthew. "He not only wants influence in Rheged, but Gwynedd as well."

Tybion nodded with an uncomfortable smile. "We took his money and the promise of aid. In return, we would allow him to build churches and monasteries throughout our lands."

"That was how he intended to control your people." Drysten looked toward the defeated Christians before realizing he had one more question to ask him. "You wouldn't have happened upon any Gaels while you approached Eboracum, did you?"

Tybion shrugged. "Only a handful of 'em. They wandered by us a long way off, but none chose to do more than stare."

"Which way were they going?" Drysten demanded, fully facing him now.

"The same way as the beggars..." Dagonet whispered.

Drysten heard the urgency in Dagonet's voice and screamed for Drysten's riders to mount their horses.

Tybion nervously stammered as Dagonet barked orders right next to his head. "I believe... North?"

"They weren't fucking beggars; they were the men who brought Eidion back to the bishop!" Drysten hissed. He looked to Amiram. "Unbind this one's hands," he commanded as he raced back to his horsemen. “We go North!”

Mor approached in confusion. “What—?”

“The Gaels!” was all Drysten could manage as he mounted a horse and spurred it on toward the presumed traders. “Cut them off and kill them!” he bellowed to the men at his back. He peered forward to see both Dagonet and Cynwrig had begun the chase ahead of him, with only two others at their sides. “Wait!” he commanded to no avail. Both men couldn’t hear him from this far off.

Before Drysten’s band of men could catch up, a black arrow shot from the side of the road and pierced the neck of Cynwrig’s horse, hurdling him forward from his saddle. Dagonet halted and ripped his blade free, raising his shield to block another arrow from the same direction. “Hurry!” he ordered his men. After a few short moments, Drysten had caught up to see about twelve Gaels huddled near some overgrowth at the edge of the road. “Shields!” An arrow pelted into his chest, but harmlessly fell to his horse’s feet as he dismounted and raced toward Cynwrig. Out of the corner of his eye, he could make out the faint shape of a horseman far off ahead. He looked to see Argyle’s familiar shape stopping for a look behind him. “Kill that one!” Drysten shouted to five of his riders. “The rest of you with me!”

Drysten turned back to Cynwrig and watched the man sprawled out in the dirt. He was clearly dazed as he tried to sit up, with his eyes going wide before Drysten could reach him.

“No!” Drysten pleaded. “Stay down!”

A black arrow danced through the air, and time began to stop. All Drysten could do was slowly follow the black projectile through the air and watch it slam into his old friend’s forehead. Cynwrig’s head was thrust backward, producing a low thud as it slammed into the ground.

***

Drysten had draped Cynwrig's body over the back of his horse. Dagonet had helped, but neither one of them wished to speak. Drysten had known the man since childhood, but still not as well as Dagonet. The two worked closely with one another through the times Drysten was imprisoned. Of the five others who raced off to stop Argyle's escape, one returned. He had draped the bodies of the four dead men over the backs of their horses in the same manner.

"What happened?" Bors asked as he eyed the bodies.

Drysten simply shook his head.

"Did they get away?" Dagonet nodded.

Argyle had been the only man to have a horse of his own, making his escape much easier. The rest of the Gaels were put to the sword and slaughtered once Drysten's men saw Cynwrig's body. That was only the first man Drysten would find to be killed.

The Powysian whose wife painted his shield had died second. Drysten hadn't seen it, but saw the man's body lying close by. Two more joined him until the Gaels who fired the arrows from the tree line became overwhelmed by Dagonet and the rest of the horsemen.

Drysten only had the opportunity to end one of the Gaels himself. One of the emaciated fiends with the strange look in his eye. The fool had tried to rush him as he stood over Cynwrig's corpse, and all he had to do was jab his blade forward into the man's neck.

"Lord Drysten?" Matthew whispered. "Mor's army follows Germanus," he explained. "The king and prince seem to be fine, but we need to join them."

Drysten nodded. "Wrap the bodies," he commanded, harsher than intended.

"Yes, Lord."

A few short moments went by before Drysten mounted his horse and led his men South, marching down the same road they arrive from. He had Matthew on his left and Bors on his right, with Amiram and Dagonet just behind them. Nobody chose to speak until Mor's army was within view.

"Lord Prince," Drysten called to Mor, who was riding in the rear with a handful of others. The prince turned. "Where's your brother?"

Mor shrugged. "He's being marched in the front with the king," he called back.

"I mean the shitty one."

Mor looked ahead for a moment before pointing a finger just in front of him.

Drysten spurred his horse forward until he finally caught up.

"I expect Germanus wished to dangle him right in front of us as bait in case someone chose to kill him. He could kill my father in response."

Drysten shook his head as he looked on the lowered head of Prince Eidion. "He's here because he chose to be. Germanus had nothing to do with it." He dismounted and marched behind Eidion, hearing the protests from Matthew and Mor. "I will not kill him," he stated as he gripped the prince's shoulder, turning him. "Why did the Gaels take you here?"

Eidion shrugged, his arrogance had vanished.

"Why?" Drysten demanded.

"They knew we were desperate," Eidion muttered. "You'd just beaten them and made them desperate too."

"So they took you to Isurium and made a deal with the bishop."

Eidion nodded.

"What deal?"

After a long sigh, Eidion finally looked Drysten in the eyes. "They were to go to some place in the North and keep their war going. In return, Germanus would give them safe passage. When the bishop would eventually return, the Gaels would attack Ebrauc from the North and him from the South."

"Would he have kept up his end of the bargain?"

Eidion nodded. "Why should he care if the Gaels attack

Britannia?"

"He? Not the both of you?"

Eidion shook his head. "You and I both know you won't allow that," he whispered back. To Drysten, it seemed like the man wished to die. "I know what I did to you," he added in a soft tone.

Drysten was taken aback. He found it hard to speak when recalling the torture he endured at the hands of Eidion and Vonig. He expected to hear this from him at one point or another, but never in this manner. He seemed almost apologetic.

"Let me… let me kill him," Eidion rasped, tears forming in his eyes. "Please," he begged. He lowered his gaze to Drysten's waist, nodding toward the ornate dagger once owned by his father.

"What did he do to you?" Drysten wondered.

Eidion stuttered and stammered something inaudible before looking away to compose himself. "Took something I can never get back," he whispered. Tears streamed down his face.

Drysten looked back to Mor, who was listening to the conversation from just behind him. "What does he mean?" he wondered.

Mor simply shrugged and stared into his brother's eyes.

"How would you do it?" Drysten asked as he turned back.

"Put that," he gestured toward the dagger, "under my mail." He pulled the shoulder of his Roman-made chainmail aside to show there was space. "I will do the rest once my father is back in your hands."

"How do I know you won't try and kill your father instead?"

"I don't care about the people Germanus has hurt. I don't care about the nameless people we buried in fields or left to rot in forests." Eidion stopped marching and held out his hands for the dagger. "But there is one person he took from me who I cared for more than anyone I ever met."

"Give him the dagger," Mor suggested. "What do we have to lose?"

Drysten considered turning Eidion around and shoving the man forward, but somehow felt pity for him. He nodded and removed the dagger from its sheath and, with Eidion's help of pulling his mail to the side, he slipped it just under the man's arm.

Eidion nodded and turned around, with Drysten looking to Mor in confusion.

Mor offered another shrug. "I have never seen him like that, even when were somewhat close as children."

"It was a woman," Drysten replied. "Only a woman could do that to a man. Germanus took a woman from him." He remembered the moment he thought he'd never see Isolde again. He then came to realize he had just seen that same anguish in Eidion. He shook his head and sauntered over to his horse, mounting it and clicking his tongue, ushering it forward.

CHAPTER TWENTY-SIX

The march to Petuaria was miserable. The large, strange mix of men trudged on through the night, with Drysten's men clinging to the reigns of the horses carrying their fallen brothers. Their shields were hung at the sides of the saddles, with Drysten having trouble stopping himself from staring at the misshapen raven looking like a chick.

What will his wife think? he wondered. Was theirs a happy marriage?

They passed Eboracum in the dead of night, with one of Ceneus' officers leading a group of men from the city to find out who the large group of strangers were.

"A deal has been struck, Eliwlod," Mor stated. "The bishop is about to piss off. All we have to do is swap hostages when we get to the town."

Drysten recalled the anger in the officer's face when he was told of Garbonian's fate. He seemed angered, yet downtrodden. It was almost as off-putting as looking to Prince Eidion and seeing the man staring off into nothing, as he had been for most of the march. Yet both men seemed to share similar looks in their eyes, and Drysten couldn't help but wonder.

That was the most exciting occurrence during the march. The Christians caused no trouble, the Visigoths remained mostly silent, and the Britons did little more than usher everyone on.

Drysten spent most of the walk with Bors and Matthew, both getting to know Tybion. It turned out the man was second in line to the throne of Gwynedd, and their kingdom was being assailed by Gaels in much the same way as Ebrauc had been. The main difference was the group and their tactics.

"They aren't those crazed loons your lot's been facing," Tybion explained. "They're a mix of Christians. They were simply seeking a safe place to carve out their place in the world."

"One away from the druids?" Maewyn asked, riding beside Tybion.

Tybion nodded. "Abhartach forced them out some time ago."

Drysten let loose a heavy sigh. "Too bad their first thought was to make enemies of the Britons."

"I agree, Lord," Tybion returned.

The whole way into the town, King Ceneus had a knife held to his throat by a Visigoth while Germanus would occasionally glance to him and cackle.

"Move aside, boy!" Germanus ordered the nearest guard. It was Petras, who Drysten had ordered to stay behind with his brother. Paulus was wounded but was expected to make a quick recovery.

Drysten saw the bishop being stalled and locked eyes with Petras, giving a casual nod. Even through obvious confusion, Petras slowly moved aside and allowed the bishop entry into Petuaria.

The few townspeople who dared walk outside in the face of a large group marching toward them were utterly shocked by who was leading them. They grew even more confused by the Visigoths wearing their black cloaks yet holding no shields or swords.

Drysten finally entered the city alongside Bors and Matthew, looking out to sea. "Ships?"

Bors nodded. "Two sets of sails, but only one is nearing the town."

"Then that is the one he intends to board." Drysten dismounted and waved for a handful of his men to follow him.

Germanus was walking toward the pier along with Ceneus and his Visigothic captor. Eidion had caught up and was giving Drysten a knowing, yet glazed over stare.

"Only a few moments and it looks like we'll be rid of you," Drysten stated with a scoff.

Germanus grunted, looking toward Ceneus and the knife to his throat. He waved for the Prince Gwrast to be brought forward. "I expect you to keep your end of the deal," he hissed to Drysten, who nodded.

"I have no intention of being the reason your people do further harm." Drysten waved King Lledlwrn and Tybion forward, spying Gwrast approaching alongside Gaius. "Lord Prince," Drysten greeted, receiving a nod from Gwrast in response. Gaius neglected to meet Drysten's gaze through swollen eyes.

The ship approached, with Drysten finally being able to discern a large cross painted onto the linen sail. It was fully crewed and looked to be of the same make as the Fortuna, albeit without the additions Drysten's father made to his own vessel.

"Line the men along the dock," Drysten commanded.

Bors nodded and relayed the order.

Germanus heard as well. "If I feel you're about—"

"I want you gone, Your Excellency," Drysten interrupted. "I merely don't want my men overwhelmed by fresh troops."

He knew those sailing under the Christian cross were likely as far from fresh as one could get. There was no wind for most of the day, meaning they had rowed their vessel into Petuaria's port. Most of the men aboard were likely exhausted.

Germanus furrowed his brow and looked away, with Drysten seeing Eidion stepping closer. He shook his head, signaling for him to wait before any attacks on the bishop, and Eidion nodded before slinking back a pace.

The ship finally docked, and a line was thrown, with two

heavily armed men disembarking and walking toward Germanus.

"Your Excellency," the larger of the two greeted. He had a large black beard and broad shoulders. There were a handful of scars across his left cheek, one extending over a blinded eye. "We weren't expecting so many. The message stated most of your people had been killed."

Germanus glanced behind him. "Half are yours; the rest remain here." He began stepping aboard before Drysten held up a hand.

"You board last," he commanded.

The bishop scrunched his face and looked over Drysten's men, all ready to pounce at a moment's notice. Germanus turned toward the Visigoths who had marched behind him and waved a hand forward.

King Lledlwrn and Tybion had joined Drysten and Bors when the last Visigoths boarded the vessel, with Germanus and Eidion being the only two who remained.

"Well?" Germanus squawked.

Drysten nodded. "You will release the prince first," he stated, knowing Gwrast was more valuable than Ceneus. The king was older and had fewer years in front of him. Gwrast was a good man with a bright future, a future king who had learned from his father's mistakes.

Germanus waved Gwrast forward, and the Prince's bindings were cut and both him and Tybion walked to the opposing groups.

Tybion gave Drysten a subtle glance before stepping forward. "Is it strange I'd rather not?" he whispered.

Drysten smiled and shook his head. "He'll likely leave you off near the mouth of the river. Your uses are few to a man in his position." He stepped closer and gave a reassuring nod. "I'll send riders after you," he whispered.

Tybion nodded and stepped aboard the vessel, eyeing the Christians as he went.

"Now for the kings," Germanus declared as he neared the

ship.

Drysten looked to Rheged's king and pointed toward the vessel. He noticed Dagonet and Petras had strung their bows and were huddled behind Bors and Jorrit, the two biggest men who could obstruct the view of the Christians. He waved them forward. "If His Excellency tries to board before Ceneus is safely in our hands, kill him," he ordered, loud enough for the bishop to hear.

The Rhegedians began to follow until the leader of Germanus' ship held up a hand. "Not enough room for them, Your Excellency."

Germanus didn't seem to care, waving the Rhegedians off.

Lord Amalech began to protest until his king whispered words of encouragement into his ear, of which Drysten heard little. It seemed the Rhegedian king would journey off without his fellow Rhegedians.

Drysten looked back and noticed it was now Eidion who led his father toward Drysten, stopping just in front of him as he unbound his father's hands.

"This will be the last memory you have of me, father," Eidion whispered, holding Ceneus' gaze.

"What...?" the king muttered.

Eidion returned a nod and turned back to the ships.

All hostages had been exchanged, and the Christians had surprisingly held up their end of the deal. No blades were drawn by either side, and Germanus had indeed waited to be the last man to board.

"I will see you again, Lord Drysten!" Germanus yelled from the prow of the ship, his mocking tone on full display.

Drysten smiled, seeing Eidion subtly step up behind him, reaching into his mail coat. "I don't know about that, Your Excellency," he yelled back.

It was foolish.

Germanus was fabled to be one of the most paranoid individuals alive. Hearing Drysten's snide tone gave the man pause as he began surveying the faces of those who stood along the pier. Drysten was able to see the moment the bishop knew his life was in peril.

Whether it was the antsy gaze of Matthew, or the silence of Prince Mor, or possibly the fact everyone along the pier was staring just over his shoulder, Drysten couldn't tell. But Germanus now knew what was happening. He ripped a small dagger from his robe, a Roman dagger from his days as a military commander and plunged into the nearest man just behind him.

That man was Eidion, who had raised Drysten's own dagger over his head for a brutal strike into Germanus' neck. The prince's eyes went wide, his momentum taking him to the very front of the ship as Germanus' thrust caused him to fall forward. His head now dangled over the edge as Germanus turned the blade before ripping it free. For a man of roughly sixty years, his strength and speed were impressive. He kept plunging the small blade between Eidion's ribs before ripping it out, eventually stopping and flipping the prince onto the pier with a low grunt.

Drysten wasn't quick enough to respond. The sight of Eidion and his father's dagger clattering to the ground gave him a moment's pause. That hesitation was long enough for Germanus to slink behind a pair of shields. The vessel's line was cut in that instant and the ship's rowers began pushing away from the peer.

"Shoot him!" Drysten ordered, his voice was frantic and cracked from surprise.

Petras and Dagonet each released an arrow, both of which thumped into the cross-painted shields of men who had come to Germanus' aid. As the ship slowly moved away, more were shot with the same result.

Eidion's bloodied corpse was lying on the pier, untouched until the Christians were too far off to throw spears or shoot arrows of their own.

It was at that moment King Ceneus began the slow walk

to his son's body, followed by the two Princes and Drysten. All four men simply stared into Eidion's vacant eyes. Each man silently understood the irony in placing their trust in someone they'd grown to hate.

"He said that would be the last memory I would have of him," Ceneus muttered. "He said that thinking..."

Gwrast glanced to his brother in confusion before Drysten stepped alongside him. "Suppose there was a shred of good left in him."

"There was more than a shred. He was just... gullible," the king returned.

Drysten looked back and ordered Dagonet to take riders to the mouth of the river. The estuary he had once fought a battle at sea against a Jorrit's Frisians. He bent low and scooped his father's dagger from the wooden planks near Eidion's corpse, carefully placing it back in the sheathe at his waist.

Despite the sadness of the royal family, the people cheered. The Christians had been driven off, and Germanus was gone.

CHAPTER TWENTY-SEVEN

King Ceneus had disappeared, but nobody chose to go looking for him. Drysten heard rumors he left in the night with Maewyn, but could find no more than that. Maewyn eventually showed himself in Arthur's court not long after, but was reluctant to divulge any knowledge of the man's whereabouts.

Surprisingly, Ceneus' children showed little interest in finding their father. Considering the man's past mistakes, Drysten couldn't blame them. After two months of Gwrast ruling in his stead, they eventually decided the man must have killed himself in shame.

Ebrauc was then split into three separate kingdoms. Bryneich was given its independence, with Gwrast's final act as regent, citing the sacrifice of his uncle. He wished to reward that sacrifice.

Ebrauc's lands below Hadrian's Wall were split between Gwrast and Mor, as was the way of the Britons. It was always tradition that a king would divide his lands between sons. This being the case, Mor received Eboracum and Isurium with their surrounding lands, while Gwrast received the lands to the North.

But there was one more kingdom placed right in the middle, which would now be Drysten's home. Its proud mountain ranges split the two right through their Southern territories.

Arthur, or rather King Arthur now, had taken to calling it The Kingdom of the Pennines. And that kingdom was now his. The lands it occupied stretched from the Northern wilds of Ebrauc, down to the safety and security of Powys' Northern border. The mountain ridge forming Britannia's spine in its center was now Arthur's, and he would secure the trade between the kingdoms of Ebrauc, Linnuis, Rheged, and Powys.

Drysten recalled the forcefulness Arthur's father had displayed when the negotiations over the borders began. He had many grievances to cite, few of which could be refuted by Ebrauc's royal family.

"Your lot plunged Britannia into more of a hole than the Romans did when they abandoned us," the lord had screamed when Mor scoffed at his original demands. "And you believe you're... what? Entitled to this land. What of the Powysian blood spilled in the name of your king and his bishop?"

All men had gone silent, with Drysten observing their shame from the doorway with Matthew.

"Any word from Dagonet?" the priest wondered though a hushed whisper. The scout had been sent after Gaius when it was learned Germanus had indeed offloaded all those who were no longer useful to him. Gaius and Tybion were tossed ashore near the estuary East of Petuaria, while King Lledlwrn was simply thrown into the sea and drowned.

Drysten shook his head. "Nothing."

"Agh," Matthew replied. "He'll likely be hard to find."

"Yet I'm sure we'll manage."

"You're awfully optimistic at the moment, Lord."

Drysten smirked. "They're debating the borders of my soon-to-be home," Drysten whispered back. "And not even one of them seems to be able to make a decent argument other than Lord Aurelianus. I'd say I have much to be optimistic about."

Matthew snickered as he watched both princes of Ebrauc doing their utmost to avoid Lord Aurelianus' gaze. "The other kingdoms already pledged their support for Arthur's borders.

They're the last two to do so." The priest nodded his head toward Gwrast and Mor.

"Then he'll likely get whatever is asked."

So he did.

Neither prince, nor any of the random lords of Ebrauc could mount a defense to Powys' demands. It was at that moment Drysten finally understood the kingdom was the last vestige of Rome's might in Britannia. They were no longer Romans; they were simply the best that the Empire had left behind.

The following night, a large feast was prepared in King Arthur's name. Many lords came to swear fealty to the new king, and Arthur made certain his scribe, Maewyn, jotted their names down onto a ledger. He knew the importance of remembering those lords' names and did what he could to make each one feel important to his lands.

There were only a handful with a sizeable force worth mentioning. The man who commanded the largest number of troops was an individual from Rheged named Amalech. He was the one who laid the trap in which Ceneus had fallen, and Drysten whispered this knowledge into Arthur's ear the moment the Rhegedian pledged himself to Arthur.

"You were the man who placed King Ceneus into the bishop's hands?" Arthur asked in surprise.

Lord Amalech had adopted the most awkward stare Drysten had ever seen. He eventually nodded. "I... yes, Lord King. That was me."

Drysten recalled the moment Arthur stared off into the rafters above the feasting hall. Everyone in attendance had fallen silent until the noble looked back to Lord Amalech and smiled. "It was a good plan, Lord," he whispered. "I would expect that same... dexterity as you serve me." He stood and walked around the large table, stopping right in front of the lord and gesturing for him to stand. "You will be my Legate," he announced. It was a high-ranking title the Romans gave to many of their officers. "You will be in charge of securing the lands bordering our West."

Lord Amalech stood and returned a proud nod. "Thank you, Lord King. I will serve you well, I swear it."

Arthur placed both hands onto the man's shoulders and offered further encouragement before gesturing to a seat at the end of his table. Amalech was beaming as he marched over and sat right beside Arthur's father.

"I have one last charge to give," the new king announced. He turned and looked to Drysten, gesturing a hand for him to come forward.

Drysten did so and kneeled in front of the man who would become his greatest friend.

"Your charge will be the protection of the roads extending East from Navio," Arthur had explained. Navio was now the new capital of The Pennines, and rested right in between Deva and Lindum, two large cities of neighboring kingdoms. "Petuaria will once again be your home."

Drysten nodded with a huge, brimming smile. He raised his head and met the man's smile. "Yes, my king," he returned.

Arthur waved a hand for Drysten to stand. "The Fortuna should meet you there, as will the rest of your people. I sent for them a few days ago."

Drysten nodded and looked to the other kings and lords who graced Navio with their presence. There were representatives from far off kingdoms such as Dumnonia and Atrebatia in the South, as well as Bryneich, Ebrauc, and Rheged in Britannia's North. A small party from Dyfed showed themselves as well, with Arthur overseeing the peace talks between them and Gwynedd. It seemed their small war had begun because of petty cattle raids, and both sides found it easier than expected to come to an accord.

All men were joyful in that moment, and the feast raged on far into the night.

But what came in the morning, and only to Drysten, was rather unexpected.

He was nursing the healing wounds he'd sustained in recent weeks when a messenger arrived, only asking for him. He was young, roughly the age Drysten had been when he arrived in Britannia, but was curiously sporting the same number of scars across his arms and face.

"Do I know you?" Drysten asked him, weary the man was one of Abhartach's hunters until he noted the presence of a tongue.

The man shook his head. "Wouldn't mind a quick word with ya, lord, but no more than that."

Drysten peered over his shoulder and saw his wife still fast asleep in the room Arthur granted them until these formalities were concluded. Looking back, he nodded and gestured for the man to walk a ways down the hall and away from prying ears.

"When I heard about what ya done, I was… impressed…"

Drysten side-eyed the man for a moment until they stopped near a window overlooking the courtyard. There, Arthur and Bedwyr were apparently arguing over something as Ystradwel looked on in little to now interest. "Well, I —"

"What will you do now, if I may, lord?"

Drysten looked back, seeing Maewyn walking up the stairs. He initially wanted to wait until the priest passed them by, but was taken aback when the man stopped and slapped this odd visitor's shoulder.

"Told you to wait, —"

"No names, if it pleases, ya."

Maewyn nodded and looked back to Drysten. "You'll like him."

"I have yet to come to that conclusion for myself."

The stranger grinned. "Well, we're of the same mind regarding the Gaels, lord, I'll have ya know." He leaned closer. "You went and did sumtin which I apparently could not!"

Drysten squinted and thought back on the last few weeks. "Your from Hibernia?"

The man nodded.

"You must be speaking of Abhartach, then."

"That I am, lord, that I am..."

Drysten suddenly realized who this stranger may have been. "You led the wars against him," he stated. "You were the reason they were here in the first place."

"I am."

"So what does that have to do with me?"

The stranger leaned closer. "You are privy to certain things which I believe should be... repurposed..."

"Repurposed?"

"You understand the magics Abhartach used, or at least where to find someone who does."

Drysten cursed under his breath and turned away. "I will never speak of those things —" But a sturdy grip over his forearm stopped him.

"I mean you no ill will," the stranger assured him. "Ya don't be neadin' to worry 'bout that. What I *do* think you need to worry about is me brother."

Drysten turned back.

"Argyll, was what you called him. Turned by Abhartach against his own kin. Taught the same ways to fight and roam. You are both an interestin' parallel, if ya don't mind my sayin."

"Fuck off," Drysten hissed. "I have no time for this."

"What will you do with it?"

"With what?"

"Their knowledge."

Drysten paused, considering the idea of another band of hunters roaming the wilds. Only this one would serve him instead of a crazy cannibal. "People like that are much too dangerous to exist," he finally decided. "I will never —"

"Enticin' thought, though, isn't it?"

"Why are you here?"

"I represent the man who nearly killed Abhartach. I represent the true followers of The Morrigan."

Drysten fell back a pace and instinctually put a hand to his waist, feeling a twinge of apprehension when he realized his blade was currently beside his bed.

"As I said, I mean ya no hard, lord." The stranger leaned closer. "But the ones you fought, as well as the Saxons? Ah, now there's a lot I'd like to get a piece of for myself."

Drysten paused, wondering why he suddenly felt a flare of rage building in his gut. Not rage for this man standing in front of him or his irritatingly confident smirk. But rage for the invaders who were killing his people.

"Fine," he flatly said, "let's here what you have in mind."

1
2
3
4
5
6
7
8
9
10
11
12
13
14
15
1. Dal Riata
2. Gododdin
3. Strathclyde
4. Bryneich
5. New Rheged
6. Ebrauc
7.The Kingdom of The Pennines
8. Gwynedd
9. Powys
10. Linnuis
11. Dyfed
12. Saxon Londein
13. Dumnonia
14. Atrebatia
15. Saxon Cantia

BRITANNIA 431 CE

Manufactured by Amazon.ca
Bolton, ON

26182326R00249